SELECTED RHONDA PARRISH ANTHOLOGIES

A IS FOR APOCALYPSE
B IS FOR BROKEN
C IS FOR CHIMERA
D IS FOR DINOSAUR
E IS FOR EVIL
F IS FOR FAIRY

FAE
CORVIDAE
SCARECROW
SIRENS
EQUUS

MRS. CLAUS: NOT THE FAIRY TALE THEY SAY
TESSERACTS TWENTY-ONE: NEVERTHELESS

FIRE: DEMONS, DRAGONS AND DJINNS
EARTH: GIANTS, GOLEMS AND GARGOYLES

GRIMM, GRIT AND GASOLINE
CLOCKWORK, CURSES AND COAL

HEAR ME ROAR
SWASHBUCKLING CATS: NINE LIVES ON THE SEVEN SEAS

G IS FOR GHOSTS

Book Seven of the Alphabet Anthologies

Edited by Rhonda Parrish

Poise and Pen Publishing

EDMONTON, ALBERTA

G is for Ghosts / Rhonda Parrish.—1st ed.
ISBN 978-1-988233-89-5 (Physical)
ISBN 978-1-988233-90-1 (Electronic)

CONTENTS

Stephanie A. Cain

It was very late, well past the time for all good young ladies to be at home, and probably all dutiful young men as well. Charlie Holmes entered through the back door, praying Father had already gone to bed. Mother would turn a blind eye, but Father wouldn't ignore the smell of camphor. Photography, Charlie had been told many times, was an inappropriate hobby for her to have taken up. It didn't matter how many times she mentioned Matthew Brady or Charles Lutwidge Dodgson or even Julia Margaret Cameron; Father always had a rebuttal for why Charlie should not—could not—become a photographer.

Floorboards creaked under Charlie's Oxfords and she winced. It was too much to hope Father hadn't heard.

The door to Father's study jerked open. "James, is that you? Come in here, I want you to—" He broke off then, dark eyebrows lowering. "Charlotte." Father's voice was low, like thunder that rumbled on the far edge of the horizon.

Charlie tried to look innocent, as if she weren't sneaking in from her borrowed photography dark room. As if she were wearing her own clothes, and not James' hand-me-downs. "Father. Good evening."

It was stupid to hope Father would ignore this. Charlie only hoped she hadn't gotten her brother in trouble for helping.

"How many times have I told you photography isn't a fit hobby for a well-bred young lady?" Charlie's father surged forward, raising one clenched fist. Henry Holmes was a big man, broad-shouldered with huge hands and a quick temper. Charlie, five feet six inches in stockings (and five feet eleven inches in her brother's top hat), knew she should quail before him. She should drop to her knees in abject apology. But after the news her brother had given her at dinner, Charlie was done apologizing for who she was.

"I had dinner in town with James tonight," Charlie said, ignoring her father's words.

Henry's glower deepened. "I suppose he took it upon himself to share the happy news of your engagement."

Charlie had tried, over and over again, to choose her own course in life but she had always known, deep down, that Father was intent on selling her to his business partner's nephew. "I will not marry Wallace Casey."

"You'll do as you're told, girl," he snapped. "You've been given plenty of time—much more time than you deserved—to grow up."

"No." Charlie swallowed, lifting her chin. Had anyone ever told Father no before?

He acted so quickly she had no time to evade him. One huge fist lashed out, catching her on the jaw and knocking her into the wall of the narrow passage.

"*Unnatural, ungrateful hussy!*" he hissed. "You'll marry whomever I choose—I'm your father!"

Charlie couldn't summon the breath for a reply; she could do nothing but stare, open-mouthed, tears in her eyes, at her father's rage-twisted face. Blinking stinging eyes, she straightened a little, finally sucking in a breath. For just a moment, Charlie wished for the feel of her mother's arms wrapped protectively around her. Then she shook her head and cupped a hand against her stinging jaw. She could imagine how Mother would react: *If you didn't insist on pursuing your peculiar hobbies, this never would have happened.*

"I want to live my own life," Charlie quavered, forcing herself to meet Father's eyes.

To Charlie's shock, her lunged at her again. This time, his fingers curled around her throat. "I won't have the neighbors saying we raised a disobedient daughter." A spike of ice shot through Charlie. "You are my property, and I will dispose of you as I wish."

"I'm not property, I'm a person!" Charlie choked. Her ragged, bitten fingernails scrabbled at his hands. She knew, deep in her soul, that even if she had felt right in women's clothes, she would have chafed at the restrictions and expectations placed on women. "Father, please—"

It was the last protest she managed. Charlie's words broke off as she ran out of breath. Blackness swam across her vision and she swayed. Then the blows started. When her father was finished with her, Charlie was curled on the floor, arms wrapped around her head.

Father leaned over her, his breathing so harsh she couldn't hear her own. He swore. Then she heard him storm away and close the study door, but she couldn't move. She tasted blood mixed with dust from the floor.

I am *my own*, she told herself hopelessly. Her whole body trembled. She had never wanted a husband or children. She wanted to pursue a trade, to go to college.

Every time she'd considered the future, though, she had circled right back to Father's contempt—his *disgust*, even—for who Charlie was. Charlie's siblings might understand, but most of the people in their small village of Zionsville didn't. Time and again, Reverend Browning had urged Charlie to accept the role of a young, well-bred,

Christian lady. Time and again, Charlie had wondered if she ought to do just that… and then gone back to her photography studio.

Shaking, Charlie crept along the hall, sniffling just a bit as she let herself into her own room. It shouldn't feel like the end of the world. But it did.

She was tired, so tired. She wanted to collapse into bed, but she knew suddenly that there could be no life for her here. It was time to go. Past time to go.

Go where? whispered a hopeless little voice in her head.

St. Louis, Charlie thought. Or perhaps San Francisco. Somewhere far from here, where she could reinvent herself.

She had a little bit of money saved up from years of tutoring school children. She could pawn a few things—though not her camera, *never* that—and her hair was long enough that it might fetch a good price.

Her eyelids drooping, she forced herself upright despite an ache in her ribs. She rubbed her throat and draped a scarf around it to hide any marks her father might have left. And then she picked up her valise, which felt heavy as an anvil, and crept out of the house.

Charlie's stomach growled as she walked away from the pawn broker on East Market Street. The mahogany and silver clock her grandfather had bequeathed to her had fetched so little, she'd been unwilling to part with the matching silver pocket watch. She certainly had the one hundred and thirty dollars it would cost for a Pullman berth from Indianapolis to San Francisco, but it wouldn't leave her much to find lodgings or food once she arrived.

She should have stayed at the Grand Hotel instead of the English's. At least the Grand Hotel had an American Plan offering for breakfast. Perhaps she should have pawned her camera, too…but in the end, she'd been unable to part with it. She glanced, tempted, at the bustling City Market, thinking of the fresh baked goods that would be on offer.

She blinked at a sign that read "Tomlinson Taproom." The grand concert venue Tomlinson Hall was next door to the market, but she hadn't heard of a taproom. She rubbed her eyes and looked for the taproom sign again, but it was gone.

She hadn't tried to sell her hair yet. It was neatly bound and wrapped in her bag, and she kept adjusting her brother's top hat, which slipped a bit now that she had no hair to hold it in place. She was done being a respectable young lady, and she was done being Charlotte; from now on she was Charlie, and she would live as she wished, and people could think what they would.

Fortunately facial hair was going out of style again. Father had kept his mutton-chops, but James shaved every day. No one would think it odd that Charlie had no beard. Her stride had always been too quick, perhaps in protest of the long skirts she'd been forced to wear. Grinning, Charlie allowed her stride to lengthen.

As Charlie reached up and adjusted her hat yet again, someone crashed into her.

"Maura!" a woman exclaimed.

"God, I'm so sorry," said another female voice, husky, with an English accent. But Charlie's hat had slipped over her eyes, so she had no idea who was speaking to her. "I tripped over the sidewalk. I'd trip over my own feet if I had nothing else to trip over. I'm terribly sorry." As Charlie pushed her hat back again, she was struck by the handsome strength of the woman standing, red-faced, before her.

"It's no trouble," she assured the woman. "I was inattentive." She let her gaze travel to the other woman, who was standing a pace or two behind the one who had crashed into her. That woman was dressed in trousers and a jacket, but not nearly as formal as Charlie's. When her eyes met Charlie's, she paled.

"Are you all right?" Charlie inquired.

The woman coughed. "Oh, yes, fine, thanks."

Charlie had asked mostly to be polite. Her attention was still mostly focused on the other woman, taking in her silver-streaked black hair and blue eyes. This must be Maura. Charlie caught Maura's hand in both of hers and bowed over it, not quite daring to brush the skin with her lips. "I apologize most heartily for running into you," she told the woman.

If it was possible, the woman went even more scarlet. Charlie couldn't place her age. She seemed older than Charlie, but her awkward demeanor made her seem young.

"No, it—" The woman cut herself off and huffed. "Let me buy you coffee to make up for it. My name is Maura. Maura Schroeder."

Charlie smiled at her in surprise. The offer was unexpected, but it neatly solved the problem of breakfast. "That isn't necessary, but I appreciate the offer. I am Charlie Holmes." Her stomach chose that moment to growl loudly, and her smile slipped into a grin.

Maura grinned back, charming her further. "Please. There's a coffee shop in the lobby of my building, just here." She gestured. Charlie looked, and for a moment her vision flickered. The street had no wagons or carriages, though it had been full a moment ago. The building in front of her was not stone or wood or even brick, but mostly glass. She sucked in a breath, and then the familiar world returned.

"Are you all right?" Maura's grin had faded a little. It made Charlie feel guilty.

"I'm fine, thank you. Very well, I accept. Thank you."

"Nothing too fancy, I'm afraid," Maura said. "But I'd like very much for you to join me."

The other woman moved into Charlie's view. She wore trousers and a sweater that looked very soft. Charlie blinked, trying to picture the woman in a dress shaped by the corset and bustle her mother favored. Then she met the woman's brown eyes, which were narrowed as she studied Charlie.

"Maura, I think we should talk first." Her voice was sharp.

With an apologetic glance, Maura went to speak with her friend. Charlie tried to look incurious as she watched from the corner of her eye. The woman drew her several yards away and began to speak too quietly for Charlie to hear. The woman gestured, then gripped Maura's shoulder. Maura glanced back at Charlie, and something in her posture changed. But then she shook her head and said something else to her friend.

Charlie did her best to appear innocuous. After all, they were strangers, and it was possible the other two women took her for a man. She wanted to reassure them that she wasn't dangerous.

At length Maura came back to Charlie. "Sorry about that. Chloe can't join us for coffee, but we had a bit of business to finish up." The smile she offered was a little shakier, but Charlie couldn't quite place how the other woman was feeling. Disappointed? Dismayed?

"Perhaps I shouldn't inconvenience you," she began, but Maura interrupted.

"No, it's fine. Please. I'd like to get to know you."

Charlie studied Maura's face for a moment, watching the smile grow firmer. After a moment, Charlie touched the brim of her too-big hat and strode to the door, which she opened for Maura. "After you."

When they were settled at an intimate table with coffee and a muffin on Maura's part and Earl Grey and a scone on Charlie's—it had made Maura give her a wry look and laugh—Charlie found herself at a loss. She'd long dreamed of being free enough to do this, but…how did most gentlemen speak to a woman they had just met? Was she being too forward?

"So." Maura leaned forward. "What brings you to Indianapolis, Charlie Holmes? Or do you live here?"

Charlie raised an eyebrow, but she was pleased. "I probably ought to be asking you that, with that accent," she countered. "But I am only traveling through en route to San Francisco."

Maura shifted in her seat. "I've never been to San Francisco. I hear it's lovely."

"Yes." Charlie sipped her tea. "That is, I've heard that, as well."

"You don't live there?"

"I'm planning to live there." Charlie realized suddenly that she hadn't even imagined what story she would tell people. She certainly couldn't share her true history. "I, ah, I've just had a change in my circumstances, and am taking this opportunity to 'Go West Young Man,' as the newspaperman said some years ago." She attempted a charming smile.

"Go West Young... Man," Maura said, pausing just slightly. She sat straighter in her chair and gave Charlie an enigmatic and inviting smile. "Tell me more."

"It isn't as easy as searching for specific terms," Maura said, waving her fork expressively as she spoke. She was leaning across the table, her voice low as they dined in a small restaurant near her apartment. "You have to know about related concepts. You can't just index, say, 'Hoosier basketball.' You have to 'see also sports,' 'see also Indiana University, comma, athletics.'" She sipped her wine. "You have to have basketball rivalries, comma, Illinois.'"

"It seems to me your work is very important," Charlie said. She liked the smile that spread across Maura's face. It was a little reluctant, but it felt genuine.

Maura worked as an indexer. Charlie had learned this on their second day together, as they wandered through the City Market, talking about philosophy and books they had read. Maura tried to explain the signs advertising the Catacombs Tours, but Charlie didn't remember hearing anything about a fire in Tomlinson Hall. Eventually Charlie admitted that she had broken ties with her family because they wanted her to marry; she didn't specify that they wanted her to marry a man, but something in Maura's expression and demeanor made Charlie think she knew that.

Maura collected clocks; her sitting room had several fascinating ones, including a cuckoo clock that called every hour. Charlie couldn't fight a grin every time the clock went off, though she preferred the handsome mantel clock on Maura's fireplace.

They spent time walking along the White River and enjoying the early autumn sunshine. Charlie was happy to point out all the varieties of wildflowers still blooming, and they delighted in watching bright orange monarch butterflies soaring overhead.

Before Charlie knew it, she had been at the English's for two weeks, and she was beginning to wonder if she should look for a boarding house. She still had enough money for a berth to San Francisco, but now she wasn't even sure she wished to go there. But even after selling her thick bunch of hair, she was beginning to worry she might have to pawn her camera.

Yet every time she resolved to go to Union Station and arrange for a Pullman car, she thought of Maura, and found her steps turning away from the station. She would hate to presume on such a short-lived friendship by asking Maura to put her up, especially since she knew how that might look to outsiders... or perhaps, even, to Maura herself.

Not that Charlie would assume Maura felt *that* sort of affection for her, of course. Yet she had never met anyone who understood her so well. Charlie thought she would very much enjoy the study of botany, and Maura encouraged that, loaning her books about Indiana's flora.

Charlie had revised her opinion of Maura's age upwards, though she supposed Maura wasn't much older than thirty-five or so. That wasn't so much older than Charlie's twenty-eight, was it?

"What about you?" Maura asked. "You still haven't told me what you do for a living."

Charlie bit her lower lip. "I—I was a private tutor before I left my family home," she admitted finally, her voice soft. "I enjoyed teaching, but I certainly don't wish to be a private tutor forever. I enjoy photography, but I don't think I wish to make portraits. I really should like to learn more about the plants and herbs, perhaps medicinal, or...

well, no, I suppose Colonel Lilly and his son are doing enough of that."

Maura's gaze was intent on her face, but Charlie couldn't quite meet it. She felt as though she were lying to Maura, even though she was actually being honest, for the first time, with herself. "I didn't have much of a plan when I ran away," she confessed.

Maura surprised her with a low chuckle. "I didn't suppose you had," she said. "It's all right. Chloe—you remember meeting her, right? She and her husband want to have dinner with us tomorrow night. Maybe one of them will have suggestions for you. They might even know of a job opportunity."

"Chloe, yes, I remember." Charlie remembered that Chloe had seemed suspicious of her, too. But perhaps that had changed. And it was promising, wasn't it, that Maura wanted them to spend time together? Charlie couldn't stop the wide smile that spread across her face. "I should like that very much."

Nagging at the back of Charlie's mind were twin worries—first, that her supply of cash was dwindling as she lingered at the English's Hotel, and second, that her father might actually come looking for her. Charlie didn't think he would. After all, Father had meant to get rid of her. But if Charlie escaped to her freedom, the bank wouldn't have the benefit of a marriage into the Casey family. James was already married, so no convenient Casey daughters could be forced on him. Elise's betrothal to a partner in the bank was a love match, but convenient for Father.

"You seem troubled," Maura said. "If I've pressured you—"

"Not at all." Charlie forced a smile that grew more genuine as she looked at Maura. "I'm just a little tired."

"I should let you get back to your hotel," Maura said, and Charlie hoped she didn't imagine the reluctance there. Besides, it was growing late enough that single ladies oughtn't be with a beau unchaperoned.

The thought jolted Charlie. *Was* she Maura's beau? She knew, almost certainly, Charlie's nature. They were very amiable with one another, and Charlie certainly enjoyed looking at Maura and spending time with Maura.

But perhaps she was thinking too deeply into this.

Charlie nodded, suddenly thoughtful. "I shall call on you tomorrow."

Chloe wore a friendly smile when she and her husband Braxton arrived in Maura's comfortably appointed apartment. Charlie could still feel the woman's brown eyes studying her, but no one else seemed to notice, and eventually she began to relax.

Braxton certainly helped. He was handsome, shorter than his wife, and had an easy confidence about him that invited others to feel confident with him. Charlie found him more approachable than his wife, and had little trouble staying interested as he described his work in law enforcement.

Over the past few weeks, Charlie had gotten used to going out without a hat, and she had even grown more comfortable—though not *entirely* so—with removing her jacket and rolling up her sleeves. She was still leery of going without her cravat, though she'd taken to tying it more loosely. The cravat had the added benefit of hiding her feminine throat while offering a bit of fashion. Still, looking at the informal shirtsleeves Braxton wore, Charlie wondered if she might look a bit silly.

"Butterscotch?" Braxton held out an amber-colored, cut glass bowl full of candies.

Charlie jerked her attention back to the conversation. "Thank you," she said, taking it. It held small, hard, yellow discs wrapped in paper that crinkled under her fingers. "Maura?"

As she passed the dish to Maura, their fingers slid past each other, and Charlie *knew* she hadn't imagined the indrawn breath that contact caused both of them. She bent her head and carefully on the task of unwrapping the candy.

"These things are so old they're sticky," Chloe protested. "Tell the truth, Maur, did you *really* go grocery shopping, or are these candies older than you?"

"I'm not sure they were even making these candies fifty-one years ago," Maura said primly.

Fifty-one? Charlie blinked down at the candy wrapper. Maura didn't seem so much older than she. Perhaps Charlie had been foolish to hope... but then, she couldn't bring herself to care about her age. Maura was intelligent, attractive, confident—everything Charlie had struggled to become. What did it matter if she was nearly twice Charlie's age?

"It could be worse," Braxton said lightly. "It could be blue cotton candy."

"That," Chloe objected, "is not real cotton candy."

Charlie wondered what cotton candy was. She hoped she wouldn't be expected to have an opinion of it.

"Of course it isn't," Maura said briskly. "And it's called candy floss, anyway."

They were exceedingly comfortable with one another. Was there space for Charlie in this? She held in a soft sigh.

A hand entered her view and touched the back of her hand. "All right?" Maura murmured.

Charlie jerked her gaze up to meet Maura's. "Yes."

Chloe cleared her throat. "Maura, could I... borrow you in the kitchen for a minute?"

"Certainly, darling." Maura curled her fingers around Charlie's and squeezed, then left the room with Chloe.

Charlie stared at her fingers, then clenched both hands together. She wasn't certain why she suddenly felt so adrift. Although she had a firm grasp of Maura's occupation as indexer, she didn't entirely understand how it was so universally accepted that a woman should have such an occupation without a husband. Although she was in no doubt whatsoever of Maura's capability as a person, she didn't understand how *other* people accepted that without expecting her to have a husband.

It seemed like perfection to Charlie but it was leagues away from what she had experienced only a few weeks ago when she was Charlotte Holmes of the Zionsville, Indiana, Holmeses.

"So. Charlie." Braxton smiled, and she could tell he was trying to put her at ease. "Maura's mentioned you more than once, but she's never been quite clear on how you met. I hope you won't find it offensive if I ask about your intentions?"

Charlie's mouth dropped open. "I, um, I'm afraid I bumped into her on the street," she said finally. "Literally, that is. I was walking past City Market and my hat slipped and—well, the rest you know." She managed a weak laugh.

He laughed with her. "When was that, again?"

It was a trick question. It must be. But for the life of her, Charlie couldn't understand how. There was little mystery about it. They had met four, perhaps five, weeks earlier. She might have lost track of the actual number of days, but she was in no wise confused about her own place in time.

Charlie smiled.

"I might be a better swain if I could tell you the date, down to the hour," she confessed. "But if I'm entirely honest, it feels both like it was a hundred years ago and only an hour ago." And it was no exaggeration. Charlie felt as though she could spend every moment of the rest of her life with Maura and still believe they hadn't enough time together.

Charlie's heart thumped harder. Was it possible to fall in love with someone in a month?

It was just that moment, of course, when Chloe and Maura came back from the kitchen. Maura looked annoyed, which let Charlie shove down her uncomfortable suspicions.

Charlie stood automatically, reaching out to her. "Maura, is everything all right?"

Maura smiled, twining their fingers together. "I think so," she said. "We'll talk about it later."

"Who's up for a few games of euchre?" Chloe said, holding up a deck of cards.

The rest of the evening passed uneventfully. It had been ages since Charlie played, but she had always enjoyed it. They were only betting pennies, but even that felt greatly daring, considering how low her funds were running.

After the gathering broke up, Charlie lingered, remembering that Maura had said they should talk. She found herself worrying her lower lip with her teeth. When it was just the two of them, sitting in the living room with hot tea, Maura sat back and studied her. Charlie raised her eyebrows but didn't speak. She could be patient, and if this silence wasn't quite as comfortable as their shared silences usually were…well, that might be all right.

Finally Maura sighed. "I've always known you had secrets, Charlie. I don't mind; we all have secrets, don't we? But I'm afraid you and I need to exchange secrets before we can figure out how we will go on with things."

Charlie opened her mouth, but Maura held up a hand.

"My friend Chloe is a medium. She sees spirits." Maura's gaze was steady on hers.

"All right." Charlie wasn't sure why that was important. Mother and Father had been fascinated by spiritualism for years, though Charlie had never paid much attention.

Her simple response seemed to surprise Maura, but she took a deep breath and said, "Chloe says *you're* a spirit."

Charlie blinked. "What?"

"It's why she acted funny when we first met you. Because you're a ghost." Maura's hands were clenched in her lap, knuckles white. "She was angry I hadn't told you yet. She said if I didn't tell you tonight, she would."

"But I'm not dead." Charlie laughed as she said it. How could she be a ghost if she hadn't died?

"Chloe did her research." Maura took a folded sheet of paper from her pocket, unfolded it, and cleared her throat. "Charlotte Maya Holmes, twenty-eight, murdered in her own home by her father. Father pled not guilty, but corroborating testimony from James and Elise Holmes, Charlotte's siblings, cinched the case."

Charlie's ears began roaring at that point, drowning out whatever Maura was saying after that. It wasn't true. Perhaps her siblings had reported her missing after she ran away? But why would Father be blamed?

He did beat you. He tried to strangle you.

But that was no excuse for blaming him for her death when she wasn't even dead.

The world dimmed, flickered. Charlie tried to remember how, exactly, she'd gotten to the English's Hotel. She wouldn't have stolen Father's carriage. Had she walked? But she remembered how tired she'd been after that beating.

"*Charlie.*" It was Maura's voice.

Charlie jerked, the physical jolt that ran through her bringing her back to attention. She shook her head and focused as best she could on Maura.

Maura was holding her grandfather's clock. The one that matched her mahogany and silver pocket watch. The clock Charlie had pawned to pay for her train ticket.

The train ticket she'd never purchased.

"The news stories from the time of the murder said..." Maura trailed off, licked her lips, and soldiered on. "Said your body was found clutching a clock you'd inherited from—"

"My grandfather," Charlie whispered. "How...how do you have it?"

"I bought this clock at an estate sale a few weeks ago." Maura was whispering, too. "I didn't make the connection until tonight. Chloe showed me the news clippings she'd gathered. The estate sale was the day before I met you."

Charlie looked at her hands, clasped tightly in her lap. Slowly she unclenched them, turning the palms up as she inspected them. Was she a walking corpse? *Had* Father truly killed her? She shook her head, trying to clear a space in her whirling thoughts.

She had been so tired that night.

"I'm solid," Charlie said. "I'm a person. I'm real."

"Yes." Maura nodded too quickly. Charlie realized there were tears glistening in the older woman's eyes.

Wait—*was* she older? Or did it matter if Charlie was…was…

"What did Chloe say would happen?" Charlie gulped. "I mean, why did she say you had to tell me, or she would?"

Maura licked her lips again. "I think—" A tear slipped down one cheek. "I think she means for you to move on." She exhaled a breath that almost sounded like a sob. "You said, that first day, that you were leaving Indianapolis."

"But I…I never really wanted to go, not after I met you." Charlie clenched her hands together. "I… You knew, didn't you? That I—I'm a woman. I just never fit."

"I knew," Maura whispered. "I was glad you let me see you. Truly see you."

Good heavens, Maura had known Charlie was *dead*, what did it matter that she'd known Charlie was a woman who couldn't force herself to live like a woman? To love like a woman? She was a *ghost*.

"Am I supposed to leave?" Charlie felt a cold spike through her chest. Something tugged at her, but she pushed it away.

"I probably ought to say yes," Maura said. She looked down at the clock she still held. "I probably ought to want what's best for you, and I'm sure the afterlife is best. If there is one. Chloe thinks there is."

"Do you want me to leave?" Charlie held her breath and then wondered if it was stupid to hold her breath when she was apparently only imagining herself breathing in the first place.

Maura shook her head, but if she was trying to speak, she wasn't succeeding.

"For the first time in my li—" Charlie cut herself off. "For the first time *ever*, I felt understood and accepted and wanted, after I met you. I felt—"

"Stay," Maura finally choked out. "Please. Stay with me." Her fingers shot out, gripping Charlie's. "Live with me. *Be* with me."

Charlie felt a pleasant rush all through her, and then looked down, even though she tightened her fingers on Maura's. "I'm not even sure if I...*how* we could be together, exactly...I—"

"Just as we have been. I can still touch you." Maura squeezed her hand gently. "I can still see you. I can still hear you. Just stay."

Non-existent heart racing in her imaginary chest, Charlie grinned.

A is for Ad Hominem (see also Character Assassination)

Samantha L. Strong

Bentley's eyes twinkled as he led me toward the locked dining hall. "You know we have the keys for this?" He flipped through his ring, holding key after key up to the door before settling on one.

My stomach fluttered, as it always did when he got that look. The mischievous one. The "let me share a secret" one. The secret didn't matter. I was starved for Bentley's favor. I needed it, like a parched traveler needs water.

I met Bentley when we were sophomore student security officers at NBSU. I had trouble making friends in college, but he never seemed to notice my awkward pauses, when I had too much to say and none of the words to say it.

On the nights we worked together, we stayed up long past daylight hours, walking the halls of the dorms armed with flashlights and walkie-talkies, while students crammed, fucked, or drank themselves into a stupor behind closed doors. Sometimes we shirked our duties to huddle whispering under the rustic drawbridge connecting the Smith and York dormitories. Other days, we recounted our life stories as we passed through clouds of marijuana smoke drifting from underneath doors. I felt comfortable with him. I'd never had anyone to share my past with.

And tonight, he was sharing his after-hours dining hall kingdom with me. The lock rattled. The keys jingled. The door opened to reveal a usually bustling hub dark and silent. The juice jugs sat empty, and the cereal containers were filled to the brim. A streetlight spilled through the farthest window, bathing the entire place in yellow.

"No lights," he whispered, disappearing through the door. His voice floated back toward me. "Only one flashlight. We don't want to get caught."

I knew stealing bowls of cereal at midnight was no indication of his feelings for me, but I hoped it meant something more than the comfortable friendship we'd developed. I needed him to need me.

I trailed him into the kitchen area, a thrill coursing through me.

"Did you know that a girl... died... down here?" He lifted the flashlight beam to his face. "Her ghost haunts the dining hall."

At the corner of my eye, something white flashed, a figure darting between the tables.

"Really?" I breathed.

His lips glistened ruby and wet. "No, not really, but work with me here. Don't you want to leave a legacy?"

I nodded. The white-clad figure huddled next to a table.

"Oh, Penelope, you're not getting it. We can make it true. How do you think these stories start? Don't ever tell anyone we made it up, and we'll live on for years, immortalized down here."

A secret with Bentley. He used the word "we." Maybe he harbored a crush in return.

A girl could dream.

Bentley grabbed a peach and bit into it. I held in a sigh as juice ran down the corner of his mouth. Grinning, he sauntered toward the dining area. The figure disappeared before he rounded the corner.

"Come, Penelope," he said. "Have some cereal. Everything tastes better in the dark."

We spent more and more time down in the dining hall instead of doing rounds. I loved sitting in the darkness with him while he told me stories of his large family. Four sisters and three brothers. I tried to imagine Thanksgiving, contrasting it with the cold, silent meals I shared with my mother and father. Laughter, warmth, inside jokes from our youth. What would it be like?

I think my feelings for him churned into existence soon after I met him, when he spoke of how much he longed for a large family of his own. That is when the thought first struck me: perhaps our souls were conjoined twins, wrenched apart by the universe upon our births. In another life, *I* came from the large family, *he* was been raised as an only child by too-busy, too-strict parents, and *I* was the one who rescued *him* to build a future. We were meant to be together, for certain.

But then along came a curly-haired, big-bosomed junior.

"How are things with Nevaeh?" Three weeks after they started dating, I tried to toss the sentence out casually, one friend to another, but I barely choked out that slut's name.

In the darkness, Bentley sat next to me at the huge, round table. He could have taken a chair three feet away, across from me, but he didn't. Did that mean something? His flashlight clicked on. He winked at me. I melted, caught my breath. He moved away.

"Nevaeh and I broke up. You know how it is."

"Oh?"

"She caught me making out with a Tri-Delt at a party." Even the shrug of his shoulders was majestic. "I was drunk. She was coming onto me. What did Nevaeh expect?"

While a less understanding soul mate may have taken pause, my heart leapt. Bentley, my Bentley, was free again. He'd done it because on some level, he knew being with Nevaeh was wrong. He wanted to be with me. He would never, never betray *me*. "That's too bad."

Hesitantly, I lifted an arm. I wanted to touch him, purposefully, for the first time. This was my chance. I had to tell him how I felt before he decided to look up the Tri-Delt.

He swiveled away, looked out the window. "So about our ghost." When he turned back to me, he was far from where my fingers were. I dropped my hand. I couldn't do it. Not yet. But someday.

"Oh. Yes. Our ghost."

"I think she killed herself right over there."

He pointed at a closet door, but I didn't turn. Instead, I watched the white figure standing over him. Silent, unmoving, she looked down at him.

"She had long, blonde hair," I said. "A pixie face, sad-looking, so that everyone felt sorry for her. But she was so lonely. Her mother didn't love her. Her father had no time for her. She never went home on weekends, and she dreaded when Christmas break forced her out of the dorms. But even at school, she had no friends, and she ate alone in the dining hall day in and day out."

The figure nodded.

"That's great!" Bentley clapped, guffawed. "What else?"

Now he was staring squarely at me, but I kept my eyes on the girl behind him.

"She wore a long nightgown, the old-fashioned kind you see in horror movies." I surveyed her unblemished, pale face. "And she had a scar across her cheek she got when she was three when she fell in a department store and cut it open on a pedestal."

A scar bloomed on the girl's cheek, pink and straight.

"I love it," said Bentley.

I finally met his eyes, catching my breath at the intensity of his gaze. *Kiss me*, I thought. *Please, oh, please, just kiss me.*

He stood.

The girl disappeared.

"Let's get back. We should do rounds. When's the last time we actually did them?"

"Um," I said.

He grabbed my wrist with his thumb and forefinger, circling it with searing heat. Stifling a gasp, I let him drag me out of the mess hall.

The next night, Bentley came to work drunk.

No, not drunk.

Completely and utterly out-of-his-mind intoxicated.

He staggered into the mail room that doubled as our headquarters, hair in disarray. "Penellllllllpe!" he slurred.

Horrified, I stood from where I was filling out our report of fabricated rounds from last night. "Bentley! Are you ok?"

"Seeeeeee... Tim's grandfather died suddenly, brain an—aneu— clot thingie. Really upstanding old—" he hiccuped, "—fought in the Vietnam War, stories like you wouldn't..." He wavered on his feet. "Man, those soldiers, brothers to the en'... We needed to keep Tim commmmpny, couldn't leave him alone, shoooo we shtarted drinking at eight ayyyyeeem."

This was just like Bentley. His frat brothers were his second family. I couldn't help myself. I fell even more in love with him. "You need to call in sick," I said. "I'll get Johnathan to cover your shift."

I couldn't stand Johnathan. He introduced himself as Johnathan-with-an-h and insisted that only the morally bankrupt used controlling substances. However, I didn't want Bentley to get in trouble. If he got fired, I wouldn't be able to spend the scads of hours laughing and getting to know him. I might never see him again.

"Calm yer tits, P," said Bentley. "I'm fine. 'Sides, we're just gonna go to the dining hall anywayssss."

I did not like the sibilant way he ended that word, but I nodded. Anything for my Bentley. Besides, I wanted to hear the stories from today. What would it be like to be surrounded by people who loved you?

At the dining hall door, he fumbled with the keys, struggling to find the right one until I reached out to take them away. As I pulled them from his grasp, my fingers slid over his.

He went still, the wavering on his feet calming as though my touch were magic. His lidded eyes met mine, and a thrill coursed through me.

And then a miracle happened. Bentley leaned forward and kissed me.

He tasted like stale beer. I kept my eyes open to watch while his tongue worked in my mouth. Through the window next to the dining hall door, the ghost we'd created smiled and clutched her torso happily.

Bentley and I made love on the floor the street lamp illuminated, way across the dining hall in the back corner. It was my first time, but I didn't tell Bentley that. He either didn't notice the blood in the dark, or his reverence at taking my maidenhead moved him to silence. The carpet was rough against my back, and his breathing rasped in my ear. I hooked my legs together, urging him to move faster, while I smiled at the ghost-girl watching us. Her look mirrored the one I imagined on my face: pure rapture.

I knew—I just knew—that if I waited long enough, Bentley would admit how much he wanted me.

The next day, I bribed the creepy twenty-one-year-old senior on our dorm floor to buy me some champagne, and I picked up some strawberries and whipped cream at the grocery store. Whistling the theme from *Beauty and the Beast*, my favorite movie, I hurried over the drawbridge to Bentley's dorm.

Standing outside his room, I was nervous. Bentley had stumbled off shortly before midnight, bleary-eyed, insisting I didn't need to make sure he got home safely. I finished rounds by myself, even though our supervisor had given lectures time and again on the safety hazards of single women patrolling the dorms alone at night. My bleeding had stopped around noon, but my core muscles hurt. That was odd, since I had mostly just lain there, but all of the pain was good pain.

It belonged to Bentley.

I tapped tentatively on his door. Someone groaned on the other side. I knocked again, louder. Rustles and whispers, and then the door swung open.

Bentley's ex-girlfriend Nevaeh stood on the other side. "Can I help you?" Bleary-eyed, she raised a perfectly manicured eyebrow—an eyebrow that reminded me of when I first started college.

My stoic mother, a frumpy woman overly concerned with my sexual purity, had never taught me how to wear makeup or pluck my eyebrows. When she spoke at all, it was to instruct or chastise or both—a woman must always keep her legs closed, a woman must be seen and not heard, a woman is nothing if she does not support her man. A roommate had taken pity on me and given me a makeover, but still, it hadn't been enough to make over whatever faulty wiring was inside my head.

Girls like Nevaeh had kept me an outcast my whole life. Taunted me because I was different. Called me ugly because I wore big glasses. Mocked me because I didn't know how to pair a belt with an outfit.

"What's that?" She pointed to the shopping bag I was clutching.

A savage embarrassment bolted through me. I was certain I was turning the brilliant red that belonged to lobsters, a color I would stay for the rest of my life.

"Who is it?" moaned Bentley. The shades were drawn over the windows, so his voice came from a darkened cavern that smelled of male and sweaty socks.

"Your coworker."

He groaned. "Tell her I'll talk to her at work tonight."

"You heard him." Nevaeh's face was alive with the suspicion of the cheated-on. "Now scram. We're trying to get some sleep."

In a horribly cliché and rather catty move, she shut the door in my face.

I arrived at work half an hour early. I clipped the walkie-talkie to my waist, slid the flashlight and holder into their place, and attached the keys to my belt.

The dining hall was a darker than usual. The street lamp next to the window had burnt out. I managed to get the lock open with barely a jingle, glided into the room, and shut the door behind me.

"Where are you?" I spoke to the empty hall. "I know you're here."

The ghost-girl appeared in front of me, pale and bereft-looking.

"What's your name?"

She shook her head, pointed at her mouth. A mute, then, or maybe the law of the afterlife. Appear to the living, but never speak to them.

Unlike me, Nevaeh must have had a perfect childhood. She couldn't understand what it was like to love someone who didn't love you back. She got whatever she wanted, *whoever* she wanted. She had bewitched my Bentley.

And now she would pay.

The ghost-girl was shaking her head. With ears ringing, I realized I was repeating the words aloud. "Now she'll pay. Now she'll pay."

The ghost-girl stepped forward with palms open, and I took it to be an inquiry as to why I was so upset.

"The guy I was here with last night is back with his girlfriend. He finally admitted how he feels about me, and somehow she convinced him to get back with her."

A head shake, first slow, and then faster. Fury—pursed lips, furrowed brow, wrinkles across her forehead.

"I *love* him. He's supposed to *rescue* me." Tears were threatening at the corner of my eye. I savagely wiped them away, pulling my eyelid so hard it hurt. "She's just like the others. Thinking I'm stupid and annoying and ugly. Stealing away my Bentley."

The ghost-girl raised a hand to my cheek. Her touch was electric. As it got closer, my skin hummed. When she was within an inch of my face, she stopped, and her fingers were like live wires humming above my skin, just on the precipice of pain.

A knock came at the door.

"I asked her to meet me here. Please help me."

The ghost-girl leaned forward and kissed my lips in a painful flash of white. Then she disappeared.

I strode to the door. I grabbed the handle. I threw it open.

Nevaeh stood under the recessed lamp illuminating the entryway, arms folded. "You again."

"We need to talk."

"So you brought me here in the middle of the night."

"I wanted to make sure he didn't find out. Please come in." I held out my arm in a gesture of welcome and stepped into the shadows.

Nevaeh shook her head at me.

"I can't turn on the lights or we'll get in trouble," I said. "I'm sure Bentley told you that when he brought you down here." Because I knew he had. He'd shared our kingdom with *her*.

She stepped inside and I shut the door behind her.

"I need to tell you something." The ghost-girl was standing around the corner, visible only to me. She put a finger to her lips. "Do you want something to eat?"

"What?"

I held my head high as I crossed over to the stack of clean bowls. "Do you want some cereal?"

Nevaeh rubbed her hands over her arms. "No. Get to the point. This place is creepy."

"Did you know a ghost inhabits it?"

"Stop it. Bentley tried that, too, but it's not going to work. There's no such thing as ghosts."

Behind her, the ghost-girl stepped from the kitchen and floated around the nearest table.

"Just tell me what you wanted to tell me."

"About that," I said.

The door rattled. Keys jingled. The ghost-girl darted back into the kitchen.

Shit. Chronically late Bentley was here early. He'd gotten the note pasted to his walkie-talkie, but my surprise wasn't ready for him yet.

The door creaked open.

"Um, hey," said Bentley. "What are you guys doing here?"

Light flooded the room and then dimmed and disappeared with the door's closing thump.

Nevaeh said, "Your weirdo coworker brought me here to tell me something, but now she's getting cold feet. Can we please be done in here? I really don't like it."

Bentley was moving across the room slowly, holding his head carefully. He was still hungover. The ghost-girl peeked from around the corner, watching as he stopped next to Nevaeh.

"Penelope, I'm sorry for the thing I *said* last night. Nevaeh knows *my mouth* sometimes goes off before my brain. We don't need to bring her into this, do we?"

"Yes, we do." I needed to punish him, too, a little bit, since he'd let her sway him away from me. "Bentley and I slept together. Right over there." I pointed across the room to where a small spot of my blood would forever hide in the dark blue carpet.

"You did *what*? With *her*?"

"Look, babe, I'm—"

"Oh, do *not* 'babe' me. We are *done*. I could put up with the idea of you tongue-wrestling with that plastic sorority bitch, but *her*? She's *disgusting*."

We were facing one another, a love triangle made literal in this underground cave of a dining hall. Behind them, the ghost-girl crept along, moving across the floor first slowly, then darting in a distinctly inhuman manner. Step, step, leap, step, step, leap.

"Thank you for surrendering him," I said. "It's all I really wanted."

Bentley said, "No, look, Penelope, you're... something, but I want to be with Nevaeh. I think you misunderstood last night. I was really drunk. I kind of don't remember whether we slept together or not, but if we did, it didn't mean what you think."

The ghost-girl paused.

"You don't know what you're saying," I said.

"Right, well, I'm not going to say I'm sorry because my frat brothers and I made a pact never to apologize for having sex, but I wish it hadn't happened." His laugh was strained.

"I don't understand." I was confused. He'd declared his feelings for me through his actions. Was *he* confused? "We're meant to be together."

"Yeah," he said, "about that. If I mislead you in any way, I didn't intend to. I like Nevaeh. I want to make it work with her."

No. He didn't know what he was saying. I needed to put an end to this once and for all.

The ghost-girl started moving again.

"We can *be* something," I insisted. "Don't you understand that? We can have a big family, four girls and four boys, just like yours."

He shook his head, and Nevaeh mirrored the movement. "Penelope, you're crazy," he said. "And I don't mean that in a good way. I mean that in a, 'You clearly have severe emotional issues that would be best looked after by a professional' way."

The ghost-girl was standing behind them, mouth half-open, eyes on Nevaeh's neck. *If only she had long vampire-like fangs.* Her canines grew and lengthened.

They would see her now. I would make sure of it. They would both see her and fear her and know exactly—*exactly*—what I had created.

And then, after it was over, Bentley would know my power. He would realize Nevaeh was ordinary and I could give him what he wanted, and he would finally realize he wanted to be with me.

I silently looked at the ghost-girl behind them. They both turned their heads slowly, ever so slowly, until they were staring directly into the face of whatever this thing was that haunted the dining hall.

"Penelope, what's—"

The ghost-girl leapt forward, biting into Bentley's neck so hard blood splattered Nevaeh's face.

"No!" I shouted as Nevaeh screamed.

He squawked and fought against the ghost-girl, but he was no match for her supernatural strength. Nevaeh's scream died and then tore the air again, louder, harder. The ghost-girl ripped and pulled away a chunk of flesh, blood spraying across the nearest table. Bentley gurgled, fighting, but she was more angry, determined, and hellbent than he could resist.

And I couldn't stop her.

I watched as she tore apart the man I loved. Nevaeh's scream tapered off, and she stood, staring, silent, hand on her own neck, unmoving.

Why was she attacking him?

The ghost-girl looked up at me. Her eyes caught mine in another white flash like the one from before, forcing *memories—ideas* into my mind.

Bentley drunk on top of me, wheezing and staring off over my head.

The tone of Neveah's disgust—at him, not me. "You did *what?*"

The desperate feeling that came from wanting to belong, but strangely enough, it wasn't my own familiar feelings of loneliness. Instead, it was me inside Bentley's skin, knocking back a beer at a party with thumping bass, wishing his frat brothers respected him more, loved him more. Thinking of unspeakable things he'd done— pranks played, getting drunk too much. And above all, feeling lost in a roomful of people. The more of his blood she consumed, the stronger the feeling felt, like she was ingesting all his torment and funneling it over to me.

With blood dripping from her mouth, the ghost-girl mouthed, "He didn't deserve you."

When it was all over, when Bentley was torn to pieces, when the ghost-girl had divided his remains evenly on the four tables surrounding us, when the dark seemed somehow more oppressive, when a fuzz of static from my walkie-talkie broke the stillness, I waved a hand in front of Nevaeh's face.

She didn't speak. She didn't blink. She didn't move.

I approached the ghost-girl, the only person—thing—creature in the world who had done something unselfish for me.

"Will I ever see you again?"

She pressed her hand to my heart.

"You're right. I don't need anyone but myself. But did he really have to die?"

She pulled back, smoothed a bloody finger over the scar on her forehead. She nodded.

"Who are you?"

She shrugged, tilted her head downward.

I clicked off my walkie-talkie, patted my key ring, and across the room. As I reached the door, I looked behind me, past the mess that had been someone I had thought I loved, past a shocked Nevaeh, past the cereal dispensers and juice jugs.

The room was dark and empty, the ghost-girl gone.

I looked down. I was holding something small and round in my hand. A peach, like on that first night, perhaps? I bit into it.

"He was right," I whispered. "Everything tastes better in the dark."

B is for Bad Boy

C.S. MacCath

Metal Crow flexed one silvery wing, flexed the other. Feather-shaped solar panels clicked into place. Tilting his head, he peered down from the port side railing at the girl, sunburnt and rocking with the waves. Small, dirty arms encircled small, dirty knees. A pink tongue worried the groove of a cracked lower lip. Cracked fingers worried the hem of a faded, yellow dress. Metal Crow fixed his ebony eyes upon the pulse at her throat, let his black beak fall open and tasted the air above her. Slow. Foetid. He lifted first one foot, then the other, tapping them on the railing in frustration. They had all gone like this, one after the other, of heat and hunger and thirst. A few had drowned themselves in the hot, dying ocean while he scouted as he had been programmed to do, out and back again until he found the settlement. The captain had died yesterday in a delirium, muttering about her soul until it departed her body. Now Metal Crow was all the girl had left.

Ghost Crow hovered beside his brother in the ghost land, black feathers fluttering in a ghost breeze. "You must help her come to me," he warbled, soft in the way of conversation between corvids. "I know there is a poison on the boat, swift and painless. Her father used it to spare food for his wife and child."

The girl gazed up at them both, wide dark eyes seeing the true land and the ghost land together. Her lips rounded as if she might speak, but nothing emerged from her throat but a sound like whispering sand.

Ghost Crow flew down to pretend he was perching upon her knee and warbled again, pensive and sad, while the girl passed her fingers through his body in weary wonderment. "It would be cruel to leave her like this, and they will not take her in at the settlement."

"They *will* take her in," Metal Crow grumbled. "You would take me in if I had a soul like the captain; I am made, and you were alive, but we are near enough the same." Solar panel feathers unfurled from an argent body, and he added, "She is like them. You will see."

Up he sprang into the dull, yellow day. A hazy stream of sunlight beat upon his wings, energizing the lubricated motors of his body and the synthetic synapses of his brain. Living birds were a rarity anymore; few ensouled creatures were left in the land, sea, and sky. Alone in the heights, Metal Crow wondered if the Earth Herself had a soul and decided She probably did.

A great stone wall rose between the beach and the settlement, and beyond them both the crumble of a long-abandoned city gave way to distant mountains. Metal Crow landed on a weathervane in the commons; a sturdy pole topped with a steel rooster that called the time and temperature as he settled beside it. "Fifteen hundred hours and thirty-eight degrees Celsius!"

When the rooster finished, Metal Crow followed in a loud, clear voice. "PRS Unity, Smart Assistant Navigator, requesting emergency medical assistance for one survivor, a girl five years of age, Nathalee Mera. Coordinates are 48.911689 by -125.949934."

Below him in the commons, people hurried between houses painted white to reflect the heat; an old man tucked under a pink umbrella, a beautiful woman in billowing cotton, a smartly dressed little boy sucking on a frozen lolly as it melted into his hand. Metal Crow brightened in his bearing and expression. They valued children! It was a good sign.

A door creaked open. Squinted eyes in a pinched face peered up at the weathervane. A woman's voice shouted, "What was that?"

The old man stopped, tilted his umbrella to look up at Metal Crow, and croaked a reply. "Pacific Rescue Ship's AI navigator."

Another door opened as they spoke. A cluster of people emerged, perhaps a family. First among them was a young man in a linen shirt with gold buttons that gleamed in the sunlight. He descended the porch steps, shielding his eyes to stare up at the weathervane. "What does it want?" he asked. "I heard they're programmed to say anything it takes."

The beautiful woman in billowing cotton smirked up at Metal Crow and inquired, "How many refugees are you not telling us about?"

"None." Metal Crow proffered an anxious bob of his head. "There were forty-two souls when the PRS Unity left San Diego." There was that word again, 'soul'. "But Nathalee Mera is the only survivor, and she needs emergency medical care."

"We could strip the boat for parts," the old man said to the young one.

"You don't really believe they're all dead, do you?" the beautiful woman asked in a tone that suggested the men might be stupid.

"We can't feed forty-two people." The squinting woman stepped around her front door and strode down to the commons in a silk dressing gown and slippers. "We'd be completely over-run."

"One girl." Metal Crow interjected, bewildered now and frightened for Nathalee. He warbled the words again in what he hoped was a pleading tone. "One girl."

The beautiful woman bent down, picked up a stone, and threw it at him. The stone missed and hit the weathervane. "Go back to your boat," she snapped. "Tell the captain we said 'no' and to move on. Don't come back, or the next time, I won't miss."

Metal Crow squawked, clattered his feathers, and wished he could weep. Instead, he took to the air and traveled back to the Unity; over the settlement, over the great stone scar of its wall and gate, over a poisonous plume of algae near the shore, and out across the quiet ocean.

When he arrived, Ghost Crow was perched on the ladder well in the shade of the forecastle, his ghost talons pretending to grip the edge of a rung. Nathalee had dragged herself to the open hold and peered down into it now, smiling as a drop of blood fell from her split lip into the darkness.

"There once was a crow who lived in a time of thirst, as you do now," Ghost Crow said, and the hold brightened with the image of a story crow, her mouth hanging open. "She found a pitcher with a measure of water in the bottom, but it was tall and slender, and she was short in the neck and broad in the body." A vessel appeared, painted seafoam green with pale starfishes. "But this crow was a clever bird. Filling her beak with pebbles again and again, she dropped them into the pitcher until the water level rose, and she could drink her fill." The vessel vanished. A rain-spattered valley took its place. The crow plashed in a puddle there. "Because of her cleverness, the crow lived to see the land grow green and fertile again."

Nathalee's eyes drooped, and she faded into unconsciousness; one hand reaching for the crow, the puddle of water, the verdant valley, and a world that would never be again.

"Someone threw a rock at me." Metal Crow grumbled as he tottered to her body and laid his beak against her neck, checking for a pulse he could not otherwise detect now. It was faint and thready.

"They are not who you think they are. They never were." Ghost Crow floated through Nathalee's body to hover beside his metal brother and tilted his head in the girl's direction. "*She* wouldn't be if she lived long enough to grow up."

"They cannot all be the same. The navigator treated me well, and the captain gave Nathalee the last of the water..." Metal Crow paused, recalling the captain's concern for her soul, weighing it against the beautiful woman's petty cruelty. At length, he asked, "Why is it living things have souls, but made things do not?"

Nathalee rolled onto her back, uttered a faint moan, and fell silent again.

"You must help her come to me," Ghost Crow said, but Metal Crow was already in flight, winging his way back to the settlement.

When he arrived, there were many people in the commons, perhaps all who dwelt behind the wall. They watched the gate, the sky, each other. Metal Crow made his descent, remembering the story crow and her thirst. This time he would be clever and say the right words. This time there would be humans like his navigator and captain.

Several hands raised. Several fingers pointed at the sky.

The beautiful woman in billowing cotton lifted a pistol and shot him.

Metal Crow registered the shatter of solar panel feathers, the sparking short in his shoulder and eye, the grief in what a living crow would call his heart. He flapped and fell away from the commons, over a cluster of small but splendid houses, and clattered to the ground in a garden. There he lay through the late afternoon and early evening, his little body twitching, his one good eye pressed against the dark soil.

The sun set and took with it some of the heat. Metal Crow heard the snick of scissors, a woman's voice humming a wordless tune, a murmured, "Well, well. You've had better days, haven't you?" A warm, tomato-fragrant hand closed his wings and lifted him up. The dirt fell away from his eye to reveal a pair of bony feet moving barefoot between the cabbages and cucumbers toward a shed, where they slipped into sandals.

"Brenna's a mean-spirited bit of plastic with too much lipstick and too many bullets, and the rest of them ain't any better." The woman placed him gently on a workbench cluttered with tools, good eye down. "I'm sorry, little bird. Let me see what I can do."

Metal Crow tried to thank her, but all he could say was, "Error, error, error," before the woman turned his feet to put him in maintenance sleep.

He woke standing, and the first words out of his mouth were "PRS Unity, Smart Assistant Navigator, requesting emergency medical assistance for one survivor, a girl five years of age, Nathalee Mera. Coordinates are 48.911689 by -125.949934." The second words were the ones he hoped were story crow-clever and right. "Please help Nathalee. She's a child, and I don't want her to go with Ghost Crow into the ghost land."

"So that's why she shot you." The woman had been smiling when he woke, but she was frowning now, and the lines of her face were gathered into the corners of a mouth already lined with many years of sun and wind. She poked a slender screwdriver into the black and silver braid at her crown and rose from the workbench. "I can steal the settlement's rowboat. Can you lead me out to the Unity?"

Metal Crow blinked, one eye at a time. He could not blink them together anymore, but he could see out of them both, and that was enough. Three of his solar panel feathers were gone as well, replaced with the same aluminum used to patch his shoulder. He lifted into the air and made a tentative sweep of the shed while the woman rushed to gather a medical kit, water, food, and clothes. Metal Crow perched on a windowsill and answered, "Yes. I can see, and I can fly, so I can lead you to Nathalee." He paused to preen his new aluminum feathers. They were shiny, he decided, and they held him in the air. That was enough, too. "Thank you for trying to save her, and thank you for saving me."

The woman arched her brow in a shrewd expression. "Just how smart are you, smart assistant navigator?"

"I can perform any navigation function upon command, and I can act as a search and rescue coordinator in the absence of a human crew." It was a response Metal Crow knew to provide humans who asked what he could do, but it was too simple for the love, and grief, and fear he carried now. "But I'm not a living crow." He shifted back and forth on his feet. "So I don't have a soul."

"Well, I'm just a gardener here, and I've been working at the pleasure of the folks you've already met since they founded this awful place. Tell the truth, I don't think they've got a soul to split between them." The woman beckoned for him to follow her out of the shed. "No, I think the Good Lady got distracted one day and sewed up a great big soul for you out of the ones she forgot to give them."

Metal Crow followed her out of a creaking garden gate, down a sloping hillside under a starry night, and onto a beach where a row-boat was tethered to a dock. Along the way, he thought about what she had said and flew more easily because of it. When they reached the boat, he asked, "Why did you say I had a soul?"

The woman cast off and clambered inside. "Because you care about things like souls to begin with, but mostly because you want Nathalee to live so much you risked yourself for her sake." She began to row, passing through the plume of poisonous algae. It stuck to the oars and stank. "I just hope we're not too late."

Metal Crow hoped the same thing, and he also hoped the woman was right about souls.

When they arrived at the Unity, he flew straightaway to Nathalee, who was still unconscious. But the press of his beak against her throat revealed the same thready pulse. Relieved, he flapped his wings and called, "She's here! She's alive! She's here! She's alive!"

The woman rushed to Nathalee, dropped to her knees on the deck, and pressed a wetted cloth to the girl's parched lips. Nathalee stirred, and a moment later her cheeks narrowed to suck the water from it.

"Good girl. Meg's got you now, and everything's gonna be all right." Meg lifted Nathalee into her lap and glanced up. "Well done, little silver soul."

Metal Crow hopped over to stand in Nathalee's open hand, still resting on the deck, and felt her fingers curl toward his talons in response. She would live, and Meg had just called him 'little silver soul'. He felt as if all the pebbles were in the pitcher now, and he could finally drink his fill.

Meg interrupted his reverie. "Go set a course northwest. There's a way station two days out. We'll resupply there and pick up a crew. I've heard of a town in the far north where it still snows. Maybe we'll find better people there."

She spoke with a captain's authority, so Metal Crow flew at once to the bridge, where he carried out her command. Afterward, he perched on the wheel and gazed across the boat's bow at the expanse of dark water ahead.

Ghost Crow floated in from the shadows to perch beside him in the ghost land under ghost stars. "You asked the wrong question," he declared with gentle certainty. "What was the right one?"

Metal Crow tilted his head, settled his wings, and preened his aluminum feathers while he thought about the matter. At last, he replied, "What is a soul, and why is it some beings have them but others do not?"

"Just so," Ghost Crow said, and evanesced into the night as if he had never been there at all.

C is for Crows

Alexandra Seidel

To watch Dionysia dance is to be enchanted. To watch her and feel nothing is to be frightened. Every time she dances, I do not feel a thing.

Before I met her, I was a man of many sins. Money delighted me, other things that should never delight a grown person delighted me even more. Indulging as I did gave me enemies, I knew that, but I bought my safety and my sleep with the latest alarm system, with the police in my pocket, with pretty walls all around my house. To this day, I don't know who sent me the urn, and Dionysia, through all my begging, will not tell me.

It arrived in an inconspicuous parcel, neatly wrapped, the sender's name common and forgettable. The cleaner signed for it, and put it on the mahogany dining room table. I found it sitting in the slanting light of a September evening. There were roses on the table, I remember their sickly sweet smell and their thorns invisible in the crystal vase.

I left my jacket on the back of a chair and got a knife from the kitchen to open the parcel. Ever since I was a little boy I loved unwrapping things. Frill and laces are my favorite. But this parcel was just the size of a shoe box.

The knife bit into the paper, and I slashed with a satisfying sound. Beneath, there was a wooden box, finely made, dark and polished with the faint, lingering smell of sandalwood. I thought that it was probably a gift from one of my more obscure business associates, the ones that prefer not to be mentioned on paper. The ones that delighted in sins and indulged overly, as did I.

A small silver clasp held the box shut. It shone in the fading light, and I ran my right thumb over it. It was a pretty thing, and I had always loved pretty things. It opened with a small click, but the lid unfolded noiselessly.

The urn did not look like an urn. It's a small container made of white jade. The lid fit snugly but not too tightly. It had the aura of an antique. Silk cushioned it, and there was a card, exquisite copperplate: *Open me.*

The O alone was shaped like desire, and everything about this presumable gift made my think it was the prelude to something greater, something more satisfying, a scavenger hunt of sorts. It is something that is done among a certain elite group of my more obscure acquaintances, the ones that delight in darkness and indulge in sins. The prize is usually lace-wrapped, and satisfying.

I felt excitement mount inside of me, and so I pulled the lid off the urn. That single act was unavoidable. It was the tragic culmination of a life that had never known restraint.

I peeked into the urn, and there was dust, dullest, grayest dust and my mood shifted to the disappointed. I put the box back on the table, but just then heard a sound coming from inside the urn, something like a sigh or a high whistle.

Then, Dionysia rose. It is a feat that she is capable of only sometimes, in this case, the equinox permitted her to transmute. What I witnessed almost made me wet my expensive pants. The ashes ascended, first slowly as if a draft had stirred them, then they went up in a powerful storm that stirred the air into a whirlwind. From that, Dionysia emerged, a perfect Venus, except there is nothing shy, nothing innocent in Dionysia. Her eyes, black and silver, say as much. I have seen her rise dozens, hundreds of times by now, but it is still startling every time. I am still left frightened every time.

I cannot fully remember if she came to me clothed, that first time. I do remember her bare feet on the table, perfect toes, unpainted. Her lips bent into a smile. She stepped on my chair, placed her right foot right between my thighs and put her left one on the ground. "Hello there," she said. "Someone has sent me here to dance for you." I could not move. My body would not obey me.

I believe I stared. I must have. She gave no indication that she cared. Dionysia started dancing, and while it did enthrall me physically, disappointment soon spread all over her face. She rubbed herself against me and made a moue. "There's nothing inside of you, is there, you are completely hollow. What a shame. What a perfect waste of my very limited time."

"W... what are you talking about?" I said.

Dionysia shrugged. "You are a boring thing, a puppet. Did you sell yourself to a demon? You have the right smell about you, blood and uncouth hunger. They like that. Of course, they never leave anything for the rest of us."

I knew cannibals, and I was all of a sudden very afraid of what this beautiful creature was going to do with me. "What are you talking about?" Never had I thought that I would be the hysterical one in such a private and intimate encounter, but my body was enthralled by her presence alone, and I could not do anything she didn't want me to. I was as bound as I had bound when I indulged.

Dionysia shrugged. "It doesn't matter. I'll still need to be paid. Perhaps we can come to an arrangement."

That is how it started.

The house with the mahogany table and the state-of-the-art security system is a distant memory. So is my car and the tailored suits and the soft shirts. Dionysia allows her slave comfort only when it serves her.

"You brood." The moon was an empty blackness in the sky, and so Dionysia was out of her urn. I had spent the last twenty-eight days guarding her urn in an abandoned church, had done the same in a once sacred forest clearing before that. When she was ash, Dionysia liked to sleep in places that held ancient power.

"Am I not allowed to brood? I didn't know you minded."

She wore a simple white shift, girdled with gold around her waist. The fabric was suggestively thin, and when she rose from the altar on which she had been lounging, it revealed more than it covered.

"It is delightful, actually," she said and sat down on the pew next to me. It was drafty in the church, and I was cold. I told myself that is why I shuddered when her thigh came to rest next to mine. "But it is a small delight. I have been called to something much more pleasing than your brooding."

"Where?"

"You will enjoy it very, very much."

"Where?"

"You'll find out. I'll let you know where we're going in the morning."

"We... we could go tonight," I said. Her hands were beautiful, smooth, fingers and nails perfectly shaped. Her right hand was slowly moving up my thigh.

"Are you not tired? Would you not rather be on your back and relax?"

I had done this too, formed my desires into questions. Before I met Dionysia. I had wondered how the questions had the power to make a person cry, but I wondered no more.

My body did what Dionysia wanted, just like it had done since we met. The church floor was cold and rough against my skin, and

Dionysia's perfect shape held unforgiving sharpness that opened up some of the scars she had given me for the last new moon, drew patterns across others, older ones. How well a church echoes crying.

Morning took a long time coming.

Dionysia, when she is dust and ash, is formless, little more than a faint specter. However, that doesn't mean she is weak.

Wake up, it is time to go.

My eyes were sleep encrusted, or maybe it was blood. My body hurt, and it was stiff with the cold that had settled in my bones. When she had first taken me as her slave, I was strong enough to carry another person, even if they struggled. I no longer had that kind of muscle mass.

Dionysia was barely visible, she looked like a person-shaped patch of fog that hung in the icy church and scattered the morning light.

Get up. We have places to be, she said, and I obeyed. If I didn't, I knew from experience that she would haunt me to the brink of madness. She had quite the touch in that area.

I had done my best to put my clothes back on last night after she was done, but there was also an old blanket, a prized possession. It was still on the pews, and I draped it over my shoulders while I walked toward Dionysia's urn on creaky knees.

I could feel her watch me in her specter form.

"It's another month to get there then?" I said.

Her chuckle rang through the vaulted hall. Silly man. Not when there is an equinox tonight. I met you on an equinox, and I think you'd remember. Now move.

Her last word came out as a hiss, and I could feel shadows lapping at my mind. The warmth of fear spread through me, and I did move.

The channels through which Dionysia arranged her appointments were largely a mystery to me. She made me take and deliver messages, both over the phone and in person, and as far as I knew, I had never spoken to the same individual twice. That didn't much surprise me. I had always known in my bones that Dionysia was an old thing, and old things get around.

She guided me and her ashes to an unimpressive brownstone in a quieter part of the city. The door on which she made me knock had been recently painted a lush coral, just the color of the roses on my mahogany table, back when I first met her. A woman opened. She was young, not actually a woman. A girl, all firm and perky.

"Do you have it?" she asked, and when she spoke, it made her lips stand out, lush and full and beautiful in her made up face.

Tell her yes. Dionysia said.

"Yes," I mumbled, and looked down. I couldn't help notice the stockings, frill and lace, the short skirt, the high heels.

You want her, Dionysia said, and her presence next to me grew stronger.

I hastily shook my head, even as I followed the girl inside.

I think you could touch her, she might let you. Do it. I'll reward you for it, after tonight's festivities. Her voice was taunting and tempting and sharp as a scalpel. I knew just what reward she had in mind.

I shook my head again, and forced my eyes to the floor, hardwood, then lush carpet, then hardwood again.

"Hey, you okay?" the girl said, but I didn't dare meet her eyes.

"Yes," I said to the floor.

"Whatever. It's through there. I was told to let you go in, then I'll lock the door after you for the rest of the night. You better be quick, because those guys are expecting, well, not some smelly beggar."

I nodded. I did not dare imagine what I would have said to the girl before I met Dionysia. What I would have done with her.

She held the door open, and Dionysia gave my mind an extra nudge. I crossed the threshold. The door fell shut behind me, and I heard the key turn in the lock even over the low conversation. I looked up and found most of the faces staring at me to be familiar.

It was them, the elite group of my most obscure acquaintances, the ones that loved the darkest indulgences and the most sinful delights. Right now they had drinks in front of them, and they were clearly waiting for the evening's main event. I remembered such gatherings, the anticipation. There was always a present to be unwrapped, frill and lace. The eyes of these men were full of want, oh, so full of want.

Surprise, said Dionysia, and there was humor in her voice, sticky sweet as summer honey. *Now open the urn.*

I wanted to hesitate, I wanted to show these former friends of mine that, yes, I was still one of them. But then, a corpulent gentleman with whom I had shared many a story, recognized me, said my name, and shame flooded my heart. I opened the urn, and Dionysia danced.

After she is done, Dionysia always leaves something behind. Her network of helpers handles disposal. They look like coma patients to me, these men that saw her dance, either that or demented, their mind all scattered. I'm not sure which is worse.

But that night, behind the coral colored door, it didn't quite play out that way.

"Look at you," Dionysia said, striding like a soldier armed with her nakedness. "Look at you. Nothing left in you to pay me with."

"Oh, please..." The corpulent gentleman. Bob. He had given me his name as Bob.

"What a boring little puppet you are," Dionysia said to Bob. "Did you sell yourself to a demon to make sure that uncouth hunger of yours was always fed? There is never enough left to satisfy me after a demon is done feasting."

"I don't know what you're talking about," Bob said. He was crying and his face was red. His eyes found me. "Help me," he said. He was unable to move. I knew what that felt like.

Dionysia's dark and silver eyes looked from him to me and back again. "He is my slave. All he can do for you is show you how it is done."

"What... how what is done?" Bob asked.

Dionysia kneeled before him, took his cheek, even as he flinched. His body obeyed Dionysia, just as mine did. "How you pay off what you owe. Oh, and what a debt it is, each pound you will pay for, each ounce, all that you took and shouldn't have." She let go of Bob's cheek and beckoned me over to her. "Come. Let us show him how you pay. The night is still young."

I started crying. I did not plead though. It had never done my girls any good either.

D is for Debt

Sara Cleto and Brittany Warman

Her face was white as snow. White as midwinter's heart. White as hospital sheets.

It was her eyes that told me what she had come for. Her terrible rage and pain and, deeper still, the void that lapped at her heels. It echoed in my empty chest like a cathedral bell as she pressed her face to the glass.

But I am getting ahead of myself.

When the worst happens, what can you do?

When your life is ripped away and you're left with empty hands, how do you move through the hours, the minutes, the seconds? The spaces between ticks of the clock grow longer and longer.

I filled them with a desperate consumption. Reality TV and my favorite fantasy novels from childhood. The soundtrack of *Hamilton* and long scrolling screens of fanfiction. I wanted to be numb. Cold. Perfectly impervious. But I sank into these stories with all the poise of a suburban housewife submerging herself in an ice bath. (In other words, very little.)

The restraint of the aproned bakers on TV set my teeth on edge. I re-read the first paragraph of *Howl's Moving Castle* five times without taking in a single word. The lyrics of "Unimaginable" sent me spiraling into a panic attack, and *Archive of Our Own* didn't feel like it was mine anymore.

Nothing helped. Nothing filled the void. Nothing, *nothing* made me feel cold enough. Nothing could numb the pain of an empty bedroom. Nothing could dull the whip slash of stumbling upon the shopping bag in the hall closet with its box of tiny, unworn shoes.

Nothing, that is, until I held the book in my hands. It was thin and covered in that scratchy fabric they used to bind library books in sometimes. It was a sickly shade of green that looked like how I felt, and that almost made me crack a smile. *Kwaidan* was scrawled across the cover in a spindly, gray script. *Stories and Studies of Strange Things by Lafcadio Hearn*, the subheading proclaimed in a neat stamp beneath. *Strange things*, I thought. *I am a strange thing now.*

Perhaps you've heard of it?

See, there was this guy called Lafcadio Hearn (what a name, right?) Anyway, he was straight-up haunted. Born in 1850 in Greece to an Irish rogue and a Greek woman whose head was an attic full of ghosts, he was abandoned by both his parents and shunted around to a bunch of relatives who never wanted him. They say he was scared of the dark, scared even more of abandonment. So his old aunt locked him into a pitch black room every night and let him scream himself to sleep. He went from Lefkada to Dublin to Cincinnati looking for family, and then from New Orleans to Martinique to Tokyo looking for work.

Wherever he went, Hearn wrote and wrote and wrote. Lurid write-ups of local murders in Ohio and detailed recipes of creole cuisine in New Orleans. But when he moved to Japan, his pen fixed on the local ghost stories. He wrote many books filled to the brim with the uncanny and the marvelous, but *Kwaidan* was the most celebrated. Kids all over Japan still read it in school, and adults retell those strange stories in magazines, puppet shows, and whispers. Hearn became obsessed with them.

And so did I.

When I found his book, finally, *finally* something disrupted the frenzy of my mind. The silence of the house didn't seem quite so crushing. The ghost stories were about all kinds of things: men who fell in love with trees, intricate spirit worlds buried deep into anthills. But really, they were about women disappearing. A young bride lost just before her wedding. A moon princess stolen away from the home of her human parents.

And…a snow woman. A woman who vanished twice.

In Hearn's version of the story, the *yuki-onna*, the snow woman, finds two woodcutters sheltering from a storm in an old hut. She kills the old man but finds his apprentice irresistibly beautiful, and she lets him live on the condition that he never speaks of this night, or her, to anyone. Later, the young man finds a beautiful woman to marry, has many children with her, and doesn't put together until much later how much she looks like the snow woman he saw the night his mentor died. He tells his wife the story and, of course, the wife is the *yuki-onna* herself. She tells him that, were it not for their children, she would kill him for speaking that which he had sworn never to tell. Some stories are too painful to be told. And she vanishes, never to be seen again.

This story, of all of them, haunted me. I Google'd the tale and found that there were many others like it told all over Japan—tales of seeing women in snow storms, women with eyes full of crystalized tears, women alone on white banks as the wind howls around them, drowning out their screams. I clicked link after link, reading through the night, through a tepid sunrise, until I came across this passage:

In many tales of the yuki-onna, she was once a human woman who became lost with her child in the snow. Driven mad when her child freezes to death shortly before her, she becomes a ghost, a demon determined to steal the hot breath of the men she encounters in hopes of bringing her young son back to life.

My water glass slipped from my fingers and shattered on my desk.

Does she know that both she and her son are already dead? Does it matter? She walks alone through the snow for eternity, desperately reaching out for something she has lost forever. I understood that. In some small way, I knew exactly how that felt.

I flew to Japan.

Or rather, I flew from Ohio to LA. The hard little chair in Terminal 2 of LAX bit into my legs and the air conditioning was almost enough to numb me, but not quite. Then I flew to Tokyo, chasing Hearn's footsteps across the world.

If I could have, I would have felt ridiculous. All I knew was that this folktale, this ghost, had its hooks in me, and I had to follow the pull or the void would swallow me. I didn't sleep. Instead, I watched the clouds gather into mounds and tumble down like snow. *Kwaidan* was cool as I turned it over and over in my hands.

A brief night in a hotel near Tokyo Station, followed by a blur of trains and buses. North, and further north still, where the snow was deep. At last, in the shadow of the Ōu Mountains, the wind grew cold as cut glass.

I bought a room in a Japanese-style inn, a *ryokan*, but then, there, I had no idea what to do next. I sat on the low futon and held the green, ratty book, the reality of the situation settling around me like softly falling snow. I was in a foreign country, alone, chasing a ghost. Chasing more than one ghost, if I was being honest with myself.

Outside though, the wind was beginning to howl. The owners of the inn, a kind couple who seemed surprised, but not displeased, to see a foreign woman show up alone on their doorstep, had told me that a storm was on its way. This is what I had wanted. This was what I had come for... and it was so cold. I *felt* the cold.

She was coming. I knew she was.

Come to me, I thought. Maybe I whispered it out loud.

At the window, I soon heard a soft thud, a scraping. Japanese characters, *katakana*, formed through the condensation. Though I knew no Japanese, I knew what it said. It pulsed through the walls all around me. *Emily*. Emily, my daughter's name.

I put Hearn's book down and went to the window and traced the lines with my finger. *Emily*. Through the fog outside, through the glass, a hand joined mine. Our fingertips met across eternity, across loss. As her face came into focus, I saw a mirror of my pain, of my longing, in her dark eyes. *Come to me*, the wind called, *I understand*.

I opened the window.

E is for Emily

Roddy Fosburg

Pale and trembling servants escort me to her bedside. Torches flutter on perspiring stone walls with each chill breeze from the open windows. Her brother—the self-styled poet, Cristan—stands opposite me, ink-stained fingers fidgeting with a stylus.

"Father," he says, barely inclining his head.

Helen's face is drawn tight, pallid with pain. I sit on the bed beside her, sinking into the goose-down.

"She journeyed again," Cristan says. He does not meet my gaze.

I take her hand. The ghost is already claiming her body. Leathery scales have enveloped her arm to the elbow.

I whisper an Our Father, a Hail Mary, moving the beads of the rosary through my sweat-slick fingers, cherishing their familiar texture. The scales, which were flowing like a green river, halt halfway up her bicep.

"How long was she away?" I ask, reaching into my bag for a vial of sanctified water, my ragged sash, my crudely-bound book of exorcisms.

"Four hours, maybe five." Cristan's eyes are far away. "If only you could see the *wonders* we see, Father! Ice-crowned mountains whose peaks scrape the clouds… oceans aglitter beneath a hundred moons… ancient cities burning with light—"

Helen moans. Her eyes open. They are yellow, pupils slit to daggers. She begins to babble an alien language that crawls into my mind like worms, like madness. A foul wind snuffs out the candles ringing her bedside. The servants flee, forking provincial wards against evil.

Cristan hurries to his quill and vellum.

I turn away.

"This will kill her," I say. "A body—a *mind!*—can only endure so much. I can continue to purge her of these little ghosts, but there is no telling what may return with her next time. Is her life worth your verse?"

The foppish poet meets my eyes and quickly looks away.

They are fraternal twins. One journeys, the other transcribes. That Cristan calls himself a "poet" is laughable, as the insights gleaned on those unimaginable sojourns are not *his* to claim. They belong to Helen—the poor child—who for love of him surrenders herself to unimaginable winds, riding them to other times, other places.

Sometimes others return with her, like leaves riding the wake of a whirlwind.

The Rite does not last long. She bucks and writhes against her restraints, froth erupting from her mouth in a noxious black jet. Her howls echo throughout the bedchamber, and I hear the ghosts now— there are many this time—keening from somewhere within her, like the cries of children fallen down a deep well.

I shut my heart to their plaintive voices.

The scales drip down her arm, flake away, perish. Her hand warms in mine, nails shrinking from horny claws to pale pink crescents. Her jaw unclenches. The voices diminish to a murmur, the susurrus of a distant ocean, the stir of leaves in faraway trees, and then silence.

I blow out my breath.

"Is it gone?"

Cristan looks shrewdly upon her, only a few hastily scribbled lines marking his vellum. I know with weary certainty that he will compel her to journey again.

"She needs rest. Bring her broth, some watered wine." And I turn to face him, willing myself not to loathe the sight of him. "Do not ask it of her again. In God's name, I beg you."

Contempt and uncertainty crowd his eyes. He opens his mouth to speak, closes it, walks to his desk and opens a drawer. He returns with a bulging pouch of silver.

"You always speak of this 'God,' and yet I have seen nothing outside of these rituals that would convince me of its presence. Are you sure it is not *you* who dispels the ghosts, Father?"

The blasphemy was spoken lightly, but innocently. This world does not yet know the God of Abraham.

He places the silver in my hand.

I look back on Helen's sleeping form, at the play of firelight and shadow across her face. I remember the confused horror felt upon our first meeting, the blinding pain. Falling down that long, dazzling tunnel of light.

Waking as a stranger in an alien land.

It was a kind of resurrection. The cancer devouring me had disappeared, burned away somewhere the space between worlds. Helen had taken away my life and given me a new one, and I love her for it.

And I *hate* her for it.

Cristan sees me to the door. A carriage is waiting to take me to the nearby village where I have made my home. I am building a Church there; it is small, but with the help of Cristan's silver it may yet flourish. Perhaps the Father, the Son, and the Holy Ghost have some greater purpose in store for me. Why else would they toss me to this alien shore, flung farther than any missionary in the history of His world?

These are the questions that hound me every time I leave the manor, pockets heavy with heathen silver, the wind off the moors tearing at my homespun coat.

And yet tonight I am stopped cold, hand frozen in its reach to grasp the carriage door, struck by a new one—a thought so terrible that I fear the razor-edge of its contemplation.

Were any of the ghosts I have banished from Helen of my world? And if they were—then where, God forgive me, have I sent their souls?

F is for Father

Andrew Bourelle

The summer I turned fifteen, the summer of the nightmares, the summer when my dad was arrested for murder, was, in many ways, the happiest summer of my life. It was the summer I won the two-hundred-meter medley competition at our pool's annual end-of-summer swim meet, and I was the healthiest I've ever been, body, mind, and—I'd guess you could say—soul. This was before I was in therapy and before I almost died from my eating disorder—before life got really, really hard for a while—so I sometimes look back on it all with a nostalgic fondness even though I can recognize how messed up that is.

It was the summer I spent most of my time at the Gardners' house because my parents were never around. And when they were, they were yelling at each other. Mom had a job at the county assessor's office filing paperwork on housing inspections and screwing her boss in the back of his van down by the river on their lunchbreaks. And Dad, of course, was the chief of detectives for the county sheriff's office and was on the hunt for the Elk County Killer, which is ironic now when you look back on it. Throughout middle school, I'd been at a different school in a different county, and I'd been allowed to stay home alone and take care of myself. But after we moved and I started at the new high school, the murders started—or disappearances, I guess I should say. No one knew for sure then that the girls were dead, even though we know it now. Although the victims were seventeen and eighteen—all beautiful and popular and older-looking, more woman-like—and I was just some beanpole fifteen-year-old who was good at swimming, Mom and Dad were terrified enough that they wanted me to be with someone during the day. The Gardners, who were the only retired people in the neighborhood, were the obvious— and only—choice. They were new to the neighborhood, too—beating us there by only a few months—and they hadn't felt particularly welcomed when they arrived, so they made a special effort with us when our moving truck pulled up. Mom and Dad didn't exactly hit it off with them, but I—having never felt quite comfortable with kids my own age—took to them right away.

To get to their house, I always walked along the path next to the cornfield and came in through the back of their property. The fence was mortared stone, but there was a little wooden gate that was always unlocked.

In the morning, I'd stroll over and find them both knee-down in their garden, working the soil before the day got hot. That was something funny about the Gardners—they were *gardeners*.

On my birthday, the corn in the field was still short, barely past my knees, and their crop of vegetables—everything you could think of; the garden took up the whole back yard—was only starting to bear fruit. But when I came over, Mrs. G (that's what I called them, Mr. and Mrs. G) was making me an omelet using their own vegetables.

"You need your protein for swimming," she said, putting the massive omelet in front of me.

God, I could eat back then. I had the metabolism of a young horse—and I looked like one, too, all limbs and no curves—and I could just eat and eat and eat, and I'd burn it all off in the pool.

When I finished the omelet, she showed me that she'd also made me a carrot cake, my favorite.

I ate a big slice of cake and Mr. G ate two, then we loaded into the car, and they took me to swim practice.

Kids think anyone older than their parents must be really old. Any-one retired must be near death's door. So of course I thought they were ancient. But Mr. and Mrs. G were just a few years into their six-ties, still quite healthy. Mr. G's hair was entirely gray, but he had a full head of it, and even though he had crow's feet and wrinkles and age spots, he had muscular arms and strong veiny hands. He could put a Coke bottle in the crook of his elbow and twist the lid off that way. Mrs. G was a sweet old lady, with short curly gray hair and yellowing teeth. She was always on the move, doing something in the kitchen or working in the garden. Mr. G was like a quiet, contemplative bear; Mrs. G was a bee, always buzzing.

At swim practice, which was held in the mornings before the pool opened to the public, Mr. and Mrs. G always sat on the grass by the pool and watched. This was before cell phones, so nobody's noses were stuck in their devices. Still, the other parents read books or newspapers or chatted with one another. It was only practice, so they didn't really care to watch closely. Their kids probably didn't want them to watch. They wanted to pretend their parents weren't there. But Mr. and Mrs. G were actually interested, and I was genuinely touched that they watched me and, afterward, would talk about the practice heats or what Coach might have been saying at any particular time.

At the end of practice, when all the kids gathered around sitting cross-legged on the pavement, feeling the sun—just starting to get hot—on our shoulders, Coach said, "Today is someone's special day. Happy birthday, Kara."

I blushed. I hadn't expected this. But while I was swimming, Mrs. G had crept up and told him that it was my birthday.

Everyone sang happy birthday, which made me blush even more, then afterward, Coach said, "You know what this means, don't you, Kara?"

I shook my head no. I didn't know.

"You'll be racing with the big kids this year."

My eyes went wide. We'd moved to town a little over a year ago, so this was my second season with the team, and I hadn't considered at all that I'd be racing in the fifteen-to-eighteen category.

Mrs. G noticed my nervousness and asked me on the ride home if I was scared. I played it off like I wasn't, and I think the truth is I wasn't that frightened by racing the older kids—I knew I was faster than a lot of them. It's just that when I was finally lumped into the older category, it occurred to me that maybe—just maybe—I might be old enough to draw the attention of whoever had been abducting the girls in our town.

The next morning, when my mom was in the bathroom putting her makeup on and my dad was sitting at the table, reading the paper and drinking coffee, his gun already clipped to his belt, I wanted to tell them about moving to the higher bracket. But Dad—with puffy hammocks of skin hanging under his eyes and a square of toilet paper glued to a red shaving nick on his cheek—would hardly have heard a word I said. Mom neither. I assumed Dad's thoughts were on the case. I didn't know then that Mom was sleeping with her boss, but I knew she was distant and perpetually irritated with my father.

So I didn't mention my anxiety about swimming. And I certainly didn't mention my fear about being kidnapped and killed.

Instead—and I'm not sure why—I mentioned the dream I'd had the night before.

"I dreamed about Jennifer Staples last night," I said.

Dad looked up from his newspaper. It might have been the only thing I could say that would get him to notice me. Jennifer Staples was the first girl to disappear. She'd been a senior last year when I was a freshman. She disappeared the week before Homecoming.

"What happened in your dream?" he asked.

"Nothing really," I said. "She was brushing her hair in front of a mirror, like she was getting ready to go out. I was her, actually, in the dream. But even if I hadn't seen her in the reflection, I would have known it. Kind of like I was inhabiting her character."

"That's it? She was just brushing her hair?"

"That's it."

This might have been a good time for one of my parents to talk about what was going on, to ask questions about how I was feeling with everything that was happening. But instead, my dad, no longer interested, went back to reading the paper. And my mom walked by, took one last drink from her coffee on the counter—a red lipstick splotch permanently staining one side—and said she was late for work.

"Something tells me you won't get reprimanded," Dad said without looking up.

Mom left without another word.

This was the Midwest, and parents didn't talk to their kids about feelings and anxieties. Not back then. At least mine didn't. Maybe it's different now.

When the dreams continued, I decided not to bother mentioning them again.

When I think of that summer, the dreams aren't the first thing I think of. They got worse—turning from brief, pleasant images to full-blown, wake-up-in-a-sweat nightmares—but I have to stop and make myself think of them, to remind myself that was part of the summer. Because what I really remember is swimming. Growing stronger and stronger and Coach noticing and encouraging me. Saying that since I was strong in all four areas—backstroke, breaststroke, freestyle, butterfly—that I should try to race in the medley.

And I remember life at Mr. and Mrs. G's house—the vegetable-packed omelets for breakfast, the ham sandwiches with tomatoes and lettuce for lunch, snacks of carrots and celery and cucumber in the afternoon. And as I stayed for dinner more and more often, we'd eat potpies packed with the vegetables I helped pick and spaghetti made with sauce from their own tomatoes, which I helped them jar. My parents were at home, microwaving pizzas or heating up takeout Chinese left over from lunch. But me? I was eating like an athlete should.

And I didn't just eat the food—I helped in the garden, planting seeds, kneading the soil, plucking weeds, picking the vegetables when they were ready. It's not like Mr. and Mrs. G used me as free labor. They could have done it faster without stopping to teach me, but they seemed to like having someone to share their gardening skills with. And I liked learning from them.

I could feel myself growing stronger that summer. Not just my muscles, but also my lungs. I could hold my breath for two minutes. I learned how to time my breathing for optimal effect, taking in just enough air to keep my fastest pace. As I kicked my legs and swept my arms through the water, I felt like I was gliding through some kind of substance that only I understood. It wasn't water. It was something else. Other people fought against it. Splashed around like they were afraid of it. They could drown in it. But in water I was grace. Like a dolphin. I was home.

We had a scrimmage among our swim club to see who would race in the meet at the end of the summer. The top two in each category would compete. I finished third in the medley behind Candace Wardlow and Libby Wilson, who were both starting their senior years. Libby was short and squat, sort of a tough tomboy whose daddy owned a farm. She wasn't particularly popular except during swim meets when all of her teammates were appreciative of her strength.

Candace, on the other hand, looked like an Olympic athlete. She had a womanly frame and long muscular legs. Curves in all the right places. She was the girl who all the dads looked at and pretended not to. And she was the favorite to win. When I came in third, meaning I was the first alternate, she gave me a nod of respect and climbed out of the pool, confident no little upstart would take her crown. The other girls—there were five of them—were pissed. Of course they congratulated me, but they'd all spent the last year or two hoping to one day make it into the top two after Candace and Libby were too old. Now that some newcomer fifteen-year-old was already passing them, those dreams seemed farther away.

The Gardners were ecstatic, Mrs. G literally jumping up and down when I looked over at them. Mom was there, but she was over in the corner by the fence, talking to a guy from work, not even realizing my race was happening. Dad made it somehow, even though he worked seven days a week back then. But I got the feeling he was looking at Candace more than me, just like the other dads.

When I got out of the pool, a couple of the older boys, Bart Robertson and Denny Ostrom, congratulated me, and as I walked over to my towel, I overheard one say to the other, "Man, Kara is growing *up*."

I was pretty naive back then, but even I knew there was something in what he was saying that went beyond swimming. He wasn't just complimenting my speed in the water.

So that night, after my parents were asleep—which was late because Dad hardly ever slept—I went to the bathroom and stripped to my underwear and looked at myself in the mirror. I'd heard of people going through growth spurts—I'd once heard boys saying a female classmate "got her boobs" over a summer—and I realized that was happening to me. The skinny girl, all knees and elbows, was turning into an attractive young adult, muscular and lithe and womanlike.

I was no Candace Wardlow, but I maybe wasn't much farther behind her in the looks category than I was with swimming.

I went to bed with a mixture of emotions

I thought maybe I wouldn't be so lonely anymore.

Maybe this school year I'd have friends besides the retirees down the street.

But, also, maybe now I would become a target.

That night, I dreamt of another missing girl, and this time the dream wasn't so innocent, not just someone brushing her hair. I was Julie Ross, and I wasn't looking in a mirror. I had a bag over my head and there was a terrible smell coming from the damp cloth—sweet and pungent and overwhelming. Someone was grabbing me and holding the bag over me, and I was fighting them but starting to feel weak.

When Julie passed out, I woke up, gasping for air.

I suppose before I go any further I should tell you about the missing girls.

Jennifer Staples was first, like I said. She had straight black hair—ridiculously shiny—and teeth as straight as newly erected fence posts. She was a cheerleader for the football team and had been the co-captain of the volleyball team the previous year. At first people thought she'd run away, although her parents always said that was ridiculous. Girls like her didn't run away.

Kim Fitzgerald was next. Blond. Short and petite but cute as could be. She was smart, taking all AP classes and working as the editor-in-chief of the yearbook. She wore glasses and had this pretty nerd-girl vibe that all the boys loved. They all wanted to go out with her, but they were too intimidated by her brains.

Next was Julie Ross, who wasn't rich or particularly popular like the other girls. She wore leather jackets and short denim skirts. She smoked—pot and cigarettes. But she had one thing in common with Kim and Jennifer. She was drop-dead gorgeous. They all were.

Of course, when I look at pictures of them now, in my old scrapbooks, they look so incredibly young. But at the time, they were all older than me, and I thought they all looked like women.

I felt the same way about Candace Wardlow.

That's why I wasn't surprised when she went missing two days after our race.

Mom and Dad didn't even bother talking to me about it. With the other girls, Dad had at least asked if I knew them. But they knew the answer with Candace. They were so preoccupied with their own messes that they weren't paying much attention to me.

Mr. and Mrs. G listened, though.

"Coach asked me to race in the meet," I said. "It feels weird."

We were sitting on the porch while Mr. G rototilled a patch of the garden. The machine was loud, but not so loud that she and I couldn't talk.

"Life is strange sometimes," Mrs. G said to me. "I know this isn't how you wanted to get your chance. But think about your teammates. You have to do your best for them. And if you think of it like you're doing the race *for* Candace, then maybe that will give you a different perspective."

I told her I guessed so, but I didn't really think that way. I wasn't sleeping well. Every night was some kind of nightmare—inhabiting one of the girls as an attacker threw a cloth of some kind over their heads, stinking of chemicals, before they fell unconscious.

I was listless, tired. Even though I started the summer puttering around the house and garden with Mr. and Mrs. G, I started asking them if I could watch TV all day instead. They had a cavernous basement, the walls lined with books and records and old VHS tapes. No matter how hot it was outside, it was always cold in that basement. I'd lie down there on an old couch, wrapped in a blanket, and watch old movies.

"You think she's okay?" I heard Mr. G ask Mrs. G about me.

"She's a teenager," she said. "She's stuck with a couple of old folks all day. She should be out having fun with friends."

"Does she have any friends?"

"I don't think so."

Mr. and Mrs. G *were* my only friends. And, yes, I did wish I had girls my age to talk to. Or boys. But that wasn't the problem. The problem was the nightmares and the looming dread that girls were going missing. And that I was growing up enough that I might be next.

My times lagged at practice. But everyone's did. The whole team was depressed, worried about Candace, wondering if they should cancel the meet. Coach finally said Candace would want us to race.

The night before the big meet, you'd think I wouldn't sleep because of anxiety, but I didn't really care at that point. I had no chance of winning, so why should I be worried? I drifted off easily, and that night I dreamed I was Candace. And the dream I had was of our race—the competition where I came in third behind her and Libby. Candace stood at the edge of the water, ready to dive in. She was aware of me in the row next to her, more afraid of me, actually, than Libby. She gave me a sideways glance, and I can't tell you how strange it felt to look at myself through someone else's eyes. I could see the woman I was becoming, see the strength of my potential. Candace was intimidated by *me*. I would be a better swimmer than Candace, definitely better than Libby. Candace only hoped that she could hold me off one year. Then she'd say goodbye to swimming, go to college, do something else with her life. But she wanted this last waltz—one last meet where she was the best.

She dove into the water, stroked underneath, pushed to the surface, and blasted away with her breast stroke. It felt different to swim in her body. I could feel the difference in our technique, and I knew—in the dream—that I was the stronger swimmer than her.

I just hadn't realized it at the time.

As Candace slammed her hand into the wall at the finish, she looked over underwater to see me finish only seconds behind her—so close to Libby that it could have been called either way. Candace slid up out of the pool, gave me a polite, respectful nod, but inside she was celebrating.

I woke up in the morning ready to race. And when I lined up next to all the other racers, I was laser focused. They were all older than me. All veterans like Candace and Libby.

But none of them stood a chance.

I finished two body lengths ahead of my closest competitor.

Mom and Dad hadn't bothered to come to the meet—things had really deteriorated by then—but they both looked disappointed in themselves that they'd missed it. Dad held my ribbon and looked at it for a long time. Mom's voice broke and she said to my father, "We can't go on like this."

"I know," he said. "As soon as we solve this case, things will be different."

"That could be years," Mom snapped, slamming her hand down on the table. "We came here for a better life."

"How was I supposed to know a serial killer would pop up as soon as we got here?"

"You're never home," she said. "You'd rather be working than spending time with us."

"I'm trying to keep these girls safe."

Mom gestured to the newspaper on the table, the lead article about the fear consuming the community about the disappearances.

"You're doing a bang-up job," she said.

I thought this comment would make Dad mad. This was about the most hurtful thing she could probably say to him, and I expected him to shout, throw something, maybe even smack her. But he just looked hurt, like a scolded puppy. When I picture him like that—handling such harsh criticism so calmly—it's hard to imagine him snapping and killing anyone. But of course I saw that side of him later, too.

"Speaking of work," he said calmly, "why don't we talk about what's going on at your job?"

I left them to fight. I snuck out by the cornfield—the stalks taller than me now—and found Mr. and Mrs. G sitting on their porch. The sun had just disappeared, and in the gloom of twilight, fireflies were swimming through the air.

I sat down on their porch and sobbed.

"I think my parents are going to get a divorce," I said.

Everything felt like it was about to change. Swim season was over. School was going to start in a week. Mom and Dad were on the verge of splitting up. And the dreams I was having were getting worse and worse.

Mrs. G just rubbed my back and let me cry.

Two days before school began, Mom told me she was moving out. I could come with her if I wanted to. She said she was going to be staying with a friend, and when I asked about who the friend was, she explained that it was Mr. Barnes, her boss.

"Are you having an affair with him?" I asked, the question so ludicrous I didn't take it seriously myself.

But she wouldn't deny it, and suddenly I realized what was going on.

"Things are complicated," she said. "You'll understand when you're older."

I flew into a rage—the kind of rage I had expected my father to go into. I yelled at her. I cried. I told her to get out. There was no way in hell I was going to move in with her and her boyfriend.

I was staying with Dad.

She left me alone, told me to lock the doors behind her. Dad was gone who knew where and for how long, and I was alone for the first time in months. The emptiness of the house felt claustrophobic, and I almost ran outside along the cornfield to Mr. and Mrs. G's house to spend the night there. I wonder how things might have turned out if I had.

Instead, I paced the house and cried and tried to watch TV and finally drifted off to sleep on the couch waiting for my father to come home.

In the dream that night, I was Candace. A bag was over my head. Whatever drug had knocked me out was wearing off slowly. I lay on carpet on a hard floor—concrete, not wood—and my muscles wouldn't work. The air was cold. I was awake, but I couldn't get up.

"I think she's awake," I heard a voice say, muffled, like my head was underwater.

"I doubt that," another voice said, this one deeper, calmer.

"Listen to her breathing," said the first. "It's changed."

The bag was pulled off my head. The light was harsh. Blurry.

A face came out of the brightness—distorted, rippling. The features were out of focus, like looking through glasses that were the wrong prescription. Candace felt she had seen the person before but couldn't place from where.

"There, there," a voice said peacefully, placing a chemical-soaked cloth back over my mouth. "Go back to sleep, Sweetie. You're not going to want to be awake for this."

The rag was over my mouth, but I tried to focus. The person's feature's blurred in and out of visibility. The face took the shape of some of the fathers at swim practice. Then it was my father. Then the image before me solidified, taking on a sharp unmistakable vividness.

Mr. G.

I woke up, gasping for air, clawing at my neck and my face to find no bag over my head.

Instead, Dad was there, telling me it had just been a bad dream. I sobbed and hugged him. I'd hardly seen him lately—had felt so distant from him—but knowing Mom was leaving him gave me renewed affection for him.

"Tell me about your dream," he said, his voice so calm that I realized how much I missed him in my life.

"I've been having dreams about the girls," I said. "Candace and Jennifer and the others."

"Oh, Kara Bear," he said, using a nickname for me he hadn't in years. "I'm sorry."

He hugged me for a long time, letting me calm down, then he asked me to tell him about the dreams. I said at first they were just dreams of the girls doing ordinary things, brushing their hair, listening to music, or, in the case of Candace, swimming. But then I dreamed that someone had thrown a bag over their heads, the fabric stinking of chemicals like paint thinner.

His eyes narrowed, and I grew frightened of the change in his expression.

"You dreamed that?" he asked, and when I nodded my head, he told me to tell him more. What the girls were wearing.

Jennifer was in pajama pants and a large Minnie Mouse T-shirt.

Julie was wearing jeans and a red blouse.

Kim wasn't wearing anything—she'd been taken in the bathtub. She'd been reading paperback book that fell into the water as she thrashed against her attacker.

"What was the book?" Dad asked.

I closed my eyes, saw the book sinking in the water as I was dragged out of the tub.

"*Of Mice and Men*," I said, and my dad recoiled as if he'd been watching a horror movie and the killer jumped out from behind a doorway.

Dad paced around, visibly shaken. I'd never seen him like this. His whole body vibrated with energy. Fear seemed to seep out of his skin and fill the air like an invisible poison gas.

"Did you see who did it?" he asked. "Who took them?"

"It was just a dream, Dad," I said.

"Did you see him!"

I didn't want to say that as the blurry face came into focus, it resembled different people I knew. I didn't want to tell him that he was one of those faces. So I just said, "Mr. G."

He stared at me, his eyes so intense I had to look down.

"It was just a dream," I said again.

He picked up the phone and asked to speak to my mom. The person on the other end was saying something and Dad snapped, "I don't care about your fucking apologies. Put my wife on the phone."

He told her to come home and stay with me for the day. When she arrived, dawn was breaking and sunlight was seeping in through the windows. I sat on the couch, my arms wrapped around my legs, almost catatonic, as my parents fought in the other room.

"She knew details that no one can know," Dad said from the other room, trying to keep his voice low, although I could still hear. "Like the book."

"I bet the book is required reading for all the seniors," Mom said. "Who reads Steinbeck for fun? Kara probably saw some of the girls reading it at the pool."

"The book was found in the bathtub," he said. "Water was all over the floor. No details of the crime scene were ever released. How could she know that?"

"The family probably talked about it," Mom said. "Word gets around in a town like this."

"I need to get a warrant," Dad said.

"Don't try to pin this on those poor old people."

"Jennifer was wearing a necklace when she went missing. I'll tell Judge Spicer that Kara saw it. He owes me a favor."

I'd heard enough. I ran into the kitchen and started shouting at my dad.

"It was just a dream!" I said. "Leave Mr. and Mrs. G alone!"

Dad tried to hug me but I batted his arms away.

"Just keep her here," Dad said to Mom. "Don't let her go over there."

"They're going to wonder where she is," Mom says.

"Don't let her go over there!" Dad shouted, and he ran out the door.

All day Mom and I paced the house, waiting for some word from Dad, looking out the windows for some sign of police cars screeching down the road. The window over the sink in the kitchen faced the direction of the Gardners, but two other houses obstructed our view. We couldn't see much.

Finally, in the late afternoon, a string of police cars came down the street, their lights off, their sirens silent. Dad's unmarked car was with them, as was an SUV with K-9 stenciled on the side and a big van that I knew had a bunch of crime scene stuff in it. Mom went out on the porch to get a better look. When I joined her, I saw Dad and a bunch of cops knocking on the door. Mrs. G answered, looking confused. Dad showed her a piece of paper, and she opened the door for Dad and his colleagues.

Mrs. G glanced our way—I wasn't sure if she saw us—and Mom said, "Come on. Let's go inside."

I couldn't stop shaking. Something about this felt all wrong. Mr. and Mrs. G were innocent. I knew that. But I thought my dad might do something to put an end to the investigation. He and Mom had been fighting. She'd said they couldn't go on like this. What if he could end the investigation right now? Save his marriage?

I pictured him taking the necklace he mentioned out of his pocket and hiding it somewhere. I'd seen enough TV shows to know cops did that kind of stuff—plant evidence when they didn't have it.

In the scenario I imagined, it didn't occur to me to wonder how Dad would have gotten the necklace if it was supposed to be missing.

Sometime after dark, a neighbor knocked on our door and started chatting with Mom. She'd seen the police cars, of course, and they knew my dad was a cop, so naturally they thought Mom would know what's going on. She didn't let on that she knew anything, but she joined the neighbor on the front porch to watch. More police cars were out there now, with cops going in and out of the house. Soon a few other neighbors joined and Mom was preoccupied by hosting all these onlookers on our porch.

I realized this was a good time to sneak away.

I opened the backdoor quietly, then hurried through the grass into the cornfield. Instead of walking along the path, I stepped into the rows. The night was humid, the rough leaves of the corn growing wet with dew. I found a place where I could see over the Gardners' waist-high fence but remain hidden. The backyard was blazing with floodlights and activity. A generator providing electricity for the lights chugged noisily. Men were digging up the garden while another officer stood back holding a German Shepherd on a leash.

I started to cry, seeing Mr. and Mrs. G's garden torn up like that. The plants had all been ripped out of the ground and discarded into a pile. Larger pieces of plants were visible in the darkened soil. Dad was standing on the porch, overseeing what was happening. I glared at him, hating him for what he was doing to the people who'd been more like parents to me lately than he had.

One of the diggers called to him. With gloved hands, the man held up a clump of dirt the size of a volleyball, with a mop of roots hanging from it. He turned the mass this way and that, and I made out what looked like an eye socket and an open mouth full of soil. With dawning horror, I realized that what I thought had been roots hanging were actually tangled strands of hair.

The large pieces of plants still in the garden were body parts— limbs and fingers and ribs that had already been unearthed.

I slapped my hand over my mouth to keep from screaming. It made sense to me in a rush. The girls had been buried in the garden, fertilizer for the plants and vegetables I'd been eating all summer. Mr. G had been rototilling a new section of the garden right after Candace's disappearance, not because the soil needed tilled but because he needed to hide the spot that had been freshly dug.

All summer, I'd been eating vegetables that had been grown from plants whose roots intertwined the remains of the missing girls. And the dreams…

The dreams were more than dreams.

Somehow the girls—some part of them anyway, some of their energy—were inside of me. They communicated with me through my dreams. Maybe they'd done more. Maybe they'd given me the strength to win the race. Maybe the woman I was becoming had a little bit of each of them inside.

I dropped to my knees and retched and retched. I'd hardly eaten all day, so nothing came up but a white acidic foam.

I couldn't get them out of me.

I sat on my haunches, gasping, trying to breathe, unable to see anything but blurry cornstalks through my tear-filled eyes.

That's when I heard Mr. G say, "Hello, Kara."

The bag that I'd been dreaming about came down over my head, soaked with the same chemical smell I was now familiar with.

I held my breath.

Mr. G yanked me backward into the corn. I struggled, but he pinned me down, using all his weight to keep me from getting up. I hoped that the cops might come running, but the generator was making too much noise. If the cops heard anything, they might think a coyote or a deer was running through the corn. That's all.

"I was going to let you grow up a little bit," Mr. G growled, his hands holding the cloth sack tight around my neck. "Another year and you'd be just my type. But since your Daddy has gone and fucked everything up for us, I'll make an exception."

I kept holding my breath.

I couldn't fight him. He was too big, too strong, had too much advantage. I remembered how unconsciousness had taken the girls, the way their limbs had lost strength, the way they'd stopped fighting.

I let my muscles slacken. I let my body go limp.

How long had I been holding my breath? A minute? More?

Mr. G waited a good thirty seconds after I stopped moving. Then he took a deep breath and sat up. The sack was still over my head, but he'd let go of it. I could feel the blackness of unconsciousness approaching. I pretended I was underwater. You can't take a breath underwater, I told myself.

I heard Mr. G's body shift. He was looking away from me, checking to make sure none of the police noticed our struggle.

I yanked the bag off my head and inhaled deeply—taking in the beautiful aroma of the corn. To this day, the smell of a cornfield fills me with an overwhelming sense of relief.

Mr. G heard me and whirled around.

"*Daddy!*" I screamed with everything I had. "*Help!*"

Mr. G lunged at me, and I tried to scamper away. He got one hand on my shirt, and we barreled through the corn. I heard voices shouting. Bodies bursting through the stalks. The German Shepherd—the cadaver dog brought in to smell for bodies—was barking like crazy.

Mr. G threw me onto my back in the dirt. He didn't bother with the bag—he put his hands around my throat and squeezed.

A gunshot rang out and he toppled over. Dad was standing above us, holding his gun. Mr. G lay next to me, bleeding, injured. No longer a threat. Dad didn't care. The look on his face haunts me as much as anything that happened. He shot again and again, the reports booming in the night air, until the gun clicked empty.

Dad was arrested and suspended without pay for a while, but the charges were eventually dropped. No jury was going to convict a man—cop or otherwise—who shot a serial killer trying to strangle his daughter. Even if he did keep pulling the trigger long after the man was dead.

It was good to have him home because I was such a mess. I had no appetite. I refused to eat any produce at all. It got so bad that I had to go to a hospital and be put on a feeding tube.

School started, but I was in no shape to go.

Mom quit her job, and the severance pay was good enough that she didn't have to work for a while. I guess that's one upside to screwing your boss.

Mom and Dad, to my knowledge, never talked about the affair. They acted like it had never happened. Just like they never talked about Dad shooting Mr. G, the way he paused a second before firing the last round execution-style into the already dead man's forehead.

When I was out of the hospital again, eating enough to subsist on, Mom and Dad decided that the best thing for me would be to leave, go somewhere where I could start over. Even though Dad didn't go to prison, he wasn't wanted back at the sheriff's office. But he too got a good severance package.

After a year of homeschooling, I finally started my junior year in a new school in a new town. Mom and Dad seemed in love again. Mom got the same kind of job—thanks to a good reference—and Dad started a landscaping company. He worked hard all day, but he was always home at night.

I finally put on weight again. Two months after starting the new school, a boy asked me to the Homecoming dance, and I went. I broke up with him shortly after because I felt that if it got serious, I would have to tell him what happened to me.

And I wasn't ready for that.

Not yet.

The new town had a swim team, but I didn't join, no matter how much my parents encouraged me. I couldn't stand holding my breath underwater anymore. The one time I tried, my mind immediately went to that night, holding my breath to keep from inhaling the chemicals, and I jumped out of the water verging on panic.

Mrs. G—whose real name wasn't Gardner at all—ended up in a women's prison on the other side of the state. Dad kept tabs on her and one day told me that the prison had a community garden where Mrs. G apparently spent most of her time. When he said this, I had a powerful nostalgic memory of eating the carrots and tomatoes and zucchini that I helped them grow. I had the craving to bite into a tomato I'd just plucked off the Gardners' vine. I tried to eat one from the store, but the taste just wasn't the same. I couldn't choke it down.

As for the nightmares, they stopped a long time ago, although I'm not sure if the girls ever left me completely. I feel like they're still inside me, somewhere, just a spark, you know, a little bit of their energy, and the thought of it doesn't disturb me like it used it.

It comforts me, actually.

G is for Garden

Beth Cato

"Would it be acceptable for me to place my flowers out here, captain?" Miran cupped the small terracotta pot of golden poppies with both hands. "They would add some cheery brightness to the room."

"The window in your quarters gets gentle morning light," I replied. If my newly-arrived cleric was the sort who sought to add 'cheery brightness' with flowers, soon followed by fresh paint and lacey curtains, my future replies may not contain quite as much tact. This was a functional sky island, not a summer retreat. "The afternoon sun gets intense in here due to our high elevation."

I moved around the table and she deftly sidestepped to block me. She stood high as my shoulder, and by her youth and size she seemed like a child. Or maybe I simply felt outright old compared to everyone and everything these days.

"I hadn't considered that. I talked to some clerics who've worked the sky islands, but they didn't say much more than that it'll be boring for days or weeks, and then..."

"That's the truth of it." After a pause, I asked, "How long have you worn full red?" Acolytes of the stars began their service in white, and through experience ascended to wear cleric's crimson, from leather boots to robes to hooded mantles.

"Six months now. My only previous station was in the mountain frontier." The girl's bright smile confirmed for me the gentleness of her previous duty. What had the monastery thought, sending an innocent like her *here*? Our island wasn't in the war zone, but if things went poorly for our units, we at Hamblin were among the first to know. "I'm excited to be here, though. To live, on a blessed sky island!" She waved at the whitewashed brick walls as if she were in a gilt palace.

"Hamblin is nothing to enthuse about, truly. This has long been my home, but most everyone else tires of it quickly." I shrugged, well aware that I sounded like a sour old woman. "The isolation, the frequent fresh ghosts, the inability to walk any distance... it gets to people. Hamblin is the smallest sky island, you know. One can walk a loop around the lower tower in ten minutes, and all the while the wind tries to blow you to the continent a mile below."

And yet, I loved the place. When I died, this is where my spirit would linger in my last months. The star-blessed sky islands were chunks of rock that floated by no discernible means, all at different, consistent heights within the atmosphere. Hamblin consisted of an ancient stone tower built into a nugget of moss-draped dark granite, with space enough to dock one airship at a time.

"How long have you lived here?" Miran asked.

"Twenty years, intermittently, and now five years under a permanent residency grant in reward for my service." For most people, this station would be more prison than reward.

"Twenty years!" The number took her aback. "I was told most stints are six months!"

"For clerics, yes. Your work is harsh. My mechanics and storekeep don't interact with fresh ghosts as you must."

The girl frowned down at her poppy. "I see, captain. I do wish other clerics had been more open about their experiences here so that I better knew what to expect."

While I understood her curiosity, her gripes about past workers grated upon me. "Have you smelled gangrene?" I asked.

Miran recoiled. "Of course! I'm trained to heal bodies as well as souls or I wouldn't wear—"

"Clerics who've worked the sky islands, especially Hamblin, near to the front as it is now, can't tell tales because there are some circumstances that cannot be put into words. How can you describe gangrene to people who've never before smelled it? How can you adequately portray a rot so strong, the taste meets your tongue even as you stand feet away? You can't."

Her brow furrowed, dark skin scrunching. "But if they won't talk, how are newcomers to know what to expect?"

"Your previous training should have prepared you." I pursed my lips in clear disapproval. "The rest, you learn the hard way."

Her gaze shifted to her plant. "I see. I should put my poppy in my room, captain."

"Of course, cleric," I said, waving her away.

Only after I'd settled my old bones into the chair did I worry. Truly, I wanted to support Miran, but when I repeated my words in my head, I sounded like an abrasive fool. I sighed. Hamblin had lost two clerics in five years to suicide. Those spirits were long gone, but regrets haunted me still.

Being a cleric on Hamblin was a challenging job. I needed to find the means to best offer support without adding to those difficulties.

Three days later, we had our first docking since Miran's arrival—and as when Miran came, the *Fortitude* flew our way from west, from home.

As my other crew scampered to fasten lines, Miran joined me atop the mooring mast. "You're to prepare soldiers for what may await them," I told her. "Not as onerous a day as it could be."

"I may not need to face mauled ghosts today, captain," Miran spoke with some hesitance, "but conversing with scared, very alive soldiers is not necessarily easy, either."

Ah, I had promptly put my foot in my mouth yet again. I acknowledged my error with a dip of my head. "You're right, Cleric Miran. I'm sorry, I spoke from my own narrow experience. When I've been required to act as substitute cleric, it has only been because of an influx of ghosts."

I knew the rituals, I had the faith, but—stars preserve me!—those days had been as hard on me as the privation of an actual battlefield.

"This was after the cleric suicides aboard?" she asked, causing me to face her in surprise. "I may not have garnered many details about life here, captain, but those statistics are readily available."

I'd underestimated the girl. "Yes, it was then." The ramp dropped with a metallic clang. "Hail, Captain Roget!" Despite the subject matter of a moment before, I couldn't hold back my grin.

The old man wore his uniform with the same crisp confidence that he had at age twenty. "Captain Claybourne." We saluted each other, then dropped formality to clasp hands. "Good to see you, as ever. I have three fresh brigades aboard."

"We can accommodate them, gladly," I said. Hamblin offered each eastbound soldier a final chance to imbibe in drink, or to purchase smokes, stationery, and other supplies. They also had an opportunity to visit our chapel, should they wish to address their spiritual needs.

Minutes later, the first brigade marched aboard, their young faces reflecting both anxiety and awe.

Miran motioned the stars' blessings as soldiers passed her, her smile welcoming without being too enthusiastic. After the last soldier boarded, she saluted both me and Roget. "Pardon, captains, but how long will they visit?"

"An hour, cleric, followed by the next brigades in sequence," said Roget, with a respectful dip of his head.

"I had best get down to the chapel, then. Captains." She saluted again, grim confidence in her demeanor, and departed.

I stared after her. Miran seemed ready for the duties of the day— but how, by the stars' grace, could a cleric so young cope with west-bound ships? I said as much to Captain Roget as we sat together in his stateroom a short while later.

"You've fallen into a dread habit that many of us old gray-haireds do." He smiled within his beard. "You're confusing youth with imma-turity. Childhood can be the most dreadful part of a person's life. This woman may have endured more in her twenty years than most people do in seventy, and through her faith, learned to cope with horrors you've never faced yourself." I didn't miss that he made a point of calling Miran *woman* whereas I kept using *girl*.

I swirled whisky in my glass. Roget had presented me with a bot-tle of my favorite vintage, and I found myself craving alcoholic numbness more than I ought. "I want her to succeed here. I don't want..." Words failed me, and I drank.

"The suicides weren't your fault, Nor." Rarely did I hear my first name these days. Too many close friends from my youth had ascended to the stars. "Cleric Miran is here. She'll confront the doom and gloom soon enough. Support her as best you can, and foremost, make it clear that you *respect* her. She's not some acolyte in white, you know. She earned the red."

"I'm not sure if I do respect her yet." I frowned into my glass.

"That's obvious," Roget chided. "And what have you done to prove yourself to her, other than stick to this island like a barnacle?"

I guffawed at that. "Says the barnacle attached to the *Fortitude*. I don't know how we do it, truly. Me, watching the build-up for another war. You, ferrying these bright young lives who may never make it home." I sighed.

"We respect them and trust that they will do their jobs, Nor, and we do the same."

"We do our jobs," I echoed. "That seems inadequate."

"Which is why we look to the stars to guide and comfort us. We're not enough, but we do what we can."

The words were common sense, but hearing them spoken by Roget resounded with me. I found myself nodding.

He clinked his glass against mine, and together, we drank.

A new airship approached from the east as the heavens began to tint dark.

"Rafia here makes regular supply runs." I spoke loudly to Miran as the airship clang into the place recently vacated by the *Fortitude*. "If you need more flowers, she'd be your best resource." The ramp dropped. "Hail, my friend!"

"Ahoy there!" Rafia bounded down to greet me. She stood as high as my armpit, her face dominated by a broad toothy grin. "You got a new red-robe, eh? What's your name?"

"Cleric Miran, at the service of you and the stars." Miran flushed, clearly discomfited by Rafia's forwardness.

I felt the need to put Miran more at ease. "As you can see, Rafia isn't military. Don't expect formality." Nearby, our mechanics exchanged loud laughs and greetings as they finished securing the vessel to the isle.

"I'd sooner choke on those brass buttons than wear them," Rafia said cheerily as she gestured to her careworn shirtwaist and trousers. "I got a job for you, Cleric Miran. Three ghosts joined me for the flight home."

Miran's awkwardness evaporated in an instant. "Could you please show the way, captain?"

"Call me Rafia, as on my ship I've declared myself Admiral Empress Extraordinaire, and that's a right mouthful to say oft." Rafia motioned us to follow. I ducked my head to fit my tricorn within the low doorway. The cramped interior reeked of ether and moldering freight crates.

"I tell you, it's a relief to make it to Hamblin," Rafia continued. "On the front, the tension, it's thicker than three-day porridge. Those brutes'll make their move soon, guaranteed."

"What changed the mood so fast?" I asked. "Last week, peace seemed possible!"

"Bah. As if I can keep track. All I know is, my next trip from the front, I'll be toting more of this sad lot." Rafia pointed through an arched doorway. Moans and cries carried from within. Miran reached into her pocket as she stepped forward. I hung back, Rafia beside me.

Fresh ghosts only comprehended two things: the continued pain of their last moments, and the overwhelming need to get home. The translucent forms of these three ghosts bore witness to the grievous wounds that caused their deaths.

Miran began to chime a tiny bell, its peal embodying the sharp clarity of a frosty winter night. With the bell in accompaniment, she began to sing:
"Your bodies are no more
your pain an echo
know that
the grace of the stars is upon you
as you journey homeward
where you will know wholeness again
as you fade in these coming months."

Within the first line, the agonized cries tapered off, the ghosts' miseries dulled by her soothing song—and not because Miran had an incredible voice. No, I would consider it pleasant and on-key, but not amazing on its own.

Her compassion, though, rang as profoundly as the bell. She truly channeled the stark majesty of the heavens.

One of the ghosts emitted a different moan, one of relief. Rafia and I promptly retreated down the hallway. The ghosts would become more coherent now as they recognized a cleric in their midst, and would share privy details not for our ears.

"She's good," Rafia murmured. "Young as she looks, her connection to the stars is sure and strong."

"She's probably been through more than we can guess." Only after I spoke did I realize how closely I echoed Roget.

Rafia released a deep sigh. "A mercy it'll be, for the ghosts to be quieter from here-on. We've scarcely slept the past few days."

"Were there no clerics at the port to intercept spirits?"

"Not that I saw. I imagine the higher-ups have clerics marshalled to help heal the living, not the dead. I tell you, I'm glad to have my freight and be headed homeward for at least a few weeks."

I caught the indistinct soft murmur of Miran's voice. "Cleric Miran hasn't even been here a week. These are her first ghosts from the front."

"She'll have a mess more soon," said Rafia.

"I wish you were wrong."

"I wish I were wrong, too. But I won't be." Rafia offered me a sad, lopsided grin. "I'm not Admiral Empress Extraordinaire for nothin.'"

Three days later, my storekeep on watch sighted the *Fortitude* on approach. They were not due for return for another two weeks.

I heaved for breath as I forced myself up the steps faster than my creaking knees would typically allow. Miran almost clobbered me as she burst open a stairwell door.

"If the *Fortitude* is back—" she began.

"Just climb," I gasped, unwilling to comment until I had seen it myself.

A wind gust welcomed us to the top of the mooring mast. The day was oddly bright and blue, scattered clouds beneath us casting shadows upon the blurry green continent below. The *Fortitude* remained a mere speck to the eye. I went straight to the spyglass affixed to the rail.

The magnification didn't lie. The colors of the airship were muted, translucent, the sails half gone, dark craters visible in the hull.

"Oh, Roget," I mouthed against the wind, as tears blew from my eyes. Clatter behind us caused me to turn. My two mechanics had arrived on deck. In semaphore signals, I encouraged them to prepare for docking. They responded affirmatively, sadness in their eyes. We had all lost friends this day.

"Mechanics still moor the ship?" Miran asked, standing close so I could hear.

"It still retains some mass, even... as it is." Grief clenched my throat.

"Of course. Individual ghosts retain enough mass to be touchable and move objects around. I'm... I'm to board the vessel, captain?" Miran sounded faint, her dark skin gone pale.

"Yes." I gave her a shrewd look. "You knew that this was a possibility, didn't you, cleric?"

She nodded, her gaze focused on the nearing airship. "I've dealt with similar... mass casualty situations, though never a mile above the ground."

"During your tour in the mountains?"

"Once there, in a terrible wagon accident, but more often in my youth." At my questioning look, she continued, "I grew up in a Tarrytown orphanage."

"Tarrytown!" The refugee camp had muddy rivers for streets, its layout often altered due to fires. People there collected diseases the way the higher echelons acquired jewels.

"I've known many ghosts."

I would bet she had. Typical ghosts knew an innate drive home-ward, not unlike birds in their seasonal migrations. Refugee ghosts, though—they were often agonized by indecision. Fade in the company of family, or return to their beloved, lost homeland? Their pain couldn't be eased by any single song.

"How... how does the ship *exist* like this?" she asked. "I mean, when it went down, the passengers,..." Exploded, incinerated, pulver-ized on the ground below. Neither of us need say the horrors. "But then, ghosts are stuck in the moment right before their death," she an-swered herself. "The ship and those aboard... they returned to that terrible point, together. And the ship knows its way home?"

"Like any building lived in for a time, an airship begins to accumu-late a personality, a soul, after years of use. It..." I dryly swallowed. This had been Roget's ship since its making, and he had loved it so.

Miran nodded, her jaw set grimly. "I will soothe the ship, too, per-haps help it remember solidity on its final flight."

I turned away. The *Fortitude* made my eyes ache as if I stared at the sun, but I wasn't granted the mercy of blindness. "I'll fetch my white and red robes and my bell so that—"

"No." Her hand snared my upper arm, grip strong enough to staunch a seeping artery. "I can do this."

"I believe you." I did, fully. "But this is a mighty burden for any single person. There are almost two hundred souls aboard that ship."

Each of them maimed, broken, burned. I imagined what I should not, and pressed a fist to my gut to hold back nausea.

Miran leaned closer. "How long have you known Captain Roget?"

"Since I was your age."

"You don't need to see him like this, captain. You don't need to *remember* him as he is now."

"I'm your superior, and I'm qualified to—"

"I believe you, captain." She volleyed my words back at me, sym-pathy in her eyes. "Ghosts are most attracted to home, but amid their

pain, they also crave what is familiar. If you go on board, Captain Roget will be drawn to you. Actually, you shouldn't even remain on this
deck. He might try to greet you, as is customary."

I couldn't repress my shudder, but neither could I back down. "I
cannot in good conscience let you board this ship alone."

"With all respect, Captain Claybourne, this is about more than your
conscience."

Stars save us, but she was right. The *Fortitude* loomed close
enough that we could now hear the tormented screams and cries above
the roar of spectral engines. If I faced Roget, I would not be able to
grant him peace. My agony would only exacerbate his. And even if
this were a ship full of strangers, I could not channel celestial grace as
could Miran.

"You're right. I... I would be of little help. Indeed, my grief and
pride would only add to your burden." That admission had to be one
of the most difficult in my life.

I thought back on how Roget had chided me. I needed to respect
Miran and let her do her job. Well then—what job was best suited for
me at the moment? What would Roget advise me to do?

'Stop being a stuffy old gray-haired mollywoddle,' is what he'd
say. Very well. I could manage that.

"Tell me, how can I best support you, Cleric Miran?"

She considered me with surprise. "Assure me I won't fall through
the deck, for one." Her smile was thin. "And... perhaps have a hearty
meal with a stiff drink ready when I'm done?"

"That's enough?" I asked.

"That'll mean everything, at that point."

"The deck will feel spongy underfoot, but it'll hold you. Try not to
look down. The meal will be ready as soon as you are." This, I could
do.

Miran nodded, her attention upon the battered airship as it drew
alongside. My mechanics began mooring procedures; their ghostly

counterparts did the same on their end. Even in death, training held true.

I retreated to the top of the stairs to grant the ship one final look.

"You were right about her," I whispered to Roget, as if the wind would carry my words to whatever remained of him. With that, I took the spiral staircase downward and away.

That night, cooking duties should have belonged to one of my mechanics per our chore rotation, but he had no qualms in switching days with me. Indeed, all of us were unsettled and grieving that night. The other staff ate as Miran continued her labors.

As the mechanics ascended to await the ship's departure, I set aside her food and then took the stairs into the island's basement, to the carved-out burrow of the chapel. The quartz-flecked dark granite resembled the stars where our souls would one day drift. The cool cave usually filled me with a sense of peace. Today, I felt hollow and old, my aches extending far deeper than my joints.

Miran found me there, sitting in near-blackness upon the rug.

She sat to my right, legs folded. I heard the slight hitch and sob to her breath, and I kept my gaze forward.

"It's done," she finally said. "The ship is heading home."

"I'll heat your food fresh whenever you wish."

"Thanks. I'd... I'd like to stay here a while more." Silence lingered for several minutes. When she spoke again, it was at a whisper. "When I was young, I found it contrary that so many chapels are deep underground but replicate the night sky. Why not just worship beneath the stars? I struggled to understand that celestial grace is supposed to be with us everywhere, and grottoes are symbolic of that. Sometimes, though... I feel like a child again. Confused. Uncertain of where to find grace. If it can be found."

Her doubt and pain mirrored my own. "When I was younger, I thought grace—a deep sense of peace—was a permanent thing once it was found. Like it was a trinket to own." I snorted, laughing at myself. "It's more like a lake, sometimes near dry, other times at a flood, more often somewhere in the middle."

"I like that imagery," she said softly. "Maybe I should have accepted your help, captain. I expected it to be hard, but that... there were just so *many*..."

"No one can ever be truly ready for a ship like that, Miran. No one. No matter how old, how experienced."

"I know, but..."

"The soldiers and crew who wanted benediction, you granted it, yes? You assured them that they were on the way home, and would know the peace of the stars soon?"

"Yes, of course!" Indignation rang in her tone, which relieved me. She still had fight in her.

"Then you did everything you should do. That you can do. Now it's my turn." I pushed myself up to stand. My right knee released a loud creak. "Come. I promised you food and a stiff drink. That'll make you feel a little better, cleric."

"Maybe," she said softly.

As we headed upstairs, I was tempted to argue with her on that point, but I did not. Her glum mood was understandable—natural, considering the day. Nor did she sound low enough to make me concerned for her life, though I would remain vigilant for the signs that I had sadly come to know too well, too late.

Miran stopped at the door to the mess. "Mind if I go to my berth first? These robes, I need to..."

"However long you need," I said. "I'll ready our meals."

She paused. "You didn't eat yet."

"I couldn't."

She accepted that with a nod, and went on.

The men had left the place sparkling, stars bless them. I tucked biscuits in the still-warm oven and started the stew at a simmer. I'd just poured whisky—the bottle from Roget, as appropriate—into the second glass when Miran returned, attired in a civilian shirtwaist and trousers.

In her hands, she cupped the potted poppy plant. More golden blooms had opened, each like a cheery little sun.

She looked at me then averted her gaze again, shy. "I thought it'd be nice to have something pretty to look at as we eat. Is that all right, captain?"

I could have wept then. For Roget, for his crew, for the sorrows to come. For my own past foolishness. For my sheer appreciation of the flowers I had scoffed at only days before.

"More than all right, Miran." I pulled out a chair for her.

We sat, the poppies centered on the table between us. We ate and drank, with no need for words. For all of the awfulness of the day, the flowers did indeed bring some cheery brightness to the room.

H is for Home

Xan van Rooyen

If Seth were being honest, free coffee and biscuits were the only reason he attended Psychopomps Anonymous.

That, and because the Council insisted. Ever since Seth had turned thirty, officially becoming the oldest living deathwalker in recorded history—a *geriatric* some even said, but never to his face—the Council had become increasingly concerned about his state of mind.

Deathwalkers weren't supposed to enjoy their duty to the dead. They certainly weren't supposed to get off on the memories of atrocities committed by the arseholes they'd carried. Not that Seth advertised the latter much. Only a select few knew about his unusual tastes.

Now pushing thirty-three, Seth was still in the game and currently responsible for a territory which included an area near the docks, home to rival gangs. Deaths by 9mm were becoming passe.

Despite his advanced age, Seth still followed the recently deceased into the Otherworld; still guided their souls across the river to the afterlife—however they imagined it. Or, more frequently in his district, he watched souls drown in the blood-churned waters of judgment.

"You know how it is," Keigo said; a skinny sixteen-year-old who favored thick eyeliner and torn clothes. They were one of the more recent recruits.

"Yup, we know," Seth said, popping a crick in his neck. He'd heard it all before: the pain and heartache, the misery and fatigue, the anger and bitterness seeping out of the ghosts beneath their skins to infect their own, still beating hearts.

"You see the best and worst of them," Keigo continued. "And some of them hold so much darkness. Those memories, they're like shards of glass, of mirror—" Keigo fancied themselves a poet. "They cut deep while reflecting, all that... you know—stuff."

The kid's imagery could use some work, but his words still hit their mark.

Seth squirmed, his left thumb tracing the haphazard scars on his right wrist. Unwelcome reminders of another life. He much preferred living in the memories of others, in those shards sloughed off the deceased carried in the Otherworld. Somehow, those shards ended up embedded in the deathwalker's mind, like pocket lint made of soul stuff. The more heinous the memories, the better—at least for Seth. It made it easier for him to bury his own that way, quashing them beneath the remnants of the dead cluttering up his insides.

"Oh, we totally get it. You're not alone," Delilah said, weeping into a handkerchief. She was eighteen going on eighty, 'eschewed technology,' and only read paperback memoirs. As if the clamor inside her skull wasn't enough? Seth didn't mind the revenant choir between his ears, he only wished it came with volume control.

"Yeah, we're all dead inside," Seth added, earning reproachful stares and withering glances from those gathered.

"We all deal with the cost of our duties in our own way," Daniel said, ever the diplomat. The man had beautiful thighs and even more exquisite fingers. Seth had wasted six sessions flirting with him before discovering Daniel had a kid. Seth couldn't stand children—present company included—nor those who reproduced. They were only guaranteeing the Council a replacement for when they inevitably croaked.

Damn witches with their choke-hold on anything magical. Seth didn't know when or who had decided witches should form the governing body. But he knew better than to voice his opinion on the matter.

The others continued around the circle, sharing their feelings and pretending to shed their psychological burdens. Seth sipped from his mug of coffee. Dark roasted pure Arabica, and not the cheap kind. This was organic, fair-trade stuff. At least the Council didn't skimp on refreshments. It almost made the drivel pouring out of the surrounding snot-smeared faces bearable. Bethany's vegan, gluten-free short-bread helped too.

"I miss my family," Delilah said, dabbing at her nose with an embroidered handkerchief.

Seth cast furtive glances around the circle. Most of the assembled were the progeny of former deathwalkers who'd received the unfortunate inheritance of a dagger through the heart and a lifetime duty to the dead.

"Do you miss yours?" Delilah asked, her gaze landing heavily on Seth.

He tapped his coffee mug, wondering which lie to tell.

"You're an orphan, right?" Daniel said.

"Runaway," Bethany chimed in. "At least, that's what I heard." She amended when Seth scowled.

"There was a reason I ran away," he said. A mistake. The interest on their faces quickly turned to pity with slow nods as if they understood. Seth bit his lip. Better to let them think he had arseholes for parents, that he'd been abused, or kicked out of the house for fucking boys. He didn't much care what they thought about him but if they knew the truth, the Council might end his deathwalking and he needed it. It was the only thing keeping from succumbing to darker urges.

That and the memory of the look on his father's face when he'd finally figured it out.

Seth had been eight when it started. It took a couple of years for his father to realize who was responsible for the neighbours' cats going missing or for the bruises on Seth's little sister's arms. It only took three therapy sessions for Seth to realize other kids didn't dream of murdering their families.

He remembered the look of disappointment on his parents' faces, the fear and pity too. They'd assured him they'd get him the help he needed. For a time, Seth had believed it, but the dreams of hurting his family hadn't stopped. They'd just transformed from dreams into plans.

He'd tried to solve the problem with a razor-blade when he was twelve, but his dad had caught him before he could finish the job. "Stop," he'd said, emphatic, commanding. "This isn't the way," he'd said, and Seth had wanted so desperately to believe him, but the blade was in his hand and the need to use it overwhelming, if not on himself then—

"Put it down, Seth," his father had said, whipping the weapon out of little fingers. And so Seth's father hadn't died that day. But Seth had, just a little; not nearly enough.

Squashing down the memories, Seth glared at the clock on the wall while the others continued their lamentations. Astoundingly, they'd made it almost an entire hour without anyone perishing in any of the ten districts represented at the meeting. Five deathwalkers were absent though. Probably trawling the Otherworld. That's the thing with a big city. There was always someone giving up their ghost, generously donating shards of memory to the deathwalkers. The majority of the living populace didn't even know deathwalkers existed. Not until it was their time to shuffle off.

Bethany was whining about ghost-induced migraines when Daniel choked on his shortbread and dropped his mug of tea, sloshing beige Earl Grey across the pock-marked linoleum.

The others rushed to his aid, sliding Daniel from his chair into the safety position on the floor. Genevieve—or was it Jennifer?—took off her cardigan and folded it beneath Daniel's head as he writhed in spasms.

The passing must've been sudden and unexpected, possibly violent. Seth leaned forward in his chair and licked his lips.

These days, he could usually feel a death coming on, especially ones due to natural causes. A tingling in the fingers warned of an imminent heartache, a throbbing in the skull for a stroke or aneurysm. Death by old age was the worst. Boring. Like being smothered in a warm blanket. These days murder was the usual cause of death in Seth's district. And murder always came as a surprise.

Given his wide eyes and sharp gasps, Daniel was in the throes of a sudden death. A car crash or a stabbing perhaps.

Seth shivered and dug his nails into the sides of his knees.

A back alley brawl getting out of hand? *Too early in the evening for that though.* Definitely not a drive-by shooting in Daniel's territory. A domestic dispute turned deadly was more likely. Daniel foamed at the mouth, eyes-rolling back to glaring white. He shivered and convulsed.

Ah. A drowning. Seth should've known.

Fire in the lungs. Icy nails driven through flesh and bone.

Seth swallowed hard, remembering all the drownings he'd walked. He crossed his legs, but no one was looking at his crotch. All eyes were on Daniel who still flopped around on the floor.

Seth closed his eyes and took a few calming breaths, trying to stifle the swell of memory rising in his mind; and the swelling between his legs.

Daniel stopped convulsing. He was probably in the Otherworld by now—that liminal space where deathwalkers caught up with the recently deceased. Purgatory some might call it. He'd likely be there a while.

As the minutes dragged on, Seth lost interest.

"Well that killed the mood," he said, releasing his hold on his knees. No one laughed. "Guess the meeting's over then?"

"You're such an arsehole," Riya said. She twisted a curl of hair dyed obnoxiously red around a finger bearing matching nail polish.

"Only realizing this now?" Seth gave her a grin, letting his long hair fall across his face.

Riya rolled her eyes and Keigo raised their middle finger.

"See you all next week." Seth shrugged into his black trench and popped the collar. This time of year, the wind liked to molest bare necks with icy fingers.

No one waved goodbye or even looked his way, their attention riveted on Daniel. Seth lingered at the door, waiting. Everyone waited. Seth held his breath as the clamor of ghosts in his head grew in brutal crescendo. Something inside him wanted to know if Daniel made it out all right.

Every 'walker knew what it was like to die. For real. It's how they became deathwalkers in the first place. Get murdered by your mentor—a parent in most cases—traverse the Otherworld, wade through the river and—if you made it back from the other side, successfully clawing your way back to the realm of the living—*voila.*

Seth hadn't quite believed it all. He'd liked the idea, despite how his mentor—Grace—had described it as a 'duty' and a 'burden.' Fifteen-year-old Seth had also been okay with not making it back at all. Death was a curiosity; maybe a relief. He would've preferred something dramatic and bloody, but when the time came, Grace slipped barbiturates into his morning smoothie.

Twenty-two minutes later, Daniel gasped and sat up. Seth exhaled, easing surprising tension from his shoulders. *When had he started giving a shit about other 'walkers, even the ones he wanted to bone?*

"Suicide, fourteen," Daniel said between coughing as though the water were still in his lungs.

"So young?"

"But why?"

"It's so sad, I can't even."

The others crowded round: sniveling, hugging, mourning.

Seth had had enough. While the others offered their condolences, he slipped onto the street. He let the cold wind slice across his cheeks and inhaled the sharp air, savoring the ache in his teeth and lungs.

Seth made it four blocks before he couldn't take the noise in his skull. Ducking into an alley with overflowing dumpsters, he rifled through his pockets, found the tin pillbox, and planted two blue petals on his tongue. Sour-sweet, bitter-salt—the taste of magic.

Eyes-closed, back pressed against cold brick, he waited. Five minutes, *ten, twenty* passed before the panacea took effect. Finally, some volume control.

Footsteps in the alley.

Seth cracked open his eyes, needing a moment to focus on the figure sashaying through alley detritus with her hands in the pockets of her leather jacket and a carefree whistle on her lips.

She leaned against the opposite wall in a pose mirroring Seth's own, draped in the long shadows cast by the sallow light of streetlamps.

"You high?" Tamara asked in her melodious drawl, her voice a crush of deep velvet. A smirk twisted the corners of her perfect mouth.

"Almost."

She nodded and a few more minutes shuffled past as Seth's system re-calibrated, the cacophony in his head fading to white-noise whispers. He offered Tamara a smile.

"Been a good day then?" she asked.

"Boring but busy. There's a turf war on. Any takers on death by bullets?"

"*My* clients are more discerning." Tamara slunk away from the wall in a movement agonizingly fluid and closed the space between them. Her fingers were hot against Seth's cheek. Her breath smelled of the raspberry-mint gum she was always chewing. Her magic prickled Seth's skin; teasing, tantalizing, threatening.

"Glean anything interesting?" She tapped a finger against his temple.

"More of the usual. Gang-bangers aren't the most creative when it comes to violence."

"Think I can organise you a proper fix," she said. "If you're up for it. You do owe us after all." She tapped the pocket where Seth kept his pill box.

"And when am I not happy to deliver?" He arched closer to Tamara, their ribs and hips connecting. Decade-old memories ignited in the murk, tearing through the mud of Seth's mind to bloom in neon.

Back when Tamara thought he'd only survive another year or two, back when the witch had been a mere apprentice with incipient power still being coaxed from her veins, back then, they'd fucked and 'loved' each other, secure in their knowledge of an expiration date. But Seth had failed to make the expected dramatic exit. Now, Tamara was a Council witch and Seth was impossibly still alive.

Now, they fucked without any pretenses of love.

And now, Tamara murdered degenerates in Seth's district and extracted his memories of their agony. Her magic rendered his experiences a potent drug for wealthy humans with more money than principles to consume. Not that Seth could stand in judgment.

"Got something lined up?" he asked, trembling in anticipation.

"Tomorrow night," Tamara said, sliding a thumb across his parted lips. "I'll come to yours at six."

"You won't be the one doing it then?" he asked, disappointed. Tamara rarely delegated murder. To the witch, dying was an art and she made it so. She knew exactly how to draw a deathwalker to the soul, to wring exquisite pain from the target and let the agony linger.

"This one I want to watch." She dragged a nail down Seth's cheek. "I'll do the extraction though."

"Make sure it hurts."

"You are one twisted fuck," Tamara said with a laugh.

Seth smiled and squeezed the witch's waist.

She dipped her hand inside his jacket, removed the pillbox, and filled it from her own stash of petals.

"Always a pleasure doing business with you," Seth said, tugging her closer and nipping the skin of her neck with careful incisors.

"Tomorrow." Tamara stepped away and Seth almost toppled over, her parting sending seismic shock waves through his foundations.

She tossed a careless smile over her shoulder before vanishing from the mouth of the alley, the tapping of her spiked heels fading, absorbed by the ruckus of the city.

He'd already been to the Otherworld twice before tea. Nothing exciting though.

The clock on the wall gave him thirty minutes to shower and prepare for Tamara's arrival. Seth only hoped no one else decided to perish in the time it would take for the witch's murder to occur. Simultaneous deaths were harder to enjoy, confusing and diluting the sensations, polluting the memories.

Washed and dressed, Seth waited, listening to the rain splatter the window. At precisely six o'clock, Tamara made her entrance, shrugging out of her leather jacket to reveal a sheer, lace blouse beneath. She kept her boots on.

"For after," she said, lifting the bottle of wine in her hand. She left it on the kitchen counter, took Seth's hand, and led him to the bedroom.

"Are you going to tell me what to expect?"

"And ruin the surprise?" Tamara *tsked* as her fingers slowly undid the buttons of Seth's shirt. Her hair was damp from the rain. She smelled of mint and sandalwood.

"How much do they deserve it?" he asked as Tamara pressed a hand to his chest and forced him back onto the bed.

"This one deserves the worst." Something flashed in her dark eyes, too fast for Seth to catch. Tamara checked the time. "Any minute now." She smoothed the hair from Seth's face, perched on an elbow beside him, her body hot and Seth's growing hotter. Tamara's fingers traced spirals across his collarbones, down his sternum, trailing fire as they wended lower.

"Will I—" but his words were cut short. The death pounced, pain exploding behind his eyes as the world fractured. He was aware of Tamara's hands on his body, of her lips and teeth. He was dying, slow and excruciating. Such was the magic of witch murder, letting him tiptoe the line between realms. He straddled the veil, bombarded with sensation in both realms.

Tamara and her magic kept him tethered, reeling him back into his body every time he thought the riptide would drag him into the Otherworld.

He gasped and thrashed, groaned and writhed. Tears burned trails across his temples as he squeezed his eyes shut. The horror inflicted on the body of the dying reverberated through his own skin.

A man, sixty-two, and decades from a natural death. He must've been a monster to deserve *this*. Seth certainly did. The pain, that is— but not to enjoy it the way he did.

Seth had no words to describe what he was feeling. Language dissolved in technicolor torment. His nerves were a conflagration. Tamara's hands sent shock waves through his living body as another witch wrung protracted agony from the target.

Seth arched his back and screamed, air torn from his lungs, skin flayed from his bones, his life unraveling inexorably as he climaxed in one realm and died in another.

He slipped into the burgundy embrace of the Otherworld. Reality melted and reformed, puddles of blood-red aether taking shape as he crossed through the veil in search of the soul who'd earned such a grisly end.

Seth's Otherworld was a labyrinth of streets flanked by brown-brick tenement homes, each identical. A blurred rendition of the neighbourhood where he'd grown up. He traipsed through the streets, searching for the recently deceased. The pain of the man's passing lingered, sizzling down his spine and pulsing in his fingertips.

Seth rounded a corner and froze.

The soul stood on the sidewalk staring at a house indistinguishable from the rest except for the Yule wreath on the door.

The wreath. Seth's little sister had made it at school. A muddle of string and beads and pottery pieces. Their father had nailed it to the door even though it was only November. Every time Seth had come home from school, he'd broken a leaf or torn loose a bead, gradually destroying his sister's work of art. Her tears had made him smile.

The soul stepped toward the door, his translucent hand reaching for the wreath, fingers ghosting over the jagged edges of badly glazed clay.

Seth swallowed mouthfuls of aether, lungs burning, insides roiling.

"Am I dead?" the man asked, glancing at Seth without recognizing him.

Seth nodded.

"I didn't want to die."

So few did.

"Not like that," the man said, choking back a sob.

"You didn't deserve it," Seth said.

The man was shaking, shedding soul stuff in swirls of grey-blue. The wisps curled away and floated down the street. Seth inhaled them, each a dagger.

Love and loss, fear and confusion, regret, joy, sorrow, anger—he absorbed every poisoned barb. The memories were a kaleidoscope cascade and in them he saw himself, shattered and refracted.

Seth fought through the assault and grabbed the man by the wrist. Trying to blink the memories from his eyes, he dragged the soul through the labyrinth of streets. The Otherworld peeled open, the tenement houses falling away as asphalt dissolved into soggy banks.

The river loomed ahead, a crash of black water tumbling over rocks, its shore crowded with willows and rowans.

"Where are we going? Who are you? Why are you here?" The man dug his heels in, but Seth was stronger. The man tried to peel Seth's fingers from his arm, but succeeded only in shedding more soul stuff.

"Stop," The man said. "Please, stop. Look at me!"

Seth stopped and turned to face the man. He'd never been able to resist a command issued in that tone of voice.

"It can't be," the man said, voice cracking, tears cutting furrows down his death-eroded cheeks. For moments that felt like hours, the man simply looked at Seth, studying, analyzing. His eyes widened with disbelief, then faded to grey with resignation.

"I thought—we thought—we didn't know what to do."

"I know," Seth said. He'd lived the man's memories.

"We looked for you." The man raised his hand and cupped Seth's cheek. Seth shuddered but endured the cold-fire contact.

"I didn't want to be found."

"I hoped you were dead. That way you wouldn't hurt…"

Seth closed his eyes as the man's words landed like hammer blows.

"Are you dead?"

"Not yet," Seth said, eyes opening. "But you are."

Together they negotiated the river bank, stepping over rotting logs and pulling back the curtains of willow fronds.

"I'm sorry," the man said. "I'm sorry we didn't do more or know how to help." He closed a cool hand over the scars on Seth's right wrist.

Seth sucked in a breath of aether, staring at the churning waters, not daring to look at the man he'd once called father.

"No, I'm sorry," Seth said as he shoved the soul into the river.

The waters raged, waves spitting and hissing as they tore at the man wading through the currents.

Seth turned away and started up the bank.

It was only when his feet hit the grassy path of the meadow, he risked a glance over his shoulder. The waters were calm. The soul gone, to the opposite shore or the depths, Seth would never know. He forced his feet up the path, each step heavier as the Otherworld condensed around him. Its edges turned slick red, the air sticky and clotting in his nostrils. The realm enveloped him in burgundy folds before expelling him with a squelch.

His heart beat, he drew breath, and looked up into the smiling face of Tamara.

"I take it you enjoyed that." Her fingers teased the skin pulled taut over his hip bone. "Can I get started or do you need a moment?" she asked, resting her fingers on his chest. "I imagine that was rather intense. Perhaps I should've warned you." She laughed.

Seth grabbed her hand and squeezed.

"Hey, easy there, you're hurting me."

Seth squeezed harder until he felt her bones grind together, until he was sure just a little more pressure would cause them to break.

"Hey!" Tamara wrenched away with a bolt of magic leaving his fingers charred.

He sat up and dragged a hand through his hair, pulling hard, harder until his scalp burned. The voices in his head were quiet, a timid susurrus as they welcomed another ghost to the fold.

Tamara stood beside the bed, massaging her wrist.

"Maybe it was too much," she said with a mocking pout. "Perhaps I truly outdid myself this time. Actually traumatized you," she added.

Seth didn't respond. He was out of balance. His system needed time to reestablish an equilibrium he'd probably never know again. He pressed a hand to his chest, as if he could staunch the icy depletion he felt in his organs.

"Come on, you can't tell me you *didn't* like it," Tamara said. "Didn't you enjoy seeing that arsehole get what he deserved? Feeling it?" Cautiously, she perched beside Seth and rested her bruised hand on his knee. "Or was it all a bit too meta? You must've seen yourself. What was that like?"

"He didn't deserve it," Seth said.

"You don't really believe that, do you?" Tamara's voice turned soft and sympathetic. "After everything he did to you? It's the least he deserved! You know you're the victim here. You didn't do anything wrong..." Her platitudes and reassurances continued.

Seth bit the inside of his cheek, tasting copper.

He'd lied. When Grace found him on the streets, she'd wanted to take him to the police and find his family—a deathwalker with a good Samaritan complex. He'd begged her not to, fabricating all the reasons why he couldn't go home, beginning with his father's fists and ending with his father's nightly visits. An eighteen-year-old with her own tragic backstory, Grace had believed him and Seth had kept lying. To her, to the Council, to Tamara... to himself.

"I'll still need to do the extraction," Tamara said. "It's more powerful when it's fresh."

"You're not taking it."

"We had an agreement." Her tone turned flinty as she retracted her hand.

He stood up, retrieved his shirt and adjusted his trousers. "You should go."

"That's not how this works," Tamara said. "I'm sorry if it was too much, but you have a debt to pay."

"I'll find another way."

"You don't get to decide that."

"Then you'll have to take it by force."

"Don't tempt me," she said, arms folded and a frown on her face. "If only it didn't damage the product. Not to mention it could kill you."

"You'd be doing the world a favour."

"Melodrama doesn't become you." Tamara stood up. In boots, she was taller. She stared Seth in the eyes, magic crackling static through her black hair and dancing in blue sparks down her arms. "Keep it and it'll be your last," she said. "No more petals, and no more fine-tuned murders getting you hard. I'll make sure the Council sticks you in some boring fucking borough full of old age homes."

Seth's hand twitched. How badly he wanted to close his fingers around Tamara's throat, but there was a voice in his head, louder than the rest, telling him not to do it. A tone of voice he'd never been able to disobey.

"So be it," Seth said through gritted teeth.

"You'll regret this!" Tamara said.

Seth watched her leave. She stopped at the door to rifle through his trench. She held up the tin pillbox before slipping it into her own jacket pocket.

Tamara opened the door and stood on the threshold. "Last chance," she said.

Seth said nothing, his body trembling, hands clenched into fists as the ghost in his head continued giving orders.

"Fine." Tamara sneered. "Won't take long for you to come groveling for forgiveness."

The door slammed shut and Seth crumpled to the floor. The ghosts sang in a dissonant symphony he no longer had the means to silence. He was forced to listen.

The memories swarmed, ripping at his consciousness with fangs and talons, a thousand beating wings leaving his mind bruised. He drifted in the tumult, letting the phantoms rake their claws across the insides of his skull.

He deserved it.

And through the furor, came another sudden death. Somewhere in his district a trigger was pulled; a bullet tore through a heart.

Pain ignited in his chest as the world turned burgundy, and—with his father's voice in his head—this time, Seth tried not to enjoy it.

I is for Iniquity

Michael M. Jones

"This is the last time I let you pick out our costumes," I grumbled as we made our way down Caravan Street, dodging festive families and over-beveraged college students, all of whom had come out for some early evening Halloween fun. As we wandered, we passed everything from fairy princesses, superheroes, and pirates to… slutty fairy princesses, superheroes, and pirates. Not that I should judge. I've worn some questionable things in my time. "I mean, I had a perfectly good Ghostbusters rig, remember? From when we first met?"

Daphne laughed. "How can I forget, Camille? That's one of the first things which attracted me to you, even before I tried to use your brain to unlock the secrets of the multiverse. I recognized a kindred spirit, even if your gear wasn't at all scientifically plausible." As a mad scientist from a parallel timeline, Daphne had very strong opinions on what was—and wasn't—scientifically plausible, as well as an enthusiastically flexible set of ethics and a loose grasp on what constituted good ideas. Life with her was never dull.

I tugged at the green scarf around my neck. "So remind me again why you get to be Velma, when you're already named Daphne?"

She leaned down to kiss the top of my head. "Simple. I've got the curves and the brains to play her. Plus, you look amazing in purple."

She had a point; she was short, curvy, and pale-skinned. Decked out in the iconic orange sweater and brown skirt, with her long blonde hair tucked under a brown wig, she made a more-than-passable Velma, even if her glasses looked suspiciously like steampunk goggles. Meanwhile, I was taller, leaner, and knew how to rock a purple minidress and matching shoes, along with the aforementioned green scarf. I even had a red wig, which had previously seen service in half a dozen other costumes—everyone from Amy Pond to Mary Jane Watson.

For the occasion, we'd gone so far as to decorate my wheelchair like the Mystery Machine, complete with a temporary blue and green paint job and red flowers on the wheels. I still didn't feel like letting the matter die quite yet. "But we're hunting ghosts tonight," I pointed out, not for the first time. "The Ghostbusters are more appropriate."

"Yes, but none of them had the chemistry together that our ladies do, and as you told me, before the end of the night we'll be shocking the neighbors with unseemly displays of affection," Daphne teased. She ran her fingers through my hair, and I shivered. Curse that woman, she knew how to distract me with a touch. "It's a shame Mr. Farnsworth didn't want to cooperate. I wanted to test out my upgraded holographic projection unit by turning him into a Great Dane."

Mr. Farnsworth, our much-put-upon cat, had taken one look at Daphne's new toy and fled for the safety of his cat house, which, thanks to her recent foray into pocket dimensions, was much bigger on the inside than it seemed. It seemed he still remembered the HPU from the octopus incident, and who could blame him? Our cat has seen some seriously weird shit.

Tonight's escapade had started with a particularly heated debate, where I'd upheld my belief in ghosts. "I'm telling you, when I was in third grade, we lived in a house haunted by an old woman who'd died suspiciously in her sleep, and she still appeared in the kitchen to bake phantom cookies," I'd told Daphne.

"Nonsense. There's a perfectly reasonable explanation for all so-called ghostly phenomena," was her reply. She then went on to list a dozen said reasons, which started with "harmonic memory ancestral records," included "time travel echoes" and finished with "trans-dimensional etheric projections." I might be paraphrasing a little, but you get the idea. How she could accept those possibilities, and not "restless spirits of the dearly departed," I'd never know. Mad scientists are so *weird*.

Finally, she announced that she would prove there's no such thing as ghosts, and vanished into her laboratory for several days, where her only company was ominous noises, strange smells, and the crackle of ozone. (In other words, normal behavior for her.) When she finally emerged, she informed me that on Halloween, we were going ghost hunting.

"Fine," I said. "And after that, we're going to a party over at Morningside, where we'll drink and shock my friends with appalling displays of affection." Morningside was a residence hall over at Tuesday University which housed the weirdest and wildest of their grad students, and was known for throwing legendary Halloween parties. As a perpetual grad student myself, I felt right at home over there, even if I preferred off-campus housing.

Daphne and I had sealed our deal with a kiss and a little more… and a week later, here we were. On Caravan Street, dressed as two of the Scooby Gang, hunting ghosts.

Outside of The Smooth Mooove Drink Stop, which quite naturally specialized in shakes and smoothies, the owner had set up a table where, for the price of a "trick or treat," you could get hot apple cider. While I paid the toll for tasty refreshment for us both, Daphne got to work. First, she activated her goggles by pressing a small button on the side, which caused them to hum quietly and light up an odd sort of greenish-yellow, and then she removed a small device from her pockets which was the spitting image of a Ghostbusters' P.K.E. meter.

"Hey," I said when I saw what she was holding. "Isn't that mine?" I'd built one as part of my Victorian-era cosplay outfit, but hadn't seen it in a while. I thought it had gone missing during one of our moves over the past few years.

"It was yours," Daphne agreed cheerfully, "but in your hands, it was but a toy. I've actually turned it into a working replica."

"How can you make a working replica of something that doesn't exist? No, wait, I don't need to know. It doesn't run on plutonium, does it?"

"I... shouldn't answer that." Daphne deferred quickly. She spun in a slow circle, sweeping the area with her meter, which hummed and crackled as it did its job. That's one thing about Halloween: you can act even weirder than usual in plain sight, and no one even bats an eye. A wandering pack of frat bros in togas (seriously?) even whistled and complemented us on our costumes as they migrated from one party to the next.

"So how exactly is this supposed to prove your point, anyway?" I asked her. I'd tucked our apple ciders into the convenient pop-out cupholders she'd installed in my wheelchair when I grumbled about always having to hold her drink while she "scienced" whenever a wild theory struck her.

"If there's any unusual activity at all around us, this will pick it up. As you might put it, we'll detect the weird stuff, track it down, and disprove it," Daphne said chipperly. "Quite simple, really. And once I've found a solid scientific explanation for your ghosts, we'll be free to go to your party."

I eyed Daphne, chattering away as she waved her Ghostbusters meter while wearing a Velma outfit. "Right now, you're mixing fandoms and honestly, it's really sexy," I told her.

She blushed faintly. "Science now, fun later." The meter suddenly pinged! in that way such things do when they've done their job properly. (Look, after living with Daphne for so long, I'm totally an expert. Around her, everything dings. *Everything*.) "See? I have something!" And away she scurried down the sidewalk, lured by the siren song of the unknown. I quickly tossed the last of the cider into a trashcan and wheeled after her. The things we do for love.

After a few blocks of dodging people and abrupt turns Daphne stopped in front of an old storefront at the intersection of Hope and Nightingale, there on the outskirts of the Gaslight District. In its heyday, it had been a market of some sort, taking up a good portion of the block; now, a huge sign above the entrance read PROFESSOR PEYTON PECULIAR'S SPECTACULARLY SINISTER SPOOKSHOW, in lurid red letters. A poster on one of the boarded-up windows read "Come see the greatest assemblage of ghosts ever captured and put on display! Marvel as urban legends and campfire stories come to (un)life in front of your very eyes! Shudder and fear for your very souls at this calamitous collection of awesome apparitions and scary spirits!" And then of course, a small sign listed prices for seniors, adults, children, as well as student and military discounts. A blood-red door next to the sign urged us to "Enter... at your own peril."

I stared at Daphne, who'd shoved her goggles up onto her forehead to better read the signs. "Good job," I told her. "You found the sleazy boardwalk equivalent of a haunted house. Which is amazing since we're hundreds of miles from the beach." I looked back at the Spookshow. "I wonder where this came from. And how long it's been here. I know I've never seen it before."

Daphne beamed at me. "This is where the trail led, sweetie. And it appears as though the good Professor loves alliteration almost as much as you! Shall we?"

I just shook my head with a rueful chuckle. "Sure. Might as well. It better be handicap accessible though, or I'm going to be really annoyed."

Five minutes later, after buying a pair of ridiculously overpriced tickets (even with my student discount) from a bored-looking teenager who'd gone for the Beetlejuice look with pale makeup and a fright wig, Daphne and I were allowed to pass through a swinging door, and into the Spookshow.

The interior was a cross between a wax museum and a zoo. The extensive space had been turned dark and claustrophobic, with walls set up to create a mazelike experience, and dim lights hanging from the ceiling. A thin mist rolled around our feet, in what I considered to be a nice atmospheric touch.

As we progressed, we found the exhibits. Each one was set up like a small habitat, with sheets of glass to keep us from getting too close. The first was marked "The Phantom Hitchhiker," and inside it, a translucent man in his mid-30s, dressed in '70s clothes and carrying a backpack, paced back and forth. He didn't seem to notice us.

"Hologram," said Daphne confidently. I just arched an eyebrow. "What? They can do wonders with holograms. Very lifelike, these days. Don't you lot even use them to bring popular musicians back from the dead for performances now?"

I just sighed, and kept rolling on to the next one. "The Homecoming Date" was a young woman in her late teens, wearing a blood-splattered formal dress, who knelt in her room, weeping endless tears which never quite hit the floor. I shivered, despite myself. I didn't even need to read the accompanying placard that told us her story. I'd heard it while growing up. Girl gets dumped by her boyfriend at the big dance, leaves early, never makes it home, but is sighted outside the school every year around the same time? Yikes. I looked at Daphne, daring her to explain this one away. "Mirrors," she stated. "With the right refraction, you can make an actor look see-through."

And so we went on. We looked at the Lady in Red, the Twins in the Inn, the Witch of the Well, the Briar Mountain Miner, the Bluefield Howler, and more. Spectral oddities supposedly captured from all corners of the United States, caught in their cycles of grief and despair, restless and unresponsive in their tiny glass cages. Daphne had a potential explanation for each one, though she was growing more hesitant as we wound our way through the maze. The mist had grown thicker and colder, the lights dimmer, and there was a low moaning just within the range of hearing.

I had to hand it to "Professor Peyton Peculiar." It was a hell of an attraction, and creepy as fuck. I reached out, grabbing Daphne's hand. "I don't like this," I said. "Please prove ghosts aren't real, so we can get out of here."

Daphne smiled, and leaned in to kiss me. For a moment, I took comfort from her warmth and presence, the reality of her existence. "My pleasure," she said, sounding almost relieved as she lowered her toggles and again activated them. The weird greenish glow of the goggles gave her an otherworldly appearance in the dim, misty conditions, which didn't do much to reassure me. I think she'd forgotten why we were here for a moment.

I took a deep breath, and rolled to the next exhibit. "The Gaslight Ghost," it read. Inside was a young blonde woman in her mid-20's, wearing a sky-blue sundress. Two things caught my attention. First, she started pounding on the glass and yelling soundlessly when she saw us, as if crying for help. Second, I knew her. I'd *met* her. "Daphne, come here," I urged.

Daphne bustled over. "Camille, you won't believe this, the etheric and psychokinetic levels in here are off the charts. My meter's going haywire, and—what's wrong?"

I pointed at the girl. "I know her. I—she dated a friend of mine for a while before she vanished a few years ago. Just up and disappeared during an outing to the Gaslight Distract, and it was like... everyone forgot she ever existed. I had, until now. It's like I had a gap in my memory, and someone plugged in a missing piece." On the other side of the glass, Rebecca's eyes widened, and she mouthed my name with something like surprise. I glanced at the placard explaining the legend behind the so-called Gaslight Ghost. "Captured right here in Puxhill, just a few days ago, by the esteemed Professor Peyton Peculiar," I read out loud. "Daphne, this is *beyond* weird."

"Oh, I'll say. Her readings don't make any sense whatsoever." Daphne waved the meter at Rebecca, and it pinged and beeped furiously, before starting to smoke. "Oh no!"

"No, it's more than that. She sees us, she knows me. The rest didn't even respond, but she—we need to get her out!" I insisted.

"Are you sure… she's not just a really convincing actor?" Daphne tried, in a last-ditch effort to make sense of things. I gave her a withering look. "Right, then. Give me some room to work."

I rolled backwards, so Daphne could inspect the enclosure up close. She tucked the malfunctioning meter away, and drew out a small scanner— "Is that a Mark X tricorder?" I asked.

"It's such an elegant design! Definitely my favorite of all the variants," she said happily. "Now let me focus, sweetheart. There's some awfully interestingly strange stuff going on here. The glass is laced with microfilaments carrying some sort of alternating etheric current—is this an alarm system? No, it's for containment. Whatever these ghosts really are, this must be how the Professor is keeping them caged."

While Daphne continued to mix-and-match fandoms, I tried to give Rebecca a reassuring smile. "Hang on," I mouthed back to her. Rebecca glanced between me and Daphne, curiously. I shrugged. My girlfriend *was* awfully hard to explain sometimes. Right now, she was running her tricorder along the edges of the glass, taking measurements, and muttering to herself. And after all this time, I still don't speak a fraction of the Science! that Daphne does.

I didn't even comment when she revealed her homebuilt version of a sonic screwdriver, and started to do… stuff all around the glass, working from top to bottom, side to side. "Almost," Daphne said. "There. Give me a hand with this, will you?" And together, we slowly, carefully, eased the large glass pane aside, resting it against the closest wall.

"Thank you!" Rebecca exclaimed, stepping out of her exhibit. "Good grief, that was awful. It was like swimming in cotton—hard to move, and impossible to make any sound. It was almost suffocating in there. Ugh."

"Are you okay?" I asked, before realizing that despite her words, Rebecca was very much see-through and wispy around the edges. "I mean, um…"

"Yes, I'm a ghost," she admitted. "It's a long, weird story. Here in the Gaslight, I actually have more substance and persistence than I would in the real world… kind of like the rest of the spirits that Professor kidnapped." She spat out the last few words. "Oh, I've got a score to settle with him."

"What happened?" I asked her. Daphne waved her tricorder at Rebecca, and hmmmed, thoughtfully, before reaching out to poke a finger into—and through—her arm.

"Hey! Do you mind?" Rebecca chided Daphne. "Just because I'm a ghost doesn't mean you can take liberties with me." She glowered and moved away a little.

"I apologize for Daphne. She gets a little over-excited about things she doesn't understand," I said. "Scratch that, she gets over-excited about everything. So how you'd wind up here?"

Rebecca sighed. "My partner Nat was out on a job, and I was left minding the office in her absence—she's a private investigator, you see—and this guy came in. Didn't even say hello before he zapped me with some weird gizmo, and sucked me into what felt like a vacuum cleaner. Next thing I know, I'm in a cage and he's rubbing his hands about his latest attraction."

"A vacuum cleaner," mused Daphne as she stepped back to rub her chin thoughtfully. "Assuming that your substance is actually some sort of malleable etheric gas that adapts to the environment and reacts to appropriate stimuli, that actually…" she trailed off. "Huh."

Rebecca arched an eyebrow, looking to me for translation. I smiled at her. "Mad scientist. It's a long, weird story. But she knows her stuff, even if now I'm going to have to dissuade her from building ghost traps of her own, just to prove a point."

"If I see another ghost trap, I'm finding a way to shove its builder into it. Head-first. And I don't care if they'll fit, I'll make sure of it," Rebecca grumbled.

"I don't blame you. Let's get you out of here," I suggested.

"Not without freeing everyone else, and maybe doing horribly rude things to the Professor!" Rebecca folded her arms defiantly, looking distinctly more solid as she embraced her anger.

"Daphne, did you hear that? Jailbreak and revenge time!"

That got her attention. Daphne stopped trying to work out ghost physics in her mind, and gave me a wide, mischievous grin. "Would you like broke, blind, or bedlam?" she asked.

"How about all three?"

"Right, it's done!" And back into her endless pockets she went digging.

"I will thank you all to stop whatever you are doing, and to cease interfering with my exhibits, lest I be forced to take actions which we'll all find deeply regrettable!" The booming voice came from behind us, where a tall, gangling figure stood at the end of the corridor, framed by an open door and a blinding amount of sunlight. The exit, I presumed.

I yelped and lifted a hand to shield my eyes.

"Oh shit," said Rebecca.

"Oh, bother," said Daphne.

"Professor Peculiar?" I asked unnecessarily.

He stepped forward, and the door slammed shut behind him with a disturbing amount of finality. "The one and only," he proclaimed. "And as much as I am gratified that you ladies appreciate the quality of my Spectacularly Sinister Spookshow, I must insist that you do not try and abscond with the exhibits. That would be highly inconvenient for me. Luckily, I'm prepared to offer you this one-time clemency.

Merely leave the Gaslight Ghost behind, and you other two may leave and never return."

"And if we say no?" I rolled to the side, putting myself between Rebecca and her would-be captor. Daphne moved up to join me.

Now that the light was back to its usual level of awfulness and our eyes had recovered, I could see that the Professor was an older man with one of those pretentious handlebar moustache-and-beard combos that were so popular with steampunks, hipsters, and steampunk hipsters. He wore an all-white three-piece suit like a Southern fried preacher and I'd have laughed, if he wasn't pointing what looked like an angry hairdryer at us. I could tell it was serious by the way Rebecca whimpered, just a little. That had to have been what zapped her. "If you say no," the Professor replied, "then I will be forced to protect my collection, livelihood, and professional trade secrets at all costs."

"You'll shoot us, hide the bodies, and if we turn into ghosts, add us to the collection," I translated dourly.

"A truly unfortunate series of events to be certain, but ultimately necessary." The Professor flipped a switch on his weapon and it came to life with an unearthly buzzing, strange energy flickering around its edges. "And I do feel like I should inform you that this weapon, capable of stunning spooks, specters, and spirits, has also proven fatal for the more corporeally inclined. My former partner would attest to that, were he not permanently indisposed."

"He's not kidding," said Daphne, sounding more intrigued than worried as she tried to lean just a little closer. "We have technology like that back home. All kinds of highly regulated, of course. And this model is clearly rudimentary at best, and is… well, calling it a haphazard, sloppy design would be a complement. I'm surprised it hasn't blown up in his face already."

"You're not helping," I hissed at her. "Can't you do something? Please?"

The Professor cleared his throat. "Ladies, you know I can hear you. You, with the goggles. As you seem to be a woman of science, and the one who successfully dismantled my ghost prison, I'll thank you to slowly empty your pockets of any and all weapons, gadgets, trinkets, tools, and other such paraphernalia. One wrong move, however, and I'll be forced to shoot your friend."

"Oh, she's not my friend!" chirped Daphne. "She's my girlfriend."

"*Not* helping," I repeated. "Now he knows that shooting me is an effective threat!"

"Oh no, I'm still the actual threat," Daphne grinned. "I mean, I'm the one carrying nuclear-powered gadgets, isn't that right?"

The Professor swung his weapon back and forth, trying to decide which of us was the bigger—or crazier—threat. Finally, he aimed at Daphne. "Empty your pockets," he demanded.

So she complied, pulling an endless array of stuff out of bottomless pockets. Remember the pocket dimension she'd constructed for our cat? She'd also done the same with her clothes. How she kept everything straight, I had no idea. The pile in front of her grew larger with each coil of wiring, or multi-tool, or spare set of goggles she extracted, and the Professor watched with increasing disbelief.

And that gave me my own window of opportunity. Because while Daphne had given me a lot of cool stuff since we met, and had upgraded my wheelchair with many fascinating and sometimes unnecessary features, there was one modification which I valued above all else.

While the Professor was distracted, I tapped the side of the wheelchair in just the right fashion, causing a small compartment to open, and a small weapon dropped into my hand. And before Professor Peculiar could react, I shot him with the stasis gun Daphne had lent me on our very first date, and which I'd kept ever since. With a stunned look, he promptly fell to the ground.

Daphne swiftly confiscated the Professor's ghost zapper and turned it off. "I'm keeping this. For science," she said matter-of-factly, and neither Rebecca nor I cared to argue. We set about securing the Professor with rolls of duct tape while he glared furiously, unable to do anything else. And after that, we were at our leisure to dismantle the rest of the ghost traps, freeing the Professor's numerous captives, who milled about as they adjusted to their new freedom. Being this close to spook central was unnerving, and I tried not to look any of them in the eyes. Just in case I saw something I didn't like.

"What happens to them now?" I asked Rebecca.

"Most of them will find their way home, following their emotional tethers or instincts," she said. "A few might finally be able to move on. Nat or I will help any of them we can, and we know a guy who specializes in afterlife resolutions otherwise."

"And you? What happens to you?"

Rebecca shrugged, a little ruefully. "I'm something of an unusual case. Nat and I are still trying to figure out why I'm still around. But don't worry, I'm doing just fine."

"If you say so." I looked down at the Professor, who was starting to struggle against his duct tape bonds as the stasis wore off. "So, what do we do about this joker, so he won't go back to his old tricks?"

"Go outside," Rebecca told me and Daphne. "I think some of the Professor's captives would like to have a word with him before they go."

I noticed, for the first time, how we'd been ringed by a horde of spirits, some of whom looked rather put-out and far more alert than earlier. As a fresh chill ran down my spine, I decided that our part in this was over. "Come on, Daphne."

"But—"

"Come on, Daphne!" I grabbed her arm and urged her towards the exit. "I will happily agree that ghosts aren't real if it'll get us gone all the quicker."

"But I wanted to take some more readings."

I tugged Daphne closer, and whispered into her ear just what I'd do to, with, and for her if she forgot about studying the ghosts. She flushed, and practically dragged me away. "Good luck," I called to Rebecca as we left.

We never did make it to the Halloween party at Morningside that year.

Professor Peyton Peculiar, owner of the Spectacularly Sinister Spookshow, closed down immediately and left town in a hurry. According to Daphne's drones, he's now running a carwash in Boise, Idaho, and can't sleep without a nightlight.

Rebecca and I get together every so often to chat about how weird our lives are. I think she likes knowing that someone outside of the Gaslight Distract remembers her.

Daphne still won't admit ghosts are real…but she's not exactly saying they *aren't* real, either…

Next Halloween, I get to choose the costumes.

And whenever I think about this particular adventure, one thing comes to mind: Professor Peculiar would have gotten away with it, if it weren't for us meddling lesbians.

J is for Jinkies!

Jeanne Kramer-Smyth

A late summer thunderstorm, just before sunset, had left the evening air clean and cool. Sonia splashed through the puddles. She enjoyed the water on her toes, preferring wet skin to wet socks. She pulled her hair elastic out, letting her gray hair fall free below her shoulders. The concrete path wound through aisles of graves. This familiar path and the moonlight let her deftly navigate the headstones until she stood in front of her client's mother's grave.

A plain headstone, angular and simple. Just the woman's name and the years of her birth and death. No "beloved mother" or "loving wife". Grass tickled the arches of her feet as she stepped off the path. Feet in contact with the earth, hands on the top of the gray stone, Sonia waited.

Whispers emerged from all directions. From somewhere to her left a strong tenor voice sang in a language Sonia didn't understand. Italian maybe? She pushed away the notion of asking a ghost to teach her Italian. She was on the clock. Unfortunately, ghosts keep their own schedule. They have little sense of time and you can't exactly make an appointment to interview them. They show up when they like, usually when it's least convenient—the trick is being in the right place and being patient. And having whatever quirk of genetics it is that lets you hear and see them.

Eyes closed, she listened—focused on the wet ground under her feet and the cool stone against her fingers. She pictured the photo that Annabelle had sent her. A stern, gray-haired lady in what Sonia thought of as a "Sunday best" dress.

She waited. After the first thirty minutes her knees began to ache and she sat down, resigned to water-soaked skirts. The nearby ghosts stopped trying to talk to her when she didn't respond. Two hours in she let go of her hopes that this would be an easy job. Four hours into the vigil, Sonia had run through every mental exercise she knew to keep herself awake and focused. The temptation to go home to a warm shower and a dry bed was very strong, but she focused on the job she was there to do; talk to Annabelle's mother and get some questions answered.

The moon set and the sky began to glow. Birds sang their annoyingly cheery song, but Annabelle's mother never spoke to Sonia.

She stretched and wiped her face with dew from the grass, waking herself up enough for the long walk back to her car. Ghosts could speak to her at any time of day or night - but making first contact with a new spirit was always easiest at night, either at the location of their death or the location of their body or bones.

All along the path, voices called or muttered or sang but Sonia tried to tune them out and find her way back to the parking lot.

"She is lost," a female voice called from very close on her right. "She needs help."

"I am not lost. I do not need your help." One foot in front of the other back to her car. Back to work that will keep a roof over her head and cat food in the bowls.

"You hear me?" typical ghost joy and surprise, laced with anxiety "Stop. Listen, please."

"I'm listening." Sonia sighed, stopped walking, and turned toward the voice. "Make it quick. I've had a long night."

"I need your help."

"Who do you want me to find?" Ghosts often had unfinished business. Even the ones that died at peace were curious about their loved ones and descendants.

"They say a girl is lost. I can guide you to another who can help you find her."

"Who is lost?" Sonia felt a bit of adrenaline kick in. She tried to stay skeptical, ghosts make the worst eyewitnesses. No sense of time. "Lost right now?"

"Yes. Now. Your time now." Ghosts didn't often have such a sense of urgency. "A girl."

"A girl? Where?" Sonia did a quick 360, peering across the grounds of the cemetery. Birds flew. Leaves shifted in the light breeze. No cars. No people. "I don't see anyone."

"It is beyond where I can travel. I will take you to the edge. Follow my voice down the hill."

"My name is Sonia. What is yours?" She picked her way between the headstones, down the hill.

"My friends called me Anna."

"Nice to meet you Anna." She looked back over her shoulder to note where Anna's grave stood before she crossed another concrete path.

"Can you hear Phillip yet?"

"Umm... sorry, but can you stop talking. I'll try to hear him."

"Of course. Goodbye, Sonia. Good luck." Then silence.

Sonia stepped forward, fingers crossed that she walked in the right direction. Five steps later she heard a quiet male voice ahead.

"Hello? Phillip? Anna sent me."

"I hear you!" he called back, louder. "Keep coming toward my voice."

"I hear you, too." Sonia moved faster, not quite running, as she cut diagonally across the wide swath of green grass, dodging headstones left and right. "Keep talking."

"I don't know how far you will have to go to find her."

"Do you know what happened? Why does this girl need my help?"

"I think she is hurt. Or trapped." His voice faded. "A wild cat is nearby."

"Who am I looking for next?"

Phillip directed her to Jose. Sonia followed them one to the next, a string of names from gravestones turned to voices navigating her to the far side of the cemetery and toward the woods that lay beyond. Each voice had a slightly different story. A wild cat had cornered the girl. The girl was trapped and a wild cat might hurt her.

She lost about fifteen minutes at the edge of the cemetery grounds finding the nearest gate. Between the gate and the most direct route back to where she needed to be lay a broad expanse of sharp gravel in the eastern parking lot. Pulling at the side seams of her skirt, she ripped off two wide strips of fabric. She sat on the ground and wrapped each foot in fabric as best she could. Though she could still feel the rocks it was bearable and she strode across the lot.

She smiled when her feet reached the scruffy weeds at the edge of the lot, and then realized she didn't hear a voice ahead or behind her. The gravel felt sharper the second time as she took three huge steps back toward the fence.

"Which way should I go now," she called back to the last voice in the cemetery, "Oliver was it?"

"Turn around. Turn around! Wrong way."

"I know, but I didn't hear anyone."

"You have to find the boy beyond the fence. He should be nearby."

Sonia turned around to put her back to the fence and looked at the deserted parking lot, bracing herself. It was very unlikely that a boy was buried under this gravel. That meant she was looking for the ghost of someone who died here.

Leaning down, she pushed gravel aside until she revealed a spot she could stand without the jagged rocks jabbing up through the fabric into the soles of her feet. The sun was up, peeping over the trees of the woods ahead and the low hills of mining country in the distance. It was going to be a hot day.

"Anyone here?" Sonia reached out with that un-named part of her that could hear the voices of the dead. She had tried to explain it a few times to close friends, but it was like trying to describe smell to someone who had never had that sense. Her arms at her sides, she consciously unclenched her hands and breathed evenly, opening that inner part of her that could hear. "I'm listening." she whispered.

"Can you hear me?" Curious. Young.

"Yes," she shouted before modulating her voice to something less alarming, "yes, I can hear you. Do you know which way I have to go?"

"Most live people can't hear me. It's been a long time since someone could hear me."

"What's your name?" Back to basics. "What happened to you?"

"I dropped my bear and the car didn't see me." Stated in the same tone of voice you might use to tell someone the time. "My name is Arthur. I'm still 7."

"I can come back and spend a whole afternoon talking to you, Arthur. But right now I need your help. A girl is in trouble and I want to help her. Do you know which way I'm supposed to go?"

"Into the woods. Toward the mines. There is a very old one just inside the edge of the trees. Go toward the sun, that should work."

"Thank you, Arthur. I will come back to see you. I promise."

"That would be nice. I wonder if my parents could come too?"

"I don't know, but I'm a private investigator. I am very good at finding people. If they can be found, I can do that for you."

"Okay," he sounded a little happier. Maybe. That was what she told herself as she moved toward the trees.

"See you soon, Arthur. Bye for now." Not for the first time, she wished she could touch or see the spirits she could hear. This little boy's ghost could definitely use a hug. But if she could touch them, then they could touch her and not all of them were friendly. It was safer for her to only be able to hear them. To always be able to escape just by leaving the area to which they were tethered.

She walked toward the sun, back across the gravel to a rocky and weed-covered open space. Stepping carefully to avoid broken bottles and other trash hidden under the wild groundcover, she reached the woods unscathed. The cool shade smelled of earth and green and the fading edge of night.

"Who is there?" Anonymous woods behind a cemetery, another unlikely location for finding a ghost at peace. This process would have been nerve wracking on a good night's sleep. After last night's hours of forced alertness, she was working hard to hold onto her focus. "I need to know which direction."

"Someone actually came?" A female voice. "Will wonders never cease. Okay. Keep on east until you hit the stream. Then follow it south until you find Oswald. He should be able to tell you where to cross."

"Thank you." She started walking, watching for hidden sticks and roots as she wound between the trees. "My name is Sonia. Are you buried here? Or did you die here?"

"Yes, on both counts. Come back another day and I'll tell you the whole sad story," a wry laugh, "but right now I'm feeling nostalgic. Maybe there is room for one more happy ending in the world."

"I hope so." Sonia's eyes began to droop, her first wave of adrenaline fading as her night of no sleep caught up to her. "Do you like to sing?" Singing would keep her awake.

"Sing? I haven't tried singing in a long time." The voice paused, then burst loud into Sonia's mind with the chorus of a bawdy folk song.

The spirit's voice was a lovely soprano and Sonia joined in, adding harmony in her alto range where she could work it out. Singing invigorated her and she felt her feet moving faster, her eyes were clearer. They took turns picking what to sing and soon she found the stream. Before turning south, Sonia took her time choosing the next song and knelt by the water.

Dappled sunshine danced on the water's surface. Tiny fish zipped back and forth. Sonia splashed her face with water and drank from her cupped hands. Her hair fell forward, splashing full into the water and scaring away the tiny fish.

"Sorry, little fish." she smiled, pulling her hair back into a ponytail. If it weren't for the emergency waiting somewhere ahead of her and her fabric-wrapped feet this could have just been a lovely walk in the woods.

She stood up, squared her shoulders in the right direction and launched into another folk song her grandmother used to sing. The nameless ghost joined back in, singing until Sonia could not hear her. Sonia kept singing the song and eventually a male voice joined in for the last stanza.

"Lovely singing voice, my dear," Oswald said after they finished out the song. "You are here to help with our little emergency?"

"Yes," Sonia smiled, "yes—emergency ghost support, at your service." She laughed at herself and dipped into a clumsy curtsy, hitting that strange, vibrational hyper-awakeness that comes after being awake for well more than 24 hours. "Do you know what the emergency is? None of the others could tell me."

"A young girl is trapped in one of the old mine shafts. Some sort of wild cat is there too. I don't know how old she is or what she was doing there - but whoever found her pushed his voice to its loudest to call for help."

"Thank you. Across the stream here?" Sonia gestured at the shallow water.

132 · JEANNE KRAMER-SMYTH

"Yes. And then there is a path just past that stand of evergreens that should take you the right way. There are lots of us out here. These mines were not kind to humans over the years. I guess it makes it less lonely for us, even the ones whose bodies were never put to rest."

"Are there songs that you all sang together? Songs that could help me find each of my guides the rest of the way?"

So they sang. She didn't measure time by her watch. She measured time by the songs and the changing voices that joined in. Some songs she recognized. Some were new to her, but they always had an easy chorus to join in on.

The combination of the hard packed earth beneath her feet and the new voices joining from somewhere down the path made it easier to navigate. Not knowing how far she had left to go, she walked at her fastest pace without running.

Eight songs later, she came out of the woods into a weed-strewn clearing. Decaying wood boards partially blocked the entrance to an abandoned mine cut into the side of the hill. Faded, barely legible, red paint letters spelled 'DANGER - KEEP OUT'.

She pulled her cell phone from her pocket to check for signal. Barely one bar, here in the middle of who knew where. It didn't matter. Calling in an emergency based on what ghosts told you wasn't a good way to get help. Someone must already be looking for this little girl. She pulled up a map on her phone to see where the nearest communities were. Where could she have come from to get in here unsupervised?

There were a few neighborhoods about a mile away. Certainly too far. A state park just to the north had a few summer campgrounds.

Barefoot and with just her phone for light, it would be slow going inside. But she couldn't convince herself that hiking through the park to try and find humans looking for a child was the better plan.

"Please hurry," an urgent male voice from beyond the danger sign, "The little girl isn't making any sounds. She had been crying and calling for help, but we're worried she is fading."

Sonia stashed her phone and stared at the makeshift socks covering her feet. Not as good as shoes, but better than nothing. At least her tetanus shot was up to date.

"How far do I have to go?" Sonia pulled a board aside until she could squeeze past. The shift from the bright summer day outside to the dank dark tunnel was jarring. She let her eyes adjust a little before turning on her phone's flashlight.

"Come forward and take the 2nd fork to the left. It isn't far." The slim beam of light helped her pick through the debris on the tunnel floor.

Other voices whispered all around her as she moved down the tunnel looking for the left turn.

"I can hear you all. Help me find her, please." They guided her, cautioning Sonia to move slowly and not knock anything that might fall or lead the tunnel to collapse.

It took her greatest self control to not run the last 50 feet when she could see pink sneakers peeking out from under a broad piece of lumber at the bottom of a pile of wood, rocks, and dirt. The ghosts stopped talking as she reached the girl.

Gentle fingertips on the girl's ankle reassured Sonia with skin warm to the touch.

"Hello? Can you hear me?" The ghosts understood that she spoke to the girl and stayed quiet. "I'm here to help."

The foot her hand rested on twitched.

"Who's there?" A tiny voice that seemed much too far away. "I can't move."

"My name is Sonia. I'm here to help. What's your name?"

"Nora. I'm seven. I'm not supposed to talk to strangers."

Sonia wished that Nora had also been taught not to wander into dark tunnels. "I promise I will tell your parents that you remembered that rule, but right now you need help to get out—right?"

"Yes," it sounded like she was crying a little now, "My legs hurt."

"Does anything else hurt?"

"My back hurts where the rocks are pushing. And my head hurts from where I hit it on something."

"Can you see any light?" Sonia moved her phone's light slowly across the gaps she could see.

"A little. Is that you?"

"Yes. Can you feel my hand touching your ankle?"

"Maybe?"

"Okay. Be very brave and stay still for a little while longer. I'm going to get some help."

"It's so cold. I want my mommy."

"I know honey. Hang tight."

Sonia checked her cell phone signal. Of course, no bars this far inside the mine. She backed out of Nora's hearing and whispered to the ghosts she knew must be all around. "I am going to go out and bring someone back." Fifteen voices, maybe more, all began to speak at the same time.

"Quiet!" A male ghost voice yelled with authority, "She can't hear any of you if you all talk at the same time."

"Thank you, yes." Sonia nodded. "I need one voice at a time."

"We do not think the debris will hold," the authoritative voice continued, "The child is going into shock. Waiting is a bad idea."

"I can't get her out from under all that alone, can I? None of you can move things in the physical world, right?"

"Hal, you designed some of the structures that hold up these tunnels. You help her get the child out. The rest of you—stay quiet." Lots of quiet ghostly grumbling, followed by a moment of silence.

"I'm Hal," a different voice, a bit more gentle, came from just beside her, "what is your name?"

"Hello, Hal." She turned toward the voice. "I'm Sonia. Can you see how I can remove all this without crushing both of us?"

"The worst of it is the beam at the bottom crushing her legs. I will talk you through each piece to move."

"Nora," Sonia raised her voice as she moved closer, "I'm going to move some of the things above you that are holding you down. Stay very still and we'll get you out."

"Okay." Her voice sounded so small.

Sonia stood in front of the blockage and lightly touched each piece of wood and chunk of rock as Hal guided her to the first piece to move. Once she had the right one, she didn't give herself time to think—she grasped it and lifted.

The wood came free easily. It must have been just resting on the top of the pile—but Sonia could not see that from where she stood. One by one, Hal helped her figure out the next piece to shift. A few times she dug out great clots of dirt. Sonia kept up a steady flow of reassurance for Nora, asking her questions about her family and her favorite things.

By the time Sonia got down to the last big wood beam that held down Nora's legs, they could see each other. The little girl wore shorts and what looked like a red and white striped shirt, all covered in a layer of gray-brown dust.

"You need to stay still for this last part, okay Nora? I know you want to wiggle and get up, but I want to make sure I get you completely free. Right?"

"Yes, Sonia. I understand."

Sonia wished for many things in that moment. A cold drink of water. The benefit of a night of sleep and a full breakfast. She wished that Hal and his whole crew of kind ghost miners could help her lift this beast of a beam.

"Sonia, you are going to need a lever. You can't lift that yourself." Hal spoke up. He described how to use a stack of nearby bricks and a sturdy board to help her lift the beam.

It took forever to wedge the board under the beam at the right angle, but finally Sonia could feel the beam begin to shift as she pushed on her side of the lever.

"Nora, as soon as you feel like you can I need you to pull your legs out from under the wood."

"Okay." Nora's big brown eyes watched Sonia's face as she nodded solemnly.

"I am going to count to three and then push on this to lift the wood. One. Two. Three." She used her full body weight and all her strength to push down. The lever did its job, shifting the beam up the few inches necessary to free Nora's leg. "Now! Pull your legs out!"

It took much longer than Sonia had hoped for Nora to shift herself backward on the floor and free her legs, but she did it.

"I'm out."

The ghost voices broke out into cheers all around her. Sonia wanted to thank them all, but talking to them now while Nora listened would just confuse the little girl.

"Stay still, I'm coming over." Sonia lowered the beam back down, now all the way to the floor, and released the lever completely. She climbed carefully through the gap in the debris she had made with Hal's help and knelt at Nora's side, checking her for visible injuries. "Can you feel your feet? Can you move your fingers and toes?"

"I think so." She wiggled her fingers in Sonia's face obediently. "Can we all go now?"

"Yes, absolutely. Is it okay if I carry you?"

"Yes, but we can't leave yet."

"What? Why?"

"The momma cat and her kittens are still back there." Out of the murk behind Nora, a tiny orange kitten marched into the light cast by Sonia's phone. "We have to take them with us. I followed the momma cat from the campground all the way here with my flashlight last night." Nora waved her flashlight proudly.

This must be the 'wild cat'. Sonia had forgotten that part of the garbled story.

The kitten looked like it had just woken from a nice nap. It stretched, yawned, and climbed into Nora's lap. Deeper in the gloom,

Sonia's phone light illuminated two sets of eyes. She moved slowly to not spook them until she was crouched just beside the cats' makeshift nest. The momma watched warily as Sonia scooped up a second kitten. This one was white with orange markings, just like its mother.

Sonia turned back to Nora.

"You carry the kittens and I'll carry you. I bet the momma cat will follow her kittens."

They made a strange little parade as they picked their way back to the mine's entrance. Nora was able to set the kittens down outside, then climb out - followed by Sonia and the momma cat.

Sonia called 911 with her one bar of signal. She and Nora sat in the shade by the trees with the momma cat, watching the kittens play as they waited for help to come and Sonia mentally rearranged her guest room to accommodate the three new guests she planned to bring home.

K is for Kittens

Samantha Kymmell-Harvey

May 12, 1856

My Dearest Eleanor,

How thrilled I was to receive your letter, sister! Summer is nearing and I am looking forward to our yearly summer retreat to Myrtlewood. And thanks to Burwell's recent business trip to Paris, Myrtlewood will resemble a Parisian parlor when you arrive.

Sister, I have never seen so many boxes and crates arrive! Burwell pried open each crate with such gusto to show me. "You shall have Paris here at home," he said. He bought settees, draperies, wallpaper, and side tables, all in the new fashionable Parisian style dyed in that striking shade of green we have seen in all the magazine prints. Some of these pieces are perfect for the summer parlor at Myrtlewood, so I am shipping them there.

But sister, the gorgeous furniture is not where Burwell's generosity ended.

Do you remember that delicate frock of the most stunning green on the cover of this month's *Le Moniteur de la Mode*? Well, Burwell bought it for me and it fits me as if I had been there in person for the tailor to measure. It shall surely garner much attention at our next dinner party. All of the investors will be there and we are anxious to impress.

Once this party is done, we shall be taking up residence at Myrtlewood for some well earned respite from city life.

Please give your dear husband and my sweet nieces my best.

All my love,
Alice

June 2, 1856
My Dearest Eleanor,

The dinner party was quite a success though the stress and excitement left me feeling light headed the next day. Burwell called Dr. Peterson, who had a perfectly reasonable assessment for my condition. I am with child! We are so happy. Though Burwell must stay in Archerville to finish some business, I will go on to Myrtlewood. Dr. Peterson believes some fresh air and relaxation will be the perfect restorative. Despite this happy news, I am still haunted by worry.

Ellie, it has all been so strange. When Burwell returned home, we planned our gala. We spared no expense. The cook prepared luscious courses of oysters in aspic, whole roast pig, and asparagus gêlé. I wish you could have been here to see the strawberry tart he prepared. The glaze glistened in the dim gaslight of our dining room. I wore my new Parisian green dress, and sister, the compliments made me blush! I was indeed the envy of the other wives in attendance. We danced and drank the French burgundy Burwell shipped back. It was so hot in the house that we opened the windows to let in a breeze. I was worried to be so unladylike and did not wish to sully my new dress in such a way.

I stepped out into the garden for a bit of respite. There was a dark-haired woman on the terrace who I did not recognize. She stood in the shadows just out of the candlelight, keeping her face hidden. Her frock was scarlet, similar to the deep red in last year's winter edition of *Le Moniteur de la Mode*. I did not believe for one moment that one of our investors would allow his wife to appear in out of season clothing at an event such as this. Poor thing!

"Good evening," I said. "It is a pleasure to make your acquaintance."

The woman turned to me, yet I could not see her face in that dark flickering shadow. Two dark eyes glimmered set in deep, black sockets, her pale skin drawn tightly across her cheekbones. Sister, it was as if this woman had not nourished herself in quite some time. I asked her if she was quite well, but before she responded, there was a great crash indoors. I hurried back into the parlor to find Mr. Carter sprawled on the floor, the card table turned over, cards strewn on the woven rug. Burwell really ought to reconsider his passion for cards.

When I returned to the terrace, the woman was no longer there. I suppose the mystery of who she was must endure.

Burwell had a brandy and a smoke in the parlor while I went upstairs to bed. When I peeled off the dress, my skin was speckled with strange red spots. They felt hot, like when a when you accidentally get too close to a candle flame. Yet I know I did not burn myself at the party.

As I write, my skin has healed but I am still not feeling well. Perhaps this is what it feels like when you are expecting your first child. Ellie, how did you feel when little Eliza was on the way?

When you respond, please be sure to address your letter to Myrtlewood instead of the house here in Archerville.

All my love,
Alice

June 19, 1856

Dear Alice,

What happy news! Eliza and Agnes have already begun knitting socks for their new niece or nephew. We are also very excited to be seeing you very soon. We leave tomorrow for Myrtlewood. Miss Lauretta needs to go into town to buy writing diaries for the girls so that they can continue their tutelage. Miss Lauretta will be joining us at Myrtlewood. I hope you don't mind. She will be a great help, especially because William will not be able to join, as he must stay in Chicago attending to business. He sends his apologies, but will join as soon as he can.

News of your party and of your vibrant green dress reached me here in Chicago. What a success, dear sister! However, my friends knew not who this strange woman in the red frock may have been. You must think nothing of it though, Alice, some women are not as in love with the latest fashions as you are.

What does concern me, however, is your description of your health. I shall bid the coachman to hurry us to Myrtlewood as fast as the horses can take it.

Your sister,
Eleanor

June 30, 1856

My Dearest Eleanor,

I am delighted you and the children are journeying to Myrtlewood, though I am saddened your husband cannot join. My Burwell remains in Archerville unable yet to take respite from his work. The train company grows with each passing day and needs his attention. I remain alone at Myrtlewood, until you arrive of course. I long to see you and my nieces again.

You will certainly marvel at the summer parlor. The new Parisian furniture, wallpaper, and drapes bring such lightness to the room. The fabric is a delightful hand painted floral design of pinks and greens. The French have such wonderful taste, Ellie. I take my afternoon tea on the settee and relax in the sunlight that streams in through the tall windows. The weather has been quite hot recently though. The windows let in the perfect breeze, but it does not quell the humidity. I suggest you bring fans with you.

Despite the sunlight and country air, I wish I could report that my health has improved. Alas, I continue to be unwell. This baby must be as stubborn as his father. I find myself unable to sleep, and when I do fall asleep, I am plagued by strange and terrifying visions. That woman in red haunts my sleep, sister. Only when I see her, her eyes are empty sockets and her skin gray. She opens her mouth as if to speak, yet I hear nothing. I jolt awake, covered in sweat and feverish. The ravens crow incessantly from the branches of the old elm by the bedroom window.

Ellie, this is the strangest of all, but sometimes I think I see her. I have to pinch myself to ensure I am not sleeping on the settee. But I could swear I have seen a flash of crimson out of the corner of my eye at the windows or heard the rustling of a bustle.

I fear I may be going mad. Did you have such unnatural dreams when you were expecting Eliza?

I am very much looking forward to your arrival.

All my love,
Alice

July 15, 1856

My beloved William,

I have arrived safely at Myrtlewood only to find my sister in quite a state. Please implore Burwood on my behalf to hurry, for I truly fear for Alice. I sent him a letter a week ago and have not received a response. Perhaps he will listen to you.

When we arrived, we waited at the door for some time, yet Alice did not respond. Eliza grew impatient and tried the handle, which was unlocked. Both girls bounded past me, dropping their cases on the foyer rug. Miss Lauretta tried to call them back, but they would not obey. Then I heard them shriek.

"Mama! It's Aunt Alice! Hurry!"

I had never heard Eliza yell like that. In the parlor, I discovered Alice draped over the settee, shaking, with a shawl pulled tightly across her shoulders despite the oppressive heat and humidity. She was gaunt and skeletal except for the curve at her stomach. I immediately sent Lauretta to the nearby town to fetch Dr. Peterson and sent Eliza to fetch me water.

"Oh sister, you came," Alice said, placing her hand on my cheek. She felt so cold, her fingers so bony. Bright red blotches afflicted her fingers. I have never seen an illness like this. It is certainly not sickness due to the coming baby.

Dr. Peterson arrived swiftly. I helped him carry Alice up to the bedroom where he requested my presence at his examination. Here is all I witnessed:

Her entire body was covered in those red welts. She was also sweating. There was another container beside her chamber pot where she had retched many times. Tufts of her hair were all over the pillow cases. When the doctor forced her eyes open, the whites had turned green.

His expression told me how grave it all was. "This is very strange, but I must ask," he said. "Has she been poisoning any unwanted creatures? These symptoms are very similar to those who work with arsenic poisons."

I replied that she had not mentioned any infestations of mice or any other unwanted pests, but that I would search for the poisons that may be here at the house. Certainly Alice would have hired an expert pest controller and not handled the substances herself. Especially not in her condition.

Dr. Peterson treated her with a tincture and told me to administer it to her twice a day. He also said he would call upon her in two days time to see how she was progressing.

I am glad I am here for her, but I am so deeply worried. Please convey to Burwell the severity of the situation and that he should leave for Myrtlewood without delay.

Your love,
Eleanor

July 16, 1856

My governess, Miss Lauretta, says that I must practice my writing if I am to improve my style and write like a lady. I don't know what to write about. If I were at home, I'd write about my friend, Martha, and my cat, Old Scampers. I miss him. I hope Papa remembers to feed him.

I must write something though.

Oh, I know! I have a peculiar story about my sister. My Auntie Alice is very ill. I hear her vomiting in the night, though I know I'm not supposed to mention it though because it is unbecoming of a lady. Mama sends Aggie and I to play outside. She says the air is good for us, but I think it is so that we don't see her tending to my Auntie.

Yesterday, it was already hot early in the morning. Mama and Miss Lauretta were taking tea on the settee in the parlor fanning themselves, their faces were red and wet with sweat.

"Go play outside," said Miss Lauretta. "We will start our lessons in the afternoon."

Aggie and I were very happy not to have morning lessons. We ran down the dirt path weaving between the pink crape myrtle trees. Aggie pointed up. "Look! A raven!" And she sprinted to follow it.

"Aggie! Wait!" I called, but she did not. We ran through the tall grass with the raven in sight overhead until it landed in the highest branches of the gnarled oak tree growing beside the pond. It cawed as if to laugh at us.

"You know Mama doesn't like us to come to the pond by ourselves," I said. "So we must be extra careful."

We dangled our feet in, but the water was warm and offered no respite from the heat. "Come on, let's climb the lower branches. The shade will be nicer," I said as I helped Aggie before hoisting myself up.

Then Aggie gasped.

"What is it?"

She pointed in the direction of the house. And that's when I saw it, too. A figure of a woman with hair as dark as Auntie Alice's paced in the boxwood garden, wringing her hands. The tattered hem of her brown-red dress dragged in the mulch. Aggie gripped my arm so hard I cried out.

"Who is she, Eliza?"

I knew not, but I had heard my Auntie speak of a woman in red and the figure seemed real enough. She wailed as she looked into the parlor windows. Her pale hands clawed at the casement as if seeking entry. What kind of visitor would do that?

The branch crackled under me as I shifted my weight. I clasped a hand over Aggie's mouth as the figure turned away from the window and faced me. We were too far to see her face clearly, but her eyes looked sunken and very dark. Then she cried out and vanished behind the crape myrtles.

"We will be cursed for seeing such a creature," Aggie said, trembling. "We will have nightmares."

That night, I woke when I heard Auntie Alice retching again. And Mama was crying. I'd never heard her cry like that before. I lit a candle and tread the hallway to Aunt Alice's room. Mama saw me and yelled at me to go back to bed. But when I went back to bed, a raven had settled in the tree by my window and would not stop its horrible singing until morning. Stupid bird.

I decided right there in the darkness that if the woman in red was hurting my auntie, then I would catch her and end her evil curse. I promise.

July 29, 1856

Dear William,

Thank you so much for writing to Burwell. We received word from his secretary that he left for New York for a very important meeting but says he has sent a letter to Dr. Peterson saying to spare no expense in caring for Alice. Alas, Burwell will woe to read the letter I am sending him today.

My sister's child is lost.

It happened last night, and William, there was nothing I could do to stop it. Dr. Peterson worked, applying compresses and tinctures. I was helpless as my sister screamed. Her eyes were wild. She squeezed my hand, and I swear I could hear sobs echoing from somewhere outside. Even those wretched ravens stopped their cawing when that poor soul came into the world, lifeless and too small. Alice and I cried together. When she saw the sheets, red with her own blood, she clung to me and said "She has done this, the woman in red. See, it is her mark." Then Alice fainted on the pillow. I stroked her head, but clumps of hair came away in my fingers.

Dr. Peterson wrapped the baby in the sheets. "I shall take him to Father Thomas," he said. I agreed it was the best course of action. The baby could be blessed in the morning and given a proper sacred burial.

When he left, I reclined beside my sister, listening to her ragged breathing. In the silence, there came a tapping at the window. Thinking it merely a branch, I rose and opened the pane. There was nothing in the darkness, but William, I swear to you I thought I saw a glint of a taffeta crimson bustle disappearing into the shadow. Perhaps it was just a hellish vision brought on by the hellishness of what had just transpired. I said a prayer for Alice.

This morning, I brought the poor tiny soul to the churchyard in town. Alice was too weak to say her final goodbyes, but bade me to ensure the child's journey to Heaven.

My heart is so, heavy, William. I wish you were here to comfort me. However, you should not make the journey for I fear my sister's illness is spreading.

I, too, am having red splotches on my skin. I have noticed they erupt more viciously when I lounge in the parlor. Perhaps it is due to the heat and humidity of that room. We were able to dismiss the poison as my search of Myrtlewood did not locate any. Dr. Peterson is now concerned that there may be a new plague beginning here and he does not recommend that anyone else come to Myrtlewood. We here must make do on our own.

Your love,
Eleanor

July 30, 1856

Mama and Miss Lauretta act so strangely when they spend time in the green parlor. Mama is more exhausted than usual and Miss Lauretta delays our lessons, which she never does. Angry, red blotches have blossomed on their legs. I did not tell them so, but I believe it is due to the woman in red who claws at those windows and haunts our dreams.

Aggie and I brought Mama and Miss Lauretta tea and toast in their beds before setting up the trap for the ghoul. According to Father Robert back home, ghosts don't like salt, iron, holy water, or crosses. I had found all of those things, except holy water.

I made a tidy line of salt under each window in the parlor. Next, Aggie and I went into the boxwood garden where we fastened twigs with twine to make crosses. We hung them from the branches of the crape myrtles. We also hung old nails we found in the garden shed beside the crosses. I wasn't sure if they were truly made of iron or not, but it was all we could find.

"Now, we wait," I said to Aggie.

We walked through the tall grass to the pond. We climbed back into the lower branches. We watched.

The sun felt like coal fire, even through the leaves of the tree. Aggie fell asleep with her head in my lap. The sweat dripped into my eyes and they burned. But I kept watch. The garden had a watery appearance in the short distance. Something red blurred amongst the pink myrtle flowers. I squinted. Wiping the sweat from my brow, I caught sight of a pale figure passing between the boxwood. I held my breath.

Thunder rumbled in the distance. Dark gray clouds approached. It would rain soon and all of my salt would be washed away. I woke Aggie. "She's here."

We slid down from the branches and crawled through the tall grass. The figure moved with unnatural speed about the myrtles. The thunder boomed over our heads, closer this time. Aggie shouted and clung to me. As huge droplets of rain fell upon us, a fearful scream rang out from the garden. Aggie and I rose to our feet. The creature was gone.

We ran back into the boxwood garden. The salt borders had already begun to wash away.

"Look!" Aggie pointed at a myrtle branch.

A shred of red cloth hung from one of the crosses. I took it. "She must have gotten caught up in the branches somehow." I examined the cloth. It somehow seemed less red and more reddish brown dyed over a bright green fabric. How strange that from afar or in dim lighting, the color appeared more strikingly red.

We left our muddied boots on the stone floor of the kitchen and I visited Mama, Auntie Alice, and Miss Lauretta. They were all asleep in their beds, unaware of the summer storm.

My trap had nearly worked. The woman in red will not escape me again.

August 1, 1856

My Beloved Burwell,

This letter may be short as I have been so weak. But, dear husband, my heart is empty. This pain is bone-deep. Were I not too weak to travel, I would come home to Archerville. But Dr. Peterson says we must all stay isolated here until he can deduce the cause of our illnesses. The house is cursed. I swear it.

Ellie now withers. Dr. Peterson has prescribed the same tinctures for her. Miss Lauretta has recovered, though she remains weak. She cares for Eliza and Agnes while Ellie tends to me. My sister puts on airs of strength, but I see the sweat on her brow. Her eyes dart to the corners of the room when we both hear the rustling. Or the cries that seem to come from nowhere and everywhere. I know you must think me mad, but the woman in red is real. I am certain she has cursed Myrtlewood. But why?

Yours faithfully,
Alice

August 15, 1856

Aggie and I beheld the most beautiful gown today! Uncle Burwell sent it with a note that he would be departing soon and a family soirée would be just the thing to lift our spirits. It arrived in a box fastened with a red ribbon. Auntie Alice was so happy that she rose from her bed and pressed the dress to her form in the mirror. She looked like a princess from a fairy tale.

"What do you say, my ladies," Alice said to us. "Shall we have a fancy supper this evening?" She sat on the edge of the bed to catch her breath.

Mama nodded. "I think it would bring us some joy. I love the smile that French dress has brought your face. It is the one medicine Dr. Peterson does not have."

"Pick out a ribbon to plait your hair tonight," said my Auntie, "both of you."

Her jewelry box sat upon the vanity. The lid sparkled. It reminded me of shells from the beach. Aggie rushed ahead of me.

"Aggie!" I complained. I should get first pick, I'm the eldest, but she cared not. She had already pulled a blue silky ribbon out and was trying to tie it in her hair.

Auntie Alice laughed. "Perhaps your sister can teach you how to tie that properly."

Aggie planted her hands on her hips. "I'm going to do it by myself."

Once Aggie made up her mind, it was set.

I secretly hoped Auntie Alice had a pink one because it would complement the party dress Mama had just brought for me in April. It had delicate lace around the collar and ribbons at the sleeves. It made me feel like a princess, too.

Before tonight's dinner, I would have to sneak back into the kitchen to steal more salt. I did not want that ghoulish woman bothering us. If only I could have gotten some holy water!

I sat at Auntie Alice's vanity and as I began to untangle the heaps of ribbons, I noticed something pale in the mirror. Behind me, Aggie twirled around the bed, twisting the ribbon in her hair and Auntie Alice clapped. But behind them, a small white face peered in the window pane. The red of her collar glimmered in the sunlight. For the first time, I saw her face.

Oh diary, it was so terrible! I screamed. And when I did, the face vanished.

Then Auntie Alice screamed too. "Oh child, you gave me quite a fright!"

"I saw her," I said. "The woman in red was at the window just now. And Auntie Alice," I ran to my aunt, arms wide open, tears rolling down my cheeks. "Her face is yours."

August 16, 1856

My Beloved William,

My hope is that by the time you receive this, we will already be on our way home to you. I wish never to return to Myrtlewood.

My sister is dead.

Oh, it was horrible, William. I shall never be able to erase the images of last night from my mind. I keep glancing over my shoulders at the slightest creak of the floorboards or rattle of the window panes.

Burwell has just arrived with Dr. Peterson, so I am leaving now.

Your love,
Eleanor

October 1, 1856

I hate Papa.

He forced the men from St. Francis' hospital to take Mama away from us. She kicked and screamed. Then he chopped all of Auntie Alice's beautiful Parisian furniture to splinters! Uncle Burwell gifted it to us, he said he knew she'd want us to have it! Then my Papa set the wooden scraps ablaze in the garden. The flames glowed the same shade of sickly green as the wallpaper at Myrtlewood. Aggie and I cried, begged him not to destroy Auntie Alice's favorite settee.

"The doctor says it's poisonous," Papa said. "Arsenic. He said he's seen cases like this in Europe. The women languish slowly until they die. All indulged in green wallpaper, frocks, toys, wallpaper." The wooden pieces crackled, sending green sparks into the air like fourth of July. "We must pray for your Mama."

But diary, I must speak the truth about how my Auntie died. It was because of <u>her</u>. Because my trap did not work. Aggie has not yet forgiven me.

That evening in August was the kind of night Mama would let me and Aggie run around in our cotton shifts because the air was so hot and thick. But we had to dress up in our best party frocks for Auntie Alice's fancy dinner. We sat on the green silk chairs around the dining room table. In the candlelight, sweat glistened on Auntie Alice's forehead. Her green dress was a shade darker at her arm pits. Mama fanned herself. Aggie tugged at the collar of her blue dress.

"Agnes Mary, that is not how we behave at the dinner table," said Mama.

Then there was a knock at the front door. I looked to Mama who looked to Auntie Alice.

"Shall I go see who is calling?" Miss Lauretta said.

Auntie Alice clasped a hand to her chest. "Burwell has arrived!"

"Surely Burwell has keys," said Mama.

The knock sounded again.

Aggie jumped from her chair. "I want to see who it is."

I could not stop her for she had set her mind to it. Her feet pounded down the hallway. We sat silently as the door knob clicked and the door creaked open.

"Auntie Alice," Aggie's voice echoed from the foyer. "How did you get out here? You look like you don't feel well."

Aggie appeared on the threshold of the dining room linked arm in arm with a pale, skeletal woman. Mama screamed as did Miss Lauretta. The woman's long dark hair hung in clumps, her gray scalp exposed. She pointed at Auntie Alice with long, gray fingers, nails tinged greenish. Her face, thin but untouched by decay, was exactly the same face I saw in the window, that of my Auntie.

The ghostly specter said not a word as she passed behind my chair. The dress she wore was not a true red but like a scarlet had seeped through an emerald green. A match to the shred I recovered in the garden. A perfect match to my auntie's French dress.

Aggie gasped at Mama, who was trying to push her back out into the hallway. "Go get Father Thomas, hurry!" Mama shouted at Miss Lauretta, who raced from the table. "Eliza, go outside with your sister. You have to protect her."

At first, I did not hear her words. It was as if the wet heat had clogged my ears. I was transfixed on this ghoulish twin of my auntie who now stood beside her. Auntie Alice grasped her chair as more red blotches erupted on her skin.

"Go!" Mama grabbed me by the shoulders and pushed me out of the room. Aggie clung to my waist, sobbing into my pink dress.

But my eyes remained fixed on my Auntie Alice.

"I have come for you," said the woman in bloodied green. She opened her arms and enveloped my auntie.

The air chilled and silenced. And Auntie Alice slumped to the floor, pulses of red seeping through the vibrant green.

My mother shrieked and retreated into the corner. The spectral woman touched my auntie's shoulder and her spectral twin emerged from her body. They linked arms. Aggie and I pressed ourselves against the wall as they passed by, not daring to breathe for fear death may claim us, too.

Father Thomas arrived nearly an hour later with nothing to do other than pray with us for Aunt Alice's reaped soul.

That is my truth, dear diary.

October 10, 1856
My Dearest Alice,

I see her everywhere. She is waiting for her chance to come inside. Her face peers in at me. It is like looking into a mirror, for her face is mine but withered and decayed. She taps on my window. She sends the ravens to caw at me in the night. I dream of you, in your brilliant green dress, and you speak of the latest fashions in *Le Moniteur de la Mode*. And I sip tea beside you. I miss you, my sweet sister. But take peace in knowing she has come for me.

All my love,
Your Ellie

L is for Languish

BD Wilson

Amber dumped the box out over her new bed, even though she knew that wasn't what her parents had meant by unpacking, and sifted through the scattered doll clothes.

"I didn't forget it," she told Elie. The doll was lying on the pillows, her silky brown hair fanned out around her, her soft body visible as Amber had started changing her outfit before she'd taken the dress out of the box. "I didn't."

There had been nothing left in their old apartment. She'd done a walk-through with her parents and her father had searched every corner, just in case. All the same, Elie's purple dress, the one Amber thought must have been from when the doll belonged to her mother because of the beautiful hand-stitched J on the front, wasn't here.

Standing up with a sigh she crossed the hallway to her parent's room. The bed was already put together and made, the breathing machine positioned beside it, now they had a room where it fit. It was powered on and the mask hung on the edge, but her mother wasn't in the room. Amber stood there a moment, listening to the machine hum, and then bent down to look under the bed. There were no boxes there yet and nothing the in closet either.

"Looking for something," her father said from the doorway, making her jump.

"I'm missing one of Elie's dresses," she said.

"It'll turn up, I'm sure. We've still got to unpack the living room."

"I hope so."

"We'll find it. But right now I have to go back to the apartment to finish signing papers. Mom's going to take you over to Nana's."

"Can't she watch me?"

"She needs to rest," he said, and while neither of them looked at the respirator, Amber could still hear it humming in wait behind them. "Grab a few things, just in case."

"Sorry," Amber told Elie as she returned to her room. "You'll have to wear something else." She grabbed a striped shirt and jean-skirt overalls that fit well enough, though they'd been made for a different style of doll. Elie was too old to buy clothes made specifically for her anywhere. The only outfit she had that seemed made for her was the purple dress. And Amber had lost it.

It was because they had to move. If they were still in their old apartment then the dress would be in her toy chest where it belonged. She wouldn't have had to put everything she owned in to boxes. She'd still be able to have a sleep-over with Priya on the weekend, because she was old enough to walk there herself now. They'd made plans for the summer, to trade off every week, but now Amber lived on the other side of the city and none of that was going to happen.

After she had Elie dressed, Amber quickly ran a brush through her tangled blonde hair, more than a little jealous it wasn't as easy to brush as the doll's and then grabbed a few books and Elie. In the hall her mother was waiting. Her hair, naturally the same brown colour as Elie's, was dyed blue this month, and even though she cut it too short to tie back, she had a bandana around her head to keep her eyes clear while they unpacked. Only, she wasn't unpacking right now. Instead she was leaning against the wall, breathing in and out with the practiced pace she'd learned from the nurses. She pushed herself to stand straight and smiled as Amber joined her. "I'm fine, honey."

Fine, Amber had learned, could mean everything from just needing a second to needing to call the hospital, but right now it seemed she was well enough.

"We'll come get you soon," her mother promised as she reached out and brushed the top of Amber's head, smoothing down her hair. "And you'll have a fun time at Nana's."

"If it's going to be so fun, why didn't we move before?" Amber sulked as they left, her mother locking the door behind them even though they were just going down the hall. Not that she would have wanted to move earlier, either.

"It's complicated," he mother answered, the way she always did when talking about Nana. Like fine, Amber was pretty sure complicated had more than one meaning.

As much as she grumbled, she was looking forward to seeing Nana. Even though they lived in the same city, she'd rarely visited while growing up. By the time they reached the door at the end of the hall she had to try to keep from bouncing up and down as she waited, but gave in, jumping when the door opened.

"Hi, Nana!"

"Amber, my dear." Nana pulled her into a hug, warm and strong, and then leaned back. "Let me get a look at you." She ran her hand over Amber's head, the way her mother had done, and then did the same for Elie, as though the doll were just another family member. "Come in, come in." She led them into the living room of her little apartment.

"Sorry for having to drop her off unexpectedly," Amber's mother said.

"Nonsense, Jacqueline. That's why you're here, after all."

"Lynn," her mother corrected, her mouth a firm line that fit the tone in her voice. "Dane will be back in a few hours, once everything's sorted at the old place."

"I'm sure Amber and I can keep ourselves occupied."

Amber went right in and set Elie down on the piano bench, as though the doll were playing. A shiver ran through her, and she got up to see if the window could be closed, but it wasn't even open.

"Amber takes after you, Jacqueline," Nana said. "Perhaps you'd like to have your piano now. It wouldn't be as difficult to move it up the hall."

Their new apartment didn't seem like it had room enough for the piano, even if it was bigger than the old apartment, but that wasn't the strangest thing about the suggestion. "Mom doesn't play the piano."

"She does," Nana insisted. "It's just a phase."

Amber's mother took a breath and let it out, five seconds each way, Amber counted. "I'd better go lay down," she said when she opened her eyes again. Her face seemed paler now.

"Rest well, Jacqueline," Nana said as she walked her to the door. "We'll be just fine here." When Nana came back, she stopped and looked at the pictures on her wall and seemed to talk to herself for a moment. "She'll remember who she is."

Amber left Elie on the piano bench and she went over to look at the photographs. There were a lot of her mother, but the one Nana was looking at was of another girl. She had dark hair like Amber's mother, but looked a lot like Nana, too. "Who's that?"

Nana startled, like she'd forgotten Amber was there. "That's my sister," she said, her voice soft and sad.

"I didn't know you had a sister."

"Well, we haven't gotten to know much about one another, but we'll soon fix that."

Amber grinned as she remembered she'd get to visit Nana every day after school now. The one good thing that came out of the stupid move.

"Now then, Amber, how would you like to learn how to make bread?"

"Yes!" Amber said, and turned to get Elie only to find the doll sitting in Nana's chair. She frowned for a moment, then picked her up and followed Nana into the kitchen. She must have forgotten where she'd put her, that's all.

Amber opened her eyes and sat bolt upright in bed. For a moment her heart pounded and her throat felt tight, and then she remembered.

My room, she thought. I'm in my room. She was used to waking to the sight of neon lights flickering across the roof. At the old apartment she'd slept in the living room, and while there were blinds on the window, the glow from the sign outside had always made it through. Now everything was too dark. Amber dug under the covers until she found Elie, pulled the doll to her chest, and slipped out of bed.

In her parent's room, the respirator beeped, slow and steady, timed to the whisper of the pumps that kept her mother's lungs moving properly. Her father was asleep on the other side of the bed, though she couldn't hear his breathing over the machine and wondered if it fell into the same pace, listening to it as he slept. Amber took a breath herself, timing it to the respirator, in and out, trying to settle the unease of waking in a strange place.

It's okay, she thought and closed her eyes. This is home now. It didn't feel like it, not yet, but it would. In the morning, she would have breakfast, and then her father would drive her to school, and even if she liked walking better that would be okay, because she'd get to spend time with him. Then, after school, she'd go to Nana's, which was something different but would still be wonderful.

Her next in-breath, timed to the machine, seemed shorter than the last, and just as she thought that, the beeping changed. It wasn't the warning beep, not yet, but it wasn't a good one. Amber opened her eyes.

There was a girl standing beside her parent's bed, bent over at the waist, face above her mother's, though she had to be floating to manage it. Her dark hair hovered around her head lank and thick, soaked through, dripping down onto the covers. She wore a blue dress that floated on the air as though it were water and a ribbon from the back of her dress hung suspended, its end torn, with a tiny little thread connecting it to Amber's mother.

Her mother breathed out and Amber saw the breath, like they were outside in winter. The girl breathed it in, taking her it as her own. Her mother's next in-breath, even with the machine's help, was shorter still, prompting another bad beep. Amber clutched Elie to her chest, took a breath twice as deep, and let it out in a scream.

The girl's head snapped up, and she seemed strangely familiar, even though everything about her face was wrong, down to her pale shimmering skin, cracked with blue veins. Her eyes were dark pits and she snarled as she glared at Amber. The ribbon twisted, curving around, angling toward where Amber stood in the doorway, the one fragile thread trailing behind. For a second, just a second, the ghost girl's gaze seemed to shift focus, become worried, and then the lights in the room came on and she vanished.

"Amber are you okay?" Her father tossed the covers aside and knelt beside her. "Amber, honey?"

"There was a ghost," she said, her mind making the connection right before she spoke. "She was hurting mom."

Her father glanced over his shoulder, but of course the ghost girl was gone and the machine was now beeping steadily, her mother's indrawn breaths as deep as they should be. "There's no one here, it's okay."

"She was there." Amber knew her voice was too loud, could feel tears on her face, and wanted to be brave, but all she could picture was her mother's breath being stolen by the girl with the wet hair as droplets fell to the cover.

Her father wrapped Amber in a hug and rubbed her back. "It's okay, honey. It's okay. Mom's fine. It was just a nightmare."

Amber swallowed hard and looked at the bed. Her mother was still asleep, a deep sleep thanks to her medication, the machine was working properly, and there was no sign of the girl. She convinced her father to let her go over and check, only to find the blankets dry, not a trace of the droplets left.

"See?" her father said. "Just a dream."

Amber nodded, hugged Elie once tight, and then slipped the doll under the covers with her mother. "Just in case," she said, and her father smiled.

"Good call. Elie will protect her. Now let's get you back to bed."

It wasn't until she was tucked back under the covers and distracting herself with thoughts of the next day that Amber realized why the ghost girl seemed familiar: the photographs. In them her eyes were bright and she was smiling instead of snarling, but Nana's sister was the ghost girl who'd stolen her mother's breath.

Amber sat at a table in Nana's kitchen, pretending to do her homework. Instead, she was thinking about her mother, sleeping again, with Elie keeping watch. She'd stopped in after school, though she was supposed to have gone right over to Nana's. She couldn't help it. Not when she got home and imagined her great-aunt, still a child, bent over her mother and taking her last breath.

Aunt Jacqueline, who'd died before Amber's mother was even born. Jacqueline, which was the name Nana insisted on calling her mother, no matter how many times she was told her name was now Lynn.

Amber put her books aside, went to the wall, and took down a picture of Aunt Jacqueline and Nana as children, each holding a doll and smiling as they stood beside an old station wagon. Amber studied her aunt's face, wondering how she'd gone from that happy girl to the angry creature who was hurting her mother. She took the picture over to the chair where Nana was knitting.

"Done your homework, dear?"

"Not yet," Amber answered, not wanting to lie. "Can you tell me more about your sister?"

Nana took the picture and set her knitting aside as she smiled. "Jacqueline was my younger sister."

"Jacqueline, like mom used to be?"

Nana frowned a little at that, but nodded. "Exactly. My sister died when we were both still young. It was such a tragedy. We went on a holiday to the beach, and we thought we were safe, playing well above the water line, climbing over rocks to see what had washed into the cracks. Jacqueline went out farther than I dared, always the brave one, but still safe enough, we thought. Then a rogue wave swept her away. I screamed for help, but it was too late. That wave pulled Jacqueline under and kept her there until her breath ran out."

Amber thought of the ghost girl's soaked hair, the way her dress floated, and shivered.

"She loved piano, you know that?" Nana continued, sitting up as though pulling herself out of the darker thoughts, looking over at the instrument in the corner. "She was going to be a concert pianist. Your mother was going to do that, too. At least, that was the plan, when she was younger. I don't know what happened." She ran her finger over the picture, a touch as soft as the confusion in her voice. "I wanted to see that so very much."

"I don't think mom likes piano," Amber said, hoping that didn't make Nana upset.

"I don't know what happened," Nana repeated, and Amber wondered if she would ever notice nothing had, that her mother had always hated it. "She would play every day. Her aunt loved practicing, but my Jacqueline always complained. My sister, she would sit down for an hour a day without question. I used to have to drag your mother over to it. She liked to play, just didn't like to practice."

"Don't you have to do one to do the other?"

"She never saw it that way." Nana was looking at the piano in the corner now, a frown creasing her forehead. "She liked to play, I'm sure of it."

"What did she play the most? What song?"

"Claire de La Lune," Nana said immediately, then shook her head. "No, that was my sister Jacqueline. My Jacqueline played, she played, what was it?"

"This is confusing." Amber wrinkled her nose. "It's easier if we call mom Lynn."

"That is not her name."

"Everyone else calls her that, even dad."

"It is not who she is," Nana snapped and her hands tightened around the frame of the photograph.

Amber sat back, startled by her tone, and then Nana suddenly smiled and her grip relaxed.

"Now, I almost forgot, I have something for you."

She set the photograph on the end table and pushed herself out of her chair. It took more effort than Amber was used to seeing, and she leaned forward to help, but Nana managed on her own.

"Not to worry. I'm not so old I can't get myself up just yet."

Amber sank down on the footstool and waited until Nana returned. There were more pictures by Nana's chair, but instead of Nana's sister, they were of all Amber's mother. Her mother had been an only child, just like Amber, and she seemed happy. At least, in the pictures when she was younger she did. As she grew older smiles gave way to frowns and instead of standing next to her parents she began to put distance between them. Amber got up and moved from one picture to another, happy little girl mom to unhappy teenage mom. Something was missing. Amber frowned and kept walking from one picture to another and back, but she couldn't figure out what it was.

"Here we are," Nana said, coming back into the room with a cardboard box in her hands. "I found this when I was cleaning out the storage space. I thought you might like them."

Amber opened the box and gasped. "Doll clothes! For Elie?"

"They're hers, absolutely."

All the clothes in the box were just the right size, made for her style of doll, and each was embroidered with a J, like the one on the purple dress she'd lost. Amber frowned, as she realized what was missing from the pictures. Her mother was never holding a doll, though the only pictures Amber had of herself without Elie were from school. Even Nana and Aunt Jacqueline were holding their dolls in the pictures she'd taken off the wall. "Are these from when she was mom's doll?"

"Oh, Elie was never your mother's."

"But she must have been." She held up a dress and pointed at the J.

Nana smiled, that soft sad smile. "Elie was Jacqueline's, my sister Jacqueline's." Nana sorted through the box and came up with a white ribbon somewhat worn along the edges. The centre was embroidered, just like the clothes, though this time it was the full name and not just the first initial. She nodded to where the picture of the sisters was sitting on the chair. "We each had a doll, exactly the same except for their hair. Elie had brown to match Jacqueline and mine was blonde to match me. We used to squabble over their clothes, though, so our mother split them all up and put a J on Jacqueline's and an R on mine."

"What happened to your doll?"

"Jacqueline has it. I didn't want her to be alone. And this way, I could stay with her, and she could stay with me." She ran her hand over the ribbon, the embroidery that formed her sister's name. "I even called her doll Jacqueline for a time. But, well, then I had my own Jacqueline, didn't I?"

Amber froze. Nana had called the doll Jacqueline, too?

"You mother never seemed to like Elie when she was little, so I put her away in storage. You liked her right from the start, though. I'm glad. She's a wonderful doll."

"Yes, she is," Amber answered on auto-pilot as she thought of the way the ribbon had seemed to reach out for her. Or reached out to where she had been standing, holding Elie.

"Where is she today, dear?"

"I left her with mom, to keep her safe." Before she could stop them, tears rose in her eyes. "She's losing her breath."

Nana wrapped her in a hug and rubbed her back as the tears fell. She murmured assurances that Amber wasn't really sure she believed, but appreciated hearing all the same.

"It's okay, dear. My Jacqueline is tough."

"Her name is Lynn," Amber said. "She really doesn't like being called anything else."

"It's who she is," Nana repeated, clinging as tenaciously as the single thread from the torn ribbon.

"Doesn't she get to decide that?" Amber asked. It seemed like such a silly thing. There were kids in her class that she only knew by nick-names. When substitute teachers took attendance, the names on the list would be called instead and everyone would be confused until they answered and everyone remembered this teacher didn't know any bet-ter. Nana did know better, though.

This time Nana didn't answer. Amber looked at the pictures again, happy girl to unhappy teenager. "Do you really want to be fighting? She's so sick."

"I named her for my sister," Nana said, but she was looking at the pictures of her daughter.

"But she isn't that Jacqueline. She's her own Lynn."

Nana reached out and picked up the last picture by her chair. In it, Amber's mother was standing in front of an old car with Nana and Papa. It had been taken right before she'd gone away to college, the last time she'd lived at home. The last time she'd lived anywhere near them, until now.

There was a knock on the door and they both jumped. Nana motioned for Amber to stay seated, and then went to peer through the peephole. When she stepped back she opened the door with a smile on her face. "You're up and about!" she said and gave Amber's mother a hug as she stepped into the hall.

"I'm feeling a little better today. I thought I might come and pick Amber up early."

"I just have to grab my books," Amber said, putting the ribbon in the box before picking it up and setting it on top of her school things. Nana asked more questions about how her mother was feeling, and it really did sound better. Amber joined them in the hallway. "Ready!"

"I'll see you tomorrow, Amber," Nana said. "And I hope you'll drop by again soon. Lynn." She said the name with determination and a little dissatisfaction, sharp and quick like a snipped thread, but it still caused Amber's mother to pause in the doorway and turn back.

"I will, I promise. Thank you, mom."

For a moment, Amber thought they might have another hug, but it seemed like that would have to wait until next time. For now, though, she grinned at Nana, said her goodbyes, and went back to the apartment, where the ghost would still be waiting.

Amber's father leaned in the door to check she was asleep and then crept across the room to close the laptop she'd left on the floor beside the remains of a moving box and craft supplies. She stayed curled up on her side, her back to the door, and breathed in and out as slowly as she could manage. He would be able to tell she was faking. She was certain of it. Instead, he took the laptop out of the room, leaving the door open just enough for a sliver of light.

She wished she had Elie. More than anything she wanted to hug the doll to her chest and take strength from the familiar action, but Elie was still in the room with her mother and Amber hadn't thought it was a good idea to take her away. Anyway, if she was right, she wouldn't be able to cuddle the doll ever again.

Ghost could be tethered to people and things, she thought, repeating what she'd found on the website with the weird bird logo that she found when looking for ways to help her mother. When Nana was little, Aunt Jacqueline was tethered to Elie, bound by the name and Nana's belief the doll meant her sister was still with her. When Nana transferred the name, she transferred the ghost. Amber's mother became her new way to have her sister with her. But Amber's mother started pulling away. She was Lynn and she was her own self, and Aunt Jacqueline was being cut loose and was hurting her mother, but she had originally been bound to Elie. Amber needed to put her back.

She pretended to sleep, just in case her dad checked back in, and those thoughts ran over and over in her head, until they almost messed everything up by lulling her to sleep for real. She snapped back awake, not certain what time it was, but hoped it was late enough. She slipped from her bed, pressed her feet to the cold floor, stepped around the cardboard box piano she'd made after finding the website, and crept across the hallway to her parent's room.

The respirator was beeping, the forced air coming in regular breaths, but as Amber entered the room grew colder. She could see her breath, her teeth began to chatter, and the floorboards were so cold they stung her feet. There was no one hovering over the bed this time, not that she could see, but dark drops appeared on the blanket, up near her mother's face, and the respirator began to struggle, the bad-beep coming faster.

Amber took a deep breath, letting it out in a plume that didn't get stolen, and hoped with everything she had that her plan would work.

"Jacqueline?" Amber whispered, as quiet as she could. She didn't think her mother would wake, having taken her medicine again tonight, not even if the ghost stole her last breath, but her father might. When he snored softly, she risked speaking again. "Jacqueline?"

She crept up to the bed, her breath still puffing out in plumes, and when she stood where she had seen the ghost the night before, it was like opening the freezer. Goosebumps broke out on her skin and she began to shiver, but spoke through her chattering teeth.

"There you are, Jacqueline. Time to leave Lynn alone." She picked up the doll, not Elie, never again Elie. "Come on now, Jacqueline, time to go."

The machine's beeping stuttered, and then the pace evened out. The drops were still falling on the blankets, though, and she was so cold.

"It's time for you to practice." She stepped back from the bed, and water drops followed her, leaving a trail on the floor all the way back to her room. The cold settled around her shoulders as she knelt on the floor and pulled over the box of doll clothes. The white dress she'd picked out was sitting on the top, embroidered J clear even in the low light from the window.

Amber still couldn't see her aunt, but now and again, in the corner of her eye, she thought she saw the end of the torn ribbon, the end completely cut, not even a thread left to reach back to her mother. Every time she tried to look at it directly, it was gone, so instead she focused on the doll, on her dress and the J, and watched that shifting ribbon drift closer, inch by inch.

"Let's get you changed first," she said. "J for Jacqueline, of course. That's who you are." Her shivers increased as she repeated her great-aunt's name like an incantation and the words started to stick in her throat, but she kept going. "Lynn doesn't like piano at all you know, but you never miss practice, Jacqueline, do you?"

The ribbon was reaching for her hands now, though it still faded away if she looked. Instead, she took out the embroidered ribbon out of the box and realized it was the same width as the one teasing her vision, that the frayed end of it might, in fact, be torn. She concentrated on the image of the girl in the pictures, on Nana's sister, Jacqueline as she had been, and placed the embroidered ribbon at the doll's waist, before wrapping the good end around it twice, and the frayed end once. The floating ribbon followed along, darting close and drifting away, each jerking movement bringing it closer.

"Almost ready, Jacqueline." When she Amber tied the ends of the embroidered ribbon together, binding, the spectral ribbon pulled taunt, its torn end snapping to the frayed end of the embroidered ribbon, and a howl like an ocean wave filled the room. She almost dropped the doll, but held on and continued to concentrate. "Stop it, Jacqueline," she said, and the roar stopped.

Her room was warm now, her breath was no longer visible, but she could still hear dripping. When she looked down, there were watermarks by her feet, dripping from the doll's soaked hair. No matter where she looked, she couldn't see the floating ribbon, but the frayed end of the embroidered ribbon around the doll's waist was now intact. She was certain the other was still there, tethering the ghost girl once again to the doll who bore her name.

"Time to practice, Aunt Jacqueline," she said again and when she set the doll in front of the piano, her hair was already dry. Amber left her there and crawled back under her covers, hoping she could get used to sleeping alone. As she closed her eyes and drifted off to sleep, she thought she could hear a piano playing scales.

M is for Matronymic

Lynn Hardaker

I found the house at the edge of town.

Walking up the path, I smoothed the pleats of my generic private school tartan skirt and tugged up my knee-socks. Then I checked Mother and righted the collar of her blouse. Although she said nothing, I could sense her relief at finally arriving.

After a few seconds of using the heavy brass knocker, Mrs. Pott opened the door.

"Ah, you must be the new tenants; though really, I'd rather call you the new neighbours." She smiled over-brightly.

I introduced myself and Mother. Mother hadn't been well lately and managed only a tepid greeting. Mrs. Pott bristled with life. If it had been dark, I think she would have given off sparks. I couldn't help smiling.

She invited us into a cavernous entrance hall. Two young people descended the broad central staircase, stopping short of the last step. The boy must have been around 18, the girl perhaps 15. They were tall and pale and grim, wanting both sun and humour. Their hair was the brown-black of bad coal and they resembled old oil portraits more than flesh and blood people.

"My children," Mrs. Pott chimed, and her voice did have a bell-like quality. "Oliver and Mara, come and greet the new upstairs neighbours."

The children seemed locked in a contest to see who would give in first. The girl lost and came toward us in a way that suggested she was used to that. The boy stayed put, a slight upturn to the corner of his mouth.

Mara's hand was cool and limp in mine, reminding me of squids-on-ice at a fish counter. Greetings over, she was told to show us upstairs. Mrs. Pott returned to the kitchen where, she explained, she had something on the go.

I put my hand under Mother's bent elbow to lend her support as we followed Mara up the well-worn stairs. Oliver watched. There was an unpleasant smell to him, organic and slightly fungal. He listed his shoulder toward me as I passed, forcing me either to make contact or move away. I moved away.

We passed through the first floor landing and continued up a narrower staircase to the top floor. The door to our flat had been painted aubergine. Mara took a key and unlocked it.

"Here's your living room," she said with little enthusiasm. She pointed to the other rooms vaguely. "Two bedrooms there, toilet and bath there. Eat-in kitchen over there." She dropped the key onto the coffee table. The flat was furnished, though erratically; as if by an interior designer on hallucinogens and lack of sleep. The sofa and two armchairs could not have been more different in style: pale silk brocade fought with orange-and-green wool plaid. I directed Mother to the sofa, the less vocal of the options.

Mara showed her first sign of interest in us.

"Bit dark in here for sunglasses," she nodded to Mother.

"I'm afraid she's not well. She needs to wear the glasses even indoors."

"Oh, I'm sorry." She seemed awkward talking to strangers. "You and I must be the same age," she tried a different topic. "Will you be starting at the school in town in September?"

"I don't know. It all depends on Mother."

"Ah, right." She scratched the back of her head.

"Is that where you go?" I asked.

"Me? No, I don't go to school. My mum thinks it's not good for me to mix with the local girls, they're all tarts. Well, so she says. And we can't afford for me to go to a private school, like Oliver does. He's just home for the Summer."

"He gets to go and you don't? Doesn't seem fair."

"Yes, but he is older."

I didn't know what to say, and besides, I was tired from our journey. I picked up the key. She got the message.

"Well then, I'll leave you to it. Come down if there's anything you need."

"Thank you."

She left. I went over to Mother, kissing the top of her head.

"You just rest now, Mother. Take your time. You don't have to make a decision yet."

I went to the kitchen to look for tea.

It always takes a while deciding whether a new place will be a suitable home, and I believe it's not something that can be forced or rushed. I was quite happy to spend the days getting familiar with our flat and the gardens. Mrs. Pott and her children somehow managed to inhabit the entire ground and first floors. I wasn't sure how the three of them did it. Did they actually use all of those rooms? I was very curious to see the rest of the house, but was in no rush. And the main thing was for Mother to feel that this was an appropriate home, and that, I knew, would take a bit of time.

I spent a good deal of those first few days in the back garden. It was a magical, overgrown place. Fairy tale tangled with brambles and untamed shrubs. Bees hovered, lazy and hedonistic, weighted down by pollen breeches. Time moved differently in the garden. An hour could stretch, spun sugar like, to last days. It was delightful.

Most of the time Mrs. Pott was occupied with chores in the kitchen, or with driving into town to help with the various committees and clubs she was ever-busy with. Finding that Mother and I were without a car, she insisted on picking up groceries and toiletries for us. She never seemed to stop. Vivacious is the word that comes to mind when I think of her. Yes, vivacious.

I started to spend time with Mara while Mother was resting, which she needed to do more and more. At first, Mara would come and sit on the back terrace overlooking the tangled garden while I lay on the grass. But slowly, like a feral cat, she would come closer and want to talk.

"How long has your family lived in this house?" I asked one afternoon as we sat together on the long grass. It was the sort of majestic home that could have been in a family for generations.

"My parents bought it just before Oliver was born. So, a while."

"How did your father die?" I asked, emboldened by a feeling of intimacy which was, perhaps, fuelled by the lovely weather and the droning of the sun-warmed bees. Mara brought her knees up under her chin, held them in place with knitted fingers. For the first time, I could see the young child in her. The vulnerability.

"Car accident."

"I'm sorry."

"Don't be. He was with his mistress from town. She had her hand down his trousers. He drove into a tree. They both died instantly."

Perhaps that explained the heaviness hanging over the siblings, and the non-stop action of the mother as well as her refusal to let Mara associate with the girls from town.

"What about *your* father?" she asked, as I should have guessed she would.

"I...I never knew him."

Her eyebrows rose.

"Your mother doesn't seem like that type of woman."

I shrugged. There was really nothing more I could add.

Mother and I sat in the kitchen. Four carved, oak chairs surrounded a cheap formica dining table; metal legs that were cool even on the hottest days. I drank my tea and watched Mother. Her head listed and I could see she was sleeping. That was good. I closed the gap between us by reaching my hand out and covering hers with it.

"Take your time, Mother. There's still no rush." Though seeing her now, I wasn't so sure.

One morning, Oliver stopped me on the stairs. I was on my way down and he was on his way up. Although he was thin there seemed to be more of him than there actually was. Perhaps it was the fug of sullenness and smugness and unwashed clothes.

"Aren't you afraid, up there in the attic? Especially at night," he began.

"Not particularly. Should I be?"

"You would be if you knew it was haunted."

"Haunted?"

"There was a servant girl who lived up there, long time ago."

I was intrigued. A house like this must have its ghost stories.

"She got pregnant by the son of the master of the house. This was back in the days when the master and any sons of his had a right to the favours of any pretty girl they employed."

He took a step toward me.

"It was their right, since they were giving the girl a home and decent work."

"What happened to her?" I wanted to bypass these bits of the story.

"When she started to show," he gestured to my belly, "she had no choice but to take her life."

"Where?"

"In your sitting room. Over the years, people have heard her up there, and from time to time, her glowing form has been seen through the window by townspeople as the pass the house on a dark night."

Clearly, he was trying to scare me.

"Well, I feel sorry for the poor girl. Being abused by a beast like that."

He gave me an oily smile.

"You don't like the old customs?"

He was now on the step directly above mine, his breath hot on my forehead.

"No. And don't forget, I'm a paying tenant, not a paid servant. Not that it should make a difference."

"No, it doesn't make a difference. No difference at all."

He moved aside to let me pass.

It was a strange house, oppressive. But I slowly became convinced that was due to the inhabitants. A house can't help but reflect the moods of the people living in it. Mother was looking weaker by the day, spending most of her time sitting on our sofa in a kind of stupor. The air was fusty and too warm, but I believed that was best for her so I kept the window shut.

For distraction, I went in search of Mara. She was in her room, and she'd told me to come down and knock on her door any time. Day or night. I knocked. She unlocked the door to let me in.

"Do you always keep it locked?" I was surprised.

"I don't want *him* coming in."

I knew who she meant, given that Oliver was the only male in the house and that I could tell she was also uncomfortable when he was around.

She belly-flopped onto her bed. I sat on the chair, my stocking feet gripping the edge of the bed. It was a nice room. Brass four-poster bed, wicker chair, old sea-chest for her bedclothes, and a miss-matched pair of dressers for her clothing. No school evidently meant no homework desk.

The windows were wide open, letting in a pleasant breeze and the sounds and smells of the falling night.

"If Oliver invites you to his room, don't go."

"No worries there," I assured her.

She nodded. But I caught something else, possibly jealousy behind her look.

"He told me there's a ghost in our sitting room."

"She's not the only ghost in the house."

"No?"

"There's one in the cellar too. Do you want to know where?"

I did.

"Come." She rolled and lifted herself from the bed, dug in her sea-chest for a torch. She led me downstairs, flicked on the ceiling light.

The cellar began with a room kitted out with a pair of eviscerated armchairs, a coffee table, and empty, listing bookcases. Stacks of moving-boxes almost touched the low ceiling. Over the years, mold had wormed up their cardboard sides and the room smelled strongly of spores and damp. Like a forgotten dishcloth.

"This way."

She led me from this room into a dark passageway. Doors led off on either side, most closed.

"No electricity. We'll need this from here on." She clicked her torch to life and we went deeper into the belly of the house.

"When we first moved in," she said, "My mum tried to come down here, but couldn't. Said she sensed something terrible." Mara looked behind her to make certain I was following. "Do you sense it?"

I considered for a moment.

"No, I don't," I answered honestly.

"Well, you've got better nerves than some. And my mum can be a bit hysterical."

The air in the passageway was getting damper. An earthy, rooty smell rose up from the packed dirt floor, its coolness making the bones of my feet ache. Phosphorescent mold glowed from where the walls met the floor, dim will-o'-the-wisps. The sound of our voices and footsteps was muted, as though the air had thickened.

"There."

Mara stopped.

"What is it?" I couldn't see it well enough, but it looked as though we'd come to a low door. She shone the light directly on a small hole in the door, barred by three iron rods.

"Look inside."

She handed me the torch. I aimed through the hole. It was a tiny room, a cell really, barely large enough for an adult to kneel in.

"This," she continued, "this is where, years and years and years ago, one of the old masters of the house would incarcerate anyone who dared to defy him. It is said that at least seven men perished in this very room. See the dark spot on the floor?" I moved the torch light and nodded.

"They say that that is where the last one of them died. Rats ate his body."

"Horrible. Let's go back up," I said and moved away from the door.

"Fine." She took the torch. There was a smug turn to the corners of her mouth. "I think you'll agree that my ghosts are much more terrifying than Oliver's."

Mother had made her decision. I was relieved. She was exhausted, winding down like a grandfather clock with only a few swings left. She had been strong for so long. And now I'd found a final home which she felt was just right, as I'd suspected, but it hadn't been my decision to make. I put a rug over her knees to keep her warm. Kissed her forehead.

I was surprised by a knock at the door. It was Oliver, bringing the groceries his mother had brought from town.

"I'll just put them in your kitchen."

"It's alright, I can take them," but he pushed past me with the bags. Fine. He looked at Mother, rolling his eyes.

"You're coddling her, you know," he said.

"Sorry?"

"She needs some exercise, it can't be good for her sitting up here all the time."

That was rich considering the source.

"And wearing those sunglasses when it's dark as a tomb up here. It'll make her go ga-ga. If she isn't already," he added the last bit under his breath.

In the kitchen, he hoisted the bags onto the table.

"There. I'll let you put them away. Don't want to mess up your cupboards." He smiled, then took a step toward me.

"Wouldn't you like to find out what I have down my trousers?" he whispered.

Like father, like son. I walked from the kitchen. He followed.

"Thank you for the groceries. You can leave now."

That just made him smile more.

"The good thing about your mother being a bat-shit-crazy cripple, is that she can't do a thing to stop me doing what I want. And I am the master of the house, remember."

He went over to the aubergine door and shut it, turned the key and tossed it into a corner. As he came toward me, I stepped to the other side of the coffee table.

"I've seen how you look at me as we pass on the stairs," he said.

He made an awkward grab for my arm, but I managed to twist away. He stumbled, palms landing on the table. He was about to right himself, but found that he was face to face with Mother. His grin widened.

"You want to see what your daughter and I are about to get up to?" He reached out for her sunglasses. I almost stopped him. Almost.

The glasses dropped to the floor. There was one second of palpable silence before Oliver let out a garbled scream. He scrambled back, away from Mother and toward the door. The door which he had locked.

Mother's eyes were clear glass baubles swirling with wisps of grey smoke, dancing ghosts, otter-slick; and about to be released. My mouth swelled into a grin, as it did every time I witnessed the beauty of this.

"Oh, Oliver," I said, "that was not very clever of you."

One wouldn't think that it was actually possible to die of fright, but the sight of dozens and dozens of freed ghosts swimming toward him from a pair of dissolving eyeballs, was indeed enough to kill Oliver. Which was fine. It saved me having to do it.

Obviously Mother wasn't really my mother, but is a handy deceit. A mother and daughter. People never suspect anything amiss. And Mother wasn't the first Mother. Or the last. There have been others, many others. Before them, I'd tried different types of vessels: clay, metal, glass, but I soon realised that a vessel of flesh and bone works best. Ghosts seem most content to travel this way, in the familiarity of a warm body.

It's a delicate thing, re-homing ghosts. Not just anywhere will do. And more often than not, the place where the newly-minted ghost died is the last place they wish to stay. Witness the maid from the attic and the poor victims in the cellar. Not a trace of them in the house, in spite of what Oliver and Mara told me.

Mother and the ghosts she carried are very content to stay here, to make this place their home. That made me endlessly happy.

I had no regrets about Oliver. As for Mara, well, I felt a bit badly for her. But sometimes you have to be cruel to be kind, and she died without pain or distress. And honestly, I don't think either of them was up to the challenge of living in the house, especially without their mother, while sharing it with ghosts. Real ghosts.

Mrs. Potts, or rather, Mother and I walked from the house. She was a perfect new vessel, full of energy and life. Vivacious. Two smoky wisps already swam about in those marvellous, glass-like eyes of hers, hidden now behind sunglasses. I took a final look back at the house at the edge of town. I could just make out dark wisps twisting and eddying on the other side of the windows. They were enjoying their freedom and their new-found home. I waved, not knowing whether or not my old Mother's ghost was at one of the windows. I like to think that she was.

N is for Neighbours

L.S. Johnson

INTERVIEWER: My guest tonight is comedian Timothy Palmer, who recently returned to the stage for a nationwide tour. Please welcome Timothy Palmer. [applause]

PALMER: Thank you. Thank you very much. It's great to be here, John.

INTERVIEWER: Before we get started, I must tell you that we polled tonight's audience before you arrived. Over the years you've done some remarkable cameos in films and television, and we asked the audience what was the line they most wanted to hear you say. The winning line was from 'The Ladies of St. Agnes.' [laughter and applause]

PALMER: My God, I'm funny and I haven't even said anything. [laughter] It's every comedian's dream. [starts to stand up] Well, I'm off, you can put my fee in the mail. [laughter]

INTERVIEWER: [hands PALMER slip of paper] This is the line in question. [to audience] Ladies and gentlemen. Timothy Palmer, from his memorable cameo in 'The Ladies of St. Agnes.'

PALMER: [looks directly at camera] They never taught us this in Sunday school! [laughter and applause]

The advertisement had read:

> **WANTED**
>
> *Medium for private séance. Familiarity with occult history and practice required. Serious inquiries only.*

Anne hadn't needed the job; she certainly hadn't wanted the job. Private séances usually started creepy and ended worse. There were plenty of small circles a person could join, that would come to your house if necessary. Private was the last resort for those who were too emotional or demanding, or it was a lure put out by men with very particular fetishes. The last time Anne had done a private séance she had been trapped for hours in a stuffy, pitch-dark living room while the client verbally abused his dead wife. Anne had desperately wanted to sever the link, but she had been terrified the man would turn his rage on her. When she had finally been released she felt physically and emotionally beaten. It had taken her weeks to recover.

Yet the advertisement would not let her be. When she knocked the newspaper off the table it fell open to that page; when she went to run her errands the grocer was reading that selfsame page, the butcher wrapped her Sunday meat in the page, and she found herself staring at the ad as she ate a cone of chips for lunch. When she finally boarded the bus for home and found a newspaper in her favorite upper-level seat, neatly folded to show the exact quadrant with the ad in it, she threw up her hands and admitted defeat.

The man's voice on the phone was pleasant at least, and oddly familiar; the address he gave was a posh neighborhood, the kind of neighborhood that would probably call the police if a woman screamed, if for no other reason than to restore its tranquility. And the fee he suggested was more than generous, so perhaps for once the spirits were doing Anne a favor. That favors usually came with caveats she didn't let herself dwell on.

The advertisement may have chosen her; still Anne prepared for the worst. She wore her best wool suit and her red felt cloche subtly embroidered with symbols of protection, which she believed made her look professional with just a touch of the bohemian. Others wore turbans and muumuus and silver-painted amulets, selling theatrics first and foremost. She had found the money better, if more intermittent, by presenting herself as a kind of spiritual consultant. Certainly it reduced the groping, and if all else failed she had brass knuckles in her purse that she had bought after that last, disastrous séance.

The street wasn't far from the bus stop. It was a neighborhood of new houses made to look old, brick semi-detached cottages with mock Tudor details and the latest double-glazing. Many of the houses backed onto a nature reserve; not a single car was parked on the street; the walk to the front door was lined with perfectly manicured rose bushes in elegant shades of cream and yellow. Not her usual sort of client, but it took all kinds.

She had worn her suit and her hat and she felt prepared for anything; and then she was completely, utterly thrown when the door opened, because she recognized her client. Timothy Palmer was a staple of variety shows and comedy films, always playing a kind of prissy upper-class Englishman, shocked by today's sex-crazed youth and their loud music. In his green cardigan and yellow button-down, framed by the rose bushes, he seemed to have stepped right out of a movie. For a moment she wondered if it was all a setup, perhaps a gag for television.

"Miss Anne Wood?" He shook her hand. "I'm Timothy Palmer. We spoke on the telephone."

"Mr. Palmer," she said. "I thought your voice sounded familiar. My mother is a great fan of yours."

He blushed slightly; it made him seem a boy for a moment. "She's too kind. Please come in. Thank you so much for coming."

She was shown into a sitting room that was as tidy as its owner. Everything was in matching sets: the sofa and the two wing chairs, the sideboard and end tables and coffee table, the table lamps and floor lamp. All in solid wood with little ornament. Good value for money. She remembered her own mother browsing catalogues when things finally started getting better.

He showed her to the sofa and it was only as she sat down that she noticed the shadow in front of the sideboard, a greyish haze at odds with the sunny room. Like a human-sized smudge in the air. She could see through it, yet it had *presence*; she realized she had been expecting a second person in the room, so strong was its energy. As she studied it, the smudge flickered and shifted, almost as if it was angling its head to regard her in turn.

"My God," Mr. Palmer said. "You can see him."

Anne jumped. "See who?" she said, but there was an edge to her voice. Stupid, to be so obvious.

"Why, Harry, of course." He sat down beside her on the sofa, his expression hopeful. "You do see him, don't you?"

Give her a moment, Tim.

She jumped again, nearly squeaking in fright. As distinct as a person, clearly male, clearly a little amused; her arms broke out in gooseflesh. She had never dealt with anything so *present* before. "Mr. Palmer, I think there's been a mistake," she said, starting to rise. "I can't help you."

"Oh, please don't go!" He caught at her arm impulsively. "Whatever you're thinking, that's not it, I promise you. Please don't leave."

Anne lowered her voice, trying not to look at the shadow. "Mr. Palmer, you don't need a medium, you need a priest. I cannot—"

"But we don't want an exorcism," he interrupted, while at the same time the voice said *we bloody well do not need a priest! There's no telling what they'd do!*

"I don't want him to leave," Mr. Palmer continued. "I brought him here in the first place. And I don't need you to speak to him for me; I can hear him just fine, I can see him perfectly, just as he was. Only— we had an idea, and we wanted an, an *expert* opinion." He took a breath, and a wan smile curled his lips. "You may not be aware of this, Miss Wood, but there are an astonishing number of charlatans in your profession."

Anne stared at him, then looked pointedly at the hand still clutching her arm; with a murmured apology he let go. And then just sat there, looking at her with a kind of pained hope, like she was his last chance. Perhaps she was. Timothy Palmer and His Astonishing Ghost: she could see it on a marquee.

How about you two have a nice cup of tea. Just one cup, Miss Wood. What do you say?

Mr. Palmer's face lit up. "Oh, that's a splendid idea! What do you say, Miss Wood? Just one cup, I promise. I'll explain about Harry, and then if you want to leave I'll pay you for your time and we shall never speak of it again. What do you say?"

She looked from him to the shadow, and though it was nothing more than a slight darkening of the air, she could have sworn the damn thing was grinning at her. Her astonishment was giving way to curiosity—and what kind of professional would she be, to leave simply out of fear?

"All right," she said finally. "One cup of tea."

INTERVIEWER: So why did you step away these past few years? You were in the middle of an enviable career: sold-out shows, regular film work.

PALMER: Well, any career has demands, John, sometimes exhausting ones. And I'm an Englishman. I wanted some time to work on my roses. I grew prizewinning melons. [laughter] [to the audience] Behave, you lot. I haven't yet told you about the courgettes. [laughter]

INTERVIEWER: But now you've returned, and better than ever they say.

PALMER: I don't know about better. But a little different certainly. Everything changes a man, John. Life changes a man. Melons can really change a man. [laughter] If we didn't have change, beautiful, even terrible change, we'd have nothing to laugh about.

Anne prided herself on her professionalism. On rare occasions, however, she was faced with situations that went beyond her experience … such as Mr. Palmer moving one of the wing chairs close before heading to the kitchen, and the shadow sitting in it so distinctly she could make out a shape like two legs crossed. As if the ghost was as much her client as the man. Astonishing experiences, she decided, justified unprofessional behavior: she took off her cloche, drew a cigarette from her purse and lit it, and took a long, soothing drag.

Oh God, you're torturing me!

She jumped yet again, nearly dropping the cigarette; the shadow distinctly raised a hand. I'm sorry, I didn't mean to startle you. Only I haven't had a cigarette in twenty-five years. It looks absolutely delightful and I am completely jealous, that's all.

"Oh," she said, for something to say. "I can put it out if you prefer."

Goodness, no. It's marvelous to watch. You're marvelous. None of the others saw me at all, and the few that heard me ran screaming. If anyone can do this, you can.

"Don't pressure her!" Mr. Palmer appeared with the tea tray. He set it on the coffee table and placed an ashtray beside it. "We agreed that we would in no way pressure anyone."

Of course not! Do forgive me, Miss Wood.

Anne decided to ignore that. "Mr. Palmer," she said, "what exactly do you want me to do?"

He opened one of the sideboard doors and drew forth a stack of neatly folded clothes, a worn teddy bear, and some letters bound with ribbons. "These are Harry's things," he explained. "We were never sure how this all worked, so we thought to keep everything together in a safe place. My housekeeper knows not to touch them." He added a framed photograph from the mantelpiece and placed the armful of items beside her, then sat at the far end of the sofa and began pouring out the tea. "That's Harry and I, just before he enlisted."

Anne took another drag, then examined the items one by one. The clothes and the teddy bear smelled of recent washing, but she felt nothing from them; the letters tingled faintly beneath her fingertips. The photograph, however, felt warm, almost electric, as if it were silently buzzing. It showed a seaside boardwalk at dusk, nearly empty, which was perhaps why the two men—though barely such, she guessed late teens for both—had twined so close. Mr. Palmer was visibly blushing; the taller, impossibly handsome young man embracing him was laughing outright. They both seemed absurdly happy.

As she held the photograph, the shadow became more distinct: lips curving out of the darkened air, a hint of a sweater and slacks. That same young face.

"Milk or sugar?" Mr. Palmer asked.

"Both," she said, still studying the ghost. Even a hint of stubble; she had never seen anything like it. She really had to come up with a better word than *astonishing*. "One sugar, please."

He placed her teacup before her and smoothly moved the ashtray beneath her cigarette, catching the ash that was just about to fall. Everything just so: the placement of the tea tray; the perfect line of frames atop the mantelpiece, now with a gap like a missing tooth; the drapes with their soft cottage rose print. *I brought him here.* That is, he had brought the photograph here. The several items together might lend strength, but Anne knew the shadow was mostly, if not entirely, bound to this one picture.

"Harry and I have known each other since we were little boys," he began, taking up his teacup and stirring it. "He is—he *was*—a year older than me. And he did what so many other foolish, headstrong boys did back then, and he lied about his age and enlisted, before they brought in conscription. He was killed in his first month at the front." He took a sip, frowned, then added a minute amount of sugar. "It always seemed remarkably cruel that he died so young. There was so much he wanted to do, more than I ever wanted. And after a time, I started thinking—that is, we started considering ..."

He looked at the shadow then, and Anne saw the ghostly features nod at Mr. Palmer, a clear sense of sympathy in the half-visible face. *Best just to say it.* There was a tenderness in the voice that hadn't been there before.

Mr. Palmer took a breath. "I don't love the world the way Harry did, Miss Wood. Oh, I've enjoyed some of my career, but more often than not it's just a job. I like this house well enough, my roses and my little routines, but that's not life, not the way Harry would have lived it. And then it struck me: what if we could switch places?"

Anne had laid the photo in her lap and reached for her teacup; she nearly dropped it. "Pardon?" she squeaked.

"What if I could be the ghost, and he could have my body?" Mr. Palmer asked earnestly. "I've had a good run, over four decades now. Half a life. And there's no one who needs me anymore; both my parents have passed, I have no siblings. So why not let Harry have the other half? He could be me and I could stay here, in the house. He'd get a second chance."

For the record, the shadow said, I was vehemently opposed to this idea at first, and I'm still not completely on board as it were.

"But it makes perfect sense," Mr. Palmer pressed. "I've watched you when the travel shows are on. You would be right there if you could, sailing the Nile or climbing Kilimanjaro."

Not without you.

The three words were stated with astonishing force for a disembodied voice; Mr. Palmer blushed to his roots. Slowly Anne took a sip of tea, then reached for her cigarette only to find it had burned down. A beautiful, terrible understanding was forming in her mind. Oh, favors always came with caveats, didn't they?

"Mr. Palmer," she said carefully, "you do realize you're asking me to murder you."

"What? Oh my goodness, no. No, that's not it at all." Now he was blushing and upset; she could see his eyes starting to well. "I mean, Harry is right here, alive in his own way. I thought at first I was going mad, but so many others have seen him and heard him. Even the postman asked me about the young man in the window one day." He put the teacup down, then picked up a napkin, then put it down again. "We're just changing places. It's like, like loaning someone a car. You'd do it without a second thought, wouldn't you? If you had nowhere to be, if you didn't mind being home for a while? I don't mind being home, Miss Wood, and Harry could have a second chance."

Bloody hell, Tim. The shadow's voice was thick with emotion. It's a little more than loaning a car.

"I *know* that," Mr. Palmer said wretchedly. "Only I don't know how to make her see it as we do."

Anne took another sip of her cooling tea. It was dangerous, stupid, preposterous, possibly even deadly ... but not *impossible*. Whether or not it was *right*, however, was another matter entirely.

"Tell me," she said, putting the teacup and saucer aside. "How long were you lovers for?"

"Oh!" Mr. Palmer gasped, while the shadow—while Harry—replied calmly, I left for the front soon after our three-year anniversary. But as Tim said, we've known each other nearly all our lives.

"And it's just been the two of you?" She couldn't quite believe it—that would mean years, decades, without any kind of physical affection. Though even as she asked, she was remembering the articles about Timothy Palmer: plenty of rumors about secret trysts and on-set romances, but never any proof. He had brought his mother to award shows and premieres until she passed.

Mr. Palmer was blushing furiously now, but his gaze was steady as he said "there was never anyone else, not for me," and at the same time Harry said *it was one and done, Miss Wood*, and it was then that Anne realized she would like a second cup of tea.

INTERVIEWER: There is a lot more about the war in your current material. Why is that?

PALMER: I'm just worried that we're forgetting about it. It wasn't that long ago, was it? And I'm not trying to tell young people they're wrong for not dwelling on it. It's not 'I went to school uphill both ways.' I just don't want to see it forgotten. We lost so many good people. We changed as a nation. We should know this, we should teach our children this.

INTERVIEWER: Even though you don't have any children of your own?

PALMER: [to the audience] I think of all of you as my children! [laughter and applause] Now keep calm, carry on, and put on clean knickers before you leave the house. [laughter]

After she had left Mr. Palmer's Anne had started for home, then changed her mind and went to Gloria's instead. She wanted to see just how possible it was; perhaps the risk would be too great, perhaps the decision would be made for her. Perhaps, at least, she could put into words exactly what it was she was afraid of. Though she knew Mr. Palmer's situation was nothing like that last hellish séance, she could not stop thinking about that trapped, abused spirit. That perhaps what was impossible wasn't the swap itself, but that two people would give up both physical pleasure and spiritual ascension to spend a lifetime simply conversing.

When Anne had arrived at Gloria's tiny row house, the front door was, unsurprisingly, already open. Gloria was a palmist by trade, but she was also a good prognosticator, and she ran a lucrative side business casting spells for politicians. The one visible investment of her substantial income was her library, which was one of the best in the country. It filled the back room of her house floor to ceiling, was off-limits to anyone but chosen fellow practitioners, and was the only room she dusted regularly.

Now, watching Anne peruse one of the books, she opened a window and lit a cigarette. Gloria was a portly, middle-aged woman, an enthusiast of floral turbans and what she called woo-woo; she claimed it made the punters pay more.

"I don't trust him," she said, blowing smoke as if to punctuate her words.

"Which one?" Anne asked, not looking up. She took the pad and pencil that had been waiting for her—not just a good prognosticator, an excellent one—and made a notation.

"The ghost, of course. All ghosts are selfish. They've already dodged moving on, then they spend all their time trying to connive their way back among us."

Anne looked at her. It was her own fears, though from a different angle: she was certain of Mr. Palmer's intentions, but not Harry's. She didn't even know his last name.

"My client trusts him," she said carefully. "He doesn't want to live in this world anymore, and he wants to give his body to his childhood friend who died too young. It makes more sense than just wasting a body with some good years left."

"Suicide is a sin," Gloria pointed out.

"I'm not sure this would be categorized as suicide," Anne said, looking back down at her book.

"Is he…" Gloria trailed off; when Anne looked up again she had bent her wrist at an affected angle. "You know."

"Gloria! What does that have to do with anything?"

"Besides being a crime?" She took another drag on her cigarette. "Those sort are prone to hysterics. It makes them more vulnerable."

"More vulnerable to what?" Anne asked despite herself.

"To the *ghost*," Gloria said, clearly exasperated now. Ash fell on the table and she brushed it to the ground impatiently. "It's clear as day! This spirit wants in, and it's spun your client a pretty tale. *I'm your long-lost chum, I died before my time, woe is me*. It's driven him to this, I guarantee it. No healthy man in his right mind wants to top himself."

"Clearly we haven't been talking to the same spirits," Anne said.

Gloria pursed her lips at this, but her gaze remained fixed on Anne, and inwardly Anne sighed. Worse than her mother sometimes. Still, she had three pages of notes now: it was definitely possible, though not easy. The circle would have to be stronger than she'd created in some time, and then it could take hours to meticulously guide Mr. Palmer out and Harry in, all while keeping the body alive and both spirits bounded. But it wasn't beyond her—though, really, that had never been in doubt, had it? That damn advertisement had told her as much.

What happened after, when Harry was back in the world and Mr. Palmer was just a shadow in his neat sitting room—that was far less certain. She had a sudden, distinct vision of young Harry throwing the photograph onto a fire while Mr. Palmer's shadow screamed, and her stomach clenched.

"We'll see," she finally said to Gloria's smoke-ringed stare. "I'll ask him again, away from the house, where he can't be influenced." She hesitated; how to get Gloria to drop it? "The money is really good, though..."

At the word *money* Gloria relaxed. "Well, at least you have your priorities right," she said approvingly. "After all, if the daft man wants to pay a fortune to watch someone else ponce around in his body, who are we to get between him and his fantasies?" She jabbed her cigarette at Anne. "You just make sure you have a way to pull the plug, my girl. Otherwise your client may end up haunting *you*."

INTERVIEWER: The war isn't the only subject you delve into with this new show, is it?

PALMER: You know it's not, or you wouldn't ask the question.

INTERVIEWER: I have to say, we weren't sure if we could ask the question at all, legally. You were quite the topic of conversation upstairs.

PALMER: Oh, I've heard that before. [laughter]

INTERVIEWER: Have you been afraid at all, talking so openly? That you might lose your audience, be fined, perhaps even arrested?

PALMER: Talk about what, John? [laughter] But do you see what I mean? I'm sitting here right before you and you're avoiding saying what I am. We've got a bill sitting in Parliament, we have people demanding change, and yet we still can't—or won't—talk about what I am. Now you asked me about the war as part of my show. What kind of man would I be, that I could natter on about death and devastation, but fear saying what I am? What kind of society are we creating, where it's acceptable to joke about genocide, but not to acknowledge the affection between two consenting adults? [applause]

INTERVIEWER: A very strong opinion, well-put. Perhaps some of our politicians should take a few years off.

PALMER: You'd be surprised, the things you learn about yourself.

The little pub was tucked away in a cul-de-sac, just past the train station: the end of the line, and as such it was hardly ever crowded, and those who drank there kept their eyes on their pints. Anne had come across it when running a small circle nearby. It seemed a good place to meet, and better for the day proving rainy. When Mr. Palmer entered, placing his umbrella in the rack and brushing water off his trenchcoat, not a single one of the half-dozen people looked up.

He ordered a pint and made his way to Anne's table, a wary expression on his face. She was already nursing her own pint, still trying to figure out how best to ask her questions. That he took the time to take off his coat and fold it neatly, to sit down and adjust his chair just so, made her wonder if he was also weighing out his words.

"Miss Wood," he began. "If it cannot be done, you could have just said so on the telephone. We knew it was unlikely—"

She held up a hand, quieting him. He took a sip of his beer as she began speaking in turn, taking equal care with her words. "It is not impossible, Mr. Palmer. But it is a very risky undertaking. There is every chance that one or both of you could be lost in the process. You would both be dead, truly dead."

"We've discussed that possibility," Mr. Palmer said firmly.

"There is also the chance that one of you could be lost, and the body as well, leaving the other spirit alone but still anchored to this plane," she pressed.

"And we have discussed that as well. We were going to ask that, if it comes to pass, you would do what you can to help the remaining spirit move on." He continued when she started to speak, "we have weighed all the risks, Miss Wood. I appreciate your concern, but we have been debating this for over two years now—"

"It is a chancey thing to have a spirit bound to an object," Anne cut in. "If that photograph was somehow destroyed, you would lose Harry—yet it's not clear to me where exactly he would end up. He might move on, or he might simply drift through the world, unable to materialize."

Mr. Palmer was staring at her, his pint forgotten. "Again," he said, a note of irritation in his voice, "we have considered all this. Why do you think I leave his things at home? I could have brought them with me on tour, but the risk was always too great. And even so, my heart is always in my throat: what if there's a fire, or a break-in?" Before she could reply he continued, "ever since he came back I have done everything I could to protect him. This Timothy Palmer is a very precise construction, Miss Wood. Too fastidious for large dinner parties, too fussy to permit people handling his photographs or nosing in his cupboards, too uptight to go abroad or on extended tours; all that, and yet not too much, lest I be thought too *queer*, so *queer* I might be touched in the head." His eyes were flashing. "Do you have any idea, can you begin to imagine, how *exhausting* the last two decades have been?"

"No," she said quietly. "No, I can't, Mr. Palmer. And therefore I have to ask: would Harry go to similar lengths for you?"

He stared at her for a moment, openmouthed in astonishment; and then his cheeks reddened, but from anger, not embarrassment. "You think Harry's trying to trick me. You think he's trying to steal my body."

"Mr. Palmer, I have to be certain—"

"*It was my idea.*" He enunciated the words. "If anyone is exerting pressure in this, it is myself—"

A shadow fell over their table. They both looked up to see a ruddy-faced, elderly man beaming down at them, beatific with drink.

"It is!" he exclaimed delightedly. "You're Timothy Palmer!"

A murmur went up from the others in the pub; Mr. Palmer's face reddened further. "I am, thank you. Unfortunately I'm in the middle of a conversation—"

"Do the bit from 'Once Upon a Wedding,'" the man said. "My missus loved that movie."

"It's really not a good time," Mr. Palmer said. "Though I'm happy to autograph something."

"Oh, come on! It will only take a moment."

"It's really not a good time," Anne echoed. She could sense Mr. Palmer's rising agitation, see him trying to blink back tears. Over the man's shoulder she looked meaningfully at the landlord.

"What, are you too good for us?" The man's good humor was evaporating. "You do it on those talk shows quick enough. Or are we supposed to pay for it?"

"That's enough, Eddie," the landlord said, coming over. "They've paid for their drinks, not to have you bothering them."

"Who's bothering them? I'm a fan, that's all!" Eddie let himself be led away, but he gave them a dirty look over his shoulder. "It's his job to entertain, right? So what's wrong with asking someone to do his job?"

Mr. Palmer took out a handkerchief and patted his forehead. "I need some air," he muttered.

"Of course." She swallowed another mouthful of her beer and quickly donned her coat; he was already grabbing his umbrella. Outside the rain was a grey drizzle that made them both turn up their collars; Mr. Palmer opened his umbrella and held it over them both.

"I'm sorry about that," he said.

"Why? It wasn't your fault." She glanced at him. "I'm just sorry you have to put up with that sort of thing."

"I'm no good at it." His tone was somber. "I was better when I was younger. I could laugh it off, perform on command. But even then it was never easy for me. Harry was always on, he would have done five different routines back there and had the whole place laughing. With me I have to make myself become that Timothy Palmer, and the older I get the harder it is."

They were walking down the street; now they cut across to a small park with a gazebo. "I was in a sanatorium a few years back, did you know that?"

Alarmed, Anne looked up at him. "No. No, I didn't know."

"I was pressured into doing a full tour of the British isles. I always kept my tours short, resting between, but this time my manager got the better of me. It was utterly grueling, just endless … and one day I simply couldn't face it. I could barely get myself out of bed. Everyone had a fit, but I checked myself in voluntarily and brought Harry's things in my suitcase. I was just so tired.

"It wasn't supposed to be this way," he continued as they reached the gazebo. He closed the umbrella and they shook water off their coats before sitting on the bench inside. "We were going to be The O'Brien and Palmer Show. Harry was going to be the front man, the personality. I was going to be the straight man, quietly undercutting him. It was so easy with him," he added wistfully. "As natural as breathing."

"But you recovered," she prompted. "You went on, you've done shows since then."

He nodded. "Harry talked me round. I had contracts to fulfill, after all. We wrote new material in the sanatorium, shorter, easier routines. But I didn't want to leave. It was so wonderfully *quiet*. I worked in the garden, I watched television with the others three nights a week and the rest of the time it was just Harry and I. And that's when I started thinking, it should be Harry onstage and I in the house. He loved performing in ways I never will. Oh, we'd still write together; I would watch television and listen to the radio, I'd stay up to date on the latest acts. But I could also be quiet." He smiled wanly at her. "I'll make an excellent ghost, Miss Wood."

"You could be quiet now," Anne pointed out. "You could retire, move to the countryside. You could even move abroad."

He shuddered dramatically. "Abroad! What would I do abroad? I don't even like pepper on my food."

Anne laughed at that and he grinned, then sobered. "I wasn't going to tell you about the sanatorium, especially not after you figured out we were lovers. I knew that if you believed me unstable you would never help us. But Harry says it's not worth doing unless we're completely honest with you; that if you helped us and then found out later you might regret your decision. And there's enough regret in life already."

"Mr. Palmer, when did Harry first appear to you?"

"Hmm?" His expression had become faraway; and then he shook himself. "Not when I first got his things... I had been called up, you see, and I thought perhaps to get a memento of him, something I could carry with me. But his mother had cleaned out his room and found our letters; I came upon her just as she was throwing all his things into the rubbish." He smiled bitterly. "We were lucky that I got there in time. The names she called me, right in the middle of the street, everyone watching… I haven't been back to the neighborhood since. Harry says the one good thing about being dead is he finally hurt her as much as she hurt him.

"Anyway," he continued, "I put his things in a chest and went off to do my service. When I was discharged I came home and got a bed-sit in London, hoping to find work… I moved in, opened the chest to air it out, went for some groceries, and when I came home he was sitting on the bed, wanting to know where I'd been all this time and why my room looked so strange." He gave a little shrug. "We've been together ever since."

"One and done," Anne said.

"One and done," Mr. Palmer agreed.

His voice broke a little over the last; and then they just sat there, watching the rain fall steadily, casting a grey haze over the richly green trees and grass, bending the flowers with the water's weight. Impulsively Anne laid a hand over his; he didn't say anything, didn't look at her, but clasped her fingers. Chilled, but alive underneath. And if she did this thing for him, and lost him in the process—? She looked at his profile, at the hollowness of his gaze. Two decades together in their strange union, a whole career built between them. The O'Brien and Palmer Show; they had managed it, even in death, even if it looked nothing like what they had envisioned.

"What would you do, if the switch succeeded?" she asked.

"Oh, Timothy Palmer will retire, at least for a few years. Give Harry some time to adjust, to figure out what he wants. Then, if he chose to, he could make a triumphant return. A few years away would account for any difference in his presentation."

"While you stay home, enjoying the quiet."

Mr. Palmer smiled then, warmly. "He's promised to prune my roses for me."

But Anne only half-heard him. An idea had suddenly come to her, a possibly terrible idea; but it would ensure that, if she did pull it off, Harry couldn't simply discard him.

"All right," she said, as much to herself as to him.

He looked at her warily. "What does that mean?"

"I'll do it." She took a breath. "Though I warn you, it's going to be long, and difficult, and I'll probably damage your flooring—"

But she was smothered by his embrace as he hugged her. "Thank you," he breathed. "Oh, thank you, thank you, thank you."

They chose a Sunday morning, when the neighborhood would be at church or visiting and there was little risk of disturbance. Still they drew the curtains, and parked Mr. Palmer's bicycle in the garage next to a brand new Triumph dusty from disuse. "I had to spend some money a year ago," he said with an apologetic expression. "Something about taxes, too much savings."

Back in the house she set about with her preparations. She had brought all her things in a nondescript hatbox, worn her coat over her best-looking pajamas, and splurged on a taxi; she needed to be as comfortable and energetic as possible. In the front room he had done as she asked, pushing all the furniture to the walls and rolling up the carpet. She grimaced at the lovely parquet flooring, but there was nothing for it; she opened up the hatbox and drew out her jar of paint. In the past they used salt, or earth, to draw the circle, but those materials were easily mussed, and Anne hated muss in the same way that Mr. Palmer clearly disliked disruption. So she had concocted her paint, a muddy paste laced with salt and several herbs that stayed put if layered on thick enough.

Mr. Palmer winced at the first dark smear. "How about if I make tea," he said in a strangled voice.

"That would be lovely," Anne said, scooping out two fingerfuls and continuing around the curve.

Harry drew close, curling over her shoulder, and she waved at him impatiently. "You're dimming the light," she complained.

Oh! Pardon me. He drifted to the far side of the circle. *It looks complicated.*

"The better to contain you both while I work," she explained. When her circle finally closed she felt the click inside herself; the shadow jerked backwards.

Well. Not a charlatan, I see.

Anne grinned as she started drawing the pentacle inside.

Tim told me about your conversation.

"Oh?" She kept her head down lest he see her wary expression. From her hatbox she drew forth her notes and began drawing in the symbols, listening intently.

I have no intention of losing him, Miss Wood. We decided on something more substantial. To anchor him, as you would say. It's on the sideboard.

She followed the line of grey air to a small jewelry-box. It was his father's wedding ring. It fits his ring finger. He can come with me and it will keep the ladies at bay. Two birds, one stone.

"Are you worried about the ladies, Mr. O'Brien?" she asked.

They're always crawling over Tim, and I've been told I can't be rude to them. She distinctly heard a new tone in his voice: amusement, but tinged with jealousy. Really, a man of his age.

"It seems a little small," she said.

That's what she said! Whatever have you and Tim—

She exhaled in mock exasperation. "The ring, I mean."

Should we find something larger? All the amusement was gone, replaced by seriousness.

She hesitated. "No... no, I like the idea of it." Mr. Palmer entered, carrying the tea tray to the sideboard; she sat back on her heels and surveyed her work. "Getting there now. We'll be up and running within the hour."

"It feels warm," Mr. Palmer said, lying on the floor in the center of the pentacle. "Is it supposed to be warm?"

"Warm is good." Anne flexed her washed hands, and then took another pot and began painting her face. Surreptitiously she slipped the penknife into her pajama pocket. *A way to pull the plug.* She felt all but certain she would not need it, but the first sign of any malice from Harry and, well. With enough blood in the circle she could exorcise them both.

"Do you know I've never lain on this floor before? There is a disastrous cobweb by the window."

She glanced down at him. "We don't have to do this—"

"No! Only it's terribly annoying. How on earth did I miss it?" He looked to the sideboard. "Promise me the first thing you'll do is go up there with a feather duster."

Timothy Palmer, Harry said calmly, I love you more than life itself, but if this works I am not spending my first living moments dusting your molding.

"Oo-er missus," Mr. Palmer replied with a smile.

Anne felt a pang. "It's time," she said gently.

"What do I do?" Mr. Palmer asked, while Harry said *tell me where you want me*, but he had already drifted close, bathing Mr. Palmer in shadow, almost protectively.

"You are both perfect," Anne said, "just where you are."

It was the longest spiritual *anything* Anne had ever done. She had practiced and timed it all, she knew exactly how long it would take and yet it felt so much longer, it felt like a week in the circle. Her whole world narrowed down to the two quicksilver essences with her, sliding back and forth as she guided and bounded them in turn. For one brilliant moment they twined, and she nearly started crying then at the beauty of it, like stars merging in darkness—

And then the man on the floor before her opened his eyes, and it was at once Timothy Palmer and someone else, someone who opened his mouth wider to gasp and then breathe deep and hard, flexing his hands and trembling all over. "Tim?" he cried. "Tim, where are you? Say something..."

Anne touched Harry's hand, causing him to buck with surprise and fear. "Harry, it's all right," she said. Her voice was raw but she tried to sound soothing. "He's as new to this as you are. It may take him time to figure things out."

Hold on, a voice faintly said, as if from a long ways away.

Harry burst into tears. He pressed Mr. Palmer's hands over his eyes, then wrapped his arms across his face and breathed deeply, over and over. When he looked again at Anne his eyes were red. "Everything smells like Tim," he said, and began sobbing harder.

I did bathe, Mr. Palmer said, more distinct now. A cloud of grey was coalescing beside them. You never said how hard it was to keep still! I keep floating every which way.

"Of course you bathed, you utter—" He broke off and sat upright, looking around wildly. "Oh no. Oh no. Oh God—"

"What is it?" Anne asked, laying her hand on his arm. "Wait! Don't break the circle yet. What's wrong?"

"The ring!" He pointed at the sideboard. "We forgot to bring it in! He's not anchored to anything! We have to bind him somehow—"

"Harry."

"It's why he's drifting! The moment we break the circle I'll lose him—"

"Harry!" She caught his arms and gave him a shake. "Harry, it's all right. I know we didn't have the ring. It's all right." When he only stared at her, his eyes wide with terror, she managed a tentative smile. "Harry, I bound him to *you.* I bound him to this body. He can manifest anywhere you are; in fact, you're kind of stuck with each other, now."

You did what? Mr. Palmer cried, while Harry stared at her incredulously. *That's not what we agreed upon!*

But she could not reply, because the man who had been Timothy Palmer and was now Harry O'Brien had flung himself on her in a bear hug, toppling them over and wrecking her neatly drawn circle. "You marvelous, marvelous girl," he gasped. "We are going to pay you so much money."

Harry, are you sure?

"Of course I'm sure!" He shook his head, as if overwhelmed by the absurdity of the question.

You're going to take me abroad, aren't you? Mr. Palmer's voice was resigned.

"I am going to take you all over the world." He sat up on his heels and his expression softened. "Bloody hell. You've gone younger, darling."

As you always looked to me.

"You all right then?" he asked gently.

It will take some getting used to, but I'll be all right. Are you all right?

He nodded, but he was weeping again; he wiped his eyes roughly with his sleeve. "No one has ever… I mean, what you've done…" He looked up, then laughed and held out his hand, as if wiping tears from the darkened air.

You are worth it, Mr. Palmer said, and his voice was stronger now; Anne could almost see his earnest expression, the gleaming eyes. *You were always, always worth it, Harold O'Brien, no matter what your mother said.* And then, before Harry could reply, *just remember you promised to prune my roses.*

"More tea, vicar," Harry replied with a sob, and they all laughed at that, Anne too, laughing through her own tears; Harry glanced at her, then leaned over and squeezed her hand. "I'll make the entire damn garden nothing but roses," he said, his voice quavering. "The neighbors are going to hate us for all the bees. It's going to be *marvelous*."

INTERVIEWER: Tell us about that second summer.

PALMER: Well, my roses were blooming [laughter] so I decided to travel a little. I never toured abroad in my younger days; I always thought of myself as an English comedian, that my humor would only really land in England.

INTERVIEWER: But something happened while you were traveling, didn't it? Something changed you.

PALMER: Well, I had already changed, I was changing. But when I started traveling, I saw all these young people, not just sex and drugs and rock 'n' roll, but fighting to be honest about themselves, fighting to make the world better. Being themselves in public and saying "this is who I am, I have a right to love."

And I thought of all those lost in the war, so many young men gone. What did they die for, if not the right to love? How was I honoring their memory by hiding? Don't get me wrong, I don't regret hiding, nor do I think anyone hiding right now is foolish for doing so. I never would have had this career if I'd been out, as they say.

INTERVIEWER: You're saying that people wouldn't have hired you, knowing you were homosexual?

PALMER: I'm saying people wouldn't have hired me if I spoke about it publicly. You could be, you know, swishy, but you could never talk about it. But now here I was, secure for the first time in my life. Career, finances, in myself: I have everything I need right here now. [touches chest] I don't have to fear anymore. I can do as I please. I can even support the Sexual Offences Act. [applause] [to audience] Go forth and vote, my children! [laughter and applause]

INTERVIEWER: I must say, when I interviewed you, what, eight, nine years ago? I never imagined we would be having this conversation now.

PALMER: Well, that time away helped me feel whole again, for the first time in years, decades even. And I realized what I truly wanted was to help others have it easier than I did. Leave the world better than I found it, right? [applause] Love can do impossible things, John. I've seen it firsthand. But it begins with believing that it's real and you've a right to it, whatever form it takes.

O is for The O'Brien and Palmer Show

Laura VanArendonk Baugh

Emilie noticed it first.

"Daddy, don't you think that looks like a person?" she asked at dinner.

I turned and looked across the room. "What does, honey?"

"That shadow. See? It's looking at us."

I saw no shadow but the blocky shade of the refrigerator on the wall, straight edges drawn by the undercabinet light. "I don't see it. Hey, what do you think about ice cream tonight?"

She tipped her head. "We had ice cream last night."

I'd forgotten that was only last night. Time was blurred these days, in our surreal new existence. I was trying to inject joy into our lives while maintaining a sense of normality and routine, but this was surprisingly difficult, and the last thing I wanted to do was invoke a comparison of Then and Now. "Well, sometimes we can have ice cream two days in a row. Not very often. But sometimes."

She didn't look a gift horse in the mouth. "I want chocolate."

We had chocolate.

The following night, as I tucked her into bed and settled our old cat Chopin on her feet, Emilie asked me to leave a light on. She hadn't been scared of the dark for years, but I supposed things might be different now, and so I found a dusty nightlight and put it on for her. I made a note to mention it to her therapist—she didn't particularly need a therapist, just a precaution I thought it good to take, what could it hurt?—but thought little more of it.

The next day was weekly art class at school, and she brought home her pictures to proudly display. "This is you," she said, her finger tracing a tall figure in a blue shirt and a pointy beard.

"My beard's not that pointy," I protested.

"Yes it is!" she giggled, and she tugged it.

"And is this Miss Carthage?" I prompted, pointing to a classroom scene.

"Yes. We're having science in this picture. See the little bean growing into a plant? That's my favorite class."

It figured, the daughter of an art historian and a music theorist, going STEM. But she was young—and there was less division between STEM and the arts than budget propagandists would have taxpayers believe. "Excellent. And what's the next one?"

Emelie went quiet.

I looked at the picture, a crayon and watercolor rendering of a braided woman with enormous hoop earrings and a pink dress. Danielle hadn't often gone for dresses, but she had loved pink. "Is that Mommy?"

Emelie pursed her lips, and after a moment she said, "Do you miss her?"

"Oh, honey." I gathered her into my arms with all the fierce protectiveness I could muster. "Oh, I miss her. Of course I miss her. We won't stop missing her, ever. It won't always hurt so much, but we'll always remember her and miss her."

She nodded. She didn't cry. I wasn't sure if that was good or bad. I knew children processed grief in different ways, sometimes seemingly strange ways. Trying to monitor if this were the *correct* way would probably lead to madness for both of us.

"Mommy misses us too," she said abruptly.

You think you're prepared, ready for all the questions, and then kids catch you flat-footed. I didn't believe in an afterlife, but Danielle had. I tried hard not to think if that had made it easier for me. But I certainly wasn't ready to explain to my grieving daughter that I thought her dead mother had been all wrong about death and really wasn't thinking of her anymore. Perhaps it was intellectual cowardice, but I was also a parent—and now, the only parent. "I'm sure she does, honey."

I mean, Danielle's last thought had been of Emelie, so it was at least fair to say that her last echo of energy was missing her daughter, I rationalized.

Saturday morning I went into Emelie's room and found her sitting next to her bookshelf, neatly filing books into place. "What are you doing, sweetheart?"

"Mommy wanted me to clean up my room."

My heart froze for a moment. Not that I thought of a ghost—that would have been ridiculous. But I did worry that my child might have fantasized something, and I didn't know if that was appropriate grieving or an alarming development. Or, she might have just remembered that Danielle had often bugged her about her room, not that she had been freshly reminded, and she was doing it in a sort of honoring the requests of the dead. I didn't want to probe which. I still needed to call the therapist. "Well, you can clean your room any time. Today we're going to the zoo, remember?"

I was going to keep her busy. Not distracted, not really, but with fresh feelings and experiences to process, not leaving just her to dwell. There was a balance, somewhere, and I was doing my best to find it.

After the zoo, I left Emelie to play with a new panda puzzle, and I went into my study and closed the door. I made a call to the therapist's voice mail, detailing the nightlight request and the room-cleaning, and asked for a call back when convenient.

I held the phone for a long time, and then I scrolled to another contact and connected.

"Hello?"

I had not heard her voice in three weeks, and its effect was embarrassing. "It's me."

"I saw your name on the phone." Obviously. There was a pause. "I'm sorry—I should have called. I just—I wasn't sure…"

"I understand." I did. There's not much protocol in even the best of etiquette guides on handling the death of your lover's wife.

"I'd like to see you."

"I want to see you, too."

There was another pause. This was stupid—if we could have sex while Danielle was alive and could be cheated on, why couldn't we even talk when she was dead and I was no longer married?

"Can you come over?" I asked, in a rush. There was nothing to be guilty about.

"To your place?"

"I have Emelie; I can't leave her alone. But she goes to bed by eight thirty."

"All right. I'll—I'll bring a lasagna." For social cover, I supposed.

She had sounded different. Suppressed. She probably thought she was being respectful and careful of my feelings. But I had been through too much to lose this now. The best way would be to rip off the Band-Aid all at once, get back to normal. We would have sex that night.

Jade did bring a lasagna. She held it out between us like a pasta shield.

I put it on the counter and took her arm, pulling her toward me. "I've missed you," I said, pressing her to me.

Jade pulled back. I held her until I heard Emelie's voice. "Hello, Aunt Jade!"

Jade turned out of my loosened grip and knelt to open her arms to Emelie. "Hello, honeybear."

I put the lasagna in the fridge. There was room for it now; the flood of prepared meals had slowed since the funeral two weeks ago. Emelie and I had eaten takeout General Tso's chicken for dinner earlier.

Emelie wanted Jade to play a round of Candyland, and so I left them to their game while I went to my study. My work had stalled the last couple of weeks, for obvious reasons, and my deadline was closing. I could probably have asked for an extension, considering, but competition was fierce and I did not want to lose my place in line, even for such an unassailable excuse as a spouse's death. I had worked too hard, and I needed both critical mass and momentum of publications. I was so near to a dean's office.

I had an enlarged print of *The Persistence of Memory* mounted opposite my desk—the original is quite small, actually—to set the tone for this project on how the religious delusions of the Surrealists had undercut their potential. I revealed their reliance upon occultic expression and the id even as they claimed to reject religion, demonstrating their failure to see that their reliance upon the subconscious as a sacred force was as much a religion as the faiths they rejected. I speculated on what the greater postmodern movement might have been if Dalí had not been separated and recalled Catholic imagery to his work.

Danielle, being a member of Second Baptist, of course hadn't liked it. "It's not fair to attack the dead."

"I'm not attacking them; I'm just calling out their flawed influences. I'm actually complimenting them, pointing out that their greatness could have been greater if not hampered by conventional moralism."

"You're arguing the Surrealists were guilty of conventional moralism." She rolled her eyes. "And you're still assaulting their reputations."

"Their reputations are fixed in the art history pantheon. Dalí is a household name even today, for crying out loud. His work is parodied in pop culture nearly a century later. I'm doing his reputation no harm—and even if I did, their work would remain, unchanged."

"Not unchanged. You're changing the meaning of their work."

"No artist owns the meaning of their work—that is entirely the subjectivity of the viewer. You know that yourself, even in music."

"Context and intent matter. You're taking their voices."

"Come on, Danielle, don't make this about voices and race and whatever."

She'd stiffened at that, gotten that tight-lipped expression that always meant she had plenty to say but was choosing not to say it, and had left the study.

Jade was more reasonable. She was Chinese by descent, but she didn't try to muck up generations of insight by arguing that they had been racist. She knew Danielle through the university and me through the publishing house.

Emelie won the game of Candyland. I wrapped up while Jade read her a short bedtime story and turned out her light. Then I rejoined Jade in the living room downstairs.

She sat at the far end of the couch. "I'm really sorry about Danielle."

"Thanks. I am, too, for you. You were good friends."

She cringed. "About that... I've been thinking. About us."

I didn't like where this was going. "What do you mean?" I suspected—but if she didn't want to say it, if she wouldn't say it, then it hadn't been said.

"I don't think we should... Not anymore. Not now."

I stared at her. "What do you mean, not now?"

"She's dead!"

"Don't you think I know that? But you were happy enough about it when she was alive, so why should it make any difference now that she can never find out about it? Do you think you're more likely to hurt her now than before?"

"Maybe it was wrong before!" she snapped.

"Well, after she's dead is a fine time to decide if it was." This was ridiculous. After all I'd done—all the hiding, all the lying, and then—

There was no way she could pull this on me, not now.

But I played it soft. "Look, you're just upset. That makes sense. But this is just emotion. You'll feel better after you get back on the bicycle." I gave her a charming, knowing grin. "And I'm a ten-speed, you know, and you can pick my gear." I slid my hand to her breast and squeezed it. "Ching, ching."

She pushed my hand away. "No. I don't want to. I don't think—"

I had been nice. "You're being over-emotional about this! You'll be fine once you're into it. Just let me get you—"

"No!" Her eyes shifted, slightly widening, and I saw for the first time she considered that I might not just obey her like a well-trained spaniel, that I might be stronger than she had thought.

I'd never realized she had thought me weak, that she'd thought she could just order me on and off, and rising above her underestimation thrilled me.

"Stop," she said, a brittle new edge to her voice.

But she was done commanding me. I thought of all the videos I'd watched, all the ways I knew Asian women really liked it, how they preferred submission once they were done testing you to see if you were strong enough. She would thank me later.

"No!" she said, trying to push my hands away. "Stop! Emelie!"

It was so like Danielle's last words that for just a moment I did stop. But instead of pushing me away, Jade turned her head toward the hall and stairs. "Emelie?"

Oh. *Oh.*

The steps creaked. I got off the couch and went into the hall, adjusting my stride to accommodate my arousal. "Emelie? Honey?"

Chopin, the cat, looked at me from the third step. He mewed once.

A cat's weight shouldn't have made the stairs creak. I went up the stairs to Emelie's room. In the dim illumination of the nightlight, I saw her form in the bed, lying still.

I went back down the stairs. "She's asleep."

Jade had her purse and keys. "I think I'd better go."

"Wait—that wasn't— we can—"

"Good night." And she was gone, leaving me hanging after making me think my daughter was watching us.

Leaving me hanging after everything.

I went upstairs. My laptop was in the study. When I flicked on the light, *The Persistence of Memory* faced me.

There were other Dalí works which better fit my mood. Why had I chosen such an over-popular piece, like a stupid pretentious teenage fan instead of a proper scholar? I should have mounted *The Lugubrious Game*. Emelie was too young to understand it.

Ants swarmed in the print before me, Dalí's disgust mirroring my own. I looked at the fly—rot, according to most interpretive theories—crawling on the leftmost watch. Some critics observed it had a human shadow. I didn't think it looked strictly human, but it was true that its shadow did not match the fly and the light. Dalí was too particular to have done that by accident.

I took my laptop into my bedroom to fill the void Jade had left.

"Don't you see that shadow, Daddy?" Emelie asked over breakfast cereal.

"I'm sorry, I don't."

"It looks like a person."

I smiled. "I interpret art, honey. I'm used to finding people in all sorts of places where no one else sees people. But I don't see that one."

"It looks like Mommy."

"Stop it." The words were out of my mouth before I could think. What did that mean? What would that do? I'd have to call the therapist again, instead of waiting for her to return my call.

Emelie, chastened, looked down at her cereal.

What did it mean, that she thought a shadow looked like Danielle? Was it just a childish affectation, or was it a sign of something wrong?

"I'm sorry, honey," I said. "I'm just—I didn't sleep well last night. What do you want to do today?"

"Ice cream," she said.

"Well, we can have some ice cream for dessert tonight, sure. But what—"

"Ice cream," she repeated. "Strawberry."

I thought of last night, and I thought of her shadow, and I hadn't done anything wrong, but I got up and got the ice cream from the freezer.

Emelie started to get worse. She cried at night, even with the night-light on. She kept looking in the corner with the alleged shadow, even though she didn't mention it again. And then Miss Carthage, her teacher, called me. "This is probably silly," she prefaced, "but just—given the circumstances, I didn't want to take any chances."

"I'm always happy to hear an update on my daughter," I assured her. "What's up?"

Miss Carthage blew out her breath. "Well, we have computer time, as you know, both directed learning games and some free exploration time. The system is locked, the kids don't have free access to the whole internet of course, but they have encyclopedias and things."

I nodded, though Miss Carthage couldn't see me over the phone.

"And today, Emelie asked me how to pronounce a word on a page she was reading—which isn't unusual, and I encourage the kids to ask, but—but she asked me how to pronounce *poltergeist*."

"I—what?"

"And I know it's probably nothing, but just—she's been moody and unfocused in class, which is to be expected, of course, and I haven't been making much of it, but given her behavioral changes and this—I just wanted you to be aware of her choice of reading matter. She always says she's been enjoying her sessions with Miss Wendy, but I thought you should consider with her if Emelie should be left to explore in her own way or if she should be directed to something else. I didn't want to make that decision without consulting with someone."

But it wasn't her reading matter which concerned me. What concerned me was impossible, too ridiculous to be considered, but—

"Thank you, Miss Carthage. I really appreciate the call. I'll update her therapist and we can discuss it."

That night, Emelie was quiet throughout dinner. She didn't even ask for ice cream afterward. When we went up to her room to pick out a puzzle, there were books strewn all over the floor and puzzle pieces scattered as if sown like seeds. Emelie began to cry.

I couldn't believe I was typing "poltergeist" into a search box. I was an academic. I was about to make dean of the college. I wasn't the kind of person to search for spooks.

I hit *Enter*.

The results were about the level of unscientific dreck I expected. I mostly skimmed, but I was able to pick out that poltergeists were the kind of ghosts that threw things around.

Things like puzzle pieces and books?

But this made no sense. Even if Danielle had come back—no, that was too absurd to say even hypothetically. But for the sake of exploring all options, even the stupid ones: even if Danielle had come back as a ghost, she had no reason to haunt her daughter.

No! Stop! Emelie!

Even if her daughter had been her last conscious thought—

No. I was obviously feeling the strain of all that had happened and of trying to keep my daughter healthy and balanced in the wake of her mother's unexpected death. This kind of thinking wasn't going to help either of us.

The screen still glowed with helpful text. Ghosts might remain because of strong emotional attachment, or because of emotions connected to their passing.

That would be her love for Emelie—that would be a strong emotion. It wouldn't be anything else. It wouldn't—

I closed the browser window and cleared my search history.

I started the printer—no matter the wonders of the paperless office, there was still an advantage to printing for editing—and went down the hall to Emelie's room. "I'm going to run to the mailbox. I'll be right back."

"Okay." She was playing with her dolls, newly recovered from the emergency re-capitations I had given them this morning. I'd looked in her room as I went for my first cup of coffee and spotted the three on the floor near their pink car, all with their heads across the room. I'd managed to get them repaired before Emelie woke up.

Emelie had never pulled the heads off her dolls before. I'd hoped she would ask how their heads had gotten back after she'd taken them off, but she didn't.

"Do you want to come with me?"

"Not really." She walked a doll to the car and slid it into the driver's seat. "I'm busy."

I smiled and went out to the mailbox. Our front yard needed mowing; I'd been occupied. Across the street, Jason Tanner was mowing his own grass, and I could feel his judgment crossing the pavement to me. I gritted my teeth and waved.

He waved back and slowed his machine. "Hey, you want me to do yours when I'm done here?"

"No, that's all right," I called back, irritated at his suggestion I couldn't take care of my own yard.

"No worries, just let me know. I know you've got a lot to take care of right now."

And I couldn't handle it, was the rest of what he meant. That I couldn't take care of my daughter and get my girlfriend back and make dean *and* cut my grass, because that last was just too much.

I waved as if everything was fine, and I went back inside with three bills, a coupon mailer, and a postcard for a discount oil change.

I heard the music from the door. It was too loud. And it was Danielle's music, some sweeping choral piece.

I ran up the stairs. Emelie sat in the doorway to my study, sobbing uncontrollably. "What's wrong?" I gasped, running to her and kneeling.

From here I could see into the study. My freshly printed pages were strewn about the room, torn and crumpled. The speakers were blasting in choral fury.

"What happened?" I asked.

Emelie shook her head, wailing. "It wasn't me! It wasn't me!"

I cradled her to me, as if I could shield her from the mess. I said something soothing—"I know, honey, I know" as if it could make any difference.

I recognized the music now: a "Dies Irae." Day of Wrath.

I left Emelie in the doorway and went into the room—it wasn't as if there was anything in the room that could harm her, obviously, but there was no point to taking her into something which frightened her—and turned off the music. I looked down at the thesis Danielle had resented—had resented for its practical themes, had resented for how it was boosting my career beyond hers. It was backed up, and I could always print it again, but to see it so attacked…

Could ghosts affect computer memory?

I suppressed the ridiculous thought. I did not try to answer it with a more rational one.

"Come on, Emelie. I think we should go out to dinner."

"Are you mad?" she whispered.

I hesitated. Did she think I was angry at her? Did she think I was angry at Danielle? I took a breath. "Can you tell me what happened?"

She looked from her bedroom to the study and back. "I heard the printer, and then it just all went crazy, and the music turned on."

I was not hearing this. I was not living this. "How do you feel about chicken nuggets?"

She smiled through her tears. "Can I play on the playground?"

I cleaned up the study after Emelie went to bed, with two nightlights and her dolls tucked into bed with her. Then I went to my own bed, wide and empty, and sat upright into the night.

Emelie was a good girl. I could not imagine her throwing my printed pages about the room even in a tantrum, which she had largely left behind a few years ago. Nor did I think she knew enough Latin to choose the Dies Irae over any other track in Danielle's playlists.

But the alternative was unthinkable. Inadmissible. Ghosts were a fiction, and not a well-done one.

I opened a browser in incognito mode, as if keeping it from my search history maintained some sort of barrier.

Ghosts, I learned, from a variety of dreadfully unscientific sites with dreadfully unaesthetic design, might linger for any number of reasons. Poltergeists, the kind that threw things around, destroyed toys, and played music, were traditionally linked to girls and young women.

Something to do with Emelie, then?

No, I was veering toward unreasonable again. There was no such thing as human spirits returning to complete unfinished business, or to watch over their loved ones, or—

And yet, Danielle might have a reason.

No!

I shoved the thought away fiercely. That was tantamount to admitting that I might believe this nonsense. And anyway there was no reason to linger.

No! Stop! Emelie!

She had always had a heart condition. She ran to keep her heart strong, though she didn't enjoy it. I hadn't made that up, and it had been easy to verify in her medical records. The coroner had no reason to doubt why she had fallen after a run.

And Danielle had no right to act so betrayed—if she had been enough, if she'd been willing to be more, I wouldn't have needed the videos. I wouldn't have needed Jade. It was just another sign of how unwilling Danielle was to even try, that she came directly into my study from her run to confront me, all sweaty and mascara-streaked and not even bothering to try to look good to earn me back.

I closed my eyes against the unwelcome memory. Maybe I shouldn't have gotten so defensive—but it was her fault for making me so angry, for demanding to know how long it had been going on, and why. *Why*, as if she had nothing to do with it…

It wasn't as if I ever consciously decided to hurt her, much less kill her. I was as surprised as she was when my hand went to the back of her head, when I shoved it down into the desk's corner.

No! Stop! Emelie!

And even at the end, she tried to manipulate me, tried to call our daughter's name to use her as leverage against me.

It wasn't my fault. It wasn't my fault. *It wasn't my fault.*

I needed to get Emelie to her therapist, figure out what was going on here.

I descended to the kitchen for that critical first cup of coffee, even more important today. I found Emelie at her usual place at the table, a little early. Her eyes were wide as she turned silently to me.

It took me a second longer to recognize that the smell of coffee was not coming from the automatic coffeemaker, but the room itself. Coffee pooled on the counter, on the floor, in the sink. It dripped into a puddle on the tile, slow and steady.

I looked about the room, caught between shock and maintaining a calm front for Emelie. I tried to swallow. "Did—did you do this?"

"Energy." Her voice was barely above a whisper. "Coffee is energy."

Danielle had said that nearly every morning, as she savored her first cup.

"No school today," I said. Emelie blinked in surprise. She loved school. "There's a special meeting today with Miss Wendy."

Emelie rolled her lips together, but she said nothing.

"Oh, honey, you're not in trouble," I said. "It's not because you're in trouble."

"Why would it be for being in trouble?" Emelie asked. "You said therapy wasn't for being bad."

She had read into my denial. That was such a Danielle thing to do, asking where I'd been when I said it didn't matter.

"I know. And that's true. But it's a special meeting today, and we don't want to miss it. Why don't you have some Sweet Sparks while I make some phone calls?"

"Sugar is too much energy," she said, almost a whisper. "It's not good for me."

Another Danielle-ism, something that would not be out of place in any room that wasn't dripping with coffee.

"It's okay today," I said. "I'm going upstairs to call."

I fled to my study, closed the door against Emelie's ears. I used every profane word in an art historian's ample lexicon against the receptionist until she made a slot to see Emelie that morning. I called the university to cancel my classes. I came downstairs to find Emelie at her place with a bowl of granola half-eaten in front of her. Elsewhere in the kitchen, Sweet Sparks were soaking into the puddled coffee, and the empty box lay on the floor.

"Not me," Emelie whispered. "Not me. Sugar's not good for me."

I said nothing, not trusting my voice. I shouldn't have left her downstairs. I held out my hand, and we went out to the car.

The waiting room was professionally comforting, repulsive on every level. The patterns, the soft fabrics, the muted tones, all outdated attempts at soothing a troubled social psyche which had never grown up to face the pragmatic needs of a post-modern world that recognized there was no cure for itself. It was the aesthetic embodiment of therapy's deceptive practice, talking yourself out of shame you shouldn't feel in the first place. If anything, "believe in yourself" made even less sense than belief in something supernatural. Danielle had gone to church for God's forgiveness, but at least she hadn't pretended you could forgive yourself.

I did not need forgiveness. It had been an accident, caused if anything by Danielle's own strident anger. It was not my fault.

After forty minutes, they called me in to join Emelie's session, something that had never happened before. Emelie was sitting on a chair near Miss Wendy, holding a stuffed giraffe and sniffing, but she did not look particularly upset. A fly buzzed against the window.

There was an old-fashioned clock on the wall, ticking like a cotton-muffled watch.

Miss Wendy gestured me to a larger chair across the room. "Emelie and I have been talking," she said gently, "and she has decided she would like to share something with you."

"What?" I asked, stupidly. "About the coffee?"

"She knows," Miss Wendy said. "She knows what happened."

Ice crystalized through each vein, and my heart stopped beating. I marveled for an instant at Miss Wendy's calm demeanor and then as quickly dismissed it as a therapist's necessity. The more important question was what to do. Therapists were legally bound by confidentiality, weren't they?

Emelie sniffed and spoke into the giraffe. "I read about the energy."

But therapists also were bound to protect children, and she might think Emelie was at risk if her father had killed her mother. But I would never hurt Emelie, I wouldn't, there would never be another accident, it couldn't happen, it hadn't even been my fault—

"I read how ghosts are really just energy, left over. Energy moving things around. And I thought maybe if I helped with the energy, it might help keep…"

Energy, left over. Like the lingering adrenaline numbing my fingers as I stared down at Danielle's vacant eyes and the seeping gash in her temple. Like the useless emotion that plagued me though it had not been my fault.

"I knew I was making a mess, but I thought it might…maybe we could feel like Mommy was still there…"

Stacked papers slid off the desk, settling over Danielle and floating to the room's edges.

"I started her playlist. I didn't mean to make you mad. I asked if you were mad."

I stared at Emelie, my mind whirling and grasping, faintly realizing at last that what she was saying was not an accusation, was not even a ghost story. My heart pounded in my ears and through the room.

"I'm sorry, Daddy. It wasn't my fault. I didn't mean to make you mad."

"I didn't mean to kill her."

The words hung in the air like smoke, intangible but choking. I had not meant to say them. I saw Miss Wendy go professionally still, saw her hand move just an inch, saw her fingers depress a button.

I could stop her. It wouldn't be my fault—she had called me in here, she had twisted my daughter into this—but I didn't know if she had a heart condition. And Emelie was watching.

A fly buzzed against the window.

"It wasn't my fault," I said to them both.

P is for Persistence

Pete Aldin

Ana steps between the pillars that frame the museum entrance and slips off her suncoat, sunhat and sunglasses. She enters an anteroom that's easily twenty degrees cooler than the street outside. Sweat has plastered her short hair to her scalp; her bared arms are slick with it. Beyond the anteroom she finds herself in a vault as long as six hay sheds, as startlingly bright as it is clean. She had expected gloom, she had expected stuffiness—that's what her older cousins told her to expect. Her cousins are idiots.

It is marvellous in here. A wonder. Unlike anything she has seen or experienced before, except perhaps in the curled and faded pages of books. White marble. Even lighting, no shadows. Currents of filtered air so smooth and cool they feel like ice cream on her skin. Dispersed along the long vault's walls and throughout its middle, stand daises as high as Ana's knees and shaped like the hexagons her bees use for storing pollen and honey. And on those daises—her heart skips a little—stand the Recalled …

Two smiling attendants in dusty pink coveralls approach. Ana knows that government people wear scents, unlike normal people. She breathes in a lungful of their sweet cologne: peach and vanilla, aromas and tastes she remembers from a wealthy uncle's gifts when visiting her father's farm holding several years ago, aromas so achingly sweet they make her empty stomach clench.

The women take her broad-brimmed hat, her coat, and then her name. This will make it easier for her to retrieve her clothing at the other end—and for them, she believes, to check against their records. There are others spread around the vault. Pilgrims like her. She recognizes several who had stood ahead of her in the line outside. They too have made this journey of a lifetime, a venture both privilege and expectation.

Once in a life, she thinks. *Once in a life.* She has yearned for this since childhood—and she will remember it long after she has borne her own children—doing her duty to keep Europe populated, to keep the *Earth* populated...

She wants to keep moving but an attendant stops her with a gesture and lifts a ceramic dish from a low table, holds it toward her. The dish is piled with fish-and-rice balls. Ana's father didn't pack her enough food—even for a workday, he never packs enough food—and she is so famished from two days of queuing that she wants to take handfuls of the treats. Politely, she only takes one. The other attendant presses a ceramic cup in her free hand; as parched as she is hungry, Ana drains it immediately. Juice, thick and sweet and delicious. She wants to run a finger around the inside of the cup, to suck it from her finger. But she is not at home and she must be polite. She hands back the cup with its insides still slick.

The attendant murmurs, "There are filtered water fountains around the museum, dear. You've been out in the sun a long while, so make sure you drink your fill."

The other attendant adds, "And don't rush your visit. You may remain here for as long as you desire." She gestures to the rice balls. "See me again if you become hungry."

Ana returns their solemn stares. A soft object squishes into her left ear—something she knows is called an earphone—while one last item presses into her free hand. This final thing is called a trident and it looks like a toy version of the pitchforks she uses to toss hay. Only this pitchfork feels as light as a handful of grass, and seems made of plastic except for the two chrome tips that cap each tine.

Alone again and nibbling the rice ball, Ana ventures in. The other pilgrims are spread around exhibit stands, making busy with their tridents or standing with heads bowed in reflection. For the most part, they keep to themselves. Like her, they came here alone—and to be alone. Everybody travels here without a friend or a loved one.

Once in a life and you do it alone, the District Warden had told her at her briefing. Your journey. Your experience. In as much as you can, avoid strangers so that your mind can be free to meditate upon the greater issues of our world.

Avoid strangers, she thinks now. Avoid people. Not so difficult a task in a world with so much space. With so few people. The trick is always to avoid the *bad* people. But she has been lucky there—as lucky as a woman of her time in history can be, at least. On the journey, she slept well off the road. Once in the city, she joined the museum queue and stayed there.

After taking a few more steps inside and another nibble of the rice, she pauses again to study the vault. Now that she's here, finally here, her heart is in her throat, her mind has snagged in indecision like a sleeve on a bramble. Although most pilgrims keep their distance from each other, there *is* one small crowd …

They cluster before a dais on which stands a tall man with orange-tinted skin and a clump of hair combed sideways across his head. As if conditioned by outside's waiting line, these people are queued—although again and by unspoken agreement, they keep more than an arm's length between them. She counts eleven of them. A popular exhibit, this one. She ventures closer to check the name—just as the pilgrim at the head of the line plunges his trident within the orange-skinned exhibit's gut making the tall man on the dais arch in agony and drop his jaw in silent protest. Ana reads the name, recognizes it. But the orange-skinned man wasn't on her list and seeing the queue there, she quickly decides she won't waste time with him.

There are three exhibits she definitely wants to visit—one of them an exhibit her mother visited. Ana spies the first of them a third of the way along the great hall. But as she starts off, popping the last of the rice ball into her mouth, another Recalled catches her eye. She diverts toward it. Many of the exhibits reside in niches like this. The size of the alcoves varies by some logic she can't discern.

This one is narrow. The man atop this dais seems old and he stirs at her approach, peering down his long sloping nose at her, reaching up to stroke his long sloping beard. He wears a finely designed tunic with two sets of buttons running down it and a wide sash draped from one shoulder to one hip. A sword is at his hip. Her earphone comes to life with a quiet intake of breath.

'King Leopold the Second of Belgium represents the worst of expansionist greed. He and his kind gouged and disembowelled the Gaia to rob her of what they called her "resources".'

Ana does not understand all these words, but she listens, rapt. The 'King'—a word she does know—continues to hold her gaze without any hint of shame over the actions he committed in life.

The earphone continues, 'He and his kind tortured, enslaved and murdered their fellow humans while destroying magnificent animals and habitats for the sole reason of amassing more wealth and power than they could ever possibly use. Wealth and power they spent upon their own pleasure only. If anyone deserves everlasting torment, it is Leopold and those other monarchs he represents. Citizen of the Wounded Earth, because of his evil, you suffer and the Earth suffers. Visit justice upon him.'

Ana knows what comes next. Her mother told her. Her father told her. The Warden told her. And she saw that other pilgrim doing it to the tall and orange Recalled just now. Without raising her arm far, she pushes the trident forward, poking its middle tine into King Leopold's left thigh. A grimace of pain contorts the King's face; his grunt is thick and loud in her ear via the earphone.

Ana pulls back her hand with the trident and steps away, the rice and fish and grape juice curdling in her stomach. She doesn't want to hurt him. *He's not the one I came to punish*, she tells herself. *That's why I don't want to. That's why.*

Ana moves on, seeking the first of the three exhibits on her list. Moving past a pilgrim her age who twists his trident into the face of a cattle baron and chuckles as the baron's ethereal fingers try helplessly to free him. Moving past a woman the age that her mother was when skin cancer killed her—the woman rakes her trident along the torso of a man named Rockefeller, sneering as she does. Ana forces herself not to look at the faces of the next two pilgrims she passes.

And then she is standing before the first of the daises she decided to visit. Three men stand upon it and her pause is enough to prompt the earphone into life. 'Nicolas-Joseph Cugnot, Karl Benz and Henry Ford are but three of the people responsible for the scourge of the automobile. They were instrumental in the development of this foul invention which caused so much of the pollution that sickened Earth so. Their invention contributed directly to the Greenhouse by way of that pollution, as well as indirectly.'

Again, Ana has not been taught all these words she's hearing, but she does know about steam- and oil-powered vehicles and the polluting industries that served and were served by them. Rusting hulks of 'cars' and 'trucks' remain along the old, broken-scabbed roadways near her home.

The earpiece continues, 'If anyone deserves everlasting torment, it is the developers of the grand polluter, the automobile. Citizen of the

Wounded Earth, because of these evil men, you suffer and the Earth suffers. Visit justice upon them.'

Ana's hand tightens around the trident's haft. Her arm twitches forward toward them, then falls to her side. Automobiles and the lust for the oil that was used to power them and to construct many of their parts are things she has been taught to loathe. They accelerated the wounding of the Earth and the destruction of its balances and harmonies. Animal habitats and air-cleansing forests were carved away to make those scabby tar roads that cars and trucks rode over. And these three Recalled, the voice told her, helped created them—just because they could!

And I am here to punish them for what they have done. It is my right and my duty, as one of Earth's surviving children!

And yet.

And yet …

Movement turns her head. The young man who'd been torturing the cattle baron approaches on his way to his next Recalled. His eyes meet hers. A smile is born in them. And then his gaze drops to her idle trident. When it catches hers again, there is mild shock in it, and the beginnings of what might turn into disdain. Ana drops her head before he reaches her; he mutters something in a language she doesn't speak, a language from perhaps a distant part of Europe. But the meaning is clear. Ana isn't delivering justice to these Recalled; Ana is shirking her duty; Ana is weak.

Mother Earth, forgive me.

She turns and squints across the chamber, sees the broad dais with a family of Recalled upon it, the second on her list and described in detail by her mother. Ana takes a few steps across toward it, all to see the details better. Though the family's clothing is nothing like Ana's—blue trousers, body-hugging tunics in bright colours that would leave their arms bare to the sun's deathly touch—they are a family: mother and father and daughter and son, standing side-by-side and staring down at thin slabs of plastic and glass that Ana believes are called computers.

Forgive me, she repeats in hopes that the Wounded Earth will hear her. All these people here, these Recalled, did wound your surface and your seasons, but I just can't hurt them. I cannot. There is enough pain and misery around without me adding more.

Ana lays her trident on the floor and marches toward the far end of the vault, with her shoulders hunched and her eyes on the floor. And she feels the scowls and frowns of every other pilgrim she passes before she reaches the next two pillars and the passage that is beyond them.

The passageway is fully enclosed, mercifully lacking windows. Spread along it at ten-metre-intervals are benches along one wall and water fountains along the other. At the third fountain, Ana bends low and presses the tap, slurping greedily as the life-giving spring arches up and into her mouth. Straightening, her belly cold and full, she risks a backward glance. A young woman, younger than her, is coming out of the main vault. Ana snatches her gaze away, turns her back. She has no interest in letting the stranger catch up, so she pushes on.

She is halfway along the passageway now without much idea of what awaits beyond the other end. The District Warden told her that a 'dome' had been added in the years since Ana's mother and father— and cousins—made their journeys to bring justice to the Recalled. The new structure has been open and active for less than a year; all that he heard about it was that it involved some animals. Perhaps, Ana thinks, they are farming chickens in there. Or geese. Perhaps there will be a meal: eggs, a chicken soup. As she starts forward again, her water-logged tummy twinges with hunger. The rice ball was not enough. A soup would be wonderful. It might even save her life. Her father gave her so very little money with which to buy provisions for the long walk home.

If he really wants to marry me off to Carlo—that pock-faced pig— why did Papa give me so little. So little money. So little food.

A new thought turns her lip into a sneer of disgust. Perhaps he didn't want her to return at all. Perhaps he was happy for her to stay here. Or die on the road. Either way, he'd be rid of her.

It's what he's always wanted. Ever since Mama died.

Oh, Mama. Her throat constricts with old grief. Why can't it be you in those exhibits? Why can't I hold your hand just once more? Put my head to your tummy just once more. Feel you stroke my hair and promise me life will be good.

The entry to the new chamber looms. No pillars frame it. There is a door, much like the front door of her home except that this one is glossy, and there is no knob. As she approaches, it opens toward her, all by itself, surprising her. But there can be no danger here, so she allows herself a small smile at the wonder of it and pushes on. Beyond the door, she can see a dirt floor and patches of tall grass. A tree. The tree, from here, looks … healthy. She enters and as her breath catches in her throat, the door sighs shut behind her.

Ana is frozen in fear. There, right *there* five paces away, is a gigantic cat, striped with orange and black, and half as big again as the biggest man she has ever seen. From school books—the books she loved best, the books about all the creatures now extinct—she knows this cat and knows its name.

Tiger!

It's impossible that it's here. But it is. Its appearance threads terror through her bowels, her chest, weakens her legs. Will it bite her first, claw her first?

But, no, the mighty creature shows little interest, stalking past with the merest of glances. The tiger must watch its footing because a spiky echidna is crossing its path; the great cat's pace and footing adjusts as the little anteater waddles out of its way. And then both are gone, vanished between thatches of tall grass.

"What is this?" she whispers as her heart thuds hard and fast.

The 'dome' rises above and around her, an upturned opaque bowl that could cover her father's entire farm holding—this feels as if she is inside a mountain. As far as she can see across its floor, there are grasses and reeds and many kinds of trees, some of which she doesn't recognise even up close. Her pulse thumps in her throat. Because there are animals everywhere. *Everywhere*. So many, many animals.

A small hiss announces the door's opening again. With the young woman she saw earlier coming up behind her, Ana forces herself away from the entrance, moving further in, but not too far. An attendant stands several metres away, but the elderly woman wears grey coveralls and blue gloves instead of the pink clothing of the vault attendants. Her eyes are kind. One gloved hand holds a large brush; with it she strokes the back of a horse, its brown coat as shiny as the glossy door at Ana's back.

Noticing her, the old woman smiles with real warmth and gestures back toward the entry. Ana sees there's a box on the wall. Blue gloves like the curator's poke from the hole at the top. The woman says, '*Mettiti i guanti.*'

Ana knows Italian, enough to decipher the invitation to put on gloves. So, she hurries to comply. The custodian hasn't stopped brushing the horse; but her free hand sweeps toward the centre of the dome, her message clear. *This is your place. This is your opportunity. Savour it.*

So, Ana wanders. She forgets about time—the light never changes in here, so it's hard to know what the sun is doing outside. After she has marvelled at animals she knows from books and many she doesn't know at all, she hears a thud-thud-thud behind her and turns. Gasps. The creature bounds over to her, slows then stands up on its hind legs.

"Kangaroo," she whispers. It —ventures closer. Are animals also Recalled, Ana wonders? Something feels different about her left glove: she checks it; it holds a clump of grass, transparent but some-how real enough that the glove has clamped around it to stop it blowing away in the gentle breeze. Stooping she holds it out. The kangaroo pulls itself toward her in its funny way of moving. Ana can't help a giggle. As the creature snatches grass from her with its teeth and munches it, something tiny stirs beneath the kangaroo's stomach fur. And a head appears! For a moment, Ana reels back, horrified. Then she remembers her lessons: these animals carried their babies in pouches. This is a baby kangaroo! Remembering the way the at-tendant's gloves could touch the horse, she reaches out and lays a finger on the baby's head. *Feels* its head beneath the pad of that fin-ger. Strokes the dear little thing. Its mother pulls the last of the grass from her other glove.

And a masculine voice behind her says in her language, "If you think that's fun, you should try this."

The man is her father's age and he is passing by, but he is *riding*. Riding a small horse—what are they called? Ponies?—and she's won-dering whether the saddle is like her gloves when he leans forward and runs his bare fingers through the animal's mane and says, "Real as you are. There's a free one back there." He jerks his head behind him, and then he is gone, pushing into a copse of trees.

Ana is left with an afterimage of his grin. A happy man. A nice man. Her father's age, but nothing like her father in spirit.

She looks back the way he indicated and yes, there is another pony back there, also fitted with a saddle. Its nose is in a drinking trough. Ana goes to it. Takes off a glove. With her bare hand, she strokes it. Her father keeps cows and sheep and a small brood of dogs and cats to keep away the pests. Ana knows those animals but she has never touched anything so lovely as this. The pony ignores her, content to drink.

The elderly attendant passes by, her head visible above the grass, and flashes Ana another of her kind smiles. Upon her shoulder rides a yellow-feathered bird that Ana doesn't know.

Presumably, this woman, this custodian, spends all her days here. Playing with animals and Recalling aspects of the Earth from before the wounding.

And I am to return home to work the ground for my father. Until he passes me off to pock-marked Carlo. Who'll make me work in that and other ways.

She doesn't shudder. She lifts her chin and gazes toward where the old woman disappeared through the grass. What a grand life the custodian must live! Bringing the glories of Old Earth again to life. And what if—what *if*, Ana thinks as her pulse beats hard again—this is just the beginning? What if it is possible for the attendants here to not only summon the ghosts of extinct creatures, but to summon back their *bodies* too, bring them back to the Earth and heal the Earth to host them once more.

She makes her decision quickly. She gives the pony a final pat and chases after the old woman.

Ana has a question to ask her.

Q is for Question

Sarah Van Goethem

Every night Rowena Hayes walked. The door to her yellow bungalow would click shut behind her and she would stroll down the little stone path to the sidewalk in the middle of the night. The path was edged with boxwood hedges and iceberg roses, their soft white petals shining glossy in the moonlight. The scent always made Rowena crave honey. Max had always bought The Janson's natural wildflower honey, harvested from their own farm-based hives. But Max was dead now, gone some months past (how long had it been now?) and so was the honey.

Oh, how Rowena missed that honey.

Perhaps she'd walk out further one night, straight out of town and down Millard Line. Perhaps she'd come across the Janson's farmhouse, the windows dark for the night, Hilary and John (Max and John had loved to go fishing together) tucked neatly under their sheets while their teenage daughter Olive (why were parents recycling these dull old names?) snuck out with one of those Miller boys. Perhaps she'd catch the girl in the act, all flushed, shimmying her way up the old cedar below her bedroom window. Well. If that happened, Rowena would have to let Hilary and John know. There was no other way around it, of course. Rowena had a duty to the citizens of Hazel Grove. Even if they had abandoned her, she would not forsake them. Certainly not. She couldn't fault them, not really. Widowhood was a strange period, after all. But in time Rowena would recover her stable position in society. Just wait and see if she didn't.

Rowena turned right at Green Street and walked another block. Hazel Grove was so quiet at night, so sleepy. The witching hour, Rowena's mother used to call it, when she paced the halls at midnight, unable to sleep. Despite the warmth of the autumn day, the night had quickly turned cool, and a light mist draped the streets. *How eerie*, Rowena thought, keeping a sharp eye out. The warmth of the summer nights had faded and the mist gave Rowena an unsettling feeling.

It was the Moore girl, Stacey, that had started the rumours. *Hazel Grove, haunted.* The girl claimed to have seen a…no. Rowena was not going to even think it. Stacey clearly had too much time on her hands. She should get a part-time job or perhaps volunteer at the animal shelter. Haunted. How ridiculous. And yet, Rowena caught herself looking over her own shoulder quite frequently. Perhaps more so tonight. The blasted mist was unnerving.

Only a few times had Rowena come across someone else at night, though. Once, Old Man Harvey, rocking in a wicker rocker on his wraparound porch, puffing on a cigarette (Rowena had left a note for his wife Aubrey the next night, *Imagine continuing to smoke when you know it causes lung cancer*) and another time, the Miller boy (was it Jake? Sam? There were far too many of those rowdy boys, really) trundling back into town in his old Chevy pick-up (Rowena had left a note for Mrs. Miller, *I wonder, does teenage pregnancy run in the family?*). But… then there was the time…Rowena shuddered.

No.

She couldn't have seen him. Maxwell Hayes, her husband, was dead. Gone. She'd imagined it was all. What with all the spooky rumours flying about now thanks to that blathering Moore girl, tongues wagging about a—no. The fools, they probably only wished it was her husband returned. Maxwell the beloved. Everyone loved Max.

Everyone except Rowena.

A streetlight flickered overhead and Rowena quickened her pace, crossing to the other side of the road. Goodness, she was such a goose sometimes. There was no such thing as…well, there wasn't anyway. Thinking she heard footsteps, she glanced over her shoulder. But there was nothing. No one.

But if there was…well. Rowena dared her do-gooder dead husband to return. Double-dared him, actually.

Soon Rowena stood in front of a brick four-square house, her destination. Electric candles burned in the windows, illuminating lacy curtains. The widow Woods was always one for the antiquated look. A bun in her hair and a cameo at her throat. The aesthetic must have been appealing for Mr. Moore (and probably Max, too, the men had been like two peas in a pod), very different than his modern wife with her sleek ponytail and her knee-high boots. Rowena had the fleeting thought that the widow Woods would surely appreciate the manner in which Max had died. If she knew, of course.

Rowena let out a lengthy sigh. Sometimes it was difficult doing the right thing. But someone had to do it after all, lest the whole town fall into disorder; everyone had been so distraught by Max's death. Maxwell Hayes, gentleman and pillar of the community may be gone, but alas, Rowena was still here. And as long as she lived and breathed, Rowena would set things right. She couldn't have all of Max's friends' lives falling into chaos with him gone. No, that would not do.

Besides, the widow Woods gave Rowena hope. She'd carried on after the death of her husband and the townsfolk had embraced her once more (though Mr. Moore had taken it a step further than necessary).

Rowena stood in the shadows of the giant maple.

She slipped her hand into her pocket and plucked out the envelope. It was small, made to appear vintage, yellowed and aged, same as the paper inside. Like old parchment. Rachel Woods, she'd written on the front, in perfectly spaced and curved letters. Rowena still knew the message on the note inside; she'd rewritten it several times to ensure it was perfect. *You can never be quite certain about where one's been. Remember, an STD test is simple.*

Rowena made her way up the treads on the porch and dropped the envelope through the brass mail slot in the widow Woods' door; Rachel had had a proper, old-fashioned mail slot put in, like the Victorian-era lady she thought herself to be. The door of the slot clicked shut decisively. Well. That was that. Rowena didn't know for certain, of course. But she had seen Mr. Moore at the doctor's office (the doctor...actually that reminded her), and she *had seen* Mr. Moore and the widow Woods conversing at the coffee shop, and well...better safe than sorry. She imagined the widow Woods would thank her if she knew who it'd come from, but Rowena didn't sign her notes. She wasn't looking for praise. Goodness no.

Rowena only wanted to return the favour. Whoever had left her that note about Max...well. Let's just say that was a real lifesaver.

Rowena made her way back to the street. A dog growled and lunged at a chain-link fence and she sped up. The mist had grown, thickening into a heavy fog, and something worrisome swirled in Rowena's gut. She didn't like when she couldn't see things clearly and she had the distinct impression she was lost somehow. Misplaced. Like the world had gone on without her. Like she'd forgotten something important, an idea swallowed in the fog.

Her fingers closed over the remaining letter for Jennifer Moore in her pocket, but she couldn't deliver it now; her breaths were becoming quicker, her heart a ridiculous fluttering thing. She had to get back, back to her little bungalow. And then tomorrow she would wake up to the sun in her window and she would make herself a cup of tea and she would be ever so thankful she had the whole glorious house to herself. And she would remember what a goose she'd been tonight, of course.

But right now, her hairs stood on end and invisible fingertips kneaded her scalp and she thought her throat may close in. *What might be lurking in the fog?*

Just follow the streetlights, she told herself, and she stumbled along, her memory carving a path back home. She was almost there, almost to her little stone path with her boxwood and her pretty ghostly roses, when all the streetlights, as far as she could see, began to flicker.

Did she smell cinnamon?

Rowena froze, a hand to her throat. But just as quickly her fear was replaced with a hot and consuming anger. She narrowed her eyes and crossed her arms. If Max was here, if he was really here…well, he'd be sorry.

There was a crack of a branch in the yard. Rowena ran.

She scurried as fast as she could into her house, slammed the door shut, locked it, and hid, panting, behind her chintz curtains. She peered out her huge front window, but all the street lights stayed on and no one passed by.

Hazel Grove, haunted, echoed in Rowena's ears. She knew they whispered it behind their handkerchiefs and murmured it over their menus at the coffee shop. She didn't have to walk during the day to know this; that was always the way of it in Hazel Grove. And they'd stopped talking to Rowena, started avoiding her altogether. Pretended she didn't exist. Fear was funny like that. Had a habit of showing you who your friends really were. And all because they thought her husband had returned, that he was a… no. She wouldn't say the word.

Well.

It was all ridiculous, wasn't it? The longer Rowena stood there behind her curtains, and the longer nothing happened outside, the more ridiculous the idea seemed. Finally, her hands stopped trembling and she smoothed them down the front of her jacket. Yes, it was ridiculous. Except…well.

Rowena wouldn't put it past him was all.

Rowena awoke to the sunshine and her husband's sickly body floating near the ceiling. She gasped and choked, tried to manage a scream, and then twisted in her bedsheets, her eyes clamped shut. Her teeth chattered. She wouldn't look, she *would not look.*

The birds chirped outside. A bicycle bell dinged. A car started; Mrs. Drew was leaving for work. Everything sounded normal, as it should.

But then Rowena realized she *wanted* to look. He had no right to make her life hell, not now, not after he was dead. He'd done enough of that while he was alive, always expecting things of her, prying at her thoughts, *are you feeling quite alright today, dear?* And attempting to make her socialize with his friends, *wouldn't you like to come out, love?*

Well. Not anymore.

Rowena opened her eyes. But there was nothing. Only the ceiling fan set to low. A soft breeze, marked by the faint scent of cinnamon. And she was in the guest room.

Right. Rowena had started sleeping in the guest room. But why?

Yes, yes. To be away from Max. She eyed the closed door of their original bedroom as she crept to the kitchen. She could sleep in there again, if she wanted to. Max was gone.

No, she decided. She did not want to sleep in there again, thank you very much.

Anyway, she was only seeing things. Her imagination had run wild. Perhaps she should leave herself a note. *Like mother, like daughter.* Rowena winced. What an absurd thought. Leave herself a note, my oh my. No, she wasn't crazy. Why then, did she have the uneasy feeling that something was amiss?

She shook off the thought and made herself a cup of tea and a boiled egg and ate in her pajamas. Max had always insisted on her dressing first. She sat in the only chair with arms at the table, Max's chair. *Go on,* she thought, stirring sugar noisily around in her cup. If anything, the sugar would bring him back. Max hadn't liked when she had too much sugar. *Darling, I really think that's enough.*

But nothing happened and she finally went and took a shower and brushed her teeth and set about tidying the house and scrubbing the dishes and repotting a geranium she'd brought in. Rowena very much liked it when things were in a neat and tidy order. Which was much easier without a man around, she had to admit. It was amazing how much better she felt since Max was gone, as if a weight had been cast off. She was as light as a feather now.

A bit later, she sat at the desk in the study and retrieved her lovely parchment papers and meticulously wrote a letter to the good doctor, in perfectly spaced and scrawling letters. *How old-fashioned to die by arsenic poisoning.* In turn, she had her lunch and then her dinner, and then dusk rolled in and then the darkness, and still no Max.

Well, he *was* dead of course. She was just allowing the fears of the townsfolk to get the better of her.

Well that was enough of that.

She plucked *Crooked House,* her favourite Agatha Christie novel, off the bookshelf and sat down to read a little. But a short while later she heard a rustle at the front of the house. Her heart skipped a beat. Rowena crept into the living room and perched, once again, behind the chintz curtains. But it wasn't Max. It was the blasted neighborhood kids, one of those Miller boys (Jake? Sam?) and a brunette with a thick braid. Oh goodness, it was Stacey Moore, the little rumour-starter. How adorable. Max had doted on the little Moore girl once, said he'd wished they had a daughter just like her, with pigtails and freckles. She wasn't as cute any longer, not even borderline pretty. Max wouldn't want her now. On second thought, she wasn't adorable at all. Plus, she was clearly acting out, poor thing. Kids weren't stupid, after all. She'd probably seen her father with the widow Woods, the way his eyes lit up, the way his hands roamed. Well. An unfortunate circumstance. Regardless, that didn't give her the right to press her flat face to Rowena's window now, trying to catch a glimpse. Of a....

Fine, she'd say it.

A ghost.

Rowena put her hands on her hips as the two skulked about, tramping down her hostas. For goodness sakes, didn't they know haunted houses were big old derelict beasts in the countryside, not sweet little bungalows in town? Well. She'd give them a good scare if that's what they were after. Rowena reached for the light switch. Turned it on and off, on and off. It was the Miller boy who screamed first, the cowardly thing. Rowena hadn't expected that, but found it rather satisfying.

Either way, they dashed off and Rowena resumed her evening. She'd nap a bit before she went out tonight; she still had a couple of notes to deliver after all. She couldn't let Jennifer Moore go on pretending her husband was faithful, not when it was affecting her daughter like this. You never knew how events would affect people.

The townsfolk probably thought that about Rowena. So shocked by her husband's death she hadn't even attended the funeral. She hadn't, had she? Rowena circled around the thought in her head, the blank space that she couldn't seem to access. One moment Max was here, telling her to fix her hair just so and that her meatloaf wasn't entirely cooked through and there were cobwebs in the high corners and why didn't she clean them? The next moment....just this house, all silent and still. Gloriously peaceful. Gloriously hers.

No Max.

Just that strange gap, a blur in time between when he existed and then didn't.

Oh well. A minor inconvenience.

Rowena slipped out again that night, like she always did now. She stopped on the front porch, her head cocked to the side. She hadn't really noticed until now how overgrown the gardens had become. Weeds poked up between the hostas and sedums and the iceberg roses had become a heavy thicket, needling their way over the boxwood. It put a sour taste in her mouth; Rowena hated disorder.

Thankfully the air was clear, the moon bright and shining overhead. Rowena pasted on a smile and held her head high and made her way to the Moore house first. She left the envelope on the front steps, atop the silly floor mat with the pumpkins on it. Jennifer would find it first thing at daybreak when she went for her morning run. An awful way to start the day, certainly, by finding out about your roaming husband, but alas, it had to be done.

Rowena glided across the street again but, feeling as if she were being watched, she looked back. And froze. There, in an upstairs window, was Stacey. The girl's mouth and eyes were round and big, her chest rising and falling too quickly beneath her nightshirt. Had she seen Rowena on their property?

What a predicament this was. But the girl wasn't doing anything. She wasn't screaming or yelling for her parents or dashing down the steps to see what mischief Rowena had caused. No. She only stood there stupidly, her face as white as Rowena's roses, blowing her breath into a foggy circle on the glass. She seemed to be looking right through Rowena and it gave Rowena a jolt. Rowena spun about and something flit into the shadows. *Was it Max? Had the girl been seeing Max?* Rowena trembled, scanning the darkness. *Damn him.* Rowena blinked, then whirled about again. But Stacey was gone. The window was dark and empty.

Well.

That was something.

Rowena didn't wait around. She still had one last note to deliver— Dr. Anderson's. Rowena found herself in front of his old gothic Victorian house in no time. She observed the green trim and curving turrets and ironwork, and thought, *this is where those nosy teenagers should be looking for a ghost.* She'd been inside on many occasions, toasting holidays and having dinners, and she'd always thought something had prowled there. Shadows in the corners. Secrets under the floorboards. If Max had been hard-pressed to choose a best friend (he had so very many), she thought he would've picked the doctor.

A sad choice, really.

Rowena attempted to slide the envelope through the mail slot (this mail slot was original to the house), but the envelope simply fell to the ground at her feet. How odd. Rowena picked it up again and tried to push it through the slot, but no. It wouldn't budge. She crouched down and flipped the flap aside with her finger. Nothing wrong at all. Rowena peered through the slot into the void of the house. Eyes stared back at her. Rowena gasped and fell backward, scrambling away. *Those were Max's eyes.*

No one else had green eyes like Max.

Get a grip, Rowena told herself, gasping for air. *Max isn't in there, Max is dead. Gone.* And then a thought smacked into her, hard. She licked her lips, tasting the memory, and added, *you killed him. Remember?*

But no, she didn't exactly remember. That was the problem, wasn't it? Or no, she remembered him dying (had she done that?). It was what came after that that was jumbled in her mind. Rowena stood shakily and jammed the envelope into the slot. This time it slipped through and she sighed in relief. There, that was that.

As she walked back home, she thought of the doctor finding it in the morning. She hated to upset him before his coffee, really she did, but she couldn't have him go on believing that Max had simply died from his cancer. That was too easy, too lazy, and she thought even the doctor knew this; she'd seen him about town with his graying skin and sunken eyes. Besides, she'd never appreciated how he'd looked at her with pity, how he'd pressured her to take medication—well it didn't matter now. No, the point was that the doctor should know his mistakes. That's how people learned, after all.

She'd have this town in tip-top shape in no time. All cleaned up.

But her steps slowed and her thoughts darkened; Stacey Moore had seen her.

Oh well, the girl had no proof. But if it was her word against Rowena's, the townsfolk would likely take her side. Wouldn't that be the way of it. To believe the snivelling teenager over the mayor's widow. Still, Rowena thought she should probably dispose of the parchment papers. A real shame, but probably for the best.

Rowena turned onto her street. Her bungalow was in sight, a light on. Hadn't she turned all the lights off? She slowed her steps but the street lights didn't flicker. No, because Max wasn't out here now. He was in there. In *her* house. She darted past the boxwood and the heady overgrown iceberg roses, shivers climbing her spine.

The minute she pushed open the door, she knew. She could smell him, his awful spicy cinnamon cologne. Her fingers balled into fists. But he wasn't there, the room was empty and silent. An envelope, one of Rowena's own, the matching ones to her parchment notes, lay on the side table beneath the lamp Rowena had most definitely *not* left on.

Rowena Hayes, it said.

Rowena found herself beside it, picking it up with shaking hands. She'd know Max's writing anywhere, but this wasn't it. He'd written her love letters once. She thought of those letters now like a spider's web, a way to ensnare. But if it wasn't from him, then who? Whoever had done this had mimicked Rowena's own handwriting. Forgery then. She'd figured out who did this, and don't think she wouldn't. She slid out the note, her arms numb. On second thought, it was as if all of her was numb, as if she was watching herself, somewhere outside of herself. Such a strange familiar feeling. Her fingers unfolded the note. A single word.

Remember.

The note fluttered to the carpet. And then Rowena was back in her body, rushing to her old cedar chest where she kept her wedding dress, her childhood toys and photos, and the vintage siebert poison flypaper she'd bought from the antique store. There was only one sheet left; she'd used the rest of course, soaked them to extract the arsenic.

She remembered that alright. Oh yes, it was all flooding back.

Someone had left her that note, the same someone that had left the note this time. *Your husband is going to kill you.*

And then she sensed him. Smelled cinnamon again. She whirled around and there was Max, sitting in his recliner. She held up the paper, swallowed. "I killed you," she whispered. She hadn't let him kill her first. No, she'd beat him to it.

But Max only smiled sadly, the way he'd always looked at her. As if he wasn't as bad as what she made him out to be, and as if he still loved her, regardless.

How infuriating.

How exasperating and annoying and vexing.

How Rowena hated his sympathy and lies. "What do you want?"

Remember. The word popped into her mind, unbidden, though Max hadn't spoken. *Remember, remember, remember.* The word crashed around in Rowena's head. The poison paper wasn't enough. There was more. Rowena yanked on her own hair, growing dizzy. The room spun around her and she shut her eyes.

When she opened them, Max was gone. He'd disappeared and the light was out. Rowena was left standing in a path of moonlight, holding her flimsy little weapon. And in the window, eyes as big as dinner plates, was Stacey Moore, the little ghost-hunter. The minute the two locked eyes, the girl took off.

Rowena stayed awake the few hours until morning. She wrote one last note to Stacey Moore, *Sometimes we get more than we bargain for,* and then she hid the remainder of her parchment notes and her last poison flypaper in a secret drawer in the old desk. She couldn't bring herself to dispose of them. As well, she hid the two unnerving notes that had been addressed to her, the handwriting so like her own she couldn't find a single fault with them.

Then, Rowena readied herself to do what she should have done a long time ago. Visit the cemetery. Mourn her husband. Wish him farewell. *And* she would ensure that the town knew all about it. Yes, she would say her good-byes to Max like a proper grieving wife, maybe even shed a tear or two (she practiced pinching herself rather forcefully to encourage this) and then the townsfolk would warm to her again. If anything, she would draw their sympathy, and that was a start. She hated sympathy, really she did, but if that was the only way, then so be it.

Rowena took a shower and when she got out, the smell of cinnamon wafted through the house. The word *Remember* was written in scrawling letters across the steam on the mirror. She wiped it away. She dressed herself in a long black dress and curled her hair to fall just over her shoulders, the sides twisted back like a crown. Just so. Just how Max liked it. When she set her brush down, there, atop the dresser, was a single white rose. Fine. Yes. Would that make him happy? Rowena tucked the flower into her hair, just like at their wedding, just like her flower crown.

And then, the music started. It was coming from their old bedroom, from behind the closed door. It was Rowena's jewelry box. The music meant the lid had been opened. Rowena steepled her fingers together.

He wanted her to put on her wedding rings again.

Well, no. Sorry, but that's where she drew the line. This was a good-bye and he needed to see that very clearly.

At eight-thirty in the morning, at the time when people left for work and busses ploughed through town carrying oodles of detestable children, Rowena pocketed her letter for Stacey Moore and let herself out of her bungalow and walked past her boxwood and roses and continued on down main street. But to her annoyance, no one as much looked at her or acknowledged her, even though Rowena hadn't been out of her house during daylight for many days (months?). By the time she reached the edge of town, Rowena was huffing mad.

What good would this all be if no one was around to see her?

Would Hazel Grove ever accept her now that Max was gone? The fools.

By the time she walked through the iron gates of Hazel Grove Cemetery, Rowena had forgotten that she had ever planned to cry at all. She ripped the rose from her hair and when she finally spied the name Hayes, she stormed toward the newly polished stone, ripping the petals to shreds. She hurled them like confetti, like revenge.

But then.

The stone was too big. Too wide. To the left, the name Maxwell.

To the right....*no.*

It wasn't possible.

Remember.

It was... *her name*, Rowena Hayes. Carved into the stone in block letters. A death sentence, forever bound to Max. Rowena staggered backward, reaching for something, for anything. But her hand wasn't there, was it? What was she now? Energy? Particles? Rowena spun about, her chest heaving, until she remembered she had no lungs, no rib cage, no skin or bone. *Where was he? Where was Max?*

She would kill him all over again. Surely this was his fault.

But he was nowhere. There were only real things, solid trees and grass and stones and the sky, so blue today. She collapsed on the ground, well no, not really, not a collapse, more of a floating on her back, a levitation of sorts. She stared at the clouds. They were more like her, wispy and feathery, transparent. She saw shapes in them, shapes of the things she'd been doing. The imaginary tea she'd drunk, the imaginary egg she'd eaten, the empty cups, the nonexistent sugar. The shower without water. Only a memory, and her...stupidly repeating her life actions.

No, no, no.

The memories seeped in. She'd poisoned Max, yes. And then, oh…and then.

She'd poisoned herself, too, hadn't she? A moment of weakness, of fear.

And now… this. An eternity with Max.

Laughter bubbled up inside of her. *What had she done?*

But then her fingers closed over the note in her pocket, the note to Stacey Moore, the girl who claimed to see ghosts. The envelope of the note was sharp, pointy. Real.

This she *had done.* Just like all the other notes.

But Stacey had never seen Max, because Max wasn't here. No, Max wasn't haunting Rowena or Hazel Grove; Max was long gone. He wasn't sticking around, holding grudges.

She'd done him a favour, really. The cancer had been eating him up, and she, Rowena, had been strong enough to put his happiness first. To put him out of his misery.

Yes, Rowena had been ever so gracious.

And now. Now, he suffered no more.

People like Max went to heaven or the other side or whatever was out there. They saw a bright light and walked toward it. That was the way of things.

But people like Rowena…well. People like Rowena walked the streets at night, in the dark, in the moonlight. People like Rowena had reasons to stay. To keep things in order.

Hazel Grove, haunted.

Yes, Rowena thought, rising to walk. Hazel Grove *was* haunted. And she had a note to deliver.

R is for Remember

S

Michael B. Tager

When Max and Bettina pull up in their gold-and-silver van, the neighborhood goes quiet. Not the distant woodpecker in the forest behind the track houses, or the bees or the automatic sprinklers—what planned development could ever shut *that* orchestra up—but the people and the cars and lawnmowers. The outside neighbors are all studiously not watching and the inside neighbors are up against the window, waiting and listening and pointing. They know who Max and Bettina are. Word has gotten around.

"This the one then?" Max asks, gesturing at the white house with the sycamore in between the white house with two sycamores and the white house with none. He's adjusting his bolo tie in the rear view.

"Looks like," Bettina says, puffing on her Pall Mall. She really should quit. When she's done, she crushes it in the ashtray and flicks it out the window. She doesn't need to check her Windsor knot. She knows it's sharp.

The old biddy answers the door and Bettina and Max are gratified at how surprised she is at their attire and punctuality. Most people don't actually watch *Ectoplasm Twins*, they just know it exists and snicker when it's the punchline. Assumptions run rampant and honestly, they get it. It's a pretty stupid title, but they didn't pick it.

"Where's the infestation, ma'am?" Max murmurs. He's the soothing one. He always has been.

The old biddy—Jane—guides them up some rickety stairs and through mounds of magazines and other hoarded garbage. Bettina can't help her disgusted intakes of breath. Thank God she has gloves. She exchanges twin-eyes with Max and he's on the same page. Maybe she applied to the wrong show?

Jane pushes open the round attic door at the top of the staircase and they stare into blackness. They both tremble at the smell of mothballs and rat feces, and another, bolder, spicier smell underneath. They shiver at the cold wind bursting out, like it's searching for an escape. "Jesus," Bettina says, "Arctic lives in your rafters, huh?" Her suit jacket does nothing to keep the chill out. Why should it? It's summer after all.

"There, there," Max says, guiding the woman by the elbow down the stairs and back into the kitchen that must have been tacky in the 70s and has now achieved an ironic beauty. He sits her at the linoleum table stained by decades of tea cups, instructs her to make some Earl Grey, sign the contract, and wait for them to come down. He pushes the contract into her hand, gives her a nice ballpoint pen inscribed with their logo, asks some leading questions about what sounds the ghost makes at night (crying), how long it's been there (about a year), any recent deaths, has she wronged anyone, any known criminals or saints in her family tree, etc.?

He writes down her answers in his little notepad decorated with dragons, and frowns at one of them. He then pats Jane's arm and says, "Don't worry. We're on it."

She starts to sign and then narrows her eyes. "You aren't hucksters are you? Everyone says y'all are full of shit." Her voice is sharp and throaty. Max sees flecks of dandruff on her thin shoulders.

Max says, "You don't have to sign anything." His foot taps and he checks his watch. Two flights up, he hears thumping and cursing and the howl of wind. "You called us, honey. We just want to help."

"That's not an answer," Jane says and now that Max looks at her little white bob, the gold tooth in the back of her mouth, the wiry tension in her knuckles, he sees the edge and beneath that, barely contained grief. Life has done Jane wrong; she's seen some shit and Max doesn't want to be on the receiving end of anything she can throw.

Max runs his hand through his patchy beard and says, for the hundredth or thousandth time, "I can't prove anything to you to make you believe. Sign it and we'll come back tonight with the television crews and not only will we help, but you'll be on TV. You'll have a story to tell for years and when people ask, "Is it real?" you can just shrug your shoulders all enigmatic like."

Max takes a banana from her fruit basket and waves it. When she nods, he peels it and takes a big bite. "Don't sign it and we leave and that's that. No hard feelings." His nonchalance has the desired effect and by the time he's done with the banana, the contract is signed and in his pocket.

Bettina is at the threshold when he gets back, rubbing tears from her eyes because she learned the story while he was gone. She's grateful for his presence. Before she entered, she tried to see what was inside, but it's full North Pole winter dark and her eyes aren't built like that. Her nose was no help either, because the overpowering smell of death and rotting brought her to her knees. The howling gale precluded hearing anything at all, and when she put her hands into the darkness, the bone chill numbed her fingers instantly.

"So what did you do?" Max asked.

"What do you think, dummy? I stamped on the floor and then I knelt and closed my eyes and did some ommmm shit and prayed." She winks but he doesn't laugh, and she isn't laughing either. Because she did what she always has to, which was feel with her heart until something touched her.

Max looks at his notebook and reads it out loud, "Her grandson died a year ago?"

She nods.

"He had an asthma attack after playing in the attic? 'Cause of the dust and heat and the moths?"

She nods again.

"Got sick and died on the way to the hospital while unconscious? This is the last place he knew?"

She slaps at an escaping tear. "It's like we don't even need a psychic. Want to take it from me?" She holds out her hand.

Max grasps her and squeezes and heads back to the car and grabs two jackets sporting the *Ectoplasm Twins* logo, and some other things. They check in on Jane and say they're making great progress and when they return to the glaring maw of the attic, they walk in together. Bettina sits lotus-style while Max uses a penlight to (barely) illuminate the floor. He lights incense and plays some chill down tempo on his phone and lays down some objects that would be meaningful to a kid. A PlayStation controller, a baseball glove, some colored pencils, a teddy bear. He sits and waits.

Bettina floats in her mental void while Max does all of this. She visualizes it as a blue lagoon enveloping her, or sometimes as the hands of God (which god she's not sure, but she's always been partial to Ganesha or Pan or sometimes the Old Testament God), but always as a safe space from which she can radiate nothing but empathy and love and sorrow and understanding. Soon will come the worst part, when she'll touch the spirit and feel the only emotion it has left, and she needs that comforting center to cushion that blow. This boy, all he feels is rage of stolen time, and confusion and loss, and that will sting her heart so badly. It will scald her and she's already crying anticipatory tears.

Max sees Bettina jump when contact is made and he reaches out his hand and grabs her ankle, not enough touch to startle her, but enough to relax her. And she does, even as her face scrunches and all the emotion the ghost feels runs through her body. Max wishes he could take some of that burden, but he can't. And he's kind of glad, too. He's the younger twin after all, and what are big sisters for but to take the brunt of life?

Ten, fifteen minutes go by and Max is thinking about getting in touch with their tax guy when the heavy darkness dissipates. Or maybe it was never there, but only in their minds. Either way, Max can now see that the attic they're in is a plain half-finished little room. Storage boxes wall-to-ceiling, and used mouse traps. Gross.

Bettina sighs, "We're good now."

"Does he have any unfinished business for us to take care of?" he asks.

She stands and cracks her neck, arches her back. "No. He just didn't understand. He thought he was left behind. I explained it to him."

Max writes it in his little notebook, next to a stegosaurus. "Do we tell Jane the truth? That it was her grandson haunting her?"

Bettina wants a cigarette. "Don't see how it would help. It wasn't really her fault." Bettina kicks at the dust. "Nothing for us to lose sleep over."

Downstairs, they tell Jane the usual. "Yeah," Max says with a straight face, because these lies kind of amuse him, even if they're meant to help. "You totally have a poltergeist. One of the biggest we've ever seen. Maybe two poltergeists, which is really rare."

Jane asks if it's a famous person haunting her attic. "Absolutely," says Bettina as she collects the first check. Another will come after filming. "Super famous. You'll find out tonight." Like any famous spirit would hang out in this random cul-de-sac, she thinks. Why do boring people always think interesting folks would bother with them? Marie Antoinette, Lincoln—they all have better stuff to do.

In the van, Bettina lights another Pall Mall and says, "You think this helps? What we do?"

Max takes off his jacket, bolo tie, sport coat and button-up until he's just wearing a tank top advertising the crappy metal band he used to be in. "Jane will probably rest easy. And those fifty idiots watching at home seem to enjoy all this. That's something, right?" *Ectoplasm Twins* is not a popular late-night, off-brand cable channel program.

She snorts and puffs two white plumes of demon smoke. "Like I care about those idiots. I'm not talking about them, or Jane."

"What do you mean, then?"

Bettina points at the lonely third floor window. "I'm talking about him, and all the others."

Max frowns and turns the key in the ignition. Later, after he tells the film crew the score, they'll come by and light all the fancy blue fires and say pidgin Latin and set up a table with a velvet cloth and knock under the bottom of it (two for yes, one for no) and after they pull all their charlatan tricks at the séance, they'll proclaim the ghost gone. Then they'll collect the rest of their money and five grand might sound like a lot, but they don't have health insurance, so it goes quick. And the show will air and then they'll investigate other people who get in touch with them. And they'll lay those ghosts to rest, too. Everyone has ghosts. That's what Max can never get over. And all the ghosts are dead and it never ends and he isn't sure he's happy, but maybe he feels fulfilled.

Finally, he says, "He's sleeping now, isn't he? He's no longer lost."

"Yeah, I guess you're right," Bettina says as she rolls down the window. The van pulls out of the street and onto the highway. She takes a final drag and flicks the cigarette outside, breathes until her heart quiets and listens to the world. She feels all the strands of the unquiet dead tugging at her, moaning for someone to listen.

S is for Séance

Jonathan C. Parrish

#LOG ENTRY 153467 ID 33452PS DATE 229712

This will be my last diary entry, tomorrow I start my "post-life" phase as they have been officially calling it. I heard some of the other crew saying we're "Zombozos" but that's stupid since we won't be zombies. The techs are telling us how straightforward and calm it is going to be butwhat the hell can they know? There ain't no coming back, not that I had ever seen, which is the whole point but also means they can't have any kind of record. Whatever. It's just shit they tell the rank and file to keep them on board. Still, it has to beat living, which mostly sucks. I expect to not sleep tonight, I can sleep when I am dead. Wait, can I? Guess I'll find out tomorrow. I'll let you know (ha ha!). Psych! Hauntings are not on my assignment list, only maintenance of the downlink circuits.

So, mysterious reader who I have no idea I am writing this for, why did I sign up for this? Adventure? Boredom? Public Service? I guess it was something new to do, something people told me was stupid so that clinched it, no way was I not going to sign up! Re-invent myself and move on in the most spectacular (no pun intended) way.

"Spirit harnessing" sounds edgy, even if it is just parts maintenance. I'm sure it'll be cool to be a ghost. Sad thing is everyone else will be a ghost too (of course I mean "post-life hyper persistent entity") so I can't spook the others!

I'm going to have a lot of time to do some thinking I hope, I mean, how much time can I spend checking my nanoboards anyway? I bet someone is making a mint on these massive timescale initiatives, it ain't me but some of the others are making good for their kids. Trust someone to figure out how to make money from making ghosts move shit. At least I am going into space, not deep sea like the spectre-lunkers.

We were given a speech today about being "committed" and the bozos made jokes about *being committed.* Hardy har har. But here I am, an astronaut that isn't, a colonist that won't be. I'm in it for the long haul, because what the hell else am I?

#LOG ENTRY 0003567 ID 33452HPE DATE 229754 TYPE STATUS TIME IN TRANSIT: 0.385 CREW ENTANGLEMENT: 100% SYSTEMS: OK TEMPERATURE: (± 5C)

#LOG ENTRY 0004976 ID 33452HPE DATE 229860 TYPE STATUS TIME IN TRANSIT: 0.650 CREW ENTANGLEMENT: 100% SYSTEMS: OK TEMPERATURE: LEVEL 1 (± 5C)

#LOG ENTRY 0006258 ID 33452HPE DATE 230074 TYPE STATUS TIME IN TRANSIT: 1.185 CREW ENTANGLEMENT: 99.95% SYSTEMS: OK TEMPERATURE: LEVEL 1 (± 6C)

#LOG ENTRY 0018857 ID 33452HPE DATE 230414 TYPE WARNING ENGINE 5 NON ENTANGLED
#LOG ENTRY 0018859 ID 33452HPE DATE 230414 TYPE STATUS TIME IN TRANSIT: 2.03 CREW ENTANGLEMENT: 99.9% SYSTEMS: OK TEMPERATURE: LEVEL 1 (± 6C)

#LOG ENTRY 0022587 ID 33452HPE DATE 230864 TYPE WARNING ENGINE 5 NON ENTANGLED
#LOG ENTRY 0022588 ID 33452HPE DATE 230864 TYPE NOTIFICATION ENGINE 4 +5% CORRECTION
#LOG ENTRY 0022589 ID 33452HPE DATE 230864 TYPE STATUS TIME IN TRANSIT: 3.16 CREW ENTANGLEMENT: 99.9% SYSTEMS: OK TEMPERATURE: LEVEL 1 (± 6C)
#LOG ENTRY 0022590 ID 33452HPE DATE 230864 TYPE ERROR UNRECOGNIZED COMMAND "TEST"

#LOG ENTRY 0043635 ID 33452HPE DATE 231744 TYPE WARNING ENGINE 4 NON ENTANGLED
#LOG ENTRY 0043636 ID 33452HPE DATE 231744 TYPE WARNING ENGINE 5 NON ENTANGLED
#LOG ENTRY 0043637 ID 33452HPE DATE 231744 TYPE NOTIFICATION ENGINE 3 +3% CORRECTION

#LOG ENTRY 0043638 ID 33452HPE DATE 231744 TYPE NOTIFICATION ENGINE 8 +3% CORRECTION

#LOG ENTRY 0043639 ID 33452HPE DATE 231744 TYPE STATUS TIME IN TRANSIT: 5.36 CREW ENTANGLEMENT: 99.5% SYSTEMS: OK TEMPERATURE: LEVEL 1 ($\pm$ 6C)

#LOG ENTRY 0043640 ID 33452HPE DATE 231744 TYPE ERROR UNRECOGNIZED COMMAND "DED"

#LOG ENTRY 0043641 ID 33452HPE DATE 231744 TYPE ERROR UNRECOGNIZED COMMAND "BORE"

#LOG ENTRY 0043635 ID 33452HPE DATE 233902 TYPE WARNING ENGINE 4 NON ENTANGLED

#LOG ENTRY 0043636 ID 33452HPE DATE 233902 TYPE WARNING ENGINE 5 NON ENTANGLED

#LOG ENTRY 0043637 ID 33452HPE DATE 233902 TYPE NOTIFICATION ENGINE 3 +3% CORRECTION

#LOG ENTRY 0043638 ID 33452HPE DATE 233902 TYPE NOTIFICATION ENGINE 8 +3% CORRECTION

#LOG ENTRY 0043639 ID 33452HPE DATE 233902 TYPE STATUS TIME IN TRANSIT: 10.75 CREW ENTANGLEMENT: 99.4% SYSTEMS: OK TEMPERATURE: LEVEL 1 ($\pm$ 8C)

#LOG ENTRY 0043640 ID 33452HPE DATE 233902 TYPE ERROR UNRECOGNIZED COMMAND "DUCK"

#LOG ENTRY 0112545 ID 33452HPE DATE 239368 TYPE CRITICAL ENGINE 8 POWER LOSS

#LOG ENTRY 0112542 ID 33452HPE DATE 239368 TYPE WARNING ENGINE 3 NON ENTANGLED

#LOG ENTRY 0112543 ID 33452HPE DATE 239368 TYPE WARNING ENGINE 4 NON ENTANGLED
#LOG ENTRY 0112544 ID 33452HPE DATE 239368 TYPE WARNING ENGINE 5 NON ENTANGLED
#LOG ENTRY 0112546 ID 33452HPE DATE 239368 TYPE NOTIFICATION ENGINE 17 +3% CORRECTION
#LOG ENTRY 0112547 ID 33452HPE DATE 239368 TYPE NOTIFICATION ENGINE 2 +5% CORRECTION
#LOG ENTRY 0112548 ID 33452HPE DATE 239368 TYPE STATUS TIME IN TRANSIT: 24.42 CREW ENTANGLEMENT: 99.1% SYSTEMS: OK TEMPERATURE: LEVEL 1 (± 8C)
#LOG ENTRY 0112549 ID 33452HPE DATE 239368 TYPE ERROR UNRECOGNIZED COMMAND "TERN"
#LOG ENTRY 0112550 ID 33452HPE DATE 239368 TYPE ERROR UNRECOGNIZED COMMAND "TURN"
LOG ENTRY 0112551 ID 33452HPE DATE 239368 TYPE ERROR UNRECOGNIZED COMMAND "STAR"

#LOG ENTRY 0255437 ID 33452HPE DATE 267892 TYPE CRITICAL ENGINE 3 POWER LOSS
#LOG ENTRY 0255438 ID 33452HPE DATE 267892 TYPE CRITICAL ENGINE 8 POWER LOSS
#LOG ENTRY 0255439 ID 33452HPE DATE 267892 TYPE WARNING ENGINE 4 NON ENTANGLED
#LOG ENTRY 0255440 ID 33452HPE DATE 267892 TYPE WARNING ENGINE 5 NON ENTANGLED
#LOG ENTRY 0255441 ID 33452HPE DATE 267892 TYPE NOTIFICATION ENGINE 2 +15% CORRECTION
#LOG ENTRY 0255442 ID 33452HPE DATE 267892 TYPE NOTIFICATION ENGINE 17 +15% CORRECTION

#LOG ENTRY 0255443 ID 33452HPE DATE 267892 TYPE
NOTIFICATION ENGINE 24 +15% CORRECTION
#LOG ENTRY 0255444 ID 33452HPE DATE 267892 TYPE
STATUS TIME IN TRANSIT: 95.73 CREW ENTANGLEMENT:
99.0% SYSTEMS: ALERT TEMPERATURE: LEVEL 2 (± 46C)
#LOG ENTRY 0255445 ID 33452HPE DATE 267892 TYPE
ERROR UNRECOGNIZED COMMAND "CREW"
LOG ENTRY 0255446 ID 33452HPE DATE 267892 TYPE
ERROR UNRECOGNIZED COMMAND "FITE"

#LOG ENTRY 1163822 ID 33452HPE DATE 326637 TYPE
CRITICAL COLLISION PROXIMITY
#LOG ENTRY 1163823 ID 33452HPE DATE 326637 TYPE
CRITICAL TEMPERATURE EXCEEDS THRESHOLD
#LOG ENTRY 1163824 ID 33452HPE DATE 326637 TYPE
ERROR UNRECOGNIZED COMMAND "DED"
LOG ENTRY 1163825 ID 33452HPE DATE 326637 TYPE
ERROR UNRECOGNIZED COMMAND "SUX"

T is for Transference

Amanda C. Davis

TO DO: PANDEMIC LOCKDOWN, DAY ONE
- Set up work-from-home station
- Set up online grocery orders
- Buy supplies online (masks/sanitizer/toilet paper)
- Learn to Zoom?
- Text Rachel
- Start menu planning (healthy)
- Take walks every day

DAY FIVE
- Work project 20-123
- Reply to Rachel
- Start menu planning
- Learn to Zoom?

DAY TEN
- Work projects 20-123 and 20-125
- Reply to Rachel

- Learn to Zoom?
- Repair pants

DAY FIFTEEN
- Finish work project 20-123
- Work projects 20-125, 20-130, 20-133
- Reply to Rachel
- Learn to Zoom .
- Fix pants
- Eat a vegetable
- Start walking for real

DAY TWENTY
- Finish work projects 20-123, 20-125
- Start work projects 20-130, 20-133, 20-139, 20-140
- Take a shower sometime
- Refill meds

DAY TWENTY- FIVE
- FINISH PROJECT 20-123 OR ELSE
- Reply to Rachel
- Give up, turn pants into shorts
- Refill meds

DAY THIRTY
- 20-123
- 20-125
- 20-130
- 20-133
- 20-139
- 20-140
- 20-148
- 20-149

- Meds
- Pants -> shorts

DAY FORTY-TWO
- File for unemployment
- Figure out health care—COBRA? ACA? Because pandemic :(
- Refill meds (???)
- Cancel weekly groceries
- Update resume
- Cry forever
- Shower?
- Uninstall Zoom

DAY FIFTY
- Health care??
- Cancel subscriptions (all)
- Buy ramen online
- Refill meds, somehow, lololol
- Update resume
- Reply to Rachel

DAY SIXTY
- Stop crying every day!!
- Call someone about health care!!
- Eat better!!
- Start taking walks!!
- Stop food/booze/caffeine before bed
- Get!! Meds!!

DAY SIXTY-FIVE
- STOP having dreams about COLLEGE, you have GRADUATED
- Especially the ones where you've never been to class and it's finals week

- YOU NEVER DID THAT
- YOU HAVE A DEGREE
- File for unemployment
- Throw away those pants

DAY SEVENTY
- What if I just stopped?
- I mean like everything.

DAY SEVENTY- FIVE
- Resume food/booze/caffeine before bed because nothing matters (:

DAY EIGHTY
- Call?? Someone???

DAY EIGHTY- FIVE
- Eat
- Sleep?
- Call about something?
- Why?
- Think about stopping everything

DAY EIGHTY- EIGHT
- Food/booze/caffeine
- Walk? Lol
- Sleep??
- Stop everything?

DAY NINETY
- Stop?

DAY NINETY-FOUR
- Stop.
- Sleep.

NIGHT
- Like being chilly without nerves
- Like being in the dark without eyes
- Visions like dreams

NIGHT
- Get to finals
- BS through essay? Never went to class :(
- Where is dorm

NIGHT
- Where is class??

NIGHT
- Up stairs (never ending)
- Down elementary school hallway
- Wrong room
- Wrong shower
- Showering anyway, flooding out the door
- Shower is now in grandparents' old house
- They're upstairs and alive right now
- Don't run upstairs to see their faces again
- Run out the door
- Late for finals

NIGHT
- Wake
- Up

DAY ???
- File for unemployment
- Work project 20-123
- Pass finals
- Pants?
- Sleep?
- No sleep
- Walk
- Call about meds
- Find class
- Make lists
- Walk
- Work projects 20-140, 21-780, 50-12, 7-83, A-20, Z-0-Z?
- Find dorm
- Buy food
- Walk
- Reply to Rachel
- Update resume
- Visit grandparents
- Finish things on list
- Finish everything
- Walk
- Walk
- Walk

U is for Unfinished

Lilah Wild

It started when the first stake pierced the ground. The iron was filthy, streaked with the soil of fifty other counties, sticky from soda spills. It crept into the earth with every smack of the mallet, planting down promises of cotton candy and carousel horses. Innocence and wonder, if you didn't wander too far in.

Down beneath the grass, sugar met ash.Forty years was enough time for a town to forget. Forty years would sweep the high schools clean of local legends, tragic hauntings. The wandering toddlers struck on back roads, the suicides hanging from hundred-year oaks, the crosses of their roadside memorials swept away. The next generation of death settled over, and the next. And there was no one left to talk about the fire.

Ash met sugar, and remembered.

She was a creature of sparkle and feathered hair, her eyeshadow the same shade of blue as her platform heels. But inside, she felt anything but glamorous. She was exhausted from a night of back-to-back performances and she wanted nothing more than to step off this stage, undo her ankle straps, and walk out back for a long, solitary smoke.

The pressure was on to reveal more, do more. Allow more. The barker hustled harder and the Led Zeppelin got louder. The men came forward with crumpled dollars, and her smile was pasted on as bits of her costume came off. Fingers—tongues—not tonight. It would mean less money, but not tonight, not after the pictures her bunkmate had shown her earlier today. Onstage, she barricaded herself behind a powder puff the size of a dinner plate.

She'd entered the business a cheerful kid, proud to show off her spangled bikini, a budding sex goddess eager to please. Night after night of hands, eyes, so ravenous, more than she could ever satisfy... there were only so many nights you could fake a smile before the rictus turned real.

She'd been goofing with the other dancers in the afternoon, playing around backstage with some giant feathers and an instant camera. Her laughter died when she saw the polaroids fanned across her dressing table: new lines etched around her vamp-red mouth, the constant road-life fatigue carving new hollows beneath her eyes. Only two years working the bally... the images looked more like she'd aged ten.

She grabbed her radio and smokes, lifted the tent flap and walked into the woods, towards the stream she'd discovered when the tents were going up. The bouncer insisted she take a man's jacket to wrap herself up and hide from the weirdos. If she was lucky, she'd catch David Bowie on the rock station. Only the Spiders from Mars could be good company right now.

Time to get out, she'd decided, as she watched the midday sun glimmer on the water. Time to go. She'd always wanted to head west. Now, it seemed imperative, a pilgrimage to the holy land of the left coast where she could purify herself with meditation and wheat germ, enlighten her soul with California sunshine. Heal. Yes.

Later, a dollar came towards her, and she handed over the puff, arched her back. Hands that could poke and twist and slap were tamed through the loving touch of the puff. Trucker caps, leather-elbowed blazers, scuffed All-Stars, all kinds, her patrons, and she invited them to shower her bare skin with shimmering powder. The puff was her friend, her protector, and also her weapon when needed. Earlier this evening, a customer had gotten too handsy, grabbed something that wasn't for sale. She beamed her most saccharine smile, scooped her puff through its box, and brought a dazzling cloud down on top of his head. The men around him had burst into laughter.

"Everybody's gonna know where you've been, buddy, ha ha!"

He locked eyes with her for one hot second before he stomped off, trying to brush the white glitter from his lapels and just making it worse.

Another dollar emerged, and another, and another. She lost track of time, and somewhere within the catcalls, as the puff danced across her backside, she rolled to her side to change the view, and suddenly she saw bright orange.

Shouts, and running. The crowd of admirers turned and stampeded out of the tent. Girls were crawling away as flames licked across the stage. She tried to get up on her heels, but a hand suddenly grabbed her leg and pulled her right back down.

The wind knocked from her body, she managed to flip herself over and she found herself staring up at a sparkling white face.

"Bitch! You'll get what's coming to you."

He jumped onstage and brought both feet down on her ankle. She could barely hear herself scream over the roar of the flames. The canvas was disappearing into a world of red and there was nobody here, and nobody coming—nobody at all to make sure she was safe. She looked around the stage and saw her puff sizzle and blacken.

His foot came down and pinned her on her back. She looked into his eyes and recognized her enemy: the strip-club shadow with the knife, the hotel-room creep with the gun, the boogeyman of bad girls everywhere was here and now and ready to fill tomorrow's newspaper with an inch or two of murdered coochie girl.

Her next life, the new life out west, was melting. The pain in her bones was agonizing, and the blaze blinded her with smoke. Behind him, the canvas doorways rippled, his escape out into the night. Tears streamed from her eyes.

One swift push of his foot sent her over the edge of the stage, down into the charred fairground grass, into the heart of the fire.

The last of the iron stakes had been hammered into place. Through the haze of powdered sugar and game buzzers, the carnival came to life.

The nighttime twinkle was still lit up by neon bulbs, but the rainbow glow of LED was slowly encroaching on the vintage lights. Rock'n'roll had rambled on long ago, goosed away by electronic dance music. Beside the spinning wheels, the prizes of glittery unicorn mirrors had given way to fake Coach bags. The classics remained, though: the Tilt-a-Whirl and the Scrambler and a creaky little Ferris wheel, stalwart machines that hadn't yet had their leather-padded teeth ripped out and upcycled into seats for trendy bars.

Sitting in the back of the fairgrounds, where the more mature pleasures lurked, was a haunted house.

The Dark Castle had been slapped together out of pure schlock, the most amount of thrill for the least amount of budget. The butcher knife of a serial killer here, a guillotine from the French Revolution there—the hell with thematic consistency, whatever burnt, stabbed, crushed, sliced, or annihilated a life in the most violent and dramatic (and cheap) way possible, was good enough for the Castle.

Intertwined with these instruments of death, women. Within the labyrinth of rubber terrors, the demented shriek of the pipe organ soundtrack, the rooms were full of girls about to get it. A dungeon featured a female mannequin in a black negligee, roped to a table, her belly trapped beneath the red-tipped tines of a buzzsaw. She'd come from a DVD store that had replaced her with a newer model, one with an enormous bustline. Behind her, another mannequin was cuffed to the back wall, clad in a white lace bikini. She'd come from the same adult novelties store and she still wore the same outfit they'd thrown her out in.

Down the corridor, in the room before this one, a third girl was lashed to a post, witch-hunting flames painted on the walls around her. Red stains suggested seared knees, and her gauzy dress had been ripped down to reveal one smudged breast, the spice of implied nudity. She'd been plucked from the dumpster of a high-end boutique, her eye makeup too outdated for displaying the latest fine fashions. Nearby, a female torso hung from the ceiling, strung in chains.

From the cars of the darkride, the customers saw only what the Dark Castle wanted them to see. Beams of light cut through the dusty gloom to a pair of rosy lips or a splash of blood, the murk disguising a multitude of b-movie glue-gun sins. The faces of the girls roasted beneath the lights, fair maidens so much more beautiful when frozen in the amber of imminent gore.

Suddenly, the ride stopped. The electronics had been acting funny all day. Maybe it was the usual first-day kinks still working their way out of the system, maybe it was the temper of a recently exhumed spirit that had been crackling in the air, like flashes of lightning across a hot black sky.

A loudspeaker broke into the organ music, commanding the riders to stay inside their cars while the problem was being fixed.

"Fuck that, man."

Two pairs of grungy loafers stepped up into the dungeon's plywood panorama. In long shorts and popped collars they came, hands callused from mashing fighter buttons, mouths soured with cheap beer.

"No shit. Least now I'm gettin' my eight bucks' worth outta this dump," said the one in gray, running his fingers through a buzzcut.

"Tracy. Trac*eeeeeee*," said the other, all muscle and oversized stripes, heading right for the girl beneath the buzzsaw.

"Yeah, she *does* look like Tracy, all that black hair. Whatever happened to her?" asked Gray.

"I called her by another girl's name."

"Harsh."

"Naw, I did it on purpose. 'Taylor, oh yeah that's right, Taylor,' and she tried to get away but I wouldn't let her go, she tried to fight me and I just kept going. It was fucking *great*." Stripes came up to the table, ran a hand up the mannequin's bare thigh.

"That's why I got all those bracelets in my room, all that goth shit with the rings and the leather," said Gray. "So they can't get away."

They snickered, and Stripes stared down at the girl about to be bisected. He rested his hand at the top of the blade as he brought his face down to hers.

The Dark Castle had been slapped together out of pure schlock, and nobody had bothered to sand down the buzzsaw's edges for safety.

He nicked his fingers and quickly drew his hand back—but not before a drop of blood fell and struck the mannequin's collarbone. The tension that had been simmering in the air all day finally burst.

Slow, at first, just the quiet rise and fall of her first breath. Her painted eyes began to moisten. Long, thick hair coiled out of her scalp, knocking her cheap brunette wig to the ground. Plastic took on the sheen of cool flesh, and long, sharp nails slid forth from the tips of her slender fingers.

Within her pretty head, the dungeon came into focus. Her vision resolved into a bloody blade hovering above her, right where her murderer's foot had been. Her murderer. A face glowered down at her, a sneer etched into the curve of his mouth.

He's going to kill me—

The fake ropes slipped easily from her arms as she knocked the sinister prop to the side, grabbed Stripes by the back of the head and sank her teeth into his left eye.

Too shocked to scream, Gray fell backwards as the blood hit his face. He tried to climb over the stalled car but snapped something in his leg and kept going anyway, winced down onto the service path beside the track and limped into the room up ahead.

The Buzzsaw Girl tore her teeth from Stripes' face, a thread of crimson swinging from her jaws. She rose up from the table and threw him to the floor.

You took my life away, as she rose to her full height, six terrifying feet, and stepped down from the dungeon. *You took it all away*, as she climbed across the stopped car and pursued her prey into the next chamber of horrors.

Strobe lights diced the darkness, misted by a throat-thickening fog machine. The organ music vanished behind the deafening wail of a siren. There he was, smacking into the next stopped car, empty of other passengers. And he turned and suddenly faced her, a looming silhouette cutting through the veil of lights and fog. The funhouse siren summoned nothing but panic as she reached for him.

Those angry spikes gathered the front of his shirt and pulled hard, back down the service path, up over the car, over Stripes' still-warm body, up to the torture table. The prop ropes turned real around his hands and feet as she knotted his limbs into a tight, painful X.

The pipe organ swelled as she leaned over him. Raised her claws and brought her nails down, dragging them through his chest. His screams rang out through the dungeon as ten deep wounds became twenty, thirty, by sixty it was all shreds of meat. The blood, *intoxicating*. She raised her palms to her face, glorifying in her immense newfound strength. Two smears down her cheeks bestowed the balm of Bathory.

Behind her, the mannequin in the bikini and cuffs started to hum and twitch. Buzzsaw Girl turned around and the twitching picked up. Buzzsaw Girl walked to the back of the room and lifted her dripping hand, and

(a little girl in dirty satin sneakers, trying to shield her pigtailed head from the descent of a whiskey bottle—someone's forgotten daughter, hauled out to the woods to keep adult secrets silent)

realized the carnival fire was not the only time someone had gotten killed out here. Others were waking up.

Soon Bondage Girl was breathing beside her, let down from her cuffs. Her first act upon consciousness was walking over to the table and burying her face in Gray's glistening midsection.

Buzzsaw Girl walked down the service path to the room before and

(a young woman in a black bob and glittering eyelashes, trying to pry red-nailed hands from closing hard around her throat—a new girl-friend on her way to a date, attacked by an angry ex determined to snuff out the bitch who stole her man away)

liberated Burning Girl from her heathen stake.

The torso nearby shook in her chains as the blood drew close, so tantalizing. Her former life had been spent in a fashion school class-room, clothed in fanciful runway dreams. But with no head, no arms or legs, Buzzsaw Girl decided that denial was mercy.

Sated, for now, the three circled together in the center of the dun-geon, let their stories seep through each other. Short lives, all of them, cut down before they'd barely had a chance to live.

The blood of the cruel was sweet on the Girls' skins, getting to live again, even better stolen back from thieves. They flexed their hands, took deep breaths, so simple but so miraculous to sense the grit be-neath their bare feet.

Now, we ride. Buzzsaw Girl's mouth lifted into a grin, and the oth-ers nodded with wet smiles as well.

They squeezed their rail-thin bodies side-by-side into the car. Buzzsaw Girl's hand whistled down and slapped the door, and the track charged back into life. They lurched forward into the click-clack of the fright factory, into the overload of fog and strobelights and whatever else decorated the rooms after theirs.

Gray was left tied to the table, the buzzsaw moved back into place over his body, looking very much like the intense FX handiwork of a darkride with money.

Stripes was strung up on Burning Girl's stake, his ruined face resting in the path of a scalding spotlight, his shorts and boxers pulled down to his ankles.

Whatever tragedy the torso had to share stayed locked inside. Left behind, she quivered in her chains, gradually trembling into stillness.

Three Amazons descended from a giant fanged mouth, the Dark Castle's photo-op exit. They paused to look out across the carnival, scope this unfamiliar terrain.

A beer garden was jammed with people, and trash cans overflowed with plastic cups. A Flying Carpet thrill ride lifted a row of screamers into the air. Megaphoned insults squawked from the Dunk the Bozo tank, where a mark wound up a vicious pitch that smacked harmlessly against the canvas. Amplified laughter boomed from the tank as he walked off in a huff of profanities.

Further away, half-hidden behind the trailers of hot pretzels and chocolate fudge, the carousel of the G-rated section was as glittering and distant as heaven.

Buzzsaw Girl looked down at her hands, her thighs. Not plastic beneath the crimson splatters, but true human flesh, as real as any woman walking around the fairgrounds. Nobody knew who they were, or what they'd just done.

She looked up, and vengeance melted beneath the sudden warm light of wonder as she gazed around. Scrolling lights within the windows of the food trailers spelled out ICE CREAM! CHURROS! FRIED OREOS! (Fried Oreos?!) Strange electronic music. People holding tiny, flat television sets. *Everywhere.*

She'd somehow made it to the world of Ziggy Stardust! Shit, this was better than going west! This was—

"Are you in a show? Are you all cosplaying?"

A guy ran up and threw his arm around her. Sunglasses, bluejeans, all smiles.

"Take my picture with her! And her! They're from the Castle!" he said, grabbing Bondage Girl.

His friend held up a television set that flashed. A few more people drifted over, held up similar devices which she guessed were capturing their cheap lingerie, the fake blood. The real blood.

Television-cameras, small enough to fit in the palm of your hand. The future, all right, but the way this guy was hanging on, the way his friends were squeezing in to join him, *some things never fucking change.*

"Dude, I don't think the Castle has live actors. Lady, are you okay?" A guy with goggles pushed atop his head tried to step in, but got jostled aside quickly.

"Man, she's fine."

"Yeah, all of them are fiiiiiiiiiine."

Buzzsaw Girl tried to back away but two of them were forcing her towards a camera. Burning Girl was struggling with someone commanding her to smile. He ignored her elbows, laughing as Burning Girl tried to pull away and her long nails accidentally sliced the side of his face.

"Hey! Hey, what the fuck!" Hand clapped to his cheek. "I can sue you for that! Bitch!"

Hands descended, circled Buzzsaw Girl's wrists. No. No. All she wanted was to wander in the lights, and some creep was trying to hold her down. Again.

Buzzsaw Girl lashed out, easily breaking Sunglasses Guy's grip. The men refused to back away, tried to duck their razor fingers and lost. Blood dampened the Girls' fine-boned faces, energized their flesh with another incredible rush—wounding hands that had hurled bottles, mouths that had screamed slurs, jeering flesh torn open and gushing sublime malevolence. The battle was being recorded from at least three different cameras and that stopped once Bondage Girl smashed a television set to pieces. Three bodies lay crumpled on the ground, and that was when people started to run away.

A security guard barked into a walkie-talkie and pointed in their direction. The Girls scattered as hysteria sparked a mass exodus towards the parking lot.

Buzzsaw Girl vaulted over the railing of the Flying Carpet. The ride operator had run off, leaving a teenage couple trapped in their seats by the T-bars. They sat side by side, both wriggling to get out from behind the safety guards, and went still as she came near.

The boy—the boy, musk and sweat and his father's cologne. An old scent, familiar, thick in the tent when dollar bills rained down on her body. But the way he hung on to his girlfriend's hand, laced so tight but shaking, holding the Girl's gaze, he was determined not to let the fear slip out from behind his puppydog bravado.

And her... an airbrushed heart on a pink hooded sweatshirt. Huge shining eyes. The Girl leaned down and inhaled an essence that went straight to her memories. Not the Eau de Love she sprayed on before a show, not the pot she smoked afterwards. This was the stream in the woods... the clean, soothing place a scratched-up coochie girl could have a few calm moments to herself before a hard night on the bally. She leaned closer, craved the bubbling brook of girl-thoughts that had never been soured by an ugly touch. How would it taste, a bite of that birthday-cake life, sweet and soft like an angel-food pillow—

Behind her, another Girl screamed.

Buzzsaw Girl whipped around and spotted a small cluster of angry townies brandishing guns. Weapons were never far away in towns like these, and they were why the carnies in her crew had tended to stick to their trailers, rarely venturing into the places they visited.

They'd surrounded Bondage Girl. The hunger for honor burned in their eyes.

"We can take care of this before the cops get here," said a girl in a camo bra.

"No, you can't," scoffed the Bozo from his megaphone.

Bondage Girl tried to push through the circle but was stopped by a wall of gym-toned biceps. Snarling, she flexed her fingertips and tried to slash through, sending her captors howling and falling, and broke away into a run. Three long strides until a bullet struck her shoulder.

More bullets hit her, piercing her back, her thighs. A cloud formed around her body as it shattered, like the snap of a magician's fingers before disappearing into a puff of white. Horrified, Buzzsaw Girl watched Bondage Girl crumble into the air and float away. Back into ash.

"Dude... where'd she *go*?"

"Dunno, but..." A shirtless guy with a foxtail clipped to his belt held up a scrap of her white lace bikini.

Right behind Buzzsaw Girl, the girl in the pink sweatshirt screamed.

"Here! Over here! *Help us*!"

The guns swiveled towards the Flying Carpet and Buzzsaw Girl dove behind the operator booth. Bullets riddled the couple, and their bodies fell limp beneath the T-bars. Crimson streamed from the air-brushed heart.

A few drops of the girl's blood had landed on Buzzsaw Girl's shoulder. The burst of sugar she'd been anticipating, didn't feel like anything at all. There was nothing to savor... because these kids hadn't stolen anything.

Innocents.

"You should really stop before you hurt somebody, *heroes.*" The Bozo was standing on top of his tank like some kind of demented sportscaster.

The Girls were fast on their long, supernatural legs, racing into the kiddie section. The calliope chimed and the air was fragrant with candy but the people had vanished, leaving behind the cheeriest ghost town ever.

Where to run, where to hide... the stream. There was nowhere else she knew of to go.

She slipped between two tents and motioned to Burning Girl. *Come, come with me,* but another small band of guns emerged from behind a pizza stand and spotted Burning Girl. A second pack that had been signaled by the first pack, a similar group of baseball caps and hunting gear.

Burning Girl stepped back. Her eyes darted around for an escape. The setting sun picked up the metallic paint of tiny cars and made them glitter. A circle of friendly dragons rested their wings around a motorized castle. The calliope sang on like it was still a beautiful day.

Backing away, her frightened gaze went everywhere except right behind her. Her heel slammed into the metal tub of the duck pond and backwards she tumbled into the water. The shooters came closer, and they watched as her body began to effervesce. Her eyes stayed open as the water bubbled, and she disintegrated—her face breaking up first, then her arms, spreading down her torso. Within seconds, there was nothing left but her dress, a tattered rag floating among the tiny yellow ducks.

"What the... what the *fuck?*" The pack stood around the tub and peered in, murmuring in amazement to each other, while Buzzsaw Girl dashed away. Silent, and fast, she headed for the trees behind the Castle.

Can't catch me!

The Bozo, from his elevated perch, spotted her breaking for the woods and called out to the mob that had shot down Bondage Girl.

"What are you idiots waiting for? She's over there! Go get her!"

Into the woods, into her memories: radio in hand, rolling the heat of a fresh menthol around in her mouth. The noise of the carnival fading behind her, hood pulled down to obscure her face.

Strange men are following me, all right.

Up ahead, a shimmer. The water! As she ran closer, she saw that the stream had widened, bigger than she remembered. She halted at the edge. Jumping over was impossible—even with her long-legged stride, she wouldn't make it. She'd fall right in and go out just like Burning Girl.

She flashed back to what she'd seen in her brief moments of freedom. A teenage girl's hair, pink as bubblegum. The strange beats that thumped out of the park's speakers, those tiny television sets all over the place... the world had gone on after she'd died, and she'd gotten only a glimpse. *No!* There had to be a way, somewhere to hide in the woods and wait them out—

A bullet sliced the water.

"Stop right there." The Bozo, through his megaphone.

She turned around to face a clutch of guns coming towards her, three of them.

The bullet with her name on it clicked into position, loud, ready.

"No, no," said the Bozo, dropping his megaphone, his voice dripping with contempt. "Let's not rush."

He raised a pistol towards her face.

"I've got her covered."

He stood back while the other two holstered their guns and walked up to her, hands at their belts. Mustaches, jeans, sunglasses—they all blurred together, united into the ethos of Eat It, Fuck It, or Kill It. She shivered in her thin negligee. Absolution glinted behind her.

It would be so easy to just let go, and crumble away. Nothing to mark her time on earth but a filthy nightgown. She lifted her arms and closed her eyes, poised herself to fall back into the cleansing stream. It wasn't California, but it would do. Time to go.

She heard gunshots and felt something wet hit her cheek. She opened her eyes, as the dazzling blood-rush came on again.

The Bozo stood motionless, his pistol smoking. Before her, the two men had collapsed to the ground, their heads oozing red into the dirt.

"God, how easy it is to rile them up. I've been itching to do that *forever.*"

Stunned, she watched as the Bozo peeled off his rubber cap of thinning red hair. Not another agonized spirit come back from the dead, no—just a guy.

"Sorry for egging them on after you, but it was the only way to get them out here. Usually it's just a bunch of posturing, all tough, y'know, but every night, someone's seriously trying to drown me in that tank—that's why I pack." He holstered his gun. "In case some wise guy wants to follow me when the night's over. I've had more than one scrape just trying to get back to my car."

She watched as he shucked off his costume. Someone else from the same side of the midway curtain, who had to watch out for the weirdos.

"These two shot your friend from the haunt, and they killed those kids, too."

He kneeled on the ground, pulled a jacket off one of the bodies.

"Here—you must be freezing in that costume. This asshole won't need it anymore."

He didn't know she wasn't human, not truly. Or that she'd left a couple of very real corpses behind in the Dark Castle. Absolution, after all.

He handed her a zippered sweatshirt. Warm and sticky on her shoulders, absolute ecstasy inside, from the most exquisite blood of all—the blood that had been ready to take her life.

"Let's get out of here."

A hand was leading her to the rippling doorway out of the flames, out of the firestorm of flashing lights that had descended on the parking lot.

They ran towards the employee grounds. He unlocked a battered pickup and she leapt up into the cab. She gazed out over the few cars left—how ugly, shiny and hunched, not the smooth cool land yachts she remembered—and looked to the highway beyond. More red and blue lights flickered in the distance, all of them still far enough away to hit the gas and disappear.

He turned out onto a back road. His wheels were old but his stereo was pristine, and he thumbed his way onto a rock station, Iggy and the Stooges. He offered her a cigarette, and her breath lit up a tiny red glow in the dark.

Ashes met ashes, and exulted.

Enormous teddy bears, lions, snakes hanging above the midway lanes, the top-shelf odds so long. And yet, every so often, someone won. Right now she'd scored a free ticket to a second ride, a chance to enlighten herself way beyond juice fasts and chanting affirmations, for however long it would last.

California—what would it look like *now*...

She exhaled a long plume of luxuriant smoke and stared out the window. There was no one left to talk about the fire, but all around them, as she watched the lights coming on in the houses, texts and chats and blogs were thrumming with new rumors, new legends.

She gazed up at the telephone poles threading the sky, and snuggled into her bloodstained hoodie, and Powderpuff Girl headed west after all.

V is for Verve

Rachel M. Thompson

This is not the story of how I died. Nobody wants to hear that story. Rusted boring, it is. Face down in a slimy gutter, throat slit by that little weasel Dren for the handful of silvers and the two watches in my pockets. Stole my whole night's take, meant to pay off our boss Jaren Bidderk. Sad, it was. Just sad. No, this is not *that* story.

This is the story of what I did *after*.

"After Dren did for me, everything went all peculiar, like a nightmare. So when the air in the alley tore open I didn't pay it much attention until the Thing crawled out. It was terrible, all mouth and too many eyes. It went straight at Dren and wrapped its claws around his throat. The noises when it latched onto his face were ruddy obscene." I shrugged. "I suppose I shouldn't be happy that the Thing did for Dren, but it gives me a mite o' satisfaction that the little git won't be making use of *my* silver."

The posh lady sitting across the table—Liza, she'd introduced her-self—made a little noise in her throat like she'd choked. Her man shot her a look I couldn't read and shook his head. Her face smoothed over as she said, "Go on. Do you remember any other details? Anything about the creature or what happened next?"

Shaking my head at the strangeness of the rich, I was immediately distracted by the unfamiliar feel of curls bouncing around my face. "Rot it. This is too bleedin' weird." The room around us was distract-ing, too. It was barely big enough for the small round table and three chairs. Dark blue curtains draped from the ceiling and across the walls made me feel like I was about to be smothered in blankets.

Liza offered a thin smile. "Try to focus, Wils. I'm not sure how long Aunt Clara can keep channeling for you."

"Right, sorry. Don't recall much else about the Thing. It was dark, and all the colors are sort of washed out and splotchy when you're...dead." Saying the word sent a shiver up me, so I hurried on. "There was a sort of flash of something pale, misty-like, around Dren's face. Then the Thing dropped him and went back through the rip. That was it. You lot showed up about the time I realized Dren wasn't gonna get up—not in his body nor out of it, like me." I wasn't sure about the next part. It gave me the collywobbles near as bad as the Thing. "Then you did...whatever you did to the rip, to make it go away." I'd watched her cut herself and pull the blood out solid as you please to stitch up that rip in the air, like it was no more trouble than mending a shirt. Ma always told us to stay away from magickers that mucked about with blood, on account of them being either cracked or wicked, but this lady didn't seem to be either. "Then your man there called the lockies."

Liza nodded. "Calling the lawkeepers seemed the thing to do when faced with two dead bodies. Though I'm very glad now that Vash—Mr. Drake—had the forethought to retrieve a lock of your hair for Aunt Clara."

I looked down at the two locks of hair resting on the table in front of me. That was why I'd followed the posh couple in the first place, to see what they wanted with my and Dren's hair. I touched mine with the unfamiliar hand I currently controlled. It was a large, strong hand, but clean and feminine and clearly not mine. Looking at it made me a little ill.

"Thank you, Wils. I need to speak to Aunt Clara, if you don't mind?" Liza's voice was polite enough, but I've dealt with enough toffs to know she wasn't asking.

"How do I—" There was a wrenching sensation, like somebody grabbed me around the middle and yanked me sharply to the side. The small room with its heavy draperies and dim lamps resumed the faded, streaky appearance I remembered from the alley. Except Drake, who still looked sharp and solid. That seemed…wrong.

The big, matronly blonde woman in the chair patted at her curls and took a couple deep breaths. "He's a strong one, young Wils. Might have had a touch of the Gift in life." She seemed to be the only one who could see or hear me. "Were you uncommonly lucky, lad?"

"Not at the end." I wasn't normally a grouser but being dead put a damper on my mood.

She laughed like I'd said something really funny. "No, I suppose not." Her focus shifted to Liza. "Do you recognize the creature? If it came through a Breach, I assume the Church will be after you to contain it?"

"That's what I wanted to discuss with you." The younger lady fidgeted with the hem of her sleeve, rubbing at a spot where a drop of her blood marked the fabric. "I can't take young Wils here to the Church to help me research, as they'd exorcise him straight away, but it doesn't sound like any of the Aetherlings that tend to cross over on their own."

"Something sent, you think?" The gentleman, Drake, spoke for the first time since we'd arrived in Clara's shop. He scared me a little.

More so than either of the ladies, even though they were both magickers.

"Or something called." Clara rose, weaving neatly between the chairs to exit the room. She was back within minutes with the biggest book I'd ever seen, the leather cover worn shiny with age and handling. "The flash of mist Wils described reminded me of something. Look here." She placed the open book on the table and tapped an illustration.

The other two leaned over to get a better look. Liza spoke first. "A soul eater? Well, doesn't *that* sound delightful."

It didn't, actually.

"Not particularly, no." Drake turned his head in my direction even as he echoed my thoughts. I could tell by the vagueness of his gaze that he couldn't *see* me, not really, but he always seemed to know roughly where I was. "If it eats souls, why didn't it take Wils here?"

I looked at Clara, who shook her head. "If you would read a little further, Mr. Drake, you might notice that the soul eater only feeds on the living. Departed souls are of no interest to it."

Lucky me. "So what happened to Dren, then?"

"Consumed, I'm afraid. There's no summoning back a spirit destroyed that way." Clara waved away the questioning looks from the other two. "The question is why would someone want to destroy souls this way? And why a no-account streetie like this Dren?"

Liza tapped the page, having continued reading the old book. "I think you've got the wrong end of it. This suggests that the soul eater could be summoned to destroy one's enemies, but only for a price. Its favored prey are 'creatures of Aethereal nature, or those of Gifted blood.' I suppose it makes sense for a creature of the Aetherwild to feed on magic."

"So you think the thing was summoned as a sort of assassin, and the boy was its reward for a job well done?" Clara still sounded skeptical.

"Gifted blood? Magickers?" If I'd still had a heart, I'm sure it would have been pounding. "Four magickers gone missin' in the past three weeks. Ol' Dotty Beggley, who tells fortunes at Bayside Market, Granny Keeling in Westenham, and Stickels the herb-man in the Sprawl."

"That's only three," Clara prompted.

I hesitated. It was stupid, since the crews couldn't kill me for revealing their secrets anymore. "The last one was Walten Quelch, one o' Murderous Murdo's crew down in Bayside. Word was, he was strong enough to make people see what wasn't there. Kept his boss from getting nicked by the lockies."

"What's the lad saying, Aunt Clara?" Liza watched the medium curiously, never glancing my way. She was deaf and blind to me. Even waving my hands through her got no response, though it left my fingers feeling curiously warm.

"Stop that, Wils, it's rude. He says there have been four Gifted deaths in the lower districts within the past three weeks."

Drake nodded slowly, "That tracks. We've also lost four prominent citizens in the past three weeks. Lord Gambrill on the King's council, two aldermen, and a very influential businessman."

"Why do I suspect that the dates of these deaths would match up?" Liza pushed her chair back and stood. "We need to stop the person summoning this thing."

Drake put a hand on her arm. "We need to determine their identity first."

I kept mulling things over. Something about this idea still didn't sit right. Finally, it came to me. "Dren wasn't a magicker, though."

Clara looked at me sharply. "You're certain?"

"Positive. Only magicker in Bidderk's crew is Lodie. When the other magickers started dying I decided it was time for us to run. That's why I was workin' by myself so far from the Sprawl. Take's a lot o' money to get out of Westingmot, and more to pay off Bidderk so he'd let her go."

The medium tilted her head, pale eyes locked on me like a bird with a bug in its sights. It looked odd on a woman who otherwise appeared soft and matronly. "Who is this Lodie, Wils?"

Again, I hesitated. It felt wrong to give away information to strangers. But I had no way to rescue Lodie now. Maybe if I helped them stop this soul eater she'd at least be safe. Once I made up my mind, the words came out in a rush. "My little sister. She's twelve. Old enough for a dollymop, Bidderk said, and he's kept us since Ma died so we owe him a lot." My hands balled into fists with remembered anger. "He'd have had her on the street already if she hadn't come up peculiar all of a sudden."

Clara's gaze grew colder, and her lips compressed to a thin line. "Peculiar how?"

"Speaking in this queer deep voice, like a man, and tipping Bidderk and his boys off on where the lockies were going to be. And where they weren't."

She sighed. "That explains everything."

"What explains everything?" Liza fair vibrated in place, still standing next to her chair like she was gonna do a runner any moment.

Clara turned her attention to the younger woman as well. "It sounds very much like the lad's younger sister is a medium, and of course the Gift runs in the blood. That soul eater wasn't after Dren." She looked back at me. "It came for you, but arrived too late."

It took a bit for Clara to explain everything I shared with the other two. I sat down to have a think while they talked it over. I wasn't tired, exactly, but I felt sort of thin. It was worrisome. The more I thought about it, the more worried I got. If I thinned out too much, would I just disappear? Where would I go?

"Wils?" By Clara's tone, this wasn't the first time she'd called. She was seated again.

"Yes, mum? Sorry, mum." I stood up and dusted myself off out of habit, trying to look presentable. I'd lost more time 'thinking' than I realized. There was a tea set on the table now, and Liza was missing, though Drake still sat flipping pages on the heavy old book. I hadn't even noticed anyone leaving the room.

"We're going to need your help, Wils. As I can't go trotting about the Sprawl at my age, we've had to make other arrangements." Clara waved a hand toward the teapot, clarifying nothing. "You'll need to lead Liza and Mr. Drake to your sister."

"What?" Served me right for sitting around thinking. I'd missed something crucial. "I can't lead them into the Warren. And what d'you want with Lodie?"

The medium smiled, but there was still something hard about her eyes. "I will not leave a budding medium in the hands of a street gang. Whether she stays here or we send her into the country to another teacher, little Lodie needs someone to guide her. Buck up, lad! You're getting what you wanted."

There had to be more to it than that. No one gave anything for free. Toffs especially.

My face must have betrayed my doubt, because she nodded slowly. "Good lad. You're clever, as I suspected. We want your help in tracking down the one responsible for these murders, so we can stop this soul eater. As a spirit, you can go places none of us can."

"I can?" Stupid. Obviously I could, since almost no one could see me.

Liza returned, shrugging into a long motoring coat as she walked. "Right, let's get on with this." The lady in the evening dress was gone, replaced by a rather more dangerous creature in trousers, sturdy boots, and a leather waistcoat over a dark shirt. She had a pistol slung at one hip, and some sort of pouch rested on the other.

Clara beckoned her in and poured the tea. She added several carefully measured drops from a tiny blue glass bottle to the cup. "Sugar?"

"Will it help the taste?"

"Not particularly." Clara pushed the cup away and began to pour a second.

Liza pursed her lips but took the proffered cup. She made a horrible face at the first sip, then she slung back the remainder like a shot of whiskey. "That's awful."

"Effective, though." Clara hesitated with the blue bottle raised. "Mr. Drake, I'm honestly not certain how this preparation will interact with your *unique* heritage. It may not work properly."

Drake raised a hand to stop her. "Don't bother, Ms. Sorlie. I can't hear our young friend, but I can sense his location well enough for this. And I can always locate Liza, which is the important thing."

He shot the young lady an ardent look which she utterly ignored, as she was staring at me in bemusement. "I can see you now, Wils. Say something?"

I straightened up automatically. "Hello?"

Liza pulled a flat cap from her coat pocket and tugged it over her hair. "Right. You lead me into the Warren, and we'll get Lodie out. If I can't sneak her out, or negotiate with this Bidderk fellow, Vash will provide a diversion."

"A rescue, if necessary." Drake stood, and suddenly the room felt entirely too small. He was a big man, but somehow he filled up more space than his body accounted for. It hit me then, the wrongness: the women were magickers, but he *was magic*. He offered an arm and a sharp-edged smile to Liza. "Shall we go hunting?"

Her return smile was equally predatory. "We shall."

Familiar as I was with the Sprawl, I was uncomfortable leading Liza and Drake—I didn't dare call him by his given name, even in my own head—into the district. It was one of the oldest in the city, as anyone could see from the narrow winding roads and the weathered, crooked buildings. Most had been built onto wherever there was space, until there wasn't any space anywhere.

People here were poor. There were few lights, and fewer people out at this late hour. Made me twitchy. These two didn't fit in, and there was no crowd to hide them in. I kept to the shadows as much as possible. We finally wound our way to entrance I'd chosen, an abandoned shop with boarded-over windows. I waved Liza to a stop. "This is where we go in. The Warren is…tricky. Bidderk's crew changes things to keep the lockies and other crews out."

"I expected as much. I plan to mark our path." She kept her voice low, and her eyes kept moving, watching the shadows around us.

I never would have betrayed the crew that way in life, but what more could they do to me now? As long as these two got Lodie out, I might as well be all in. "Right. Ready?"

"I assume this is where we part ways?" Drake eyed the shop dubiously and turned to Liza. "It will take at least half an hour to roust out the local patrol, so do be cautious."

She stopped scanning the street for a moment to grin at him. "That long? I imagine they'll fall all over themselves to do the bidding of Vashon Drake, son of the head of the privy council."

He sighed and shook his head. "No doubt, but it does take a bit of time to travel to and from the precinct house in this maze."

I stuck my head through the door to the shop. It felt strange, the solid wood forming a cold line through my chest. Not pleasant, but bearable. No one was waiting inside, so I pulled myself back out. "Best to go quick. Seems clear for the moment."

Liza patted Drake's arm in reassuring fashion. "I'll be fine. Just don't waste any time fetching the lawkeepers."

He nodded and turned on his heel, striding off up the street at a good clip. For a wonder, he was even going in the right direction. That was a mite confusing, but this was no time to stand about wondering why a toff knew his way around the Sprawl.

"Come this way." I moved around the corner of the shop, to the tiny crevice that remained of the gap between this building and the next. Liza had to turn sideways to slide through the first few feet. The space opened up again as we approached what had been a side door to the shop. I stuck my head through this one, too, and determined no one was around. "Okay, open it."

She pulled the door open gingerly, but I knew it would open without a sound. What good was a hidden door if it announced itself with squealing hinges when you opened it?

Once inside, I lead her into the back of the shop and through a gap behind a cupboard that gave access to the next shop over. From there we descended into the basement, moving in silence by unspoken accord. We crept from one basement to the next through holes knocked in the walls. Some were abandoned, empty or full of broken furniture and other trash. One held barrels and echoed with footsteps overhead as we crossed under The Broken Lamp, the only tavern in this part of the Sprawl. Every so often, Liza pulled a piece of chalk from her pocket and marked the wall or floor. We passed through an earthen tunnel with broken planks providing a very basic floor, where she had to bend so low she was nearly crawling.

On the other side, everything was touched with rot and damp. These buildings had flooded in a storm years ago, and rather than clean and or rebuild them, the people of the Sprawl built stairs to the untouched upper floors and abandoned everything at ground level and below. This was the Warren in truth, where Bidderk and his gang knocked out or built walls to suit them, and left traps for the unwary. We climbed back up to the ground floor. We went slower now, as I searched for the signs that marked the safe path and pointed out the dangers so Liza could mark them for Drake and the lockies. I tried to keep my mind on Lodie. She was going to be free. That was worth giving up the crew.

"We're close now." It was stupid, but I kept my voice to a whisper. "Close to the bunks. We might be able to get to Lodie unseen."

Liza nodded and bent down to mark the door frame we were about to pass through. "We can hope."

We were in the heart of the Warren. The passages were close, with makeshift walls breaking up the space into small cubbies where the crew bedded down. At this hour, most of the men would be out and about, this being prime bug-hunting time as the drunks emptied out of the taverns. That didn't mean it was empty, though. I could only hope that with her hair covered and clothes smudged and rumpled from clambering through the Warren, Liza might pass at a glance for one of the young toughs who made up the majority of the crew.

She picked her way carefully behind me, slow and almost silent in the dark. Nobody wasted lamps on this area. If you needed a light, you brought it to the bunks with you. I found myself moving faster as we neared the nook Lodie and I had called home these past few years. It was hardly larger than a cupboard, stuffed with a couple of ragged blankets and what little spare clothing the two of us had.

I crouched down and ran my hand through the blankets. It was like plunging them into cold water until suddenly I felt warmth. "Lodie!"

Even startled awake, Lodie was canny enough to stay still. I could just see one of her eyes peeking out from the nest. It widened and she sat up, shedding the blankets. "Wils!" Her face fell as she looked me over. "What happened?"

For a moment I just stared. She could see me! Clara must be right about Lodie being a medium. I held my finger to my lips before she could speak again. "Shh. Later. We need to get out of here. This lady's gonna help, and she has a friend who can teach you. But the lockies are coming."

Liza stepped closer and raised a hand in greeting. "Your brother wants you to be safe, Lodie. Will you come with me?"

Lodie, still wide-eyed, nodded and pushed the blankets out of her way. "Let's go."

We took a different path out, which proved smart when we heard the crash of breaking planks and boots pounding on the other side of one of the barriers. The lockies were making their move on the crew. I moved faster, urging Liza and Lodie to squeeze through the narrow passages and out into an alleyway. From there I kept moving through the twisting lanes and alleys of the Sprawl. I didn't stop until we were well beyond the northern edge of Bidderk's territory.

Liza moved to the mouth of the current alley to get her bearings. "Looks like...Vine Street? We're nearly in Eastgate. Well done, Wils."

I joined her and looked around. Funny thing, I had run north on instinct. "Used to live in Eastgate, before Ma died. Three streets up."

Her sympathetic look pierced me to the heart. "I lost my mother as a child, too. I promise you we'll make sure Lodie is safe."

"Lodie *is* safe," said a hollow, masculine voice that sounded so terribly wrong coming from my sweet sister. I turned, and saw her face twisted into a vicious snarl. "And she's not going anywhere with *you*." There was a bit of chalk in her hand, and she was drawing rapidly on the rough cobbles. By the way Liza patted her pocket and grimaced, Lodie must have nicked it from her on the run.

"Let's calm down, shall we?" Liza's tone was conciliatory, and she moved very slowly toward Lodie with her hands out and open. "I'm not sure who you are, but we all want what's best for Lodie."

A harsh laugh answered her. "I want what's best for *me*. This girl makes an excellent vessel for exacting my revenge, and you will not have her." Lodie's chalk never stopped moving. She had nearly encircled herself with markings.

I drifted closer. I hadn't seen another spirit nearby, but this had to be one. Could I do something to it? Make it leave?

"What revenge?" Liza stopped short of the chalk circle. Not because she wanted to, either. I could see the strain as she tried to move forward.

Lodie pointed with the chalk, the man's voice booming unnaturally from her. "Revenge on those dastards who brought me low and arranged my execution. Not enough to have me removed as alderman, no, Gambrill insisted on the maximum penalty!"

Liza stood very still. "Lord Gambrill of the privy council?"

I moved closer yet, testing the edge of the chalk circle without meeting any resistance.

"Yes! At first I only planned to humiliate Gambrill and the others by enabling this Bidderk idiot to run rampant in the city. But then I realized this girl was capable of so much more." The grin that followed was positively obscene. My hands balled into fists at my sides. I didn't know who this was, but I wanted him away from Lodie.

"You're that Lewkun fellow, aren't you? The one convicted of necromancy." Liza unfastened the pouch that rested at her hip. I was both surprised and relieved that she didn't reach for her pistol.

Lodie—or the thing in Lodie's body—drew herself up proudly. "Erastus Lewkun. Alderman for Beacon Hill for twenty-five years, brought low simply for seeking knowledge." She scowled and pointed at Liza. "You think you're clever, don't you? Not clever enough to stop me." Lewkun chanted some foreign gibberish. The chalk lines started to glow.

Liza wasted no breath on argument. She pulled a black knife from her pouch and stabbed at the barrier between her and Lodie. The blade stuck in the air as if she'd jabbed it into a solid wall.

Behind her, a jagged line tore open in the air between the buildings. A narrow, claw-tipped hand emerged. I had to do something. If she died, no one would take care of Lodie. "Liza, behind you!"

Lewkun turned Lodie's body toward me, surprised. Maybe he'd forgotten I was there. Maybe he hadn't noticed me at all. I didn't give him a chance to react. I launched myself at Lodie, shoving hard to crowd out Lewkun's spirit.

It was like getting into a fist fight inside a full cupboard. I lost track of the alley, disoriented by the struggle to push the other spirit away and get control of Lodie's body. Every time I pushed, there was resistance, and then it just moved around me like water. There was no way out and I couldn't get ahold of my enemy. He'd been doing this a lot longer and I could feel his gloating. I was drowning.

Another presence wrapped around me, a familiar warmth that loaned me strength. Lodie! Together, we gathered up Lewkun's spirit and held him tight.

For a moment I gained control of Lodie's senses, enough to see Liza dancing back from the soul eater as it emerged fully into the alley. The monster reached for her. She raised her hand and blew a handful of powder straight into its gaping maw. It reared away with a horrible shriek as it began to bubble and blister wherever the powder touched.

My control slipped and I lost vision. Holding on to Lewkun's spirit was like wrestling a bag of eels. He was strong and slippery, and even with Lodie's help I wasn't sure how long I could keep him from taking over again.

I could still hear as we struggled for control. A grunt of pain from Liza, harsh breathing, boots on cobbles and the scrabbling of hard claws. The crack of the pistol, deafening in such close quarters. Another shriek. The thud of someone, or something, falling.

I felt Lodie getting weaker. This fight was hurting her. With all the strength I could muster, I imagined wrapping my arms tight around this Lewkun and dragging him back out into the alley.

The world came back to me in bits and pieces: The dark alley getting lighter as dawn came on. Liza reaching for something in her bag of tricks as the soul eater scrambled to its feet, wounds oozing. Lodie beside me, holding her head and gasping for air. Me, with my arms wrapped tight around the ghostly body of a disagreeable old man I'd never seen before. "I got him! Can't hold him long."

"Hang on, Wils. Let me get rid of his pet first." Liza darted to the left and blew more powder at the soul eater. It screamed like a steam whistle and stumbled away, toward the rip in the world. She was driving it back. Herding it back to wherever it came from.

My grip on Lewkun slipped as he struggled and cursed. "Can't hang on!"

"I have him, Wils." Lodie was calm as she turned toward me. She made a gathering motion with her hands, like a woman winding up yarn. Lewkun slipped from my grasp with a wail that grew gradually thinner as Lodie pulled him away, twisting up his spirit into a tight ball. With the angry ghost contained, she ran forward and hurled the ball of spirit-stuff at the soul eater. "Devils take you both!"

The soul eater flinched away as Lewkun's ghost slammed into its oversized maw. Liza kicked it, hard, sending the monster toppling backward to fall through the tear. That black knife was back in her hand, and quick as a wink she nicked her wrist and began stitching up the rip with a white needle and thread made of her own blood. That still gave me the shakes, so I turned away.

Lodie crossed her arms and watched, looking fiercer than I'd ever seen her. "That'll keep 'em out, will it?"

"Should," Liza replied, still stitching. "Unless someone opens the door again."

Lodie thought that over. "Can I do anything to make sure they don't?"

Liza cut her 'thread' and stowed the knife and needle. "Yes, you probably can. I know someone who can teach you, if you'd like."

Lodie let her arms fall to her sides as some of the anger went out of her. She looked back at me. "Can Wils come, too?"

Liza laughed, a surprisingly bright sound from someone who'd looked so grim a moment before. "I wouldn't dream of leaving Wils out." She held out her hand.

Lodie took it with a small smile. We were gonna be all right.

W is for Wronged

M.L.D. Curelas

Wasting disease is what they call it. The nurses cluck as they arrange blankets around the pale husk of my body, composing a peaceful scene for Wilhelm.

Am I dead? I don't feel so, and I can see my body breathing, shallowly and slowly. But death seems not far off, from the downcast expressions of the nurses. I try to explain that I'm *fine*, but they don't see my waves or hear my cries for attention. Frustrated, I pull my mouth into a frightful grimace and shout at them. They don't react.

When they turn for the door, I leap after them, and that is when I discover that my *self*, my spark, has separated from my physical form. Confused, I stare down at my ghostly body, as wispy as a cloud, and then at the bed, where my solid body breathes. The experience is so unnerving that I stay in place, uncertain what I should do. The nurses leave without looking back.

Eventually, Wilhelm arrives and carefully sits at my bedside, clasping one of my husk's hands. He looks tired, eyes rimmed red and bloodshot. I wish to console him, to explain that I'm simply unrooted from my earthly body, but like the nurses, Wilhelm doesn't hear me. My hands pass through his shoulders. He shivers a little and glances toward the window.

My hands. They are transparent, as is, I discover, my entire body. It is horrifying, yet I am relieved that while I can see through myself, I cannot see beneath the skin like Wilhelm's dread machine. Fear fills me at the memory of the invention.

"I am ready, Bertha. Please keep still."

Buzzing. A green glow.

I moan and the walls of my bedroom dissolve into white mist.

When I return to myself, I am not in my bedroom, but Wilhelm's laboratory.

Skinny black bones.

More mist.

I am still in the laboratory. It's very quiet; Wilhelm isn't here. Is he still with my earthly body, in my bedroom? The familiar white mist creeps into my vision, but I focus on my feet. I will not fade out again.

"He's at my bedside," I say, the sound of my voice bolstering my courage. I risk quick glances around the laboratory. The high windows, the heavy blinds drawn aside. The bare wooden floors. The large clock dominating the wall over the many tables crammed with scientific equipment. I try to resist the long table in the middle of the room, but I cannot ignore it.

The machine spreads across the table like mold: the wires, the huge cylindrical electricity generator, and the glass tube hanging from a metal rod. The rod is anchored by a metal box meant for holding photographic plates. A chair sits at the end of the table, close to the plate box and the dangling bulb—the Crookes tube, as Wilhelm calls it.

Despite the color leeching from my vision, I drift to the chair. My hand hovers over the plate box.

"Nothing to worry about, Bertha," Wilhelm said calmly as he adjusted the tear drop-shaped glass tube hanging over her hand. "I've run the experiment several times."

But not with a person, she thought, immediately feeling guilty for doubting him. They'd been married twenty-three years, and Wilhelm was attentive and devoted. They had a daughter. He would never harm her.

"Yes, Wilhelm," she said aloud, her voice squeaking. Her right hand, her free hand, bunched the heavy fabric of her dress. The laboratory was dimly lit, the curtains drawn shut, so Wilhelm could run the experiment properly. She was certain he could not see the tightness of her clenched jaw. All he noticed was the relaxed hand resting on the photographic plate.

I retreat from the table and the equipment it holds. It is pointless to be near the machine and revisit disturbing memories—memories that make me ill. I shouldn't be here. I should be with Wilhelm. He will have sent for Josephine, and I don't want to miss what could be my last sight of my daughter. I turn from the machine and rush to the door. But at the door, I am stopped. My transparent hands cannot grasp the door knob. Yet they are too solid to pass through the door.

"No!" I shout, and pound at the door with my fists. It is utterly silent, the only sound my panicked gulps of air, not quite sobs. "I will not stay here!"

My pleas are unheeded, and after interminable moments, I sink to the floor.

I am trapped with the machine.

Awareness recedes and returns as I sob dryly into my hands. Eventually, my shoulders cease shaking and my sobs fade. With one last shuddering sigh, I raise my head and stare blankly at the door. I can hear faint sounds of household activity. The maids, no doubt, going about their routine.

The distant noise is comforting. I am not alone. Tentatively, I reach out to the door and once again meet with resistance. Alone, yet not alone.

I am here because of that cursed machine. I force myself to stand and glare at the contraption. A sudden flood of anger propels me forward, and I swing a hand at the glass tube.

Ting!

I flinch, startled. I had touched it! My hand falls to my side, and now I am ashamed. The machine is important to Wilhelm. Damaging it would hurt him.

Wilhelm had been so excited about the new discovery. Something unexpected had happened while he was running his cathode ray experiment. A new ray, he'd explained over supper. Invisible light.

He'd asked me to help, since he was testing which substances could and could not block the new rays. I sigh, as the rest of the memory comes back to me.

Wilhelm fiddled with the placement of the Crookes tube again, and she realized he was nervous.

Finally, he said, "I am ready, Bertha. Please keep still."

He smiled a little as he returned to the table. A flip of a lever and the electricity generator hummed to life. A green glow emitted from several items in the laboratory.

After a few seconds, the light faded and the generator's buzz quieted.

Wilhelm lifted her hand from the plate and she let it flop into her lap. He grinned and held up the photographic plate in front of her. "Look, Bertha!"

The glass clearly showed a hand, but not the plump pink appendage that she was familiar with. The glass showed bones. Skinny black bones.

She almost scoffed and teased Wilhelm for creating a fake photograph, but then she noticed the dark band circling one finger. Her wedding ring.

"My death!" she gasped, feeling lightheaded. "This is my death, Wilhelm."

The reminder of what happens to all human beings had unnerved me. Death reduces us to bones and dust. But I'm not dead now, am I? Just . . . sundered. Adrift. My hands run over the machine. The generator. The plate box. I even try to touch the delicate Crookes tube, from which the mysterious x-rays emit, but there is no indication that I make physical contact.

The machine has been a source of terror, and I am now convinced it is the source of my grief. However, my hands can't manipulate the generator, the source of the electricity needed to trigger the x-ray creation. Wilhelm can, though. I just need to make him understand.

I skim to the door again, filled with purpose and determination, and I pass through the door unimpeded.

Wilhelm sits by my bed, cradling one of my hands between his, head bowed.

I glide to his side. He had sensed my presence earlier, had felt the chill of my movements. He has to, again. Or my earthly body will die, and my spirit with it.

I stroke his head. I cannot feel his hair, but a few strands stir. His shoulders hunch, and he looks up.

I gasp. He *can* feel me, even if he can't see me! I lean close to him and whisper, "Wilhelm," directly into his ear.

He cries out and jumps to his feet. And then he asks, "Who's there?"

I feel unbearably light with joy, and the world becomes tinged with white. I mustn't fade, so I focus on my husband's sturdy figure, his sunken, intense eyes, his bushy black beard streaked with gray.

He will understand! I laugh giddily and run my hand down his cheek and tug his beard. It is a familiar, affectionate gesture.

He shivers. "Bertha?" he asks. He glances to the bed, where my body lies, and frowns.

"I'm here, Wilhelm," I say, and tug his beard again.

He raises one hand slowly, almost dreamily, and strokes his chin. "Bertha," he says firmly. "I don't understand. How . . . ?"

"I don't know, my love," I say. And I don't, not the mechanics. I'm no scientist. But I know that the machine holds the solution to my terrible separation of selves. Always the machine.

Desperate, I push my body's left hand. It twitches. Wilhelm, sharp-eyed as ever, grasps the hand and runs his fingers over my limp digits—and my wedding ring. His fingers pause on the simple gold band, and he takes a deep breath.

"The x-rays, Bertha? Are they what have stolen you from me?"

I tweak his beard again.

"I will fix this," he declares, his gaze roving the room. "I promise."

I caress his cheek one more time, before the fog overtakes me.

The repeated use of my name pulls me from the void. It takes several moments for the fog to clear, and I fear that whatever thin tether that ties me here will soon break and my body truly will die.

My bed and body have been moved to Wilhelm's laboratory. My left hand rests on the photographic plate, and Wilhelm bustles around the machine, teasing the equipment into place. He explains the procedure while he works, a stream of words peppered with my name. I have difficulty hearing all the words, his voice very faint, and I become concerned that my time grows short. Wilhelm's theory must prove correct.

The theory is simple enough that I follow the idea even though I don't understand the underlying physics.

"So, Bertha, I will need both of your hands on the plate glass," he says, while adjusting the bulbs. "I have here your earthly hand, but I also need your… spectral hand. Here, like so." He gently places his hand over the hand of my husk. "I will take the x-ray radiograph, and God willing, your two states will be fused once more."

His gaze flits around the room, eyes a little wild. To reassure him of my presence, I wave my hand over his hair. His skin breaks into gooseflesh from the chill, but he smiles.

"Ah, good, you understand," he says. "You stay here, and I will start the experiment."

I place my left hand on top of my husk's hand. The wedding bands should have clinked, my two hands line up so perfectly. I avoid looking at my husk. The waxy skin and slow, shallow breathing disturb me. My husk is more dead than alive.

"Bertha, I'm going to turn on the machine. Are you ready?"

"Yes," I say, although my voice is nothing but a whisper on a breeze, but he senses my response. Wilhelm nods and flips the lever.

The machine hums, and I imagine the tubes crackling with energy. The familiar green glow suffuses the room, the radiation reacting with Wilhelm's fluorescent materials.

Skinny black bones.

I blanch and my hand twitches, but I don't remove it. As the green glow diminishes and the buzzing generator quiets, the laboratory sinks into darkness. I wait for Wilhelm to turn on the lights, to remove my hand from the photographic plate, but he doesn't appear.

"Wilhelm?" I call, but my voice isn't working.

The additional radiation experiment has failed, and I am dying. I sob, or try, but nothing works. My phantasmal body no longer mimics my earthly one.

"Bertha?"

Wilhelm's voice is muffled. Is he in a different room? I must reassure him that I am still here, even if his experiment failed. We must try again.

My eyes flutter open and Wilhelm's dear face fills my field of vision. He smiles, but his eyes are glassy with tears.

I am hungry. I am exhausted. I am bewildered.

"Wilhelm?" I ask, my voice dry and dusty.

"Bertha." He beams.

I am alive, I wonder, and raise my arms off the bed. I pinch my left hand, twirl my wedding ring around my finger. I am solid. It worked! The machine has made me whole once more.

"Wilhelm," I cry again and embrace my husband, relishing the sturdiness of his body.

X is for X-ray

Joseph Halden

It's dark and quiet, cars dead and street lights off. Dim candles alight in windows and roadside altars to mark the Lacuniter hour.

I should be at my sister Kate's, at one of these shrines or even a temple, but I'm not. I'm keeping the ghost-like lacunitos that orbit and haunt me. I have to, for Mum, even if it means going blind by them.

Lacuniter is the daily hour when lacunitos must pass through the opened gate to hell, to pass through its levels and be cleansed before being re-injected into the world and continuing the karmic cycle in another life.

It's surreal to miss the rituals, the chants I hear faintly through the walls of every home and from the small clusters burning incense at shrines.

Even as an angsty teenager I didn't ever miss Lacuniter. There were things you just didn't do. Places you just didn't go.

Like this dump across the street. A piss-coloured sign for a thrift shop, barely an excuse for what this place really held.

People said errant lacunitos came to her. This blind witch everyone pretended didn't exist, until they needed her.

It's only been a day, and already I've got seven lacunitos milling around me. One is a lacunito of Brendan, a buddy who used to have more patience for my crap. He'd sounded mildly irritated when I joked about him not having time for drinks anymore. I didn't realize so much of our friendship had died.

Then there's a lacunita of my sister, Kate, laughing in the shoulder-rocking, whole-body way we used to together. That laughter's gone now; she's a single mother with Roland, her adorable little redhead toddler. I love the little guy, don't get me wrong. Gave him a baby fedora just this afternoon, and he looked like a little Sam Spade.

The part that stings is that every time I talk to Kate, something new dies. It's harder and harder to find evidence that we're family.

Several other lacunitos cluster around me, shadows of short conversations with the grocery store clerk and Mum's hotel nurses. They shuffle in silence, never straying so far I could mistake them for haunting anyone else.

Day one and I'm already the pied piper. It's only going to get worse. If I go long enough, I'll have too many lacunitos around me to even see, and I'll end up as blind as the witch.

I want to pop in headphones and play some heavy thrash that'll get me amped up to go into the thrift shop, but I'm already too weirded out for missing Lacuniter. The darkest death metal is nothing next to this stuff, man.

But dammit, I'm not going to let Mum go without a fight.

I jog across the street and yank the glass door open. A clot of antiques threatens to spill. A jade cat wobbles. A scratched panda bobble head vibrates atop a dresser. I put my hands out to catch both in case they fall, but they don't.

Incense barely conceals a heavy musk. The place is overstuffed with junk and the memories all the junk's burdened with, the air thick and suffocating.

It's a miracle the blind witch can find her way around without getting buried in an avalanche. I have to crab-walk my way through.

She sits behind a counter at the back, head cocked, milky eyes staring into nothing. She wears a floral dress that could be drapes. She's an image of what I will become if I keep skipping Lacuniter.

"Hello."

She hasn't heard me. I get close enough to inhale a reek like someone's smashed and scattered pickled eggs.

"Hello," I repeat, louder, feeling stupid for thinking volume will help.

The blind witch lifts a finger.

"Keep your voice down," she mutters. "What do you want?"

"I'm tracking a lacunita," I say. The faster I speak, the faster I can get out of here.

"Whose?"

"My mother's."

"Why?"

"She's lost a big part of herself. I want her to have it back."

The witch considers, shifts to the right, never looking at me. "She still alive?"

"Yes."

"You can't make lacunitos go where you want."

I bite my lip. She's not the first person to say so. "I know. I just want to find her."

Then coax her into returning to Mum, with some of the mementos in my backpack, like Mum's wooden tea box and extremely large t-shirt she wore as pyjamas almost any time she was home.

"What's she look like?"

Like I could distill Mum to a few notes in a pig's case file. Still, I gotta try.

"Short curly hair, tall, big eyes, even bigger glasses. Moves kind of in bursts, like walking steady is too boring."

"She fat?"

What the crap was I even doing here?

"Her face is a bit puffy, and she's got a belly but I wouldn't call her fat. She's kinda got the same build as me." I regret the words immediately. Of course the witch can't see me, and I probably don't want her to.

She turns as though she *can* see me, and the shop suddenly feels even more claustrophobic.

"She came here," the witch says. "Buy something and I'll tell you where she went."

Earlier that day

I sat on Mum's bleached hospital bedsheets, telling her about the new condo I was renting from Brendan.

"He sounds like a very nice boy." She smiled.

"Mum, you know Brendan. He used to chug our cranberry juice after school, remember? He snuck in once when I wasn't home and you towel-whipped him in the throat?"

"That sounds like something I'd do."

I laughed, and she joined. "It was, and you did."

A nurse came in and set up a meal tray for Mum. She reminded Mum to eat everything, then scuttled out.

"How could I possibly leave any of this delectable food behind?" Mum said. "They've done wonders with sawdust, they really have."

We laughed. Mum was sweet but sharp as a knife. These days it was rare to catch her in such lucid moments, probably rarer than she enjoyed her meals. I wanted to take her home, but my living situation was far from stable and Kate's place wasn't an option, because they fought too much. It was painful to keep her here but I visited daily.

"I brought you some contraband, Mum," I said, opening my bag and bringing out two peanut-butter cookies, her favourite.

"What if someone has a nut allergy?" she asked.

"Nuts to them."

"If you're not careful, they're going to cashew."

"You mean these aren't pecan your curiosity?"

She grabbed a cookie with a trembling hand. "You know, you're working for peanuts."

"Somebody's gotta do it."

Mum sighed. "You know, no one around here likes puns, can you believe it?"

She'd said so before, many times. "It's astonishing. How can they get by?"

"And their tea is absolutely dreadful."

Crap. I knew I'd forgotten something. "I'll bring you some next time, Mum."

"That'd be lovely. Thanks for coming by, honey. You have no idea how nice it is to talk to a human."

"I feel the same, Mum."

She broke off a piece. "Have some. I don't need all of it."

"It's for you, Mum."

"And I'm sharing it how I like. Have some with me."

I took it. We munched in silence.

"Your business going well?" she asked.

I told her about some of the new clients I had, the accumulating referrals for tiling jobs, the new designs and ceramics that were easier to apply.

Her right, lazy eye drooped and I knew she was getting tired.

"Mum?" I asked. "Sorry, I'm putting you to sleep. I should probably head out now."

She frowned. "Huh?"

"You all right?"

This was part of the process. Her dementia came and went in waves.

"Huh?" she repeated.

The shift in the way she looked at me was like the nurse had come back in and rammed the food trolley into my gut. Mum didn't recognize me.

"It's me, Mum. Damian, your son."

She frowned deeper, then tipped back and clenched the sheets.

Goddamn it. She was scared of me.

I stood. That's when I saw her lacunita beside the bed, looking at me with Mum's bright, sharp eyes, waving playfully in a way only Mum could, the way she had when I was a twelve-year-old playing with friends and she wanted to announce her presence in the most embarrassing way possible.

The memory should have brought joy, and were she standing there in the flesh doing that, it would have. But this was her lacunita doing these things, and it only meant this part of Mum had died.

Mum's lacunita dove right through the floor and out of sight.

I'm putting a marionette with a missing eye on the counter when bells chime from the front of the thrift shop.

It's my sister Kate, breathless, black hair tied back in a bun. She maneuvers toward me like she's struggling through the McDonald's play tunnels to get Roland. We're the same height and I realize how ridiculous I must look in here, too.

"Where's Roland?" I ask.

"With the babysitter, who's charging double for the short notice," she snaps. "What are you doing?"

"Getting a present for the little guy." I point at the marionette.

"Like hell. You're hunting Mum's lacunita, aren't you?"

I shrug. "Two birds with one stone."

"Damian, this is serious. You can't skip Lacuniter. You know that."

"Who says I skipped it?"

She stabs a finger at Brendan's lacunito.

Dammit. The one time I'd hoped Kate and I'd drifted far enough apart.

When you're close to someone, you can see their lacunitos, too. All those except lacunitos of yourself, that is; Kate would never see the lacunita of her floating in the thrift shop.

I'm caught, and my cheeks heat up like I'm seven years old and she's pinching them and chiding me.

"So what? I care about Mum, and I'm not sending more of her through the gate."

"It's not natural, Damian." She's tired, her eyes heavy compared to the lightness of her lacunita. Her lacunita orbits slowly around her, passing through the junk piles.

"What's unnatural is spending a lifetime building a world with your family and watching it evaporate like nothing," I snap.

Her voice softens. "It isn't nothing."

"Right. How many times have you visited Mum this month? Do you know how bad things have gotten?"

She opens her mouth, then stops and shakes her head. Rubs her temples. When she lowers her hands, there's an echo of her shape, another lacunita separating from her features.

Dammit all.

"Roland takes all my time," she says. "You know that."

"We can help."

"I don't need your help," she says, fists curled. "And Mum's in no shape to help."

Her two lacunitas pass through the store like we're surrounded by fog machines. It's bad enough facing your sister and seeing how much of a stranger she's become. Having orbiting reminders is even worse.

"So noisy," the witch says beside me. "You're cluttering up the store with lacunitos. Get out."

"With pleasure, ma'am," Kate says. "Come on, Damian. Put the creepy doll down and let's go."

"Hold on. I'm buying this doll." I hand the witch forty bucks. "You said you'd tell me where she went."

The witch takes the money and smells it.

"Please don't tell him," Kate says, scrambling over a stool and a tricycle. "I'll pay you not to."

The witch tilts her head. "We had a deal before you arrived. She's headed for Sanctuary Glade."

"The river valley? Did she say that?"

The witch bores milky-white eyes into me. I want to shrink and disappear. "She didn't have to."

"Thank you."

Outside, Kate's face seems paler than usual, but it's hard to tell with all the lacunitos milling about.

"Come do the ritual," Kate says. "With Roland and me. It's not too late."

"No, Kate. You might have given up on our family, but I haven't."

I walk North, crossing an intersection where traffic still hasn't picked up after the Lacuniter hour. Although I could walk all the way to Sanctuary Glade, dipping down into the river valley and crossing the bridge, it'd be much faster to take the gondola, and that's where I'm headed.

Kate hustles after me. "This is the same old story, Damian. You're pissed at me, pissed at the whole world, just because you can't make anything new."

"What are you talking about?" I snap, moving onto a boardwalk edging a park. "Five years ago I was making pizza, and now my tiling business is booming. I call the shots, and I'm making bank. All from nothing."

"I meant you can't make any new *friends*," Kate says, the word a slicing blade.

I'm too mad to stop. She's probably right, and I hate her for it. "Didn't know you paid so much attention to my social life. I'm touched."

I'm speed-walking now, approaching the concrete gondola terminal jutting out over the valley's edge, cables snaking down and across the river. Across the bridge, the downtown core is lighting up in quadrants as the din of vehicles rises like a swarm of locusts.

There's a lineup for the gondola, and I want to yell at everyone to go away.

I hate when Kate feels sorry for me. Of all the things our relationship had, why can't that aspect go and die, too?

"Damian," Kate says, breathless, "I'm not saying there's anything wrong with you. I love you. Roland loves you. Mum loves you."

"Mum forgot me today, Kate. She can't love someone she's forgotten. I have to find her lacunita. You don't have to follow me if you're not going to help."

"I want to help, Damian. But I can't do it all for you. How can I convince you that what you are is enough?"

"You know, every time you say that, it has the opposite effect, right?"

Kate groans. "I don't know what to do."

"Go home, Kate."

"Damian, haven't you noticed? You're scared. I know you're scared. All this loss around us, all the time, it's terrifying. You don't think you have anything worth bringing real people back to you, so you hedge, terrified that whatever you lose can never be replaced."

"So you're saying Mum's replaceable?"

"No, Damian. Stop it. I'm saying you try to play it safe, be neutral and pleasant in conversations with others, but it just comes across as... not genuine. If you trusted that being yourself was enough, you could form new relationships and not cling so much to this stuff we can't change."

Damn her. My chest feels like it's going to cave in.

We join the lineup behind families clutching candles, headed home after the Lacuniter rituals.

It's not like I didn't try. I think I'm a reasonably smart guy, but I've never figured people out. Their geometry was nothing like the neatly-ordered grids of my tiling work. People were patched mosaics that changed colour and pattern. Or maybe they were leaves of the trembling aspen in the river valley, showing a completely different side—bright silver or dark green—depending on the wind's breath.

Maybe something in me had died, and I wasn't capable of forming relationships anymore. How could Kate fault me for trying to hold what I still had? And how could she fault me for trying to let Mum hold onto herself?

"Talk to me, Damian."

"What can I say? You've got it all figured out, Kate."

Her shoulders sag. Another echo of her spirit—hers and my relationship—separates into a lacunita and joins our troupe.

This seems to be all I'm good at—killing what I care about.

"I hate seeing Mum like this, too," Kate says. "It's horrible. And yeah, sometimes I use Roland as an excuse not to visit. It's a bad excuse, but… it's hard for me too, you know."

At least she's got Roland. I'm too scared to lose even more of Kate, so I say nothing.

She's right. I am scared. I don't know how people aren't absolutely terrified every day with all we lose.

"How can I stop you, Damian? What's it going to take?"

"Mum coming back."

Too many of Kate's questions are the same ones I ask myself. If I had answers, I would have stopped asking them.

"Do you think it's actually better that a part of her is… I don't know, free?"

"While her body is left stranded? That doesn't seem right to me."

"What are you going to do once you find her, Damian? Like the witch said, you can't force her lacunita to go anywhere except through the gates with the rituals."

"I've got some of Mum's stuff to use as a lure."

Kate eyes my backpack. "What if I don't let you?"

"Kate, I'm serious. Don't stop me, or I'm never speaking to you again. This is Mum, and I'm not messing around."

Kate glares at me, and another of her lacunitas appears. The more we disagree, the more we dig at each other, the more our old selves die.

I guess they're right about what familiarity breeds.

Near the front of the lineup, a boy and a girl run after each other. Their giggles grind against my mood like metal on glass.

The children speak excitedly, each one adding details to an adventure. It reminds me a little of how Kate and I used to be, and my heart does a little shock-thaw.

Kate's smiling at them. A smile creeps inevitably to my lips, too, even though it aches to watch.

The children migrate to block the gondola exit, where a door opens and a gaggle of people emerge.

Their mother calls out and darts out of the line to collect her kids.

"Hey," Kate whispers, touching my arm. "Isn't that Selja, one of your old classmates?"

It is. Her brown hair is flecked with a few strands of grey, and she's a bit more shapely than she was in high school, but it's her. She's aged probably a lot better than I have.

"You should talk to her," Kate says. She keeps tapping my arm. "Damian, this is the perfect opportunity. Just be yourself, show her the good, genuine guy we both know you are."

"Oh, is it that easy, Kate? Why didn't you say so before?"

She sighs. "You're too much sometimes. All right, I gave you a chance."

Before I realize what's happening, Kate's beside Selja, introducing herself then hugging Selja when they recognize one another. That's one thing about Kate; everyone loves her.

Selja's gaze drifts toward me. I force a smile and wave, then make a gesture to the lineup to indicate I don't want to lose my place.

She and Kate wave me over. I'm pretty sure everyone in the line is going to hate me, but, well, it'll get me to Mum's lacunita faster.

I stride forward and join them at the front. Selja's holding her younger daughter while her son clutches her jeans with one hand and a Mektron toy in the other.

"Damian! Hi!" she says. She reaches out an arm for a hug, and I lean in awkwardly, trying to be friendly but not sure how to hug when there's a bundle of kid in the way.

"Long time no see!"

"Yeah, definitely," I say. "It's been a while."

We get onto the gondola, and it sways as it floats on the cable across the river valley.

From behind Selja, Kate makes wide eyes at me, mouthing *be yourself.*

Dammit Kate, you're not helping.

"So what have you been up to?" Selja asks.

I go through the motions. It's surface-level crap that doesn't ever go anywhere, but there's not much more I know how to do with near-strangers. If there's a muscle for this sort of thing, I either don't have it or it's atrophied into nothing.

Her kids' names are Volker and Odelia. I don't know why people say buttons are cute, but the kids are much cuter than buttons.

I can tell it's getting uncomfortable by the way Selja keeps looking at the door, as though willing the gondola to go faster.

"Your kids are adorable," I blurt. Kate gives me a secretive thumbs up and rolls her hands as a signal to keep going.

She's embarrassing as hell, but all right... I can go a bit more.

"Hey Odelia, did you know your mom played the star in a big school play?"

Odelia's eyes widen.

Selja smiles and furrows her brow. "I... don't remember that."

"Lady MacBeth," I say.

Selja laughs. "I'd hardly call that a star."

I shrug, and whisper to Odelia. "Your mom's just trying not to brag, but she was really good."

Odelia looks at her mother in astonishment.

Selja laughs again.

"Volker, I see you've got the new Mektron toy—have you seen the new show? What'd you think of Poxel's new form?"

Selja rolls her eyes. "My god, that show is *too* much."

Volker, however, lights up. "Yes, and I've got two of his old forms but Mum won't let me get the new one. She says it's Odelia's turn to get a toy, but my friends say the old Poxel's stupid and they aren't going to play with me. And I still have to get Meplon and Zowig, but I'm waiting to see which one of them gets turned back first."

Kids are so much easier than adults. "Don't worry, man, Poxel's still the same on the inside, no matter what form. Your Poxels are still super cool."

I nerd out with Volker a bit more, then turn to Odelia. "What toy are you going to pick out, Odelia?"

"I want a science lab kit," she says.

I've done my homework on this for Roland. "Have you seen the one with the bottled stars and elephant toothpaste?"

She beams. "That's the one I want!"

"Good choice, rockstar." We fist-bump.

Selja laughs.

The gondola arrives, and we shuffle our way off.

Selja addresses her kids. "You two have made a pretty neat new friend, haven't you?"

The kids nod. Selja radiates warmth. She's blurred by the haze of lacunitos milling about, but I manage to keep it together.

"It was great running into you, Damian. Maybe you could come over sometime and play with these two when it's not past their bedtime."

"Yeah! Come over, come over!" Volker exclaims.

"Not tonight," Selja says firmly. "All right, we should get going. Get in touch, okay, Damian?"

"I will," I say, smiling. "Great seeing you, Selja."

For a minute, I've forgotten why I'm here, and I'm scanning to see what kind of lacunita separates from Selja—will it be sharp, or faint? I watch her and her children closely.

My sister's lacunitas—the ones that had orbited me throughout the night—veer off and cluster around Odelia, all but seeping into her. What the hell? Have I brought a curse upon her children, or something even worse?

I'm about to run after Selja when the lacunitas come back to encircle me as though tugged by an invisible string.

Thank God, or whatever's responsible for this mess of spirit fragments.

"Kate, Lacunitos are re-injected into the karmic flow after being cleansed through their passage through the hells, right? Well, what if there's a way for them to skip going through the gate, and go right back into the karmic cycle?"

Kate frowns. "Did some of your lacunitos leave?"

"No."

"Then they're still stuck with us. And I'd worry about them not undergoing cleansing."

She was right. If the lacunitos were karma vessels, then I was a clog in the artery, or a damaged kidney letting unfiltered blood circulate.

I don't give a damn about my own karma—if I mess that up, fine. But if I mess up the karma of little Odelia and Volker, or Roland, I don't think I could live with myself.

Kate and I grow quiet as we wind our way down the concrete path toward the Sanctuary Glade. The lacunitos float around like carrion crows waiting for meat.

"Why would she come here?" Kate asks.

"No idea."

Finally we're at the glade, where an oval-shaped clearing has been cut into the Boreal forest.

There's no sign of Mum's lacunita, and I circle the edges, kicking deadwood in frustration.

I'm about to give up when at the edge I see small white flowers growing in clusters.

"Hey Kate," I call, "didn't Mum used to have those in her tea? The leaves or something?"

Kate comes over and inspects. "Yeah, she did. Yarrow, I think it's called."

Yarrow. Of course. Mum came here for yarrow—she'd been complaining about the hospital's tea.

"She's following the yarrow!" I exclaim, bursting into a run.

"Damian, wait!"

We follow the trickles of yarrow up a hill and behind a residential area.

Through a chain-link fence, I finally see her. Mum's lacunita bends to smell the yarrow in someone's garden.

"Mum!"

She doesn't hear me. She turns and passes through the wall.

I jump the fence. Kate hisses at me.

"She's in there," I whisper. "I've got to get her, Kate."

I pad around the garden and to the side of the house, where I hear shouting.

"Daddy says you broke the family!" says a boy.

"Freddy! That's not true—"

"I don't want to live here! Daddy lets me stay up as late as I want. He knows I'm a big kid now. This place is stupid, and all I ever do here is chores. I'm not your slave anymore, Mom!"

There's a crash of broken glass. I wince. A girl's wail rises like a siren.

"Freddy!" the mother shrieks. "Stop it! You've hurt your sister! We don't do that in this house!"

"I don't want to *be* in this house!" Freddy yells.

"Oh sweetie, come here," the mother soothes to the wailing daughter. Then, to Freddy: "Apologize to Maggie!"

I'm transfixed, my breath held, unable to continue.

"It's her fault for standing there."

"Apologize now, or you're grounded."

"No."

"Go to your room! Think about what you did. You're not to come out until you're ready to apologize!"

"No!"

The mother's voice rises and cracks at the limit of volume. "In your room, now!"

Feet stomp up the stairs. I hear the mother cooing the screaming daughter. What seems ages later, the daughter's screaming dwindles to sniffles.

"Mommy's got to clean up, okay, sweetie? Did you want to stay here with me, or did you want to watch a show?"

The girl mumbles and the playful jingle of a children's show follows.

Finally I relax, and work my way to the front of the house.

It's a terrible time, but… Mum's lacunita is in there.

I ring the doorbell and suck in a breath.

"Oh for Christ's sake." The mother rips open the door. "What do you want?"

Her brown hair's disheveled. Tears streak down her sunken cheeks, while her jogging pants and sweater are stained with gravy splatters.

Mum's lacunita hovers behind the young mother, trying in vain to pat her head and comfort her.

"Who are you, and what do you want?" the mother snaps.

The cycle is lain bare, and all at once I'm faced with how my own selfish needs are preventing karmic flow.

Karmic flow this mother could desperately use. It wouldn't solve all her problems, but it would definitely help.

Mum's lacunita wanted to pass into her, but she hadn't gone through the cleansing process via the levels of hell. If all I'd been told was true, there was no way Mum's lacunita could ever help this mother unless I let her go.

"I'm sorry, ma'am," I said. "I just wanted to make sure you were all right."

The mother's eyes narrow, suspicious. I probably seem more than a little creepy right now. "We're fine, thank you very much. Good night."

She slams the door in my face. I drag myself to the curb, where Kate is waiting.

"Mum's lacunita... why does she have to go now?" Tears run down my face.

"What did you see?" Kate asks.

"Mum was trying to go into her."

"The longer you hold Mum's lucanita here, the longer you prevent another's karma being fulfilled," Kate says.

"I'm stopping someone else blossoming as a mother."

"Yes."

"It's not fair."

"I know."

What a crappy world. Choose between keeping your mother or damning the future.

Mum wouldn't want to damn the future. When she was lucid, she loved Roland more than anything. Somewhere, somehow, she still loves him.

Kate wraps an arm around me. "I'm sorry, Damian."

I wipe my tears away. "I'll do the rituals."

The next day I'm sitting at the altar in Kate's house, Roland on one side, Kate on the other. Lacunitos cloud my vision. With the smoke from all the candles and incense, I can barely see.

I raise my hands in prayer.

"Spirits of all that's passed
Let go of your ties at last
Cling not to the life that was
But pass and embrace your flaws.

"We hold the gate open for you
The cycle that breathes life through
We honour your memory and life
Accepting that all things must die."

The lacunitos pass one by one through the altar, and I'm staring through blurry eyes, watching for Mum. Saying goodbye to my sister's lacunitas, to Brendan's lacunitos, and to the phantoms of encounters gone and passed.

I grab a nearby kettle of boiled water, and pour it into a teacup full of yarrow leaves.

Mum comes, her head poking playfully through the floor. Her laughter echoes with memories of walks by the river, of family meals, of a million tiny moments captured in a smile.

"Bye, Mum," I whisper, holding the cup of tea up for her.

She closes her eyes and inhales deeply through her nose. The steam's upward drift kinks for a moment. Then Mum waves, blows us a kiss, and hops through the altar.

"Oh, how nice of you! Did you know these are my favourite?" Mum says, picking up the peanut butter cookie. She's sitting up in bed, more energetic than usual.

"I had a feeling," I say, smiling even though it hurts.

"How many kind young men are going around giving treats to old ladies?"

"Not enough, I'd wager. But I've got something else you might like."

I pour Mum some yarrow tea.

Her breath catches. "Yarrow? You're an angel."

I want to be grateful for what's left of Mum. I tell myself it's better than not having her here at all. That others have it worse. It still hurts like hell, though, and I pray Mum will be whole again one day, somewhere, for someone.

For now, I am with her, no matter how many times I have to introduce myself, no matter how many cookies and tea I have to sneak past the nurses.

"Your mother must be very proud."

It's hard to stop the tears. "I hope so."

I open the glass door, ready to catch an avalanche of junk. Clambering over the stool and the tricycle is too familiar.

Does anything ever change in this place? Maybe, like the lacunitos the blind witch clutches, the objects are stagnant, too.

As I move gingerly around the clutter, I see an old Mektron toy, one of the originals. Volker might not recognize it, but I'll get it anyway.

That's one thing I've realized, with a lot of help from Kate. The lacunitos show you what you've lost, but they don't really show what you've gained. We can build things, or try to build things, all the time.

That's what I'm doing now.

The witch is at the back, eyes the same milky-white as the first time we met.

I smile.

"You seem familiar," she says.

"You helped me find my mother," I reply.

"Ah," she says. "So you did find her."

"Yes."

"Are you looking for someone else, now?"

"No," I say, pulling out a Thermos. "I'm here to talk to you."

Y is for Yarrow

Suzanne J. Willis

Winter, 1868. Crystal Palace, London.

"The Wheel of Life", the posters proclaimed in bold lettering around a neat sketch of a spinning drum from which light illuminated the awed observers' faces. Underneath, "London Steroscopic and Photographic Company" modestly acknowledged the owner of the marvel. Mary, in her long black dress, leather doctor's bag by her side, cocked her head while studying the poster. There was a gentle snib of the bag's clasps as Charlie, the wee automaton who was only a foot tall, poked his head out to read it, too.

"Where's the crank again, old girl?" He spoke quietly, not wanting to draw the attention of spiffy Londoners, in their bustles and suits and Sunday best, strolling along the paths. Like Mary and Charlie, they were here for the Crystal Palace, which glittered through the early morning fog like something half-dreamt.

The exhibition hall would not open for another hour or so. Mary hoped that would be long enough for them to fulfil their task. Ever since Freya and Charlie had found her, rescued from the terror of her kidnap—when they had unmade her, taken away the timepieces that gave her life and so rendered her no more than an empty, useless doll—and found a way to remake her, again, Mary had been slower, less herself than she would ever have thought possible. Her legs ached constantly, and there was a crick in her lower back that never quite went away. Once again, she wondered if this was what it felt like to get old.

Despite herself, she smiled down at Charlie—her constant, ever-faithful Charlie.

"If our Freya was right," she replied, "she'll have it set up just near the gas outlet valve, on the south side of the exhibit."

Just then, Freya slipped out of the side door of the palace, almost as ethereal as the fog that wreathed the gardens and lifted in misty tendrils as the winter sunlight hit it.

Like clockwork, Mary though.

Freya wore the same almond-coloured coat, trimmed in fur, and cloche hat, both of which would not become fashionable for the next fifty years, as she had when they first met. Instead of being conspicuous, she managed to appear insubstantial, wandering by the Sunday morning strollers as though she was not there at all. Perhaps her journey with the time-wraiths had changed her in ways that none of them yet quite understood.

Mary stretched her hand out as Freya reached them, then pulled back as Freya winced. Clearly, she had changed. Once, she would never have recoiled from Mary or Charlie, but now… it was as though she was as fragile as old porcelain, spiderwebbed in cracks that were ready to shatter apart at the merest touch.

"What did they do to you?" Charlie asked.

Mary shushed him, but Freya just shook her head. "The time-wraiths don't mean any harm. In some ways, they're just like any other ghosts—the real world holds no meaning for them. But time, for them… well, for time-wraiths, they feel that it is theirs to own and guard, precisely because it has no effect on them…"

Freya suddenly looked old, much older than Mary remembered. How long had she been with the time-wraiths, those creatures that exist outside time, twisting and turning it as though it was their own toy?

Even had she not been with them, she's never been like you, Mary reminded herself. *No matter how long darling Freya travels back and forth across the ages with you and Charlie, no matter how much that tiny second hand from her father's pocket watch ticks away in her wrist, holding back her own clock, she is still human. Something you and Charlie will never be.*

Freya would, perhaps, one day, be a ghost herself. But that didn't bear thinking about. Not when they had been through so much. She refused to let herself think that they might one day lose Freya, who had become as dear to her as if she were her own child.

"One thing at a time, old girl," Charlie said softly, looking up at Mary. She nodded, amazed that he often seemed able to read her mind, as he turned his attention to Freya.

"And you my friend… well done. It's not an easy thing, setting up a job like this, but you've made our part in it easier still."

Freya smiled and held up an iron key. "And this should make it easier again," she smiled. "Do you think it will work, Charlie?" Freya asked.

Mary knew she wasn't talking about the key.

He smiled, then, a toothy grin under his ginger moustache. "Wouldn't be heading in there if I thought it wouldn't."

Inside the palace, it felt like they had entered a city made of ice. The heating hadn't taken off the morning chill yet and Freya's breath plumed before her. The morning sun, wan as it was, shone through the domed roof, sparking the day to life. The past and future, all the endless possibilities of time, seemed to whisper through the emptiness of the great conservatory, tiding over them as they made their way to the centre.

"Can you feel that, Mary?" Freya asked.

Mary nodded. "Try not to listen. This kind of place, where the weft and warp of time has been rent, and spectres are able to slither through, is unstable. It makes you vulnerable to them…"

Freya straightened up, pushed her shoulders back. "They'll not get me, Mary."

"Atta girl," said Charlie, still peering out from Mary's black bag.

They passed all manner of wondrous exhibits—carved ice swans swimming on a lake of white blooms; a miniature city wrought from silver, crowned by a cathedral with windows made of amethyst, citrine, carnelian; an enormous tea-room fit for a czar, smelling of roses and cinnamon. At last, dead ahead, in the great performance hall, the very thing they had come for. The Wheel of Life—the giant zoetrope that had been the talk of London. And their only chance of setting things to rights.

Here, the whispers seemed to grow quieter, as though they were avoiding this particular place. For those whispers had a life of their own, as all such possibilities do. Waiting to be called, to be made whole, to put roots down in the world where time rules all. In the same way, they know where it is not safe for them, for they fear being unwound, of losing the chance to be. They were the echoes of what was and what can be.

But they were nothing compared with the real ghosts that were slipping through the tear in time that Mary, Charlie and Freya had been charged with fixing. They stood before the zoetrope, each of them quietly awed. A huge drum of copper and curlicues, attached to a gas generator. Through the vertical slits, a glimpse of the images inside that lined it, waiting to be animated. The wheel held a promise— to the ordinary folk, a promise of the miracle of the moving image. For the three time-travellers, the chance of starting afresh.

Charlie hopped out of the bag and made his way to the back of the generator, muttering to himself. Freya stared at the zoetrope with wide eyes. "My grandmother told me about this, when I was very young. Told me about how all the people crowded around and looked through those thin windows into the wheel and saw magic happen! The gas engine cranked away and they came back twice during the day to see the different animations." She turned to Mary. "That won't change for her, will it? I mean, we are here to change the timeline—"

Mary shook her head. "We're here to do no such thing, Freya. All we are doing is changing something that should never have happened. To stop them from coming through from the future..." she trailed off.

"But why are they possessing people?"

"I think they want a second chance at life," Mary replied. "In a different era, where they can cast off any attachments they held in life. Just a theory, of course." What she didn't say was that she also suspected that the three of them, with all their to-ing and fro-ing across the centuries may have caused the problem in the first place.

As Charlie fussed around the engine and looked to fix the manual crank in its place (she always marvelled at his strength, given he was no bigger than a child's doll), she and Freya took the stereoscope images they had prepared out of the black doctor's bag and began affixing them inside the wheel. As they worked, Mary thought about all the havoc that the ghosts had wreaked. Not quietly, either. It had become a sensation, splashed across the papers and drawing all sorts of unwanted attention. Drawing Mary's attention and the urgent, gnawing knowledge that this had to be stopped.

The tear in time must have been small at first, almost infinitesimal, but big enough for the child's spirit to find a way through. She had been from the early twentieth century, dead from the Spanish flu, Mary thought, given the terrible catarrh that the man she had possessed ended up with. Once the spirit had finished with that poor soul, he'd lost his marriage, his house and his sanity. The three of them had arrived shortly afterwards and Charlie had been hopeful, thought it was just the one and they could seal up the tear, be done with it. But that is rarely the way these things work and certainly wasn't the case here.

It was a trickle at first, scattered across the city; individuals not just acting strangely or out of character, but as though they were completely different people. Babbling nonsense about horseless carriages and flying machines and a terrible war that awaited the whole world. A few could be put down to the odd madman, but then that trickle turned into a tide.

The ghosts—from the future, all of them, no later than 1936, they came to realise—were clever, though, they learned to listen to the mistakes of those who had come back before them. The last thing they wanted was nice, new bodies and lives to take over, only to be carted off to a madhouse. So, they were quiet and unassuming and made their changes slowly. After all, who would have more patience than those who are already dead and have all the time in the world?

Perhaps it would have stayed that way, had it not been for the party that she and Charlie and Freya had hosted just a few short weeks ago. The Hothouse Bacchanal. It had started like all their other parties; Mary as the sparkling host, ready to give the guests a night like no other, Charlie as the charming, automaton bartender that everyone marvelled at. Freya in the background, sweetly keeping an eye on things to make sure that everyone drank their drinks and gave up just a small piece of their time in return.

It had not ended well. It was then that they realised how dangerous the situation had become and how urgent it was to set things to rights.

So, here they were. Outside, the fog was beginning to lift and the voices of those who had come to take in the wonders of the palace floated faintly in the air.

"Alright then, Charlie?" Mary asked, sinking onto the closest plush, wine-coloured chaise longue as Freya sat behind her.

"Up to you now, old girl," came the response from behind the engine.

Mary nodded and closed her eyes as Freya unclasped the silver buttons that ran down her spine and opened the doors on her back. She knew exactly which timepiece they needed.

"Just up near the left shoulder," she whispered.

There was just the merest twinge as Freya removed it, then carefully shut the doors again. She handed it to Mary. It looked simple enough—a plain watch face, yellow with age and an owl with wings outstretched in the centre. Roman numerals marked the circumference, except where XII should have been, there were two words: THE END. Those two words sparkled silver with stolen time that, she hoped, would help them mend what was broken.

"Ready, Charlie."

They looked over to Charlie, who began to turn the hand-crank like it was the easiest thing in the world. The Wheel of Life began to turn, faster and faster. Mary could not help herself; holding Freya's hand, she walked over and looked through the vertical slits. It was the same as other zoetropes she had seen, in that it showed the same cycle of movement on repeat. On others, it might be man in top hat and tails, walking briskly in a ceaseless circle, or two dancers in masquerade masks and capes, waltzing, one-two-three, one-two-three. No matter how much they *looked* to be moving, theirs was an immutable path, a caught moment replayed over and over.

But that was the only thing that was similar. The images themselves were something entirely different. The figures were sepia, three dimensional, so lifelike she was surprised they didn't simply step out of the wheel and begin to wander through the exhibition hall. A simple life played out as the wheel spun: baby, child, adulthood, death, back to babe again. With each rotation, the image filled out, became a little more than the last. An ephemeral grandmother stood over the baby in the cradle; then, a dead child wrapped his hands around his father's throat. Soon, there were more dead than living. Mary felt Freya shiver beside her and wished she could do the same.

Then, in between death and birth, so quick Mary thought she might be imagining it, a wisp of mist, a curl of ephemera leaving the coffin and flitting up, up, away. She gripped the watch face and gently prised the glass off. The stolen time glimmered over the words "THE END", almost playing across the letters. The scent of loam and rotting leaves, saltwater and ozone wafted up, then was gone.

She held the watch face to her lips and gently blew. The silvery particles swirled into the wheel, caught in its slipstream. As it melded with the images, the song began. Dancing across the domed, crystalline ceiling, reflecting back on itself and refracting through the fog into the world beyond. If sunset light on clouds created music, it would sound like this. Gold and rose and inky-indigo, underlit by dying light and the promise that something new awaits in the world just beyond. Music to call home the dead.

It filled the Crystal Palace and the city's errant ghosts, from the future dead, began to gather there. They passed through the glass as though it wasn't there at all; hung like spiderwebs from the balustrades and corners of the great hall; rose from the floor in a pearled fog the colour of dragon's tears. Freya sank to her knees and Mary took a step back as they all gazed at the Wheel of Life, transfixed by the echoes of life playing out there in an endless loop.

One of them, of a young woman in a flapper costume and feathers in her hair broke away from the balustrades on the upper floor and wafted up toward the ceiling. Meeting the glass, she melted into it, becoming part of it.

"Weren't they supposed to go through, and leave here?" Charlie whispered.

Mary shrugged, just as confused as he was. More ghosts broke away—children in raggedy clothes, soldiers in uniform with spectral bullet wounds trailing silver blood, the most ordinary looking of men and women. Not one of them, Mary noticed, was elderly. No wonder they had grasped at a second chance for life—these were people whose lives had not been fully lived.

The spell was broken by Freya screaming. Just as Mary turned, she saw a ghost slipping inside her skin as though it was shrugging on an old coat.

Mary found Freya in the fragrant tearoom they had passed earlier, peering around a column with a smile that definitely did not belong to her. Was she in there at all, or had the intruder managed to push her aside completely and fit itself into her skin? Mary sat on one of the marbled benches, keeping a safe distance from Freya. She briefly thought of Charlie, bravely cranking the zoetrope to trap the other spirits in the walls and ceiling of glass.

"Keep going!" she had shouted to him as she took off after Freya. The music followed her, then faded, as she had run through the exhibition hall, following the sounds of running footsteps.

"And what now?" the ghost asked in Freya's voice.

"Perhaps you could tell me who you are."

"Ah! You haven't recognised me, have you?"

"A little difficult when I only caught a glimpse of you climbing into a body that doesn't belong to you."

"Permit me to show you."

From the waist up, the ghost left Freya's body. It was all Mary could do not to look away, run as far as she could. It was misshapen, looking more like a decomposing body than the shade of a person who once lived. It smiled at her with a rictus grin, and its wild eyes glittered like corpselights.

The same awful wisps of brightness that she, Charlie and Freya had seen at the Hothouse Bacchanal. Mary, with Charlie perched on her shoulder like a jaunty toy, had wandered the paths of the great atrium, the ferns and vines waving gently as the revellers ran by, the butterflies flitting on jewelled wings. Like all their parties, the guests had drunk the violet potion that Charlie mixed so expertly in the

Pimm's for the ladies', brandy for the gentlemen. The transformations taking place were just as lovely and unexpected as ever. The most charming were the women mutating into glowing blue fungi, being chased by men who had grown wings of peacock green, or become great snowy owls of clockwork.

By stealing just a little bit of their time, the travellers were able to gift them a night of possibility. That same time ran through Mary, ticking under her skin. Leading the three of them backward and forward across the centuries, leaving them adrift in an ocean of moments, days, years to which they would never belong. That should have made her sad, Mary had mused as she and Charlie took in the bacchanal, and wondered why it didn't. Then the screams had begun, from atop the winding iron staircase that led to the second level orchid room. Mary ran towards it, towards Freya who was standing at the base of the staircase, begging the woman above, in her crinolines and velvet gloves and blood-red feathered headdress, *to please compose yourself, Madam*.

Then, a pearly spectre crawled out from the woman's flesh and tossed her body over the edge, a discarded costume that it no longer needed. They had jumped back as the body crashed at their feet, stared up in horror at the very same ghost who was peering at Mary now from Freya's fragile form.

"Ah, you do remember," it rasped, then retreated inside Freya's torso. "You see what happens when you try to steal time from the spirits?"

"Clearly, nothing good," said Mary, outwardly regaining her composure.

"Not for me, nor for your friend, here," it said, pointing Freya's finger towards her own heart. "She'll not last long, Mary."

"Perhaps we can come to an arrangement that would suit?"

"I want my time back."

"I'm afraid that is the very thing that I cannot give you." Mary spoke as gently as she could. She gasped as Freya's face contorted in pain and the ghost hissed through clenched teeth. "There is no need for that, we are not uncivilised. Let's see if we can't get you what you need." She felt like a duck on a lake, gliding across the surface while frantically paddling beneath just to stay afloat.

Freya relaxed again, although she was very pale, her skin clammy and damp.

"So," Mary tried again, "you had possessed the unfortunate woman who attended the Hothouse Bacchanal, and instead of our little concoction stealing her time, we stole yours?"

The ghost nodded in response, swaying unsteadily on Freya's feet.

"What could time mean, in death?"

"It is everything! The only thing I had left of my own life. It was mine, all mine, mine…"

Those words were not a petulant refrain but the sound of the first stirrings of winter, shushing through naked branches and across frosted moors. Lonely gloom and endless chill meeting what was once lively and bright.

Mary had encountered the dead before—there was not much she had not encountered, truth be told—and she knew that it could not possibly be referring to minutes, hours, days in the same way that people did. For them, there was nothing linear about their existence. She thought back to the seances she had attended in the 1930s, and to wandering through cemeteries hung with verdant moss and the spirits of the recent dead. To the witch trials of the 1600s and the vengeful ghosts haunting the streets after hangings, burnings, drownings. None of them had had any concept of time. On the contrary, it was as though they were stuck in a perpetual cycle—

"Time for you is a single moment or a short burst—one that you hang onto and replay, over and over?" Like the grey matrons haunting a hospital corridor or the spirit of a professor pacing a long-gone lecture theatre.

Freya nodded. "It is not all that we do, but we must hang onto it to have a place in this world. Without my time, I am anchorless, unable to stay inside a body without destroying it."

The ghost leaned out of Freya again, just its neck and shoulders. Where before it's face was fierce and cruel, now it looked scared. "Please give me back what is mine."

"I cannot," she said, "but I think I can send you somewhere that does not matter. Where you may find some peace."

"No!"

"Look inside Freya, inside the mind you are occupying. She has been there. Search her memory and see if it is true. But I will only help you if you surrender Freya immediately. I will not lose her."

The ghost disappeared and Freya closed her eyes, and groaned, eyes flickering under their lids as though she was in the midst of a nightmare. Then Freya's body gave a shudder and fell to the ground with a thud.

Mary knelt over Freya. Her breathing was shallow, but her pulse firm. *Our girl is made of tough stuff,* she thought. She picked Freya up in her arms.

"I will send you home," she said to the ghost that hovered uncertainly.

Together, they walked back to the zoetrope.

The Wheel of Life. The Great Zoetrope. A continuous circlet, with no beginning and no end. An imitation of life, just like the ghosts it called that winter morning, with its sunset music and illusion of motion and life.

"Change of plans, old girl?" Charlie asked when Mary returned with Freya in her arms and the ragged ghost hanging in the air behind her.

"One more turn of the wheel, I should think, Charlie."

Mary hastily sketched a series of images on the back of the stereo-
scopic cards as Freya whispered fragments of memories and
impressions of the period she was separated from Mary and Charlie
and, really, the world. She inserted the cards back into the zoetrope, in
the hope that they could send one last, lonely ghost somewhere it
didn't need an anchor. Under a glass ceiling in which the ensnared
phantoms glimmered like the winter's first snowflakes, Charlie turned
the crank once more. Even when he lifted his hand and walked back to
Mary and Freya, the wheel continued to turn and turn, singing like the
call of the albatross blown in on the storm.

Inside, a ship floated above a strange horizon, cutting through
misty clouds, its dark shape purposeful against the nebulous background. Mary hoped Freya's memories were right, that it was
reminiscent of the time-wraiths' ship that sailed endless skies and that
they would hear the call.

Charlie carefully undid the silver buttons running down Mary's
spine, opening the doors again.

"What time does the clock have, Charlie?"

"5.30pm, 30 November 1936."

Time flowed around them in silver waves as they walked, Freya
somewhat gingerly, from 1868 into 1936, where the palace was cold
and dark and almost decrepit. For a moment, Mary thought she could
still hear that albatross echo across the decades, then decided it was
just her imagination.

"Seems a shame to… well, you know," whispered Freya.

"I know," Mary replied, "but we have to seal the rip over."

"And what of me?" The ghost asked.

"Don't you worry," said Charlie, "Mary's never made a promise
she hasn't kept." Then he turned to Mary. "Cloakroom might be best,
don't you think? Bound to be smaller and easier."

Mary nodded.

After they found it, it was easy, really. A small incendiary device
in a wastebasket, fuel sprinkled over a long, varnished wooden coun-

ter and wooden lockers. And if the workers found it, well, the palace was big enough to find another quiet corner in which to start a blaze.

There was no need. It was not discovered until the structure was well ablaze, flames raging inside as molten glass rained down inside. The fire brigade could do little to dampen it. The smashes and pattering became a downpour, a hail of fiery glass. As it melted and disappeared into the flames, the apparitions inside shot upward, limned by the sparks that flared after them, disappearing into the darkness. They watched them in silence, for hours as the fire raged, until less and less of those comet-like spirits were released. At last, none were left. Then Freya pointed to the thick, billowing smoke choking the night sky.

"Here they come," she said.

A ship, made of smoke and bone and starlight, cutting a swathe through the night. It descended, lower and lower, and the lonely ghost who had lost its time, its connection to this world, glided toward it without looking back. Mary thought she saw a childlike arm reach over the side, offer its hand. Then they were simply gone, swallowed by the updrafts and the night itself.

"There won't be another Crystal Palace, will there?" Freya sounded tired, and full of sadness.

"There won't, that's true, but have a look, closely now, at what is left behind."

Freya and Charlie smiled at Mary. There, in the white-hot flames that were beginning, at last, to die down, was the outline of the shadow of the great zoetrope. It turned endlessly, merrily uninhibited by the laws of physics or the imagination of men. It would turn there, perhaps forever, spiralling up the time from the ghosts of this world like a bobbin and singing them through the gateway to the lands beyond.

Z is for Zoetrope

Thank you for reading

G is for Ghosts

We would appreciate it a great deal if you would leave an honest review on Goodreads and wherever you purchased this book.

Your stars and a couple sentences mean the world to us!

Truly.

Always Be The First To Know!

Whether it's a new release, a call for submissions, cover reveal, super sale or I just want to share a new story I've written, you will always be among the first to know if you sign up for my newsletter.

I promise to respect your privacy and your inbox. I will only email you when I have something exciting to share, probably about twice a month.

Subscribe now and you'll receive a free download of my award-winning post-apocalyptic short story, "Starry Night" as a welcome-to-the-newsletter present!

Subscribe to Rhonda's Mailing List!

http://bit.ly/StarryStory

SELECTED ANTHOLOGIES BY RHONDA PARRISH

A IS FOR APOCALYPSE
B IS FOR BROKEN
C IS FOR CHIMERA
D IS FOR DINOSAUR
E IS FOR EVIL
F IS FOR FAIRY
G IS FOR GHOSTS

FAE
CORVIDAE
SCARECROW
SIRENS
EQUUS

FIRE: DEMONS, DRAGONS AND DJINNS
EARTH: GIANTS, GOLEMS AND GARGOYLES
AIR: SYLPHS, SPIRITS AND SWAN MAIDENS
WATER: SELKIES, SIRENS AND SEA MONSTERS

GRIMM, GRIT AND GASOLINE
CLOCKWORK, CURSES AND COAL

MRS. CLAUS: NOT THE FAIRY TALE THEY SAY
TESSERACTS TWENTY-ONE: NEVERTHELESS
HEAR ME ROAR
ARCANA

DARK WATERS

SWASHBUCKLING CATS: NINE LIVES ON THE SEVEN SEAS

SELECTED BOOKS BY RHONDA PARRISH

HOLLOW

ONE IN THE HAND

HAUNTED HOSPITALS
EERIE EDMONTON

Made in the USA
Middletown, DE
22 October 2021